No Greater Love

Margaret Dickinson, a *Sunday Times* top ten bestseller, was born and brought up in Lincolnshire and, until recently, lived in Skegness, where she raised her family. Her ambition to be a writer began early and she has now written over thirty novels – most of which have been set in her home county, but also in Nottinghamshire, Derbyshire and South Yorkshire.

Margaret Dickinson

No Greater Love

PAN BOOKS

First published 2025 by Macmillan
This paperback edition first published 2025 by Pan Books
an imprint of Pan Macmillan
The Smithson, 6 Briset Street, London EC1M 5NR
EU representative: Macmillan Publishers Ireland Ltd, 1st Floor,
The Liffey Trust Centre, 117–126 Sheriff Street Upper,
Dublin 1, D01 YC43
Associated companies throughout the world
www.panmacmillan.com

ISBN 978-1-0350-2463-6

1 3 5 7 9 8 6 4 2

A CIP catalogue record for this book is available from the British Library.

Typeset in Sabon by Palimpsest Book Production Ltd, Falkirk, Stirlingshire
Printed and bound by CPI Group (UK) Ltd, Croydon, CR0 4YY

Visit **www.panmacmillan.com** to read more about all our books
and to buy them. You will also find features, author interviews and
news of any author events, and you can sign up for e-newsletters
so that you're always first to hear about our new releases.

For Dennis and all our wonderful family

One

Leicestershire, March 1901

Lady Elizabeth Ingham faced her fiancé of two months across the hearth in the library of her home, Ancholme Hall. She felt the tears well in her eyes and fought to stop them falling, but she couldn't prevent her voice trembling as she asked, 'Why, Oliver? I don't understand.'

Oliver Goodwin, the only son of Sir William Goodwin, who was the head of one of the oldest and most respected families among the landed gentry of Leicestershire, stood twirling his hat between nervous fingers.

'It's your brother's fault, Lizzie,' Oliver blurted out. 'I can't believe he has been so – so *cavalier* with his inheritance. So careless with his future and yours too. He's ruined everything.'

'Bruce? What has Bruce got to do with you breaking our engagement?' Lizzie felt a quiver of fear. She knew her brother led a wild life. She had heard the whispers among their servants that he frequented the nightclubs and gambling dens of London and other cities on the Continent and that he mixed with the theatre-going fraternity. There were even rumours that he had got a promising young actress pregnant but that had been successfully hushed up. Or so she had thought.

'There's going to be a huge scandal and I am to have

no part of it. My father has instructed me to ask you to release me from our betrothal.'

'Oliver, what are you talking about? What scandal?'

There was a long silence between them as they stared at each other. At last, Oliver shook his head and said softly, his tone pitying now, 'You don't know, Lizzie, do you? You really don't know what's happened.'

A surge of anger had driven away her tears now as she said tartly, 'Obviously not. Perhaps you would be good enough to enlighten me.'

'I don't think it's my place to tell you . . .'

'It most certainly is. I want to know what you have heard that has made you travel twenty miles or so on horseback to tell me this. Please –' she gestured towards a chair, though there was irony in her tone – 'do sit down. I will ring for some refreshment.'

As she moved stiffly to pull the bell cord, Oliver said, 'No, please don't do that. I – I'm not staying. I must go. You must ask your father – or your mother. They will understand. Please try to forgive me, Lizzie. This is not my wish.'

He gave a little bow, turned and left the room abruptly, leaving Lizzie staring at the closed door. Slowly she sank down into the chair beside the fire and closed her eyes. She thought back over the last year, trying to find some explanation as to why this was happening. At the start of the social season in the spring of 1900, she had been presented at Court in a long line of debutantes. That exciting, yet daunting, day had been followed by months of balls, dinner parties and charity events, visits to the theatre and attendance at various sporting occasions, which attracted the nobility and landed gentry. It had been a whirlwind. She had made several friends among the other young women, but it had been the young men, the eligible bachelors, who had queued up to dance and flirt with Lady Elizabeth. Always chaperoned, she'd had no occasion for any indiscretion, but one young man – Oliver Goodwin – had made his intentions clear from the start. He was kind, charming and attentive and had sought her company at every opportunity. Lizzie had found herself drawn to him and at the end of the season, he had proposed. Lizzie's father had given his blessing to the match and they had become betrothed on Lizzie's nineteenth birthday in January 1901. Oliver was heir to his father's estates and he and his future wife were set to become one of the county's foremost families. The engagement would last eighteen months and a date for the wedding had been planned for the summer of 1902.

With startling violet eyes, smooth skin and sleek black hair, Lady Elizabeth had been hailed as the most beautiful debutante of the year among a bevy of pretty girls. It was a compliment to her lovely nature that she was not the object of jealousy or envy. Without exception, all her peers wished her well. The only 'competition' among them now was to vie to be one of her bridesmaids. Her closest friend, Alexandra, safe in the knowledge that her position as chief bridesmaid was assured, had hugged Lizzie joyfully.

'He's the handsomest bachelor this season. Blond hair and blue eyes – what more could you possibly want? You will have an enviable position in society and he loves you to distraction. I'm sure of it. I would say that I'm jealous, but actually I'm not. None of us are. You deserve him, darling Lizzie, and he deserves you. You'll be so happy and have the most beautiful children. All the girls will look like you and your sons will be like him.'

But now all Lizzie's hopes and dreams had come crashing down. She wondered how many of her friends knew already and who would still be her friend when they did hear. But hear what? She was still ignorant of the facts that had brought about this catastrophe in her family. Lizzie pushed herself up from her chair and walked woodenly out of the library, across the hallway and into the morning room, hoping to find her mother there. The room was empty. She pulled the bell cord and waited for the butler to answer it.

It was not Timmins, the butler, who answered but Jinny, the youngest of the three housemaids, who also acted as Lizzie's lady's maid.

'Lady Elizabeth,' the young girl said as she knocked and entered the room, dipping a swift curtsy as she had been taught by Mrs Schofield, the housekeeper, when coming into contact with any member of the family.

'Do you know where my mother is, Jinny?'

The girl blushed and refused to meet Lizzie's gaze. 'I believe she's in her room, m'lady. She's resting. I – I don't think she's feeling well.'

'Is it one of her palpitation attacks?'

'I – don't know.'

'And my father? Do you know where he is?'

'He's gone away. On – on business, Mr Timmins said.'

'Do you know where he's gone?'

Jinny shook her head.

Lizzie nodded. 'Then I'll just go to my mother's room . . .'

'I wouldn't, m'lady. Mrs Schofield said she was not to be disturbed unless she rang the bell.'

'I see,' Lizzie murmured, but she didn't see at all. Her mother often retired to her bedroom during the day, especially if she had one of her attacks, but it was unlike her father to leave home suddenly without a word.

'Then I will go for a walk in the garden,' Lizzie decided,

'until my mother feels well enough to receive me. Perhaps you would fetch my cloak for me.'

The young girl dipped a curtsy, but said no more.

Wrapped up warmly against the late March chill, Lizzie left the house by a side door which led out onto the terrace and walked down the steps into the garden. It was a blaze of colour from the hundreds of daffodils planted there. She wandered among the radiant blooms. She loved this time of the year when the flowers were at their very best. Soon there would be tulips too, the colours many and varied. Normally, Lizzie loved the spring, but not today. Today, her heart was heavy with sadness and her mind full of unanswered questions. She glanced back at the house towering above her; it had been her home all her life.

Ancholme Hall and its estate belonged to her father, Edward Ingham, the fifth Earl of Ancholme. There were three tenanted farms, parkland, rivers and streams and the small village of Ancholme under his stewardship. One day, everything would pass to her brother, Bruce. She knew that under the terms of her father's will, she would inherit nothing, but she had always trusted that even if she didn't marry well, her brother would ensure she was taken care of. But now, doubts entered her mind. Something was amiss. She could feel it.

Her sharp hearing caught the sound of carriage wheels on the long driveway leading to the front door. She turned and hurried back towards the house. Perhaps her father had returned. But in the main hall she saw that the visitor was her dear friend, Alexandra Mayberry, who lived a mere five miles from Ancholme Hall.

'Alex, oh Alex.' She ran towards Alexandra and into her outstretched arms.

'My dearest Lizzie. I came at once – as soon as I heard . . .'

'Miss Mayberry –' Timmins, who was hovering nearby, began but Lizzie waved him away impatiently.

'We shall be in the library. Please have Jinny bring us tea and cakes.'

Timmins opened his mouth to speak again, then closed it and gave a courteous little bow. 'Very good, m'lady.'

The two girls moved into the library and closed the door. 'Oh Lizzie, I am so sorry. My father forbade me to visit, but I came anyway. I shall be in dreadful trouble when I go home, but I don't care. I just *had* to see you.'

'Alex, do slow down and tell me what this is all about.'

Alexandra's eyes widened and her mouth dropped open. 'You mean – you don't *know*?'

'Something very strange is going on, I know that much, but I don't know the cause of it. Oliver came this morning to break off our engagement but even he wouldn't tell me why.'

'Oh, you poor darling. Papa said that would happen. About Oliver, I mean. Look, let's wait until Jinny has brought –'

'No, tell me now. Tell me quickly.'

Alexandra sat beside her and held her hands. 'It's your brother. He's got himself into the most enormous trouble and your father is going to have to sell everything he owns to pay off Bruce's debts and keep him out of gaol. In fact,' she added hesitantly, 'to keep him safe.'

Lizzie's heart began to thump and she felt for a moment as if she might faint.

'But what . . . how . . .?' she stumbled over the questions that were tumbling around her head. 'What do you mean – everything?'

'The estate, the house, all the furniture. Just – everything.

And there will be such a dreadful scandal. Society's doors will be closed to you for ever. That's what Mama says, anyway.'

And she would know, Lizzie thought bitterly, though she did not say the words aloud. She would not hurt her friend's feelings, though it looked as if their friendship might soon be at an end if Alexandra's parents had anything to do with it. Mrs Emily Mayberry, who craved a title for her husband and recognition from society, was the biggest snob Lizzie knew. She had encouraged her daughter's friendship with Lizzie, hoping that some of the girl's popularity, especially among the season's eligible bachelors, would envelop Alexandra and lead to her making a suitable marriage. Lizzie's own mother had been the one to sponsor Alexandra to be presented at Court and although Emily Mayberry was grateful, that gratitude would not extend to a continued friendship in view of the gossip she was hearing now. All ties with the Ingham family would be severed.

Lizzie was speechless. It wasn't until Jinny had brought in tea and cakes and left the room again that she felt able to say, 'Alex, please tell me everything you know.'

'I – I don't know if I should. I mean, you should hear it from your parents. It's only gossip and might not all be true.'

'Tell me anyway.'

Alexandra poured the tea and took a small cake. Lizzie accepted the tea but shook her head at anything to eat. She couldn't face a thing, not even the cook's dainty iced cakes.

'Your brother has always been a bit of a rake, hasn't he? Even you must know that. There was the scandal of him having got an actress pregnant. I understand that your father had to pay out quite a lot of money for that to be kept quiet, but, of course, it wasn't supressed entirely. Rumours and gossip always circulate, don't they?'

7

'I didn't know about the money,' Lizzie murmured. 'But go on.'

'Then there's his gambling debts. He owes money all over London, so it's said, and on the Continent too. But worst of all, he went to Sicily and got embroiled with some very dangerous people there. Rumour has it that he was involved in a duel, killed his opponent and now he's running for his life.'

Lizzie's eyes widened and she drew in a sharp breath. 'Where is he now?'

'No one knows.'

Thinking of her brother, Lizzie shuddered. They had been very close as young children. With only two years between them, they had been brought up together by nannies, governesses and tutors until Bruce had been sent to an all-boys' boarding school at ten years old. Their separation and different way of life had begun at that time and although Lizzie mourned the loss of the closeness she had once shared with him, she understood it. But not this. She didn't understand him falling so far from grace and in such a short space of time. The last time she had seen him – the Christmas before last – everything had seemed well in his world. The scandal of the actress had been successfully squashed and he was due to set off on a world tour in the spring of 1900. Even their parents had agreed to it.

'A young man must sow a few wild oats before he settles down,' their father had said indulgently, little knowing just how wild those 'oats' would be. 'And once you return, you must find yourself a suitable wife and begin to learn the business of running an estate, where many people's lives and livelihoods will depend on you.'

But now it seemed that all those fine plans lay in ruins.

Two

It was early evening before Lizzie was able to speak to her mother. Constance Ingham, Lady Ancholme, sent her own lady's maid, Dolly, to find Lizzie and ask her to come to her bedroom. Lizzie entered the room with trepidation and yet she was determined to find out the truth. Her mother, sitting on the window seat, held out her hand towards her daughter. It was from Constance that Lizzie had inherited her beauty. But Constance was now in her early fifties and her dark hair was flecked with white at the temples, and, today, her smooth skin was blotchy from the copious tears she had been shedding. Her fine eyes were clouded with anxiety.

'Come and sit with me, Lizzie, my dear. I have some upsetting news that you should hear from me before the tittle-tattle spreads.' She sighed heavily and murmured, 'As it surely will.'

Lizzie sat beside her mother and turned to face her. She did not say that she had already heard something of their problems from Alexandra. She wanted to hear it from her mother's lips.

Constance's voice trembled as she took Lizzie's hands in hers and said quietly, 'My dear, we are in awful trouble. Bruce –' Now her voice broke and she took a moment to compose herself. 'Your brother has got himself into the most dreadful scrape. Your father has gone to try to find him, but –' again she paused for a

9

moment before adding shakily – 'but he has no idea where Bruce is.'

'Is he in London? Or abroad?'

'I – we don't know.'

'What sort of trouble, Mama?' Still, Lizzie did not breathe a word that she already knew something of the facts, hoping that what Alexandra had told her were merely rumours which had been blown out of proportion by the gossips.

'Your father has heard that Bruce was in Sicily. It seems he fell in with some very dangerous people to whom he now owes a lot of money.'

'Gambling?' Lizzie asked softly.

Her mother sighed and tears sprang to her eyes. 'I expect so. That's usually the case, isn't it?'

Lizzie waited, expecting her mother to say more, but Constance had turned to gaze out of the window at the well-tended gardens and the parkland beyond. After several moments of silence, Constance whispered, 'We shall have to sell up and leave all this. There will be no inheritance for Bruce and – and all you will have left, my dear, is the small legacy my mother gave to you in her will. That, thankfully, cannot be touched. I wonder . . .' Constance murmured more to herself now than to Lizzie – 'if she had some inkling that one day you might have need of it?'

Still Lizzie said nothing. She didn't want to add to her mother's distress by telling her that her engagement to Oliver was at an end. But she was obliged to say something as Constance murmured, 'I don't know how we will be able to afford your wedding, if he'll still have you . . .'

'There's no need to concern yourself about that, Mama.'

Constance turned her head slowly to meet Lizzie's gaze. 'He's been here already, then?'

Lizzie nodded. With a supreme effort, she managed to keep her voice steady as she said, 'His father has instructed him to ask me to release him from our engagement.'

Constance's tone was laced with irony. 'And he lost no time in carrying out his father's bidding. What have they heard? Did he say?'

Lizzie shook her head. 'No, Mama. He said I should hear it from you or Papa.' She bit her lip before asking tentatively, 'Is there – is there anything else?'

Constance sighed. 'Not that I know, but isn't that bad enough? We shall lose everything. If we don't pay what these dreadful people are demanding then – then I fear for Bruce's life.'

Trying to prompt her mother to reveal more, Lizzie murmured, 'It sounds as if there might be more to it than a gambling debt, however large that might be.'

Constance frowned as she said slowly, 'I think perhaps there is more than I am being told.'

Lizzie avoided meeting her mother's eyes. Perhaps Constance truly didn't know any more. Maybe her husband had thought to spare her further details of the scandal that was enveloping their family. Or perhaps the rumours had been exaggerated and what Alex had heard about a duel was not true.

Softly, Lizzie said, 'So you really don't know any more than you have told me, Mama?'

Constance turned her head to face her daughter's clear gaze. 'No, Lizzie, I don't, but I can see that – like me – you think there is more.' She hesitated for a moment and then added in a whisper, 'Dolly told me that Alexandra called this morning to see you.' There was an unspoken question in her eyes.

Lizzie sighed inwardly. She didn't want to deceive her

mother and yet to repeat such scandalous rumours, especially if they weren't true, would be cruel. As if sensing her daughter's dilemma, Constance whispered, 'Tell me if you have heard anything else, Lizzie. I'd rather know the truth, however painful.'

For a moment Lizzie glanced away. She couldn't bear to see the growing fear in her mother's eyes. And yet, Constance had asked for her honesty. She took a deep breath.

'Alex said there are rumours flying around but she doesn't know if they're true . . .' Again she paused for a brief moment before adding, 'She'd heard that Bruce had been involved in a duel, that he'd killed his opponent and now is, as she put it, "running for his life".'

Constance flinched and put her hand to her chest as if she had a sudden pain there. 'So – no one knows – where he is?'

Lizzie shook her head. Constance had taken this latest bombshell much better than Lizzie had expected though her mother was obviously terrified for Bruce. He was still her baby boy, whatever he might have done. She was being remarkably brave.

'I expect there was a woman involved somewhere,' Constance murmured. 'There usually is.'

'It could just have been over his debts.'

'Just,' Constance murmured sarcastically, with a brief hint of her usual spirit. 'They're certainly serious enough without anything else. Did Alexandra say any more?'

'No, Mama.'

'I am surprised her father allowed her to visit you. We shall be ostracized from all society now.'

'She disobeyed him,' Lizzie said quietly, 'so I don't think she will be able to visit again.' The lump of sadness grew in her throat. As her mother said, they would lose all their so-called friends, but being parted from Alexandra would hurt Lizzie the most, even more than the loss of her fiancé.

The household staff were loyal. Led by the butler and housekeeper, they carried on with their duties despite the threat to their own livelihoods. They still treated their employers with the deference they always had, but now gloom pervaded the household.

Lord Ancholme was absent for a week, during which time there was no more news, and both Lizzie and her mother passed the time in a fever of anxiety. When finally he returned late one evening, Constance and Lizzie were sitting in the drawing room after dinner, trying to concentrate on their embroidery.

'That's a carriage drawing up at the front door, Mama. It must be Papa.'

They both rose, casting aside their needlework and moving towards the door. In the hall, they saw Edward handing his hat and coat to Timmins.

'Have you eaten, my lord?' the butler was saying. 'I can have Cook prepare something on a tray for you.'

Lizzie gasped as she drew nearer to her father and took in his appearance. His face was grey with exhaustion and he stooped as if he had aged ten years during the time he had been away. He was shaking his head. 'I'm not hungry, Timmins. Just bring some whisky to my study . . . Ah, Constance, my dear, and Lizzie too.' He hesitated and then sighed heavily, as if realizing he could put off the moment no longer. 'Please, will you join me in my study?'

'Of course, Papa,' Lizzie said, taking her mother's arm.

Edward sat behind his desk and leaned forward, resting his arms on the surface and bowing his head. He waited until both Constance and Lizzie were seated on the chaise longue opposite his desk and for Timmins to serve him with a large measure of whisky.

When the butler had left, Edward began to speak. His voice was husky and shaking a little. 'My dears, I must tell you some dreadful news. Bruce –' he faltered for a moment as if the very name of his son brought him fresh anguish – 'has fallen foul of some very wicked people. Men who have no scruples, no sense of decency. They ensnared him into their evil ways with no thought that he was a young man alone in a strange country. They – they led him astray . . .'

Lizzie felt sick as she listened to her father, whom she had always loved and admired, making excuses for her brother when there was no defence to be given. Throughout his life, Bruce had been indulged and spoiled, allowed to enjoy life to the fullest before he was expected to settle down with a suitable wife and, in due course, take over his father's title and guardianship of the Ancholme estate. Even now, when he had brought his family to ruin, Bruce's father was still trying to shield him. Now Lizzie was angry. This past week, while she had waited and worried and watched her mother's despair, had made her feel very differently about her father and her brother.

'Is it true,' Constance ventured, 'that we will have to sell everything to settle his gambling debts?'

'If that were the only problem, my dear, it might not be so bad, but he was challenged to a duel over some – some woman, and, as you know, Bruce is an excellent swordsman . . .' He fell silent.

'Did he – did he kill someone?' Lizzie asked in a whisper.

Slowly, Edward nodded. 'He went into hiding and the people who were protecting him from the revenge of the friends of – of the deceased got in touch with Bellingham.'

Lizzie knew that Arthur Bellingham in Leicester was their family's solicitor. She gasped. 'Did – did Bruce give them his name?'

Edward shrugged. 'He must have done. Bellingham, of course, then got in touch with me. Somehow – I don't know how, because he wouldn't tell me – he has arranged safe passage for Bruce to Tunisia.'

'Then surely he can come home?' Constance said.

Edward was shaking his head sadly. 'There's a price on his head, my dear, from the family of the man he has killed, and no doubt from the law too. He – he must disappear if he wishes to stay alive. Africa is a vast continent. It will not be so easy to find him there, whereas if he were to try to travel through Spain and France to get home, then –' He fell silent.

Lizzie spoke heavily. 'And all this is going to cost a vast amount of money.'

'Everything we have,' Edward whispered hoarsely. 'Bellingham is arranging for the estate, including the farms and the village cottages we own, this house and all our belongings, to be put up for auction.'

'Where are we to go?' Constance asked.

Edward spread his hands in a gesture of helplessness. 'At this moment, I have no idea.'

Lizzie and her mother glanced at each other but suppressed their remaining questions. Edward was spent. The anxiety, the travelling, the painful decisions that he had had to make had all taken their toll. And most of all, of course, the terrible disappointment in his son.

Lizzie rose and went to him. She put her hand on his shoulder. 'Come, Papa, let Roderick help you to bed,' she said, referring to her father's valet. 'Timmins will bring you something on a tray.'

Edward gripped her hand as he dragged himself to his

feet. 'Oh, my dear girl, I am so very sorry. All this will have such an impact on your life. I –'

'Please don't worry about me, Papa. I am young and strong and you have educated me well. I'm sure there are plenty of things I can do.'

'The money that your grandmother left for you in trust will not be endangered, Bellingham said. He suggested that it should be spent on some kind of training for you. As a governess, perhaps, or a nanny.'

'But I can't touch that until I am twenty-five.' She paused then added, 'Can I?'

'Bellingham said that in these circumstances, perhaps something can be done. He's going to look into it on your behalf.'

She was heartened that even amidst all the worry about Bruce's safety, both her father and his solicitor had thought about her too. She patted his hand. 'Don't concern your-self about me yet, Papa. Let's concentrate on making sure Bruce is safe and then finding somewhere for the three of us to live.'

Edward gripped her hand as he said huskily, 'If only your brother had your strength of character, your honesty and your sense of purpose, then none of this would have happened. I am sorry to say that he's a weak young man, but I must bear some of the shame myself. I have indulged him, thinking to give him some fun, some experience of life, before he needed to settle down and take over the running of the estate from me. Instead, he has squandered his inheritance and brought ruin and disgrace on us all.' Her father's dark brown eyes looked deep into her clear gaze. 'It is you, my dear girl, who should have been born the son in this family.'

Three

Events seemed to progress with surprising swiftness. Mr Bellingham visited Ancholme Hall and stayed for three days. For most of that time, except at mealtimes, he remained closeted with Edward in his lordship's study. After dinner on the eve of his departure, he came into the drawing room. When Timmins had served everyone with drinks and had left the room, Arthur Billingham, a portly man with thinning hair and bright blue eyes, cleared his throat and addressed his words to Constance.

'I am relieved to be able to tell you, my lady, that your son is now in Egypt. I have friends there who have been able to find him safe haven. Not with them, I am afraid. That would be too dangerous, but they know where he is and have assured me that he is safe and well.'

'Can we know where he is? Can we write to him?'

Arthur shook his head. 'It would not be wise for you to contact him, my lady.'

'But –'

'My dear,' Edward put in. 'We must do whatever Mr Bellingham advises. Perhaps in the future . . .' He shrugged helplessly.

Constance's voice shook a little as she asked, 'But how will we hear of him? How will we know if – if . . .?'

'Mama,' Lizzie said, taking her mother's hand. 'I am sure Mr Bellingham will keep us informed of any news he hears.'

Arthur smiled at Lizzie and inclined his head in agreement.

Lizzie returned the gesture, but it was a weak smile that did not reach her eyes. She wondered if she would ever feel like laughing wholeheartedly again. 'Why Egypt?' she asked.

'There are many British people living there, Lady Elizabeth. I too lived there for five years until about three years ago. I am fortunate to count several of those still there among my friends.'

'And we are very lucky that you have such contacts, Mr Bellingham,' Edward said. He sighed heavily and glanced at his wife and daughter. 'The estate is to be advertised for sale by auction . . .'

Before he could finish his sentence, Constance covered her face with her hands and began to weep. 'I can't bear it. I can't bear to watch our home and all our precious things sold. Whatever is to become of us? I still don't understand why we are to lose *everything*.'

Edward's face was grey as he said brokenly, 'It has taken a great deal of money to pay off his debts and to secure his safety.'

'May I suggest, my lady, that perhaps you could go to stay with a relative until everything is settled,' the solicitor said.

Constance removed her hands from her face and looked up at him with tear-filled eyes. Her voice rising shrilly, she said, 'But when will things be settled? When will they ever be "settled" again? What are we to do? Where are we to go? Where are we to *live*, Mr Bellingham? Can you tell me that?'

'As a matter of fact, my lady,' Mr Bellingham said calmly, 'I think perhaps I can. I visited the vicarage yesterday and the vicar told me that he is about to leave

18

here. He is a go-ahead young man and he has secured a living in a larger parish some fifty miles away. The vicarage will be empty for a while . . .'

If it hadn't been such a serious matter, the scandalized look on her mother's face would have reduced Lizzie to helpless giggles.

'The vicarage?' Constance said. 'You are expecting us to move into the *village*? The village where we once owned most of the dwellings? Among folk who used to be our tenants? We'd be a laughing stock, Mr Bellingham. Oh no, no. I won't do it. I'd sooner die first. I will write to my sister and beg her to give us shelter until something more suitable can be found. Somewhere – anywhere – away from here.'

'My dear . . .' Edward began, but Constance held up her hand.

'Please – not another word. I blame you for all of this, Edward. If you had not been so indulgent with the boy, none of this would be happening.' She rose, obliging her husband and Mr Bellingham out of courtesy to do the same. 'I shall retire. I wish you all goodnight.'

Constance swept from the room. Edward and Arthur Bellingham exchanged a glance and sank back into their chairs. Edward looked grey and his hands were trembling.

'Papa,' Lizzie said tentatively, not knowing if her input would be welcomed. 'Perhaps it would be a good idea if we were to stay with Aunt Susannah for a while, as Mama suggested. There might even be a house in her neighbourhood where we might live. We are not so well known there.'

Edward appeared deep in thought for a few moments before saying slowly, 'I think you and your mother should go, though I will remain here until . . .' Now his voice faltered and he choked on the words as he realized the enormity of what was going to happen. He, Edward Ingham, the fifth Earl of Ancholme, was about to lose everything that had been built up by his forebears.

The reply to Constance's letter to her sister came by return but contained a shock for the family. Susannah Waltham wrote:

> *We are willing to accommodate you and Elizabeth for a short while until matters are settled but we must ask you not to leave the house and gardens. You will only be permitted to mix with our most trusted servants and must not speak to any outsiders. Lawrence* – Susannah referred to her husband – *will do his best to find accommodation for you. His family own properties on the Lincolnshire coast and he will make enquiries. This is a huge scandal, my dear, and anyone associated with you is bound to be tainted . . .*

The letter slipped from Constance's fingers and fell to the floor, as she pressed her hand to her chest. Lizzie picked up the letter and read it. She sat beside her mother and took her cold hand, trying to warm it between her own. 'I would never have thought Aunt Susannah could be so callous,' she murmured.

'No, nor I. I rather think it is Lawrence who is behind those words. He won't want his good name besmirched by our family scandal.' She sighed heavily. 'But we will have to go. I can't stay here, Lizzie. I just can't. There is no alternative.'

Packing only one trunk each, they travelled the fifty or so miles to the Walthams' home on the outskirts of Stamford and were at once shown to rooms at the back of the house on the first floor. They were given a bedroom each and a small sitting room, and asked to use a side entrance and to walk only in the rose garden. The Walthams' butler, Bridges, and Susannah's lady's maid, Jane, were the only servants they encountered.

'Obviously, we are persona non grata,' Constance remarked bitterly. 'We are to be virtual prisoners.'

'But comfortably housed and well fed, Mama. The rooms are lovely and the view over the Lincolnshire countryside is beautiful,' Lizzie said, trying to see the positives in their situation and to raise her mother's spirits. 'Perhaps Uncle Lawrence will find us somewhere more permanent very soon.'

'I do hope so,' Constance said, sinking into a chair. 'My sister has not even come to greet us.'

'I'm sure she will, Mama. Now, shall we unpack?'

'Ring for –' Constance began and then looked at her daughter with wide eyes. 'I was forgetting,' she murmured. 'Dolly is no longer with us. Oh Lizzie, our wonderful staff. Perhaps the new owners will keep them on.'

'I hope so, Mama. Now, you go and lie down on your bed. You look exhausted. I will see to everything.'

It was evening, after dinner, before Susannah conde-scended to visit her relatives. Constance and Lizzie had not even been invited to dine downstairs. Their meal, though sumptuous, had been served to them by Bridges and Jane.

The servants were courteous towards them and Jane even risked a swift smile at Lizzie. 'If there's anything you need, m'lady, just let me know,' she whispered as she served their food. Lizzie glanced up and smiled. 'Thank you.'

'Hodson,' the butler spoke sharply to the girl. 'You

were told not to speak. The mistress trusts you to obey her instructions.'

'Yes, Mr Bridges,' Jane said meekly, but as she turned away, unseen by her superior, she gave a huge wink and Lizzie knew she had an ally in the household should she need one.

A little later, when they had finished eating, Susannah entered the small sitting room.

'My dear Constance,' she gushed, bending to kiss her sister's cheek. 'How sorry we are to see you reduced to this. Whatever was Edward thinking of to give Bruce such latitude that he has brought you so low? But we will do all we can to help you. Lawrence has already made some discreet enquiries.'

'Thank you,' Constance said stiffly. 'I am indebted to him.'

'It's no more than a family should do to help in times of trouble. Now, have you everything you need? I expect you would like to retire soon. You must be weary, so I'll leave you for now and see you again tomorrow.'

But the next day, and over the next few weeks, Susannah did not appear again. Constance and Lizzie were well cared for and couldn't deny that they had everything materially that they needed. But they were shut away from all communication with anyone. And, worst of all, no word came from Edward as to how things were progressing with the sale.

'I can't understand why your father has not visited us here or at least written to let us know if he has heard anything more about Bruce,' Constance said. 'I am beside myself with worry.'

'I don't think he'd be welcomed here,' Lizzie said in a small voice. 'Perhaps – perhaps he has been asked not to communicate with us at all.'

22

Constance regarded her sharply. 'By your uncle, you mean?'

Lizzie nodded. 'Any visitor – or perhaps even letters arriving – might be seen by other members of the staff. Word might get out.'

'Surely even your uncle wouldn't be so – so unfeeling as to prevent us hearing from your father?'

Lizzie shrugged. 'He told us we were not to send letters to Papa. Maybe he in turn has been asked not to write to us.'

'Instructed, more likely,' Constance said bitterly. She paused and then added, 'Why is everything taking so long?'

'It would have taken some time to advertise the auction of the estate,' Lizzie said reasonably. 'And after that – even if it was sold – there would no doubt be a lot of formalities to conclude.'

It was the middle of May – eight weeks since their arrival – before Constance and Lizzie saw anyone other than the two servants who had been deputed to care for them. They had walked in the garden each afternoon to take a little air and exercise but their route through the house to the side door had always been carefully chaperoned by Bridges.

'Now I know how Mary, Queen of Scots, must have felt for all those years she was incarcerated by her relative. The sooner Lawrence can find us somewhere to live the better.' Constance put her hand to her heart. 'It is all so very distressing. I am feeling quite ill with the strain of it all.'

During the late afternoon, Bridges brought a message that Lawrence wished to see both of them. He escorted them down the stairs and into his master's study.

'Oh, Mr Bellingham, you're here too,' Constance exclaimed as they entered the room. 'How good of you to come all the way from Leicester. What news have you for us? Edward has not written. Not one word in all this time, which has surprised me.' She cast a reproachful glance at her brother-in-law. She was sure he was to blame for them being kept in isolation for so long. The solicitor rose and courteously conducted Constance to a chair by the fire.

Lizzie glanced at her uncle. She had not seen him during all the time they had been living in his home, nor for several years before that, but he had not changed much from how she remembered him. He was tall and thin with smooth fair hair, thinning now, and unsmiling eyes. He gestured for her to take a chair beside her mother. When both he and Arthur Bellingham were seated, the solicitor cleared his throat nervously. 'My dear Lady Ancholme, I am the bearer of sad tidings. I regret to inform you . . .'

Before he could say more, Constance's fingers fluttered to her mouth. 'Oh no, no. Not – not Bruce? Have you had word that – that . . .?'

Lizzie waited quietly but her heart was pounding. She had not seen Bruce for almost eighteen months, yet they had been close as youngsters and if something dreadful had happened to him, she would mourn his loss.

'No – no, it is not your son, but your husband.'

'Edward! Is he ill? I must go to him.'

Arthur was shaking his head sadly. 'He has passed away, Lady Ancholme.'

Constance stared at him, the colour draining from her face. Lizzie's whole body began to shake.

'There is no easy way to tell you, so it had better be said bluntly,' Lawrence said. 'He took his own life. He took his shotgun and went into the woods.'

Constance made a little noise in her throat. Her eyes rolled and she began to sway. She would have fallen forward onto the floor if Lizzie hadn't jumped up and caught her. Gently she laid her mother back in the easy chair.

'We should send for a doctor,' Arthur said.

'No!' Lawrence said harshly. 'Word of this must not get out. The first scandal was bad enough, but this . . .' He moved to the bell pull at the side of the fireplace. Bridges appeared and was asked to send Jane in with smelling salts.

When Constance had been revived, she began to weep and clasp her hand to her heart. 'I have such a dreadful pain in my chest.'

'Uncle Lawrence, please will you send for a doctor?' Lizzie pleaded.

'It's no doubt the shock. Just calm yourself, Constance, while we think what must be done. Bellingham, will you take care of everything at Ancholme Hall? I will visit if absolutely necessary, but I'd rather not be involved. I'm sure you can appreciate that.'

Arthur pursed his lips. He did not answer but merely inclined his head. He understood only too well. He was appalled at the callous way in which the Ingham family were being treated by their relatives. Silently, he vowed to do everything he could to help Lady Constance and her daughter. He and his wife had already discussed the matter and she was in full agreement.

'Arthur,' Caroline Bellingham had said when he told her of the further tragedy that had befallen the Ingham family, 'Lord Ancholme's family have been clients of your firm for many years and you have dealt personally with their affairs since our return from Egypt. He has always been most generous towards us, especially the wonderful hampers at Christmas. We must do everything we can to help his poor wife and daughter in their hour of need.'

'Thank you, my dear. I was hoping those would be your sentiments, for they are certainly mine.'

In the days that followed, Lizzie didn't know what she would have done without the help and support of the family solicitor. Her mother took to her bed and refused even to contemplate returning to Ancholme Hall to attend her husband's funeral. Lizzie must go alone. Lawrence finally relented and allowed a doctor to visit Constance but with the strict proviso that not a word about the family's troubles was to be divulged. The doctor, a kindly, middle-aged man, with a world of knowledge about the ailments and their causes that could afflict his patients, was puzzled. He diagnosed a serious heart condition, but was at a loss to know what had brought about such a sudden collapse. He sat for a while with Lizzie and questioned her about her mother's recent health and asked if anything had happened to cause such a rapid and unexpected decline, but because Susannah was also present, Lizzie could not answer him truthfully. Indeed, she could not answer him at all, for it was Susannah who interrupted saying, 'My sister has been in poor health for some time. We thought to help by having her to stay with us for a few weeks, but it seems that perhaps the journey here was too much for her.' Susannah put her hand dramatically to her chest. 'I shall never forgive myself. I thought only to help.'

Lizzie bowed her head, unable to meet the doctor's concerned gaze in the face of the lies her aunt was telling. But Doctor Mortimer was an astute man who was adept at reading his patients' reactions and even, on occasion, those of their relatives. He instinctively knew that there was more to this than he was being told and he also guessed that his patient's daughter could tell him a lot more if only she had the opportunity. He had caught the sudden flash of shock in her eyes at something her aunt had said before she had lowered her gaze. If only he could speak to the girl alone, but Mrs Waltham was obviously determined that that should not happen. The good doctor tried another ploy.

'I will make up some medicine for your mother,' he said, speaking directly to Lizzie. 'Perhaps you could take a walk to my surgery in the village to collect it.'

Before Lizzie could answer him, Susannah snapped, 'That will not be necessary. My maid will fetch it. Lizzie should stay with her mother. And now, Doctor, thank you for your kind attention. No doubt you will let my husband have your account. We will let you know if your services are required again. Bridges will show you out.'

Four

'Please come into my consulting room, Miss Hodson,' Doctor Mortimer greeted Jane, Susannah's lady's maid, when she arrived at his surgery. The servants who worked for the Walthams were also in Doctor Mortimer's care so he already knew Jane, having treated her for painful chilblains the previous winter.

'Oh Doctor, I can't stop. The mistress –'

'It's quite all right, my dear. I just need a private word with you. Please sit down,' he offered as he ushered her into the room and closed the door. 'Now, I need your help.'

'Mine, sir?'

'Yes, yours. You see, I'd like to know more about my patient. Let me reassure you that anything you tell me is in the strictest confidence. It will go no further than this room, I promise you, but –'

Jane was shaking her head vehemently. 'I can't tell you anything, sir. I would be dismissed without a reference if the master or the mistress . . .'

'I give you my word,' he said solemnly. 'But if I am to do my best for the dear lady, I must know a little more. I know she is Mrs Waltham's sister, but I don't know her married surname.'

Jane struggled inwardly. She wanted to answer the doctor, wanted to help the poor woman who was suffering so severely, but what little she had been told had also been said to her in the strictest confidence. Even the

28

master had impressed it upon her that not one word about their unexpected visitors was to be talked about outside the house. She cast her gaze around the doctor's room, desperately seeking some way out, and saw a folded newspaper lying at the edge of the doctor's desk. With a courteous, 'May I . . .?' she rose, picked up the paper and opened it out. The 'Ancholme Scandal' about Bruce Ingham was headline news. Without a word, she laid the newspaper in front of the doctor. He glanced at the lead article and understood. 'Ah,' he said. 'I see now.'

'There's been even worse news since, Doctor. I can't tell you what, but it'll no doubt be in the newspaper during the next few days. I – I think that's what made the poor lady faint.'

Doctor Mortimer nodded. 'Thank you, my dear, and please rest assured not one word will reach your master and mistress. I give you my solemn promise.'

'It's the daughter I feel so sorry for. She's only about my age.'

The doctor sighed deeply. 'I guessed as much and it looks as if she will carry the burden on her young shoulders. And now, I must ask for your solemn promise not to repeat what I am going to say to you.'

Jane nodded. 'Of course, sir.'

'Lady Ancholme – for I presume that's who she is – is gravely ill. I suspect she may have had a heart condition for some time and the shock and anxiety have made matters worse. Much worse. I shall visit again in a few days' time, whether I am sent for or not.'

'Oh but, sir . . .'

'I know what you're going to say, my dear, but I carry enough weight in this community to visit a patient whether invited to do so or not.' His eyes twinkled mischievously. 'Especially if I don't charge for my services.'

Jane smiled back at him. She liked Doctor Mortimer. It was known throughout the village that he often attended the poor and needy without charge. 'And now,' he added, 'I'll give you the medicine. You must be on your way. I don't want you to be in trouble for tarrying.'

'There is just one more thing, Doctor, that perhaps you should know.' She paused, again uncertain whether to confide in him. But she had gone so far now, a little further couldn't hurt.

'Go on,' he prompted softly.

'There's a very nice gentleman, who came to visit Lady – *them*. A Mr Bellingham. I think he's their solicitor from Leicester.'

'Thank you, my dear. That's very useful for me to know. And now, off you go.'

Several days passed before Arthur visited the Waltham household again to advise them of the date of Edward's funeral. Lawrence invited him into his study and sent for Lizzie.

'I'm so sorry this has all taken so long,' Arthur said to her, 'but there are a great many formalities to be gone through in such a case. But now I can tell you that the funeral will be in three days' time. Your father is to be buried in the churchyard in the village, my dear, but sadly in unconsecrated ground.'

'That's to be expected,' Lawrence said, tight-lipped. 'It is a crime to commit suicide. Lizzie will attend. Is there somewhere she will be able to stay?'

Arthur nodded. 'She can stay at the Hall. Although there is still much to be sorted out, the sale of the house and lands has been concluded and all the necessary paperwork was signed and sealed by his lordship before – well – before the tragic occurrence. But the new owner – a Mr Thomas Bailey – has graciously stated that Lady Elizabeth may stay in her old home for as long as she needs to. He has taken on all the servants, but he and his family will not be moving in until later in the year.' He turned towards Lizzie to say, 'I will return in two days' time to accompany you, my dear, if you would like me to do so.'

Before Lizzie could answer, Lawrence said, 'And may I ask who is paying for all your services, Mr Bellingham, because I am certainly not prepared to do so. It is costing me quite enough to house and feed Lady Ancholme and Elizabeth for all this time as it is.'

'Mr Waltham . . .' Suddenly there was an edge to the kindly solicitor's tone. 'The law firm of Bellingham and Son, of Leicester, has acted as solicitors for the Ancholme family for three generations – four, if we now count Lady Elizabeth. During all that time we have been well recompensed, I can assure you, and I feel now that it is my Christian duty to assist this young woman, who now finds herself with such a heavy burden to bear. I do so gladly and, I might add, without charge. I bid you "good day", sir. Lady Elizabeth, I will see you in two days' time.'

'Thank you, Mr Bellingham,' Lizzie said quietly, 'I shall be glad of your company.'

Early on the day before the funeral, a carriage and pair drew up in front of the Walthams' house. Bridges was watching for its arrival as he had been instructed to. At once he went upstairs where Lizzie was waiting. He escorted her down the back stairs and around the side of the house, almost hustling her and her valise into the waiting vehicle. He greeted Mr Bellingham with a nod and then told the coachman to 'drive on'.

As the carriage moved down the drive, Arthur took

Lizzie's hand in his. 'How are you, my dear? I am sorry that we have such a sad errand today.'

'I'm well, Mr Bellingham, thank you, but I am so very worried about my mother. Doctor Mortimer visited two days ago even though he had not been asked. He insisted that he should examine my mother thoroughly with only me present. Not even Jane was allowed to stay in the room, much to my aunt's displeasure. He – he told me afterwards that I should prepare myself. Mother is gravely ill.'

'Oh, my dear, I am so very sorry. But I promise you I will do everything I can to help you.'

'You're very kind, Mr Bellingham. My uncle has secured accommodation for us somewhere on the Lincolnshire coast. I understand the annuity, which you have been able to arrange for us, will be enough to cover the rent and our living expenses.'

Mr Bellingham nodded.

'But Mother is too unwell to travel at the moment. I fear . . .' Lizzie bit her lip and could say no more. Nor could Arthur think of anything appropriate to say to comfort the young woman.

It was just under fifty miles from Stamford to the Leicestershire village of Ancholme. With two stops for refreshment and to rest the horses, it was dusk by the time the carriage drew to a halt in front of Lizzie's old home. Timmins must have been watching for their arrival, for he ran down the steps at once and opened the carriage door. Offering his hand to help her, he said, 'Oh Lady Elizabeth, it is good to see you, but we – the staff and I – are all so very sorry for what has happened. Mr Bellingham – good evening, sir.'

'Timmins,' the solicitor greeted him.

'Cook has prepared a cold collation for you in the dining room and your rooms are ready. Jinny is waiting for you in your bedroom, m'lady, and Roderick, his late lordship's valet, will attend to you, sir.'

At that moment, Jinny ran down the front steps towards Lizzie and enveloped her in a warm hug. 'Oh m'lady. Come with me. Everything's ready for you.'

As the two young women moved away, Arthur said quietly, 'Thank you, Timmins. You have been a tower of strength these past few weeks. I will see that you are well recompensed.'

'That's thoughtful of you, sir, and appreciated, but there's no need. I have served this family for thirty years. It has been my home and the best thing you could possibly have done for me was to find me future employment, which you have done for all the staff. We are all to stay here with the new owners and so we are the ones who are very grateful to you.'

'Mr Bailey is a wealthy industrialist, who has made his own fortune,' Arthur confided. 'He is what they call "new money" and therefore despised by many in society. But rumour has it that he is a firm, but fair, employer and treats all those who work for him very well.'

As they walked up the steps and into the house, their conversation continued.

'Mr and Mrs Bailey and their two young sons visited last week, sir,' Timmins told him. 'They met all the staff and were very open about their background. They assured us that they will keep us all on, but said that they will need help in running the estate, especially from the estate bailiff.'

Arthur smiled. 'I'll let you into a secret, Timmins. I know I can trust your discretion.'

'Of course, sir,' the butler said, inclining his head.

'Mr Bailey has asked me to stay on as his solicitor and advisor too.'

'That is good news, sir. I like continuity. And there's no one who knows more about the legalities and so on of running this estate than you and your firm.'

'I suspect you will be seeing rather a lot of me during the coming months, Timmins.'

'It'll be our pleasure to attend to your needs, sir. And I'm sure his late lordship would be most pleased to hear the news.'

'It's just so sad that he felt that that was his only way out.'

'I think it was almost a question of honour, sir. He had been very depressed since his troubles began. He felt he had let his father and indeed, all his forebears, down very badly.'

'Did he not think about his wife and daughter?'

'I think when one's mind is as disturbed as his must have been, in some warped way he perhaps felt they would be better off without him. I think, though I'm only guessing, he perhaps felt that Lady Ancholme's sister and her husband would care for them.'

Arthur sniffed and said bluntly, 'It grieves me to tell you, Timmins, that is not the case. The Walthams resent having any connection with the disgrace and scandal which has sadly become national news now.' He explained briefly just how Lady Ancholme and her daughter were being treated.

Timmins was appalled. As he held open the front door for the solicitor, he asked quietly, 'So what is to happen to Lady Ancholme and Lady Elizabeth?'

Arthur sighed deeply. 'Lady Ancholme is very seriously ill, Timmins.'

Timmins's face creased with sadness. 'I am very sorry to hear that, sir. Very sorry indeed.'

'As for Lady Elizabeth, well, I have some ideas regarding her future but now is not the time to broach the subject. We will just have to wait to see if her mother improves first. Mr Waltham' – his tone hardened even as he uttered the name – 'says he has found them accommodation somewhere on the Lincolnshire coast, though I shudder to think what it might be. At the moment, however, Lady Ancholme is far too ill to travel. Even *he* must accept that.'

Roderick was waiting for Arthur in the guest bedroom assigned to him. As he left the room, Timmins said, 'Mr Bailey has written to me to say that you and Lady Elizabeth are to be afforded all the care and attention you need. He has said that he will not visit at such a time but extends his sincere condolences to the family.'

'I will make sure Lady Elizabeth is informed,' Arthur promised him.

As was custom, all the men in the village attended the funeral the following day. Edward Ingham had been their lord and master for many years, a benevolent and kindly estate owner following in the tradition of his forebears and especially of his father. The villagers surrounded Lizzie with their affection and sympathy, which carried her through a most difficult day. The vicar gave a moving eulogy, concentrating on all the positives in Edward's life and ignoring the recent tragedies that had befallen the family. Edward was buried in one corner of the churchyard in unconsecrated ground, as was the law, but the site chosen was as near to the Ingham family graves as possible.

Arthur and Lizzie stayed one more night before travelling back to Stamford. Lizzie was anxious to be back at her mother's side, but heartbreaking news awaited them on their arrival. Constance had passed away the previous evening, on the very same day her husband had been buried.

Five

Lizzie was numb with shock and grief. She lay awake far into the night, staring up at the ceiling in the darkness. She couldn't believe that so much tragedy had befallen her in such a short space of time. Losing her home and belongings had been bad enough, but at least then she and her parents had had each other. Now she had no one. Not even her brother. She knew instinctively that she would not be invited to live with her aunt and uncle. After a night of very little sleep, she rose, washed and dressed, moving like an automaton. Jane brought in her breakfast, but she could eat very little.

'Me and Mr Bridges are so sorry for your great loss, m'lady,' the girl whispered as if afraid that even in saying this she would be reprimanded. 'The mistress said to tell you she will come up to see you after breakfast.'

Lizzie nodded dully.

After being so ungracious towards her sister and niece, Susannah now seemed to be trying to make amends, but Lizzie suspected that her aunt's newfound concern was caused by guilt more than anything. The young girl who had danced the night away as a debutante, who had laughed and flirted with many a beau until she had settled on one of them as a future husband, now felt she had matured ten years during recent months. She had had to learn to deal with life's unexpected misfortunes very quickly.

'Your uncle and I have decided that we will do everything we can to help you start a new life. None of this has been your fault, my dear. I'm afraid the blame must lie solely with your reprobate brother and, sadly, with your parents' indulgence towards him. If he had been brought up in a stricter environment, none of this would have happened.' Even now, Susannah could not stop herself from being critical.

A spark of anger reignited Lizzie's resilience. She would not allow this tragedy to defeat her, to cow her. She was tempted to answer back, How would you know anything about bringing up children? You've never had any. But her natural politeness and deference towards her elders prevented such a retort. Whatever her aunt thought, Lizzie had been well brought up by loving parents. She would not forget their teachings. Besides, she told herself, she needed the help of her relatives for just a little while longer until she could arrange her mother's transport back to Ancholme Hall and her burial in the churchyard there. Thank goodness she still had Mr Bellingham's support. She didn't know what she would have done without him these past few weeks.

'That's very kind of you, Aunt,' she said stiffly in response to Susannah's offer. 'Once Mama is buried, I will then decide my future. It is most kind of you and my uncle to give me shelter until then.'

'Unfortunately,' her aunt went on, 'it is now highly unlikely that we shall be able to arrange a suitable marriage for you. Maybe it would be best if you were to look for a post somewhere. Perhaps as a companion to an elderly lady. Your uncle and I will both make some enquiries.'

Lizzie shuddered to imagine being at the beck and call of some difficult and demanding old woman. She sighed inwardly. If that was to be her future, then so be it, but before she succumbed to that, she would talk to Mr Bellingham.

Lady Constance had died of natural causes and the death certificate had been signed by Doctor Mortimer, so there was no delay in arranging her burial. As before, Mr Bellingham collected Lizzie the day before the funeral to accompany her to Ancholme once more.

'I must say,' he remarked, for once breaking the natural discretion of a solicitor, 'I am surprised that neither your aunt nor your uncle are accompanying you.'

Lizzie sighed. 'They don't want to be the object of scrutiny and gossip among the villagers.'

Once again, the inhabitants of Ancholme estate turned out to bid farewell to the woman who had always been generous towards them. Baskets of fruit had always been sent to anyone who was ill. Lady Constance had made it her business to ensure all the children on the estate attended school and she also helped them to find employment when they left full-time education. While her husband had been engaged with the running of the estate, it had been his wife who had busied herself with the welfare of their tenants, employees and their families.

The vicar's eulogy was affectionate and heartfelt once more and, in the churchyard, Lizzie was touched to see that the grave itself was lined with flowers as a mark of the respect and affection Ancholme's tenants had had for Constance. After the service, several of the women from the village approached Lizzie.

'Your parents were wonderful people, Lady Elizabeth. They will be sadly missed by everyone on the estate.'

Lizzie forced a smile. 'Thank you. I do hope you will all get along with the new owners.'

'Mr and Mrs Bailey have been to see us all. They visited

each one of us in our homes and told us to be sure to let them know if we had any problems. We all think everything will be fine. But it's you we're concerned about, Lady Elizabeth. Is there no way you could stay here?'

'It's kind of you to say so, but I must make my own way in the world now.'

'You have your aunt and uncle, don't you? I'm sure they will care for you until you marry.'

Lizzie smiled weakly but could not think of a suitable reply.

On the journey back to Waltham House, she asked, 'Mr Bellingham, do you have any suggestions as to what I might do to earn my own living? I know you said I will have a small annuity from the money my grandmother left, but I really don't want to be sent to live in Lincolnshire, nor do I wish to stay with my aunt and uncle any longer than necessary. And my aunt's suggestion that I should become a companion does not appeal either. I don't want to sound ungrateful but . . .'

'You don't, my dear, and I agree with you entirely. Life as a companion to some querulous old lady is for middle-aged spinsters, not a vibrant young woman like yourself.' He paused and then added, 'I do have an idea, as it happens. How would you feel about training to be a nanny?'

Lizzie stared at him as the carriage jolted over a rough patch in the road. 'A nanny,' she repeated slowly and rolled the idea around in her mind. She remembered the nanny and then the governess that she had had. They had been kindly, middle-aged women, strict with her but always fair.

'I took the liberty of making some enquiries on your behalf, m'lady, and there is an excellent college for young women in London, whose nannies are very well thought of. You should have no difficulty in securing a post once you are fully trained.'

'What would I do during the holidays if I couldn't stay at the college? I – I wouldn't want to come back to my aunt's.'

Mr Bellingham smiled gently. 'I rather thought that might be the case. There should be enough from your allowance to allow you to take lodgings somewhere during the college holidays, but I have discussed this with my wife and we are agreed that, if you should ever require it, there will always be a home for you with us.'

'That is so kind of you, Mr Bellingham.' Tears of gratitude welled in her eyes. She had not wept at the funerals of either of her parents but the solicitor's unexpected kindness touched her deeply. 'You don't know how much I appreciate it – and everything you have done for me and my family over the past weeks. And please, thank your wife for me.'

'Then you are happy for me to take matters further with the Davenport College?'

'Oh yes, Mr Bellingham. I would be most grateful.'

Arthur smiled. He had hoped Lizzie would agree to his suggestion. 'I did take the liberty of approaching the principal and she indicated that we might still be in time to make an application for you to commence at the start of the new academic year in September. I will keep you informed of progress.'

'There's just one thing, Mr Bellingham. I realize that I shall have to be truthful about – about my past, but I wish to be known from now on as Miss Elizabeth Ingham.'

Mr Bellingham stared at her for a moment and then smiled. 'I think that is a very wise decision. If I might be so bold, I think you have shown a remarkable maturity through all the tribulations you have had to face over the past weeks and months. I am only sorry that you have not received a kindlier reception from your relatives.'

'No matter, Mr Bellingham. As long as I have your support, I will survive.'

'You will always have that, Miss Elizabeth,' he said softly, deliberately using the name by which she now wished to be addressed.

Lizzie returned to her aunt's home where she kept to the rooms she and her mother had been given. She had her meals delivered to her room by Jane and was allowed to walk in the back garden in the afternoon. She hardly saw her aunt or her uncle as she waited impatiently for some form of communication from Mr Bellingham. She so desperately needed to hear from him before her aunt or uncle should find employment for her as a companion.

His letter came ten days later.

An interview has been arranged for you at the college for next Wednesday. I will accompany you as it will be necessary for you to stay two nights in the city. We will travel by train and I will make all the necessary reservations and appraise you of the arrangements as soon as I know them. In the meantime, I think you should tell your aunt and uncle . . .

When Jane brought her dinner to her on a tray, Lizzie said, 'Jane, please would you ask Mr Bridges if he would arrange for me to see my uncle – or my aunt.'

'Of course, m'lady. I'll do it at once.'

Lizzie had not told her family or their servants of her wish to change the way she was to be addressed in future.

She rather thought her aunt would not approve, though she doubted her uncle would care one way or the other. An hour later when she had finished eating, Bridges tapped on the door of the small sitting room. 'Your uncle will see you in his study, m'lady, if you would like to come with me.'

'Thank you, Mr Bridges.' Lizzie laid aside her needle-work, rose and followed the butler. Once inside her uncle's room, she stood in front of his desk as he frowned up at her. 'What is it, Elizabeth?' he asked curtly.

'Mr Bellingham has made some enquiries on my behalf and I have an interview in London next week at Davenport College, where I can be trained as a nanny.'

Lawrence blinked. 'You should have consulted me or your aunt about this first, Elizabeth.' He was thoughtful for a moment before saying, 'However, I am pleased to see that you are prepared to stand on your own feet and make decisions. There's one problem, though. If you are accepted, how do you expect to pay for the fees?'

'Mr Bellingham has said that the annuity I receive from the money my grandmother left me will be sufficient to pay for the college fees and,' she added swiftly, 'to provide accommodation during the holidays.' She had no intention of telling him about the solicitor's kind offer to take her into his own home should it prove necessary.

'Ah, well, that all sounds satisfactory. Most satisfactory, in fact. Does your aunt know?' There was no hiding his delight that the orphaned girl would soon no longer be his responsibility.

'No, Uncle. I thought perhaps I should tell you first.'

'Then you may go to the drawing room and tell her now. Bridges will escort you.'

Susannah was equally delighted. 'It is a most suitable profession for you, my dear. I have heard of that college.

It is most prestigious. I only hope they will accept you given the recent scandal in your family, which you will not be able to hide. I do hope, though, that it will not be necessary for you to mention our connection with you.'

Lizzie lifted her chin a little higher. 'I hope not, Aunt Susannah.' She would have liked to have added, But I will not tell lies to save your reputation.

One week later, dressed in the black outfit which had been bought for her to attend the funeral of her father, and then later that of her mother, Lizzie was sitting in front of a slim, middle-aged woman dressed in a brown costume with her fair hair arranged in a smooth chignon. Her blue, all-seeing eyes assessed Lizzie shrewdly and then they softened a little as she said, 'My name is Lucinda Davenport and I am the principal of this college. First, may I say how very sorry I am to hear of the dreadful loss you have sustained recently. To lose one parent is hard enough, but to have both of them pass away within such a short space of time and then to lose your home too –' She paused and then added, 'But I admire your resilience and your spirit, Miss Ingham, and I am cognisant of the fact that none of the tragedy is in any way your fault. Now, shall we begin the interview?'

For the next two hours Lizzie answered all the principal's searching questions. Then Miss Davenport took her on a tour of the building and introduced her to one or two members of staff. When they returned to the woman's study, Miss Davenport smiled and said, 'I will, of course, write to you formally, Miss Ingham, but I am happy to tell you that we would be glad to welcome you to this college in September. It will be a two-year course followed by a twelve-month placement with a family, which we obtain for you and which forms part of your final assessment. Are you willing to accept?'

'Most certainly, Miss Davenport. Thank you so much.'

As she travelled back to the hotel where she was staying, Lizzie felt the beginnings of hope. After such a dramatic shift in her fortunes, the deaths of her much-loved parents and the shock of her brother's conduct, to say nothing of the disappointment in her fiancé and her relatives' lack of compassion and understanding, Lizzie felt at long last that life was indeed still worth living.

Six

July, 1904

Lizzie stood on the platform of the small country railway station on the outskirts of a Derbyshire village called Alstone-in-the-Dale. She glanced up and down as the train that had just deposited her there began to move again. There was no one about apart from the stationmaster disappearing into his office and a boy porter wheeling a running barrow. The past three years had flown by and now here she was, about to be interviewed for her first proper job as a fully qualified and highly recommended nanny.

She had enjoyed her time at the Davenport College and had revelled in the busy hours that had occupied her both mentally and physically and left her with little time to brood on the past. With courage and fortitude, she was determined to look to the future. The first six months had been residential training at the college itself with daily lectures and practical lessons. The following three months were a placement in the kindergarten department of a local school, after which there were another few months back at the college. The second year was divided between the college and the children's ward of a local hospital. It was during this time that she'd read in *The Daily Telegraph* of the engagement and forthcoming marriage of Mr Oliver Goodwin to a Miss Florence

Ryan-Smith. She waited for the pain of heartbreak to arrive, but it did not. She didn't even feel like shedding tears. It was then that she realized that she had become a different person to the young, naive girl who had once danced her way through life without a care. Her marriage to Oliver would have been one of convenience, no doubt engineered by his parents and with the compliance of hers. It was the way things were done in their society and she had known no different path. She and Oliver had been fond of each other, but it had been in no way a passionate love affair like she'd read about between the pages of Jane Austen's books or the Brontë sisters' novels. She had set aside the newspaper thoughtfully. Perhaps, she thought, I have had a lucky escape. At least now my life is mine to do with as I wish.

The third year had been spent in a probationary post, found by the college, with a family whose son was due to go to boarding school in a year's time at the age of ten. Lizzie had been fortunate. The family and other members of staff there had made her welcome. The boy had been well behaved and a joy to care for.

'You might not always be so lucky,' Miss Davenport had warned. One or two of her colleagues had experienced difficult employers and unruly children and one young woman had decided the life of a nanny was not for her and had left the college.

At the end of the three years, Lizzie was presented with the certificate from the college. She had graduated with the highest marks in her year and was now ready to face whatever life had in store for her next.

Leaving the college for the last time, she'd travelled to Leicester where she stayed with Mr and Mrs Bellingham until she could secure a permanent post.

'I am very proud of you, my dear,' Arthur greeted her

when he met her at the station. He took her home to meet his wife, who in turn said, 'I'm very pleased to meet you at last, Miss Ingham.'

'Oh please, it's Lizzie,' she said, grasping the two hands that Caroline held out to her.

'Then from now on, it's Caroline and Arthur. Let me show you to your room. I hope you'll be comfortable.'

It was a charming bedroom with matching chintz curtains and bedspread.

'This room is to be yours any time you need it, Lizzie.' Caroline smiled. 'We are fully aware that the post of nanny can sometimes be a short one or a long one, but whatever happens, please know that you always have a home with us.'

'I'll never be able to repay you and your husband for your kindness. He has been a tower of strength from the very beginning of my family's misfortunes. I don't know what I would have done without his help and guidance.'

'Bellingham and Son have always been a *family* solicitor and have acted for yours for many years, even from the time of Arthur's grandfather, I believe. My husband has always followed the tradition of the firm's founders, but, if you don't mind my saying so, it is also his nature to give his help willingly to those who need it.'

'Well, I certainly did and I am very grateful.'

'All he wants – all we both want – is that you should find a post where you'll be happy.'

'I have an interview on Monday,' Lizzie told her, 'with a Mr Spendlove in a small village in Derbyshire. Miss Davenport – the principal at the college – had heard that they are in need of a nanny immediately. I made enquiries at the station and I can get there by train.'

'Then we shall have a nice weekend together first and Arthur will take you to the station again on Monday.

Now, if you'd like to freshen up, dinner will be served in an hour. Please join us in the drawing room when you're ready.'

The letter she had received from Mr Spendlove of the Manor in Alstone-in-the-Dale had said that she would be met by his groom with a pony and trap at the station on the second Monday morning in July at eleven o'clock. Now, still watching the entrance at the far end of the platform, she saw a young man, dressed in the type of clothing a groom might wear, glancing around him as if looking for someone. She moved towards him and, as he saw her, he gave a start and then hurried towards her.

Pulling off his cap, he said, 'Are you Miss Ingham?'

'I am, and you must be from the Manor.'

'Yes, miss. Have you any luggage?'

'No. I'm only here for an interview today.'

The young man's face seemed to fall. 'Ah, right. I thought you might be staying.' He sighed. 'If you'd follow me, miss. Me dad's waiting outside with the pony and trap. He's head groom and I work with him.'

Outside the station, the young man introduced his father who was standing beside the pony's head. 'This is Joe Marshall and I'm Billy.'

'I'm pleased to meet you, Mr Marshall,' Lizzie said holding out her hand.

After a slight hesitation, the man took it and shook it firmly. He was thin and stooped slightly. He was also, Lizzie couldn't help noticing, very bow-legged. His son, however, whom she guessed to be about twenty years old, was tall and broad with fair curly hair and a cheeky smile that lit up his bright blue eyes. But at the moment, his expression was solemn and, Lizzie thought, for some reason she could not understand, disappointed.

'She's not staying, Dad,' Billy said.

The older man sighed and nodded. 'I don't expect she will, lad. Anyway, let's get you to the Manor, miss, and then we'll see.'

Lizzie was puzzled by the remark, but she made no comment. Billy helped her into the trap and Joe climbed in and took the reins. Leaving the station, they travelled for about a mile through gently undulating countryside until they reached a few cottages on either side of the roadway. Then they turned to the right into a long, straight road that seemed to be the main village street. They passed a few shops and, at the end of the street, Lizzie noticed a small school with children playing in the yard.

'It's break time,' Billy told her. 'Eleven to a quarter past. I used to go there when I was a nipper. Still got the same master there. He lives in that house next to the school. Mr Holland is a good teacher, but very strict. He'd cane you if you so much as looked out the window.'

'Even the girls?'

'Oh aye. But they got it on their hands, not on their backsides like us lads.'

'Watch your language in front of a lady,' Joe muttered. But Billy only grinned as he said, 'Sorry, miss.'

'Is there only the one teacher for the whole school?'

Billy nodded. 'Not many kids, you see. When they're old enough, the clever ones go to the nearest grammar school. Chesterfield, usually. It's only about five miles away. The rest of us stay on here till we can leave. The master at the Manor – Mr Spendlove, that is – is very good. He helps those who can go to the grammar school and if they're really clever and can go to university, then he helps them with that too.'

Joe took up the story. 'And those who are left, he tries to employ as many as he can either in the lead mine he owns a few miles from here or on the farmland around the village, most of which he owns too. There are two tenanted farms and Home Farm, which Mr Spendlove farms himself. So, you see, most of the men in the village are employed by the master in one way or another.'

'Does he own the cottages in the village too?' Lizzie asked, thinking back to the idyllic time when she had lived on her family's estate and all had been right with the world.

'Most of 'em, miss,' Billy said. 'But he's a good landlord and master. We're very lucky here and we all know that. It's just such a shame . . .'

'Billy.' There was a warning note in Joe's tone.

Passing the church and the vicarage at the edge of the village, they left the cottages and houses behind and drove a short distance between grass fields on either side up a slight incline towards a grand house standing on its own. Passing through the gates, Joe steered the pony up the driveway, which was bordered on either side by well-kept gardens.

'I'll take you round to the kitchen door at the back of the house, miss,' Joe said. 'I'm sure Mrs Weston – she's the housekeeper – will want to see you first and then she'll take you to see the master.'

'The master?' Lizzie asked. 'Won't I be interviewed by the mistress?'

'Oh no, miss. The mistress is in rather delicate health these days, though it wasn't always so. The master sees to everything, with Mrs Weston's help, of course.'

'And there's the butler too. Mr Bennett,' Billy put in. 'He and Mrs Weston more or less run the house between them. They're in charge of all the servants.'

Lizzie nodded as Billy helped her to climb down from

50

the trap. 'I'll take you in and introduce you,' he said. 'Perhaps Cook will make you a cup of tea.'

'I wouldn't bet on it,' Joe muttered beneath his breath.

Courteously, the young man opened the back door of the house and ushered her through what looked like a large washhouse, with a brick-built copper in one corner, several tubs, wooden dolly pegs and three airers which were hauled up to the ceiling. Then he led her along a short passage and opened a door into a large kitchen.

'Mrs Graves,' he addressed a plump, middle-aged woman in a white apron and cap who was rolling out pastry on the large scrubbed table in the centre of the room, 'I've brought Miss Ingham from the station for an interview with the master.'

Lizzie glanced about her. It was very like the kitchen at Ancholme Hall, with a huge cooking range on one wall and shelves of gleaming copper pans and shining crockery. The sight of it and the happy memories of her old home it evoked brought a sudden lump to her throat. But she forced a smile to her lips and said, 'Good morning, Mrs Graves.'

The cook did not respond or even look up at her, but continued to concentrate on her pastry-making. Addressing Billy, all she said was, 'Have you indeed?' Then she raised her voice. 'Nelly . . .'

A young girl, whom Lizzie presumed to be a kitchen maid, appeared from the scullery, drying her hands on a towel. 'Yes, Cook?'

'Go and find Mrs Weston. Tell her the latest would-be nanny is here. She might be resting in her bedroom. She had one of her nasty headaches earlier.'

Nelly scuttled away through a door, which, Lizzie presumed, led further into the house. Billy was fidgeting, standing first on one foot and then on the other, looking extremely uncomfortable for some reason, which Lizzie couldn't understand. The cook looked like she was a formidable woman, but she couldn't believe the young man was actually frightened of her.

'I'll be off, then,' he said, as if he couldn't escape from the kitchen quickly enough. 'They'll let me know when you're ready to go back to the station, miss.'

Lizzie smiled at him. 'Thank you, Billy.'

There was a loud sniff from the cook that sounded suspiciously like disapproval. 'Aye, him and his dad running up and down to the station every few days as if there isn't enough to do here,' she muttered.

'I'd willingly have walked here, Mrs Graves, but Mr Spendlove said in his letter that I would be met at the station.'

'Aye well, he would. Wants to make a good impression.'

Lizzie was puzzled. Why on earth would an employer want to make a good impression on a possible future servant? For that is what she would be. Surely, it should be the other way round.

The door opened again and a slim woman Lizzie guessed to be in her early fifties – possibly a similar age to the cook – came in. She had brown hair piled neatly on the top of her head, and wore a long-sleeved black dress with an ankle-length skirt and a discreet, single-strand, pearl necklace.

The woman smiled at Lizzie and held out her hand. 'Good morning. Miss Ingham, is it? I'm Mrs Weston, housekeeper for Mr and Mrs Spendlove.' She glanced at the cook. 'Perhaps you would be kind enough to have Nelly bring tea to my sitting room, Mrs Graves. And some sandwiches, if it's not too much trouble. I'm sure Miss Ingham must be ready for a little refreshment after her journey.'

52

Again there was a loud sniff of disapproval from the cook. 'Whatever you say, Mrs Weston.'

The housekeeper turned back to Lizzie. 'If you'd come this way, Miss Ingham.'

Lizzie followed her out of the kitchen and down a short passageway into what was obviously the house-keeper's sitting room. When they were seated comfortably and the maid had brought a tray of tea and sandwiches, Mrs Weston seemed to take a deep breath. 'I should perhaps tell you something of our situation here before you see the master. If you decide that this position is not something you could undertake, then there will be no need to trouble Mr Spendlove.'

This was sounding very strange to Lizzie, but she said nothing and waited for the housekeeper to explain.

'You are the sixth nanny we have interviewed in as many months and even before that, during the last two years, no one has stayed very long. Master Charlie is four years old now and he is a very –' she paused as if searching for the right word – 'troubled little boy. As a baby he was adorable but, at about the age of two, things changed and the nanny he'd had from birth said she could no longer cope with his bad behaviour.' She sighed. 'After that, we began a succession of nannies, none of whom could control him. We have to – to do certain things that I don't really approve of but there seems to be no alter-native.'

'May I ask what those things are, Mrs Weston?'

The housekeeper looked away guiltily. 'It's very difficult to wash him properly and bath time is a nightmare. He lashes out so violently that even Joe and Billy, who always help, can hardly hold him. And as for washing his hair, well, we've given up on that.' She paused briefly and shook her head in despair. 'He's destroyed or damaged every toy he's been given and he won't sleep at night. We have to shackle him to his bed. Then he screams and screams and can be heard through most of the house, big though it is, and especially in the servants' bedrooms, which are just above the nursery quarters. No one gets any sleep so – so the doctor comes on a Saturday night and gives him a sleeping draught. At least that way we get a couple of nights' rest.' She paused and bit her lip. 'I don't like it, Miss Ingham, but there's nothing I can do. I know that the master is in a very difficult position. He has to think of his staff too.'

'Have other staff left because of the situation?'

Mrs Weston shook her head. 'No. You see, most of us have been here since before Master Charlie was born and we're all very loyal to the master and the mistress. She is in very delicate health now, poor lady, and I think it stems from all the trouble with her little boy. She was fine before all this started. When she first arrived as a young bride, she was so pretty and vivacious. The master and mistress entertained a lot then. We had dinner parties and balls. It was a wonderful time.' The housekeeper's face fell into lines of sadness. 'But then it all went wrong. And now, I think it is very unlikely there will be any more children. They just daren't risk whatever is wrong with Master Charlie happening again. It's so sad because when the little chap was born, there was such rejoicing here and in the village. A son and heir for the estate and the lead mine. We were all so happy.' Mrs Weston pulled a handkerchief from her pocket and dabbed her eyes. Then she straightened her shoulders and gave a wan smile. 'But we have to deal with the here and now, don't we? So, Miss Ingham, are you willing to talk to the master or would you like to leave now?'

For a moment, Lizzie was thoughtful but then her heart

went out to the little boy, even though she had yet to meet him. Perhaps, with all her training, there was something she could do to help.

'I'll definitely talk to the master, Mrs Weston, and, if he thinks I'd be suitable, I'd like to see Charlie too.'

'Oh – er – oh, I see.' Mrs Weston seemed taken aback by Lizzie's remark, but to the young woman it seemed the most natural thing in the world to want to meet the little boy who was to be in her charge. 'Very well, then. We'll go up now.'

The housekeeper led the way from her room up the back staircase that led to the main part of the house. In the hallway, the butler was hovering.

'Mr Bennett,' Mrs Weston addressed him, 'do you know if the master is free to interview Miss Ingham?'

Mr Bennett was a tall, broad-shouldered man somewhere, Lizzie guessed, in his fifties with smooth dark hair which was thinning a little. He was smartly dressed in a black suit, white shirt and tie as befitted a butler and head of the household servants.

'I believe so, Mrs Weston. If the young lady will wait a moment, I will enquire.'

Mrs Weston turned to Lizzie with a smile that did not quite reach her eyes. They had a look of permanent anxiety in them. 'I'll leave you with Mr Bennett, then, Miss Ingham. If – if you still wish to see Charlie after you have talked to the master, Mr Bennett will send word to me and I will take you up to the nursery.'

'Thank you, Mrs Weston.'

A few moments later, Lizzie found herself being shown into Mr Spendlove's study. A tall, straight-backed man with dark brown hair, greying a little at the temples, rose from behind his desk. He was clean shaven with even, handsome features. He held out his hand to her and she found herself looking into warm brown eyes. There was deep sadness in those eyes, as if he carried a great burden on his shoulders, but his voice was deep and welcoming as he greeted her.

'Miss Ingham, please sit down. You have come some distance to see me, I believe. I am grateful.'

There it was again. Why was a prospective employer grateful to her? When she was seated, Mr Spendlove sat down again and clasped his hands together on the desk. He began speaking, a little hesitantly, Lizzie thought.

'I expect Mrs Weston has told you a little of our – er – problems. Charlie is – difficult to handle and during the past two years no one has felt able to stay very long.' He smiled wryly. 'The shortest was two days. And these were, in the main, experienced nannies. Now, I see that this would be your first proper appointment after college. Although Miss Davenport's letter of recommendation states that you have just completed a probationary year too caring for a boy who is to start boarding school in September, I'm – not sure whether or not you would be able to cope here.'

'The college course was very thorough,' Lizzie said softly. 'And we were shown all sorts of scenarios as to what we might encounter.'

'I'm sure you were,' Roland Spendlove said. 'The college you attended has an excellent reputation. I believe they have trained nannies who have ended up in the service of the royals and certainly in the households of the upper class, but I doubt very much whether you have experienced any child quite like poor Charlie.'

'What exactly is the problem, sir?'

Roland spread his hands in a helpless gesture. 'That's the trouble, Miss Ingham. We don't know. None of the doctors – and there have been several who have a special interest in the development of children – can give us a medical diagnosis. One or two of the more experienced nannies have said they believe it's severe temper tantrums or just plain naughtiness, but even their . . .' he paused for a minute as if overcome with emotion and there was a break in his voice as he added, 'even their punishments were to no avail.'

'I see,' Lizzie murmured, but she didn't really. She was beginning to have a very uncomfortable feeling about little Charlie.

'My wife and I were so thrilled when he was born,' he continued, repeating more or less what the housekeeper had said. 'He was the answer to all our prayers. A son and heir. I have a younger brother who has followed an army career, so there would have been an heir, but James has no interest in farming or mining, though I am sure he would do his duty if it became necessary. Nor is he married yet. He was delighted when Cecily and I had a son. He saw it as an event that would allow him to live his own life.'

'May I see Charlie?'

Roland met her clear gaze and sighed. 'I can understand that you'd like to, but I fear if you do . . .'

'I'd like to, but first I must ask one question. Are you actually offering me the position? Because it wouldn't be right for me to meet him and then you decide I'm not suitable.'

'Oh yes, I'm offering it to you, Miss Ingham. Of course I am.'

Silently, Lizzie thought, the poor man is desperate. He'll take anyone he can get.

As if suddenly realizing he had not yet interviewed her properly, had asked no questions about herself or her background and how that might look to her, Roland said hastily, 'Your credentials are excellent, Miss Ingham, and the principal at the college speaks of you in glowing terms. If there are any doubts, they will be on your side, not on mine.'

Lizzie struggled with herself. While she did not want her family's secrets spread abroad, she was a truthful and honest girl. She did not feel it would be right to keep the facts of her former life from her employer, particularly when they had been so open with her about their own troubles. She took a deep breath. 'I think there is something I should tell you, Mr Spendlove, but I would ask you to keep it most confidential, apart from sharing it with your wife, of course.'

'Of course,' he agreed but the worry in his eyes deepened as if he feared to hear something that would oblige him to rescind his offer.

'I expect you would have seen in the newspapers a little over three years ago now the stories that came to be known as the "Ancholme Scandal"?'

Roland stared at her as he murmured, 'Yes, I do remember it. Go on.'

'I am Elizabeth, daughter of Edward, the fifth Earl of Ancholme.'

Seven

The revelation of her true identity seemed to stun Roland and he gaped at her as the details of the tragedy he'd read about filtered through his memory. At last he said, 'Oh my dear girl, I am so sorry for the dreadful time you must have had. So –' he paused and frowned slightly, 'you are actually *Lady* Elizabeth.'

Lizzie smiled wryly. 'I suppose so, but it's not how I want to be known now. I must forge a new life for myself and be known as Elizabeth, or even Lizzie, Ingham.'

'Or just,' Roland murmured, his gaze still on her, 'Nanny.'

'Precisely.'

There was silence in the room until he asked tentatively, 'Have you no relatives who would – support you?'

Lizzie's mouth tightened. 'There's only my mother's sister, but she and her husband were terrified of being linked to the scandal and planned to send me to live on the Lincolnshire coast, well away from society. Or, perhaps, to have me become a companion to an elderly lady. But I have had enormous help from my late father's solicitor, a Mr Bellingham. He and his wife have been so kind. He advised me that I had enough money from an annuity left to me by my grandmother to be able to attend the college.'

'Where are you living now?'

'With Mr and Mrs Bellingham in Leicester until I can

find a position.' There was a slight pause before Lizzie said, 'Mr Spendlove, if this has altered your opinion of me, please say so now.'

He answered swiftly, 'Oh good Heavens, no, it only increases my admiration for you that you have handled such a catastrophe that was none of your doing so well.' He noted the hint of steel in her fine eyes and marvelled at the strength of character she must possess to have dealt with everything that had already happened to her in her young life. Perhaps, he thought hopefully, this remarkable young woman sitting so calmly in front of him was the answer to his prayers.

He stood up. 'So, the position is yours if you will take it. And now, I suppose we had better introduce you to Charlie.'

Roland moved round the desk and, as Lizzie stood up, he opened the door for her. In the hall, both the butler and the housekeeper were waiting.

'I have offered the post of nanny to Miss Ingham, but she would like to meet Charlie first before she gives me her answer.'

Lizzie saw a look pass between the two senior servants.

'Very well, sir,' Mrs Weston said, moving forward. 'I'll take her up.'

'I will come with you,' Roland said.

'Oh sir, there's no need for you . . .' Mrs Weston began, but Roland pursed his lips and said firmly, 'I want to.'

As they mounted the main staircase from the hall to the first floor and moved along a long corridor towards the eastern end of the house, the sound of a child screaming reached their ears. Mrs Weston glanced anxiously at her employer, but Roland, with his lips pressed together, moved on purposefully.

They came to a door at the end of the corridor.

'This is the door into the nursery quarters,' Mrs Weston said as she produced a bunch of keys from her pocket and unlocked it. When the three of them had passed through, she locked it again behind them. Now the child's screaming was much louder. Ahead now was a shorter corridor with two doors on the left-hand side and one on the right, which Mrs Weston opened. Stepping inside she held it open for Roland and Lizzie to enter. Lizzie glanced swiftly around her, taking in the large room with a door at either end. The two south-facing windows, overlooking the front of the house, were barred and the furniture in the room was minimal. There was only a single-sized bed with an easy chair beside it, a large wardrobe, a chest of drawers and a small table and two chairs. A warm fire, with a sturdy fireguard in front of it, burned in the grate even though it was summer. But there were no toys strewn about the floor, no bookcase with children's books. Her gaze came to rest on the little boy lying on the carpet. With every scream he was kicking his legs, drumming his heels on the floor and punching the air with his fists. Although he was lying down, Lizzie could see that he was tall for his age. He was dressed in navy-blue knickerbockers and thick socks. The white collar of a shirt was folded down over the neckline of his jacket.

A young girl dressed in a nursery maid's outfit moved forward. She was a pretty girl with fair hair tucked neatly beneath a frilly white cap, though at the moment she was red in the face and tears streamed down her face. 'Oh sir, I'm so sorry you should see him like this. I – I can't do anything with him this morning. Billy had to come and help me dress him, but since then . . .' She gestured helplessly towards the distressed little boy.

'It's all right, Kitty,' Roland said gently and there was

great sadness in his tone as he added, 'it's not your fault. You've been coping on your own for weeks now and it's taken its toll. I can see that.'

Lizzie stood for a moment and then moved towards Charlie. She placed her reticule on the floor and then knelt beside him. The smell of a soiled nappy assailed her nostrils. The boy was four years old, she'd been told. He should have been toilet-trained at least two years ago, if not before that.

'Hello, Charlie,' she said softly, leaning towards him. 'My name's Lizzie and I'm going to come and help take care of you.' Deliberately she avoided using the name 'Nanny'. She guessed that his experiences with that name had not been pleasant. She reached out and gently stroked his cheek. 'There, there, little man,' she whispered. 'Everything will be all right.'

Charlie clenched his fist and knocked her hand away, but Lizzie tried again. His screams subsided a little as he turned his head to look at her, but tears still streamed from his eyes and ran down his temples and into the thick mass of matted black hair that had formed tangled ringlets. Now, he hiccupped miserably.

'Shall we change that nappy?' Lizzie said. 'I'm sure it can't be comfortable.' Lizzie glanced up and smiled at Kitty. 'Perhaps you'll help me, Kitty.'

'Of course, miss.' The young girl seemed suddenly revitalized. She scurried through one of the doors leading out of the main room into what Lizzie could now see was a bathroom. She returned with a bowl of warm water, soap, a flannel and soft towels. She set them on the floor beside Lizzie. 'I'll just get a clean nappy, miss.' She hurried to the chest of drawers and came back with a towelling nappy.

As Lizzie began to take off the boy's short trousers,

Roland and Mrs Weston moved to the other side of the room and stood near one of the long windows. However, they were still watching what Lizzie and Kitty were doing, especially when the boy's cries began to increase again.

'There, there, Charlie. Soon be done.'

Deftly, as if she had been doing it for years instead of only a comparatively few times the during the college's practical lessons, Lizzie removed his clothing and the soiled nappy and washed him.

'There's a nasty sore on his bottom,' Lizzie whispered. 'Have you any Vaseline?'

'Yes, there's a jar in the bathroom cupboard. I'll get it.' Again Kitty jumped up.

When Charlie was dressed once more but still lying on the floor, Kitty said, 'Perhaps you'd like to wash your hands, miss?'

'Please.' She got up from the floor and followed the girl into the bathroom. 'I'll be back in a moment, Charlie,' she tried to soothe him, but by the time Lizzie had washed her hands and returned to him, he was screaming and kicking once more. She knelt beside him again and held out her hands, inviting him to come to her, but his face was so screwed up, he didn't notice. So, she reached over, picked him up and pulled him to sit on her lap. 'There, there, all done for now.' She stroked his cheek and whispered soothing words to him. Gradually, his crying subsided to a hiccup once more. As she held him close, she couldn't fail to notice the smell coming from his unkempt hair and his unwashed body.

'Now, Charlie, I have to go back to fetch my belongings but I shall come back here on Thursday on the same train as today. That's three days away and then I shall be staying here with Kitty to look after you. I won't go away again, I promise. How does that sound?'

The little boy looked up at her and though tears still ran from his eyes, he was no longer screaming. Now, he really seemed to be searching her face. At that moment, Lizzie felt a warmness soaking through her dress and knew that the child had urinated in his clean nappy.

'Oh dear, I think we've had another little accident.' She smiled and glanced up at Kitty. 'Could you fetch some more water and another nappy, please Kitty?'

As they knelt together again, the maid whispered, 'What about your dress, miss? It's wet and it'll stain.'

Unconcerned, Lizzie smiled. 'It'll wash, Kitty. Don't worry.'

Once Charlie was changed again, Lizzie picked him up and carried him to the window to look out over the driveway. 'So, on Thursday, at about half past eleven in the morning, I will be coming up the driveway there with Joe and Billy. You can watch out for me, can't you? Now, there's just one more thing . . .' She carried him back to where she had left her reticule on the floor. She set him down, opened the bag and pulled out a small, soft teddy bear. 'This is Mr Snuggles and I want you to look after him for me until I come back.' She gave the bear a quick cuddle and then held him out to Charlie.

The boy snatched him and then threw him across the room.

'Oh, Charlie . . .' Kitty began and out of the corner of her eye she saw both Roland and Mrs Weston start to move towards them, but Lizzie only laughed. 'Oh, poor Mr Snuggles. I hope he hasn't hurt his head?' She crossed the space to where the toy had landed and picked it up. 'No, he's fine, but you must look after him, Charlie. I'll show you how to put him to bed because he'll want to snuggle up to you at night. Now, is this where you sleep?' She crossed the room to the bed and as she neared it, she was appalled to see ties attached to the frame that must be the restraints Mrs Weston had spoken of. But she ignored them and drew back the covers, tucking the toy beneath them so that only the bear's head showed. 'Now, that's how you put Mr Snuggles to bed and he will stay beside you all night. Will you do that for me?'

Charlie just stared up at her and made no gesture that he had understood one word of what she had been saying.

'Miss,' Kitty began hesitantly, with a nervous glance towards Mrs Weston and the master. 'Is – is that toy special to you because – because . . .' She bit her lip, unwilling to continue, but Roland came to her rescue.

'Kitty is worried about your possession, Miss Ingham, because Charlie can be very destructive.' He gestured around the room. 'You may have noticed there are no toys around. There is a good reason for that.'

'No matter,' Lizzie said cheerfully. 'I just thought it might make him understand my promise to come back.' She made no move to take the toy away, but squatted down in front of the little boy and took his hands. 'I must go now because I have a train to catch, but I will come back on Thursday.' She touched his cheek tenderly and then stood up. She picked up her reticule and then turned to face Roland. 'Thank you, Mr Spendlove. I accept your offer of employment as Charlie's nanny.'

She saw Roland and Mrs Weston exchange a glance, then the housekeeper turned to her and asked, 'Don't you want to see your room?'

Lizzie's smile widened. 'I am sure it will be fine, Mrs Weston.' She turned to the nursery maid and held out her hand. 'Goodbye for now, Kitty. I'll see you on Thursday.'

Kitty began to weep again. She clung to Lizzie's hand with both of hers. 'Oh miss, you will come back, won't you? You really will?'

'I will, Kitty.' Moved by the young girl's tears, she hugged her and whispered in her ear, 'I give you my word.'

As Roland, Mrs Weston and Lizzie left the nursery and moved back to the main part of the house, the echo of Charlie's screams followed them.

Eight

Roland shook Lizzie's hand in the hall. 'Safe journey and I – I hope to see you again on Thursday.'

Lizzie thought she could still detect a note of doubt in his tone but there was really nothing more she could do to reassure him.

'Thank you, sir. I shall do my very best for Charlie.'

He gave a quick nod, turned away and disappeared into his study.

'Poor man,' Mrs Weston murmured as she led the way back down to the housekeeper's room. 'I do hope, Miss Ingham, that you're not leading us all on, because, to be honest with you, we're all about at the end of our tether. We've had so many promises that have been broken. So many hopes smashed that none of us, especially the master, knows what to do next for the best.'

Lizzie sighed. She was at a loss to know what to say that would convince these good people that she was sincere. 'I can only guess at what you've all been through and I can think of nothing else to say to you other than, you'll see me on Thursday.'

With a deep sigh, Mrs Weston murmured, 'I hope we will. I really hope we will.' Then in a stronger voice she added, 'Do you want to sponge your skirt? That might cause a stain.'

'That's very kind of you. Thank you.'

'We'll go back to my room, then. This way.'

*

A little while later, Mrs Weston led Lizzie back into the kitchen. 'Nelly, will you tell Mr Marshall and Billy that Miss Ingham is ready to be taken back to the station.'

The girl hurried to do the housekeeper's bidding as Mrs Graves glanced up from her chair by the fire. 'Just havin' me five minutes, Mrs Weston, before setting about the preparations for dinner. I didn't get a lot of sleep last night, as per usual. Roll on Saturday night, is all I can say, when we might get a bit of peace.'

For a moment, Lizzie didn't understand the cook's remark and then she remembered. On Saturday nights the doctor visited to give Charlie a sleeping draught. It was the only way, she'd been told, that the staff whose rooms were above the nursery quarters, could get a good night's sleep.

The back door opened and Joe and Billy came in.

'You ready, then, miss?'

'I am, Mr Marshall, thank you. And please would you be able to collect me from the station at just after eleven o'clock on Thursday, as you did this morning? I shall have two medium-sized trunks with me. Will that be all right?'

Joe's mouth fell open. 'You're – you're coming back?'

Lizzie met his astonished look with a smile. 'Most definitely.'

Behind her she heard the cook's derisive snort. As she followed Joe and Billy out of the back door, she paused to say, 'Goodbye, Mrs Weston. Thank you for your kindness. Goodbye, Mrs Graves. I'll see you again on Thursday.'

'Will you, now?' the cook said. 'A blue moon on Thursday, is it, then? Or should I watch out for pigs flying past me window?'

But Lizzie only smiled as she closed the door behind her.

*

Back at the station, Billy helped her down from the trap. 'Do you mean it, miss? Are you really coming back? 'Specially now you've seen the little chap.'

'I am, Billy. Kitty tells me that you often help her with Charlie.'

'I do, miss.' He hesitated and then said in a rush, 'Me an' Kitty are walking out together.'

'Really? That's unusual, isn't it? Employers don't usually allow their domestic staff to – well – walk out together.'

'It's an unusual household, Miss Ingham,' Joe butted in before Billy could answer. 'The master's very lenient because we all do a lot extra to help him, if you know what I mean.'

Lizzie nodded. 'I can guess.'

'When the little lad needs a bath, both me and Billy have to help. He's surprisingly strong.' He glanced at her shrewdly. 'If you *are* coming back, miss, you can count on me and Billy to help you all we can. Don't be afraid to ask anything of us. Anything at all.'

'Thank you, Mr Marshall. That's good to know.'

'And it's Joe, miss.'

She smiled. 'Thank you, Joe.'

A train whistle sounded in the distance. 'I must go. That's probably my train. Goodbye, I'll see you on Thursday. Don't forget. Eleven o'clock.'

As Lizzie hurried away Joe pulled his cap back on his head and muttered, 'I don't reckon we need bother ourselves to come down here on Thursday, do you, our Billy?'

'Actually, Dad, I do. I think she will come back.'

'Don't be taken in by a pretty face, lad,' Joe said, as he turned the trap around and headed home.

'She's more than pretty. She's beautiful,' Billy said above the rattle of the wheels. 'Did you notice the colour of her eyes? They're violet.'

Joe laughed. 'Don't let Kitty hear you say that.'

Billy grinned. 'I love Kitty dearly and to me she's the loveliest girl in the world, but it doesn't stop me admiring other young women. And Miss Lizzie has an aura about her, an air of – what do they call it – sophistication. She's been well brought up, I reckon.'

'That's a big word for a Monday,' Joe teased him. 'But I think you could be right. She must have a good background to have been able to attend some posh college. So, I ask you, what on earth does she want to come here for?'

Now, even Billy, who had taken a liking to Lizzie and truly believed in her, was stumped for an answer.

After Lizzie's visit several conversations within the walls of the Manor were had. It had long been a custom for the three senior members of the household staff to meet in Mrs Weston's sitting room at the end of the day when their duties had finished. They were never completely off duty – they were always on-call if needed – but usually they could relax for an hour or so before retiring. That first evening, Nelly brought in three mugs of cocoa.

'You can go to bed now, lass. I'll make sure everything's all right in the kitchen and Mr Bennett will lock up as usual.'

'Thank you, Cook. Goodnight, then.'

As the door closed behind the maid, Mrs Graves sighed. 'The lass that came today, she'll not come back, you know. She's just another one to add to the ever-growing list. Though how poor Kitty's going to cope for much longer, I don't know. She's worn out.'

'It's a big responsibility for a young maid like her, I grant you,' Mrs Weston said. 'And Miss Ingham's very young too. Perhaps I'm wrong to believe her. But there was just something about her. Charlie can't have made a very good first impression and yet she was lovely with him. So calm and patient.'

'I understand from the master that she's more or less straight out of college,' Mr Bennett said. 'I know it's a very good one, but she won't have had much practical experience, will she?'

'She's had a year's probationary placement with a ten-year-old boy, I understand.'

Mrs Graves snorted. 'Nothing like poor Charlie, then, that is a fact.'

'Has the master said anything else to you, Mr Bennett?' Even in private moments like this the senior staff never called each other by their Christian names.

'He seems hopeful, Mrs Weston, but then he's been hopeful before and been bitterly disappointed.'

'And he will be again. You mark my words.' Mrs Graves was adamant.

Upstairs in the drawing room, Roland and his wife, Cecily, were having a nightcap together.

'Tell me about the nanny you interviewed today,' Cecily asked.

'Are you sure, my love? I don't want you to worry yourself.'

For a moment Cecily's face crumpled but she pulled in a deep breath. 'I am not being a good wife to you, Roland, I know that . . .'

He moved swiftly to sit beside her on the sofa and took her hand. 'My darling Cecily, I love you dearly and want no other, I promise you. None of this trouble we have with poor Charlie is your fault.'

Roland had first seen Cecily at a ball in the year of her coming-out. He had fallen in love with her there and then. She had been beautiful; slim with fair hair and blue eyes. She had been vivacious and captivating with a string of admirers, but had fallen for him too and they were married within a year, just before her twentieth birthday. Their son had been born a year later and the young couple, and, indeed, all their family, were ecstatic. Their household servants, their tenants and workers on the farmland and in the mine rejoiced too and all seemed well in their world. There would be an heir for the estate and their livelihoods secured. But as problems arose with Charlie, Cecily blamed herself and her health declined. She lost weight and slept badly. She no longer wanted to entertain as they once had. Roland was always gentle with her and the staff followed his example, running the household without the guidance of the mistress.

'But perhaps if I had taken a greater interest in him as a baby . . .' Cecily said now.

'You must not blame yourself in any way. We had what we thought was an excellent nanny, the same one who had cared for you until you were old enough to have a governess. It was your mother's insistence, if I remember, that we should employ Nanny Gordon for Charlie.'

Cecily gazed into the dying embers of the fire as memories of her childhood flitted though her mind. 'She was very strict,' she murmured. 'If I misbehaved, she would smack me hard and sometimes, as a punishment, she would lock me in a dark cupboard for what seemed like hours, though it was probably only minutes.'

'You've never told me this before,' Roland said softly.

Cecily shook her head. 'No, I – I think I'd shut it out of my mind.' She met his gaze squarely. 'I only began to remember some of it in a dream I had recently. Oh Roland . . .' Tears filled her fine blue eyes. 'What have we done? Is it our fault that Charlie is like he is?'

'No, my darling, I'm sure it isn't.' He patted her hand, trying to reassure her, but doubts were creeping into his mind now. Had they unwittingly employed a harsh nanny, whose punishments for what she decreed as misbehaviour had actually bordered on cruelty?

Cecily dried her eyes and said bravely, 'So tell me about the girl who came today?'

'Well,' he said slowly, 'I hardly dare say it, my love, but I am hopeful she will come back.' He went on to describe Lizzie. 'She was so calm and gentle with him. She even left him her own teddy bear to care for until she returns.'

'She sounds too good to be true,' Cecily smiled a little sadly, 'but you know what they say about that.'

Roland smiled too. 'There's something else I should tell you, but you must give me your solemn promise you will speak to no one of this, not even to your parents.'

'Of course, Roland. What is it?'

Roland told her everything that Lizzie had told him about her past, ending, 'And that is part of the reason I think she will come back. I believe she wants to disappear from a world that has been cruel to her when none of it was her fault. Her life at the college would have been – sheltered, shall we say – and I think that's what she wants.'

'So, really, she should be *Lady* Elizabeth?'

'Yes, but that's not what she wishes to be called. She's Lizzie Ingham now – or Nanny.'

'How cruel that her own relatives would not support her,' Cecily said. She was silent for a few moments as she tried to imagine what it must be like to be in Lizzie's shoes. 'You're right, Roland,' she said at last. 'We must comply with her request. Not a word to anyone, I promise. Oh, but I do so hope she comes back on Thursday.'

Nine

Lizzie stepped down from the train and looked about her. There was no one waiting on the platform to meet her. She smiled ruefully. She had half expected as much.

The young porter was wheeling his barrow towards her. 'You got any luggage, miss?'

'Yes, it's in the guard's van. There are two trunks. They might be rather heavy,' she warned, but did not add that they contained all her worldly belongings.

'We'll manage, miss. Guard'll help me.'

When her trunks had been off-loaded and were sitting on the platform, the whistle blew and the train began to leave the station. There was still no sign of Joe or Billy. Lizzie glanced at the station clock. It was already ten minutes past eleven. She sat down on one of the trunks. She'd give them ten minutes and then she would ask to leave her luggage here and walk to the Manor. She was watching the entrance when, five minutes later, Billy strolled onto the platform and glanced about him. Catching sight of her, she saw him give a start. Even from a distance she could see the surprised expression on his face. Now, he hurried towards her.

'Oh miss, I'm so sorry. Train must have been early.'

'Maybe so, Billy. But never mind, you're here now.' She stood up. 'My trunks are heavy, but I'm sure the porter will help you.'

'I'll get me dad . . .' Before she could say more, he

ran back and moments later reappeared with Joe at his side. As they approached her, Joe pulled his cap from his head.

'Well, miss, I'm never one not to admit when they're wrong and I was wrong about you. Me and Billy had a right old set-to this morning about coming down here to meet the train, even though it was the master's orders. Billy's said all along that you'd be back. I owe you an apology, miss, and I'm very glad to see you.'

Lizzie chuckled and held out her hand to the head groom. 'And I'm glad to see you again too, Joe. Now, this is my luggage. Can you manage it?'

'Oh yes, miss. This bit's nothing. You should see the luggage the mistress takes with her when she goes away, 'specially if she takes her maid with her. Come on, Billy, shift yourself. Let's get this loaded.'

As they travelled the mile or so from the station, Lizzie, now that she knew she was going to be staying here, looked about her with greater interest.

'Does Mr Spendlove farm all this land?' She waved her hand towards the fields on either side.

'Yes, miss. The land around the village is known as Home Farm and the master supervises that himself. Then there are two tenanted farms a bit further away from here. He also owns a lead mine, but that's several miles away. No one from the village works there. It's a bit far away to travel every day, but it provides employment for folk in that area.'

'And the village itself? I noticed one or two shops last time I came.'

'Aye. There's a butcher, a baker . . .'

'But no candlestick maker,' Billy put in with a chuckle.

'Ignore him, miss. He thinks he's funny.' But Joe was smiling too as he carried on. 'We have a cobbler and a dressmaker and, of course, as you'd imagine, a wheel-wright and blacksmith.'

'They're the same person,' Billy interrupted again. 'There's not enough work for two separate businesses, but Matt Naylor is kept pretty busy. He's the sort of chap who can turn his hand to most things.' Now Billy was solemn as he added, 'He's the local undertaker and makes the most beautiful coffins. He made a lovely one for my mam when she died a while back.'

Joe cleared his throat and continued with his description of the locality. 'And then there's the village shop and post office run by Mrs Smith. It's just beside the church.'

'Aye,' said Billy, pushing aside any sad memories and smiling once more. 'Also known as the local gossip shop.'

As they bowled along the village street, Lizzie saw several inquisitive glances in her direction. She heard Joe's laughter beside her. 'I know what they're thinking. There goes another one, but she'll be leaving again in a few days.'

'Not this time, Joe,' Lizzie said firmly.

They passed the church and then Lizzie turned her face to look towards the big house standing about half a mile away, up a slight incline outside the village. It was an oblong-shaped building, three storeys high with too many chimneys to count. As they went through the gates and along the driveway, Lizzie noticed again the well-kept gardens and smooth lawns on either side. Steps led up to a terrace and then more steps up to the front door, but, once again, Joe took them round the end of the house to the stable yard behind it.

'Don't forget what I said, miss, will you?' he said. 'Anything you need me an' Billy to do, we will. Let us know when you want to bath him, 'cos you'll need help with that.'

'I will, Joe. Thank you again.'

'We'll bring your trunks up straight away.'

Billy made as if to show her indoors, but Lizzie said, 'It's all right, Billy. I know the way.'

'Oh, I'm coming in with you, miss.' He grinned. 'I want to see the look on Cook's face when you walk through the door.'

He preceded her into the house and into the kitchen, throwing open the door with a flourish as if producing a rabbit from a hat.

'Mrs Graves, just look who's here.'

As she stepped through the doorway, Lizzie saw for herself the look of astonishment on the cook's face. The wooden spoon she was holding clattered to the floor and she gaped at Lizzie, her mouth actually dropping open. When she'd recovered a little, she said, 'Well, I didn't expect to see you back again, not after you'd seen him.' She sniffed, now in charge of herself again. 'But I don't expect you'll be here for long, mind. Anyway . . .' She nodded, more to herself than to Lizzie. 'We'll see, won't we? If you'd like to sit down, I'll make a pot of tea. Nelly, go and find Mrs Weston. Tell her that the nanny has come back.'

As Lizzie sat down at the table, drawing off her gloves, Billy and Joe carried her trunks through the kitchen and up the back stairs to the nursery quarters.

'Thank you,' she said, when they returned. Joe caught her glance as he pulled on his cap before he and Billy returned to their work. 'Now, don't forget what I said, miss.'

'I won't, Joe.'

As the two men left the kitchen and Mrs Graves placed a cup of tea in front of her, the cook said, 'And what has that old rascal been saying to you, might I ask?'

'Just to ask them if there's anything they can help me with. With Charlie, I mean.'

'Aye well, they do a lot for the little chap already, I'll grant you that. Kitty wouldn't manage without them sometimes.' She hesitated and then sat down opposite Lizzie and stared at her. 'Now then, miss, let's you and me get one thing straight between us, shall we? I didn't expect you to come back at all and I'm pretty sure you won't stay long. Joe and Billy will soon be carrying them trunks back down and taking you to the station, I've no doubt. But I'd just ask one thing of you. If you could bring yourself to stay at least a few days just to give poor Kitty a rest. She's exhausted. It's a big responsibility on her young shoulders and she's had no proper training other than what she's picked up here and there from the succession of nannies we've had over the last two years.'

Lizzie regarded the woman sitting opposite her. She took in the small plump figure of the cook in her pristine white apron and the frilly cap that covered her greying hair. Mrs Graves's hazel eyes were sharp in her round face that was showing the first signs of a few wrinkles. But Lizzie saw too in those eyes deep-rooted loyalty to, and concern for, her employers and the rest of the household.

She smiled across the table at the cook, whose expression remained stern. 'I know I can't convince you, Mrs Graves, that I intend to stay for as long as I am needed. Only time will tell you that, but I give you my word that I will care for Kitty as well as for Charlie.' She rose. 'And now I'd better go up to the nursery. Thank you so much for the tea. It was very welcome.'

'I'll get Nelly to –' Mrs Graves began, but at that moment, the kitchen door leading into the house was flung open and Roland Spendlove stood there with Mrs

Weston hovering anxiously behind him. He gazed at Lizzie for several moments before saying in a husky whisper, 'You've come back.'

'I have, sir, just as I promised.'

He seemed to recover his composure and he smiled at her. 'Then I won't keep you any longer. Mrs Weston will take you upstairs and see that you have everything you need.' He held open the door for her as she fell into step behind the housekeeper towards the back stairs leading up to the nursery quarters on the first floor.

When Mrs Weston opened the door into the nursery, Kitty flew across the room with a little cry and flung her arms around a startled Lizzie, weeping against her shoulder. 'Oh, miss, you've come back. Thank you, thank you.'

'There, there, Kitty,' Lizzie said, patting the girl's back. 'I'm here now. You won't have to cope on your own anymore. Now, dry those tears. Where's Charlie? Ah, there he is on his bed. Is he asleep?'

'He's worn out, miss. We had a very bad night. He cried for hours. I didn't get a wink of sleep.'

'Nor did any of us,' Mrs Weston said, but there was no resentment in her tone, just a deep sadness. 'If Charlie doesn't sleep, then none of us do.'

'Then we'll leave him to rest while I settle in. Now, Kitty if you'd show me where everything is and where I am to sleep –' Lizzie removed her grey lightweight summer cloak and hat to reveal her nanny's uniform. She was wearing her more formal attire to travel to her new post. An ankle-length dark blue dress with leg o' mutton sleeves and a high neckline with a white bow tie. When on duty, she would also wear a long white linen apron with a bib.

Kitty glanced at the housekeeper. 'I don't have a key for the nanny's bedroom, Mrs Weston.'

'I'll show Nanny her room.' The housekeeper led Lizzie back into the corridor and opened one of the doors on the opposite side. 'This is your room. I trust it will be comfortable for you. I will have Clara, the under house-maid, make up the bed at once.'

Lizzie smiled inwardly. It was quite obvious that no one had expected her to return, except perhaps Billy. She glanced around the room. It was indeed comfortable with a double bed, a wardrobe and a chest of drawers, but she would have preferred to have been closer to Charlie.

'Where does Kitty sleep?'

'In the room leading off the nursery.'

'The door on the opposite end of the room to the bathroom?'

Mrs Weston nodded. 'That's right, so that she can go to Charlie in the night.'

Lizzie gave Mrs Weston her most disarming smile. 'If it wouldn't be too much of an imposition, may we swap rooms? I'd really like to be as near Charlie as possible and I'm sure Kitty could do with some undisturbed sleep after having had to cope so long on her own.'

'Well, I – er – suppose it would be all right, if that's what you want.'

'Let's ask Kitty if she minds,' Lizzie suggested, but the housekeeper only laughed.

'Mind? Kitty won't mind. She'd be getting a much superior bedroom. I think you'd better see her room first.'

They returned to the nursery and Kitty heard Lizzie's suggestion. 'Oh miss, are you sure? It's only small. Come and see.'

The nursery maid's bedroom was indeed smaller than the one she had just been shown, but it was cosy and comfortably furnished with a wardrobe and chest of drawers. 'It hasn't got its own bathroom like the nanny's has,' Kitty pointed out. 'I use the nursery one.'

'That's no problem,' Lizzie said. 'This will be just fine for me if Mrs Weston has no objection.' She looked at the housekeeper, who shrugged and said, 'If it's what you want, Nanny. I'll send Clara to change the beds and help Kitty move her belongings across the corridor. Oh, and I'll make sure you have a set of keys.'

Lizzie smiled. 'I don't want to sound demanding the minute I get here, but I just want what would be best for Charlie, and for Kitty too.'

Now Mrs Weston smiled at her in return. 'We all wish to help you in any way we can and if this is what you want, then so be it.'

There was a small sound from the nursery.

'That's Charlie waking up,' Kitty said and hurried back into the adjoining room.

Alone for a moment with the housekeeper, Lizzie said, 'I can see that Kitty needs some rest.'

Mrs Weston nodded. 'She has been with Charlie day and night for weeks now. The poor girl is shattered.'

'I understand she is walking out with Billy. That the master has no objection.'

'This is a very different household to what you might expect, as I think you will be beginning to understand. Everything revolves around us all trying to do our best for Charlie and if Kitty and Billy being allowed to see each other – courting, if you like – indirectly helps Charlie, then the master is relaxed about it. We all know neither of the young ones will take advantage of the situation. But they haven't had much time together lately, as you can imagine.'

'Then as well as getting plenty of rest now, I shall try

to see Kitty has some time off to spend with Billy, if you have no objection, that is.'

'Kitty is the nursery maid and comes under the nanny's control.'

'But surely you have jurisdiction over all the female staff, don't you?'

'I suppose so, although the nursery staff have always been set apart. Nannies seem to think they're a law unto themselves and should not be answerable to the housekeeper.'

Lizzie frowned. 'That must make things difficult for you sometimes, Mrs Weston.'

'It does.'

'Then rest assured, I am willing to defer to you and to seek your advice. In fact, there is something I want to ask you now. If I need anything for Charlie, do I come to you, Mr Bennett or directly to the master?'

'Let me know first, Nanny, and I will take it from there. What sort of thing did you have in mind that you might need?'

Lizzie laughed. 'I really don't know yet, but I'm sure there will be something.'

'You do know that you have overall charge of Charlie, don't you? Whatever you decide is best for him, we will concur.'

'Thank you, Mrs Weston. It's good of you to clarify that because I think there will be one thing I want to change this very weekend, although you might not agree with it.'

Mrs Weston stared at her for a moment before slowly nodding her head. 'The doctor and his sleeping draught?'

'Most definitely.'

Mrs Weston sighed. 'It won't go down well with the

rest of the staff if they think they're not going to get at least two nights' sleep in the week.'

'Then let's not tell them. Let's see what happens, shall we?'

Now Mrs Weston actually chuckled. 'On your head be it, Nanny. But for what it's worth, I actually agree with you giving it a try. It's not the sort of thing that should be happening to a four-year-old.'

Hearing Charlie begin to cry, they moved back into the nursery.

'Hello, Charlie, here I am.' Lizzie held out her arms towards the little boy sitting on his bed as she crossed the room. She picked him up and hugged him. 'Have you been looking after Mr Snuggles? Ah yes, there he is.'

Charlie struggled and kicked to free himself. Lizzie set him on the floor and immediately he ran to the far end of the room to stand staring mutinously at her. Her smile didn't slip but she sighed inwardly. This was going to take a little longer than she had hoped.

Ten

The rest of the day passed in a flurry of activity as Lizzie learned the routine of the household. Breakfast was at eight o'clock for the master, mistress and any guests.

'Clara usually brings ours up to the nursery just before that because then she has to serve in the dining room,' Kitty explained. 'We have luncheon in the nursery at noon, the family at twelve-thirty and the rest of the staff at one-thirty.' She ticked off the times on her fingers. 'Afternoon tea is at four and brought to the nursery for us, though that's really Charlie's dinner. His bedtime is at seven and then we have our dinner brought to us up here. We can go down to join the staff later, if we want, but we won't both be able to leave Charlie. Dinner for the family is served in the dining room at seven and the rest of the staff have theirs at eight.'

'Thank you, Kitty. It's very helpful to know the household routine. Now, I presume I haven't met all the household staff yet?'

Kitty wrinkled her forehead. 'Well, you'll meet Clara in a few minutes and then there's Polly. She's the head housemaid and acts as Mrs Spendlove's lady's maid too, so you probably won't see a lot of her. That's all of us really. It's not a huge living-in staff, but one or two women from the village come in on wash days or to do extra cleaning when needed.'

Clara arrived to help Kitty move her belongings and

clean her old room ready for Lizzie. Clara was small in stature with mousey hair and a wide, welcoming smile. She was quick and efficient in her work and willing to do whatever was asked of her. While the two girls dusted and polished and made up the beds with fresh linen, Lizzie spent the afternoon looking after Charlie. She was surprised that there were no toys for the little boy, but decided not to broach that subject on her first day. She felt she had made enough demands already. The two maids worked hard and by three o'clock, everything had been done.

'Shall we unpack your things for you, Nanny?' Kitty offered, but Lizzie said, 'If you could just move both trunks into my room, Charlie will help me put my things away, won't you, Charlie?'

Kitty looked surprised. 'Are you sure, Nanny? He – he can be very destructive. Just be careful what he gets hold of.'

'I will, Kitty. Now, away you go and have an hour off until tea time.' She smiled impishly at the girl. 'Perhaps you'd like a bit of fresh air. A walk to the stables might be a nice idea.'

Kitty blushed. 'You – you know about me and Billy?'

'Oh yes,' Lizzie said airily. 'Billy told me.'

'That's kind of you, Nanny. Thank you.'

As the two girls left the nursery, Lizzie heard Clara say, 'Well, I hope this one stays. She's nice. I like her.'

'So do I . . .' was Kitty's reply, but that was all Lizzie heard as the maids passed through the door leading out of the corridor and locked it behind them.

'Now, Charlie,' Lizzie said, when they were alone. 'Let's go and put everything away in my room, then I'll really feel I've moved in, won't I?'

The boy took no notice. He ran up and down the

room, stamping his feet and throwing Mr Snuggles against the wall. Lizzie turned her back on him, though she was aware of exactly what he was doing. As she opened the trunks holding her clothes, she chatted non-stop to the little boy through the open door. At last, as if overcome with curiosity, he came to watch her. When she'd put all her undergarments in the chest of drawers and hung her spare uniforms and other outfits, of which there were few now, in the wardrobe, she opened the second trunk. It held a few photographs and treasured knick-knacks she had rescued from Ancholme Hall, but also some books and toys from her own childhood. When she had decided to train as a nanny, she had realized that they might well come in handy. And she'd been right; she was shocked that Charlie had no toys of his own. She picked out a wooden pull-along train and carried it into the nursery. She set it on the floor and attached the three carriages to the engine, all the time explaining to the little boy what she was doing. Then she pulled it along the floor with the string saying, 'Choo, choo.'

Charlie squatted down beside the train and then picked up one of the carriages and flung it as hard as he could against the wall, breaking one of the wheels. He reached out to pick up another but Lizzie said firmly, 'No, Charlie, that's not the way to play with the train.' She picked up the carriage he had thrown, fixed it back on to the end of the carriages and pulled at the string. 'You see, it won't run now because it has a broken wheel.'

The boy looked up at her with a determined set to his mouth. He picked up the broken carriage and flung it at the wall again. Another wheel fell off and rolled across the carpet.

'Oh Charlie,' she said, her tone heavy with disappointment. She stretched out her hand towards him. With a whimper, he cringed away from her. Ah, she thought, so that's what used to happen when he misbehaved. He'd be smacked.

'It's all right, Charlie,' she said gently. 'I'm not going to smack you. Come here.' She held her arms wide but the boy did not move. Instead, he stared at her as if he didn't understand. Lizzie dropped her arms and picked up the string. 'Here, you pull the train along.'

It took several minutes before he moved. Slowly he got up and came towards her, but his eyes were on her hands as if he still expected a blow. Lizzie put the string in his hand and, holding hers over it, showed him how to pull the toy along the floor. 'And we say "choo, choo". That's the noise a train makes.'

And that was how Kitty found them when she returned, Lizzie with her hand over Charlie's pulling the toy around the room and saying, 'Choo, choo.'

Nursery tea for Charlie was mashed potato and cheese with jelly and custard to follow. Lizzie had already noticed that the luncheon that had been sent up for him had been minced and mashed and covered with gravy. And Kitty had fed him with a spoon, often having to chase him around the room to give him a mouthful. This was not what a four-year-old should be doing. For the moment, she decided to say nothing, but it looked as if this was another problem she would have to tackle – and with the woman who was her severest critic: Mrs Graves. The child should be eating properly served food now, not babyish pap.

'We have nursery tea with him,' Kitty was saying. 'Just tea and cakes for us, but Clara will bring our dinner up when Charlie's in bed.'

Lizzie nodded. She agreed with what he was being

given to eat and when, but not the way it was presented and certainly not the way Kitty was still spoon-feeding him. But enough for today, she thought as she watched Kitty once again chasing him around the room to feed him his tea. One thing at a time.

After Clara had cleared away the tea things, Lizzie said, 'Does he have a bath before bedtime, Kitty?'

'Only on a Sunday evening, miss. He's more docile then.'

Lizzie raised her eyebrows. 'Docile?'

'The doctor comes every Saturday night to give him what he calls "soothing syrup". Charlie sleeps through the night then and he's still quite drowsy on Sunday. It's the only time any of us gets any rest, Nanny.'

'Kitty,' Lizzie said firmly, 'I'd better tell you now that Charlie will not be given any more "soothing syrup". I heard about it during my training; it is certainly not good for him and could even be dangerous if he was given too much. It contains morphine.'

Kitty looked at her blankly. 'Then we won't get any sleep at all, Nanny.'

'We'll see,' was all Lizzie would say.

As Charlie's bedtime approached, he became more and more agitated. He ran around the room, trying to avoid being undressed.

'Let's leave it until we've had our dinner,' Lizzie said.

'If you say so, Nanny,' Kitty said. She had struggled so valiantly to care for the little boy and was only too happy to hand over the decision-making to the new nanny.

When the two women had finished eating, Lizzie said, 'Now, Kitty, tell me everything you usually do to get him ready for bed.'

'I give him an all-over wash as best I can and then tie him in bed. That's when he starts screaming.'

Lizzie was tempted to say, I'm not surprised, so would I. Instead, avoiding that subject for the moment, she said, 'Does he have a drink of warm milk or Horlicks at bedtime?'

'No, Nanny.'

'Then I'd like us to start that routine. Please would you go down to the kitchen and heat him some milk or, if Cook has any, make him some Horlicks.'

Kitty scurried away. Down in the kitchen she said, 'Nanny says please may Charlie have either a mug of warm milk or Horlicks, if you have any, Cook. She thinks it might help him sleep.'

'I doubt it,' Mrs Graves muttered, but she hauled herself out of her chair.

'I can do it, Cook.'

'No, no, Kitty. We must all do our bit. I have got some Horlicks, as it happens. I like a mug myself on a Saturday night when we can get some sleep.'

Kitty sighed. 'That might not happen anymore. Nanny's putting a stop to him being given his syrup.'

The cook's mouth dropped open and she stared at Kitty. 'Ah, so even if she does stay for a bit, we're going to have trouble with this one, are we?'

Grumbling beneath her breath, the cook nevertheless prepared the warm drink for Charlie. But as Kitty prepared to return upstairs, Mrs Graves said, 'Does Mrs Weston know about him not being given the syrup anymore?'

'I don't know.'

Mrs Graves pursed her mouth. 'Then I'll make sure she does.'

As Charlie finished the malted milk, Lizzie said, 'Good boy.'

'My word, he's polished that off,' Kitty said. 'He must like it.'

Lizzie caught hold of Charlie and held him between her knees. She managed to take off his jacket and shirt before he wriggled free and ran around the bedroom.

'Oh, Master Charlie . . .' Kitty began, trying to catch him.

'Leave him be. We're not in any rush.'

'It's his bedtime, Nanny,' Kitty said, but Lizzie only smiled.

After twenty minutes, they'd managed to undress him and put on his pyjamas and dressing gown, but still he ran around the room as if to prevent them putting him in the bed.

Lizzie was about to ask if Kitty had tried sitting him on the chamber pot, but she said nothing; she had already noticed through the day that that never happened. It soon would, she promised herself. It was high time a four-year-old was toilet-trained.

'I'll just have a wash and change into my nightdress and dressing gown and then I can manage, Kitty. You can have the rest of the evening off. We'll see you in the morning.'

'Are you sure, Nanny?'

'I am. It's high time you got some rest.'

'Then thank you, Nanny. I could certainly do with an early night, though I expect I'll still hear him crying in the nanny's room.'

Lizzie chuckled. 'It's your room now, Kitty.'

'Yes, I keep forgetting.'

When Lizzie had readied herself for bed, Kitty said, 'Goodnight, then, Nanny. Be sure to wake me if you need anything. If not, I'll be here first thing.' She pulled a face. 'There'll be a wet bed to deal with.'

As the door closed behind the nursery maid, Lizzie said, 'Now, Charlie, you and I have a little job to do.'

She went through to the smaller room that was now her bedroom and from the top drawer of the chest of drawers, she took a large pair of scissors. Charlie followed her as she approached his bed, took hold of the bindings and snipped the knots. 'There, Charlie, no more being tied in bed.' Replacing the scissors where he could not reach them, she picked up the bindings and wound them into neat balls. 'I'd better give these back to Mr Marshall. He might have some use for them.' She smiled inwardly at the thought of Kitty's face in the morning.

'And now, we'll settle for the night, shall we?'

She turned down the oil lamp on the shelf just above Charlie's bed, so that there was just a soft glow throughout the room. Then she fetched a children's book she had brought with her and a pillow and the eiderdown from her own bed. Carrying them to the easy chair at the side of Charlie's bed, she arranged the pillow and eiderdown and then settled herself comfortably in the soft armchair with the book on her lap. She held out her arms to the little boy, but he ran to the opposite side of the room and squatted down against the wall, his mouth set in defiance. Lizzie just smiled at him and opened the book. It was not one from her own childhood – they were all a little old for Charlie – but one written by a relatively new writer called Beatrix Potter.

'This is about a little bunny rabbit called Peter,' she began. 'He's very naughty and disobeys his mother by going into Mr McGregor's garden.'

There was just enough light for her to read. For a while, Charlie didn't move, but then out of the corner of her eye she saw him begin to shuffle across the carpet towards her. By the time she had finished the story, he was sitting two feet in front of her. She patted her knee. 'Come and sit with me and look at all the pictures.'

It took another ten minutes of coaxing before he allowed her to lift him onto her lap and nestle him in the crook of her left arm. She pulled the eiderdown around them both, tucked Mr Snuggles into Charlie's arms and then opened the book again to point to the illustrations, which she understood had all been done by the author herself.

'There's Peter, look, and there's Mr McGregor chasing him out of his garden.' Charlie put his thumb in his mouth. Although it was something that Lizzie would discourage, she decided it was another thing she could let slide for the moment. He leaned his head against her shoulder as she began to read the story again from the beginning.

By the time she had read it for the third time, Charlie's head was snuggled into her neck, his eyes were closed and his thumb had fallen from his mouth. He was asleep.

Lizzie rested her head against the back of the chair and closed her eyes. It had been a long day and she was tired. She was not afraid to sleep. She knew that Charlie only had to stir and she would be instantly awake.

Eleven

They slept for most of the night, Charlie waking only twice to be carried through to the bathroom. By morning, there was no wet bed, not even a wet nappy. Lizzie quietly congratulated herself. They were both still dozing when Kitty opened the door into the nursery and stood staring at them in amazement.

Lizzie rubbed her eyes and yawned. 'Is it that time already, Kitty? Good morning. What a couple of sleepy-heads we are. We'd better stir ourselves, Charlie, or Clara will be bringing breakfast and we won't be ready.'

'I'll see to him, Nanny, while you get dressed.'

'Thank you, Kitty. If you would. Did you have a good night?'

'I slept right through.' There was awe in her voice, as if she couldn't quite believe it herself. 'I never heard him once.'

'That's because he slept through too. Well, almost.'

'Have you slept in the chair all night, Nanny?'

'Yes, we've been fine. It's lovely and comfy.'

'But, shouldn't he . . .?' the nursery maid began and then stopped. She should not be questioning the new nanny's methods. Especially when they seemed to be working, though she wondered what both Mrs Weston and Mrs Graves would say when they heard. All the other nannies had been so strict. Times for meals, washing, going to bed and getting up had all been meticulously observed. Naughtiness had been punished by a sharp smack. Kitty was relieved to see the change but perhaps it would be best if she didn't tell anyone else. Her loyalty, after all, ought to be to Nanny.

As if guessing what she might have been about to say, Lizzie said softly, 'All in good time, Kitty.'

Lizzie washed and dressed and returned to the nursery.

'Oh, what a pretty colour your uniform is this morning,' Kitty exclaimed. 'Such a lovely shade of rose-pink.'

'This is my "working" dress. The one I wore yesterday when I arrived is for afternoons or more formal wear.'

'They're both very smart,' Kitty said.

When Clara brought breakfast to the nursery for the three of them, she said, 'Are the sheets and nappies for the wash in the bathroom, Kitty?'

With a grin, Kitty said, 'There's nappies in the bucket from yesterday, but no wet sheets.'

Clara gaped at her. 'What?' Her puzzled glance went to Lizzie and back again to Kitty.

'We slept in the chair with him on my lap,' Lizzie said, 'and when he stirred, I took him to the bathroom. So, no wet sheets.'

Down in the kitchen, Clara couldn't wait to tell Mrs Weston and the cook.

'She slept all night in the chair at the side of his bed with him on her lap. But it must have worked because this morning there are no wet bed sheets. And I never heard him in the night, did you?'

The two older women glanced at each other. 'We were just saying the same thing,' Mrs Graves said. 'I reckon she must have given him something. She's going to stop the doctor coming, but give him a draught herself. Maybe that's what she learned at her fancy college.'

'I don't think so, Cook. I don't think that's what's behind her stopping the doctor coming,' Mrs Weston said.

'Then she's spoiling him. Nursing him all night. I've never heard the like.'

'Perhaps,' the housekeeper said thoughtfully, 'that's just what the poor little mite needs.'

Mrs Graves sniffed and banged a saucepan down hard on the range hob, giving vent to her disapproval. 'Just making it harder for the next nanny who comes after her,' she muttered, 'if you ask me.'

In the middle of the morning Lizzie said, 'Kitty, where are Charlie's outdoor shoes and coat? I've looked through his wardrobe and I can't see any.'

'That's because he hasn't got any, Nanny. He never goes out.'

'What? Never?'

Kitty shook her head. 'Not while I've been here, though I've heard that when he was a baby his nanny then used to take him out in the big black perambulator. It's in the stables now, gathering dust.'

'So, just how long have you been here, Kitty?'

'Almost two years. I worked in the village shop for a couple of years after leaving school and then I heard that the nursery maid here was leaving, so I applied for the job and got it.' She paused and then added, softly, 'I sometimes wish I hadn't, but now me and Billy are allowed to see each other . . .'

'Yes, of course.'

'Mrs Weston could tell you more. She's been here donkey's years.'

Lizzie hid her smile. She didn't think the housekeeper would like that remark. It implied she was elderly when Lizzie believed Mrs Weston was only in her late forties or perhaps early fifties. 'She often pays us a visit in the nursery just before lunch. You could ask her then.'

Just after eleven, Lizzie heard the rattle of a key in the lock of the door in the corridor and then, moments later, Mrs Weston entered the nursery. Lizzie was again showing Charlie how to pull the wooden train along.

Lizzie glanced up. 'Good morning, Mrs Weston. Charlie, say "hello" and show her how we pull the train and say "choo, choo". And then, we'll sit down for a moment and talk to Mrs Weston.'

'I hear you slept with him in the chair, Nanny,' the housekeeper said as she sat down. Lizzie sat down too and took Charlie onto her lap. He snuggled against her and put his thumb in his mouth as she rocked him gently.

'I did, but I shall get him back into his bed by degrees.'

'I see. Is there anything else you need? It can't be very comfortable for you.'

'Actually, the chair is fine, Mrs Weston. I slept well, but thank you for asking.'

The housekeeper glanced at Charlie's bed. 'You've removed the ties.'

'I have indeed,' Lizzie said, a little tartly. 'We won't be needing those anymore, but there is something I would like to ask you. How do I obtain some outdoor clothes and boots for him?'

Mrs Weston blinked. 'Outdoors. Oh, he doesn't go out, Nanny. He never goes out.'

'Why not?'

'Because – because . . . Well, he just doesn't. He might run off and – and . . .'

'Was he taken out in a perambulator when he was a baby?'

'Oh yes, he was then. That was when his first nanny was still here. She had been the mistress's nanny when she was young and Mrs Spendlove's mother was adamant that she'd be ideal for Charlie.'

'And was she?' Lizzie asked bluntly.

Mrs Weston hesitated and glanced at Kitty. The girl, intuitive that there were perhaps things the housekeeper wished to say to the nanny without the nursery maid present, tactfully said she would just go down to the kitchen to help Clara with the laundry.

'Nanny Gordon was by then in her seventies,' Mrs Weston went on as the door closed behind Kitty. 'And when Charlie began to crawl and then to walk, he became too much for her to cope with. She was a very strict nanny, even Mrs Spendlove says so. That was when he stopped being able to go out. Nanny Gordon couldn't chase after him.'

'Wasn't there a nursery maid, who could have done that?'

Mrs Weston shook her head. 'Not then. Nanny Gordon refused to have one. She said they were flighty and wouldn't be firm enough with him. They'd spoil him, she said.'

'When did she leave?'

'Charlie would have been coming up to two. After she left, we had another nanny and a nursery maid too. The two of them coped quite well for about four months but all the time Charlie was getting more and more difficult. They both left about the same time and, after that, we just had a succession of nannies, who never stayed long. Kitty came – let me think – in the September of 1902 and, bless her, she's stayed, though I think it's only because she can be near Billy, if I'm honest.'

'Has Charlie ever talked?'

'No, never. Not even first baby words. He makes noises and he cries but no, he's never tried to form proper words.'

'And his hair. Why has it been left to grow so long?'

'I can't really answer you that, unless they were too afraid to get near him with scissors. It is a dreadful mess, isn't it? I don't think it's even been washed properly for some time.'

'Do I have to ask permission from the master or the mistress to cut his hair?'

'Oh no, Nanny. Like I said, you have complete charge of him. You don't have to ask anyone. But – but how are you going to manage it? Do you want Joe or Billy to hold him tightly while you do it?'

Lizzie shook her head. 'No. I'll find a way to do it without him getting hurt, or upsetting him too much.'

'Maybe if you let the doctor give him the syrup . . .'

'Absolutely not, Mrs Weston,' Lizzie said sharply. 'That stuff can be very harmful. He won't be having any more.'

Mrs Weston nodded. She was heartened by Lizzie's words and her manner. This nanny – as long as she stayed – was going to fight for Charlie's wellbeing.

'So,' Lizzie said, breaking into the housekeeper's thoughts, 'about outdoor clothes . . .?'

'I'll see about ordering some from the store where Mrs Spendlove has items sent out to her or she might like to ask her dressmaker in the village. What about his shoe size?'

'That's a very good point, Mrs Weston. We'll do it now,' Lizzie said, standing up. Carrying Charlie on her hip, she went into her bedroom and brought back two sheets of writing paper and a pencil. Placing the two sheets side by side on the floor, she set Charlie down with his feet on them.

'Now, darling, stand still while I draw round your feet.'

It took several attempts before Charlie would cooperate enough for Lizzie to make a half-decent outline of

98

his feet. Mrs Weston marvelled at the patience of the nanny. Lizzie never for one moment became annoyed when Charlie kept lifting up first one foot and then the other while she tried to draw the shape of his feet. Indeed, Lizzie was actually giggling and making fun of the whole procedure. When she had finished, she hugged Charlie and said, 'Good boy. Now we'll be able to get some shoes and boots for you. Then we can go out for little walks and to play with a ball.'

'If you don't mind me asking,' Mrs Weston said, 'how are you going to be sure he won't run off? The lawn at the end of the house slopes down to a small lake and there are ponds throughout the grounds.'

'When they collected me from the station yesterday, both Joe and Billy said that if I ever needed their help, I was only to ask. I intend to ask Billy to be with us when we're outside. He will certainly be able to chase after Charlie if he got away from either me or Kitty.'

Mrs Weston nodded. 'I'm sure the master will approve of that.' She rose from her chair and held out her hand. 'I'll take the measurements, though I can't guarantee those will make a perfect fit. Perhaps . . .' She paused thoughtfully. 'These would do temporarily. If – if things improve, perhaps we could have someone come to measure his feet, but I'm not sure if . . .'

'Given time, Mrs Weston,' Lizzie said quietly, 'I think we might be able to do that.'

Mrs Weston found Mr Bennett in his pantry cleaning silver.

'May I have a word, Mr Bennett?'

'Of course, Mrs Weston. Do come in.'

She stepped inside the small room and closed the door. Then she proceeded to tell him what had just happened in the nursery. 'She wants him to have outdoor garments and shoes and boots. I know the master has said that Nanny is to have full charge of Charlie, but this seems a very big step forward. Do you think he'd approve? Do you think we should tell him?'

Mr Bennett put down his cleaning cloth and rolled down his shirt sleeves. He reached for his butler's jacket from the back of a chair and pulled it on. 'Indeed I do, Mrs Weston. We'll go together.'

Only a few moments later they were standing in the master's study. Mrs Weston was still holding the two pieces of paper with the outlines of Charlie's feet.

'Please sit down, both of you,' Roland said with a sigh. 'I do hope you haven't come to tell me that this nanny is leaving.'

'No, sir,' Mrs Weston said at once and she saw relief flood his face. 'But she's wanting to do things that we – Mr Bennett and I – thought you should know about.'

'We don't want to sound as if we're telling tales, sir,' Mr Bennett put in quickly. 'We all want whatever is best for Charlie.'

'Yes, I know you do. Go on.'

'Well, for one thing,' Mrs Weston began. 'She wants to cut his hair.'

'I'd be delighted if she did,' Roland said. 'He looks like a little wild thing. I'm surprised it's not been done before, but I didn't want to interfere. I feel we've been a bit lax with previous nannies, but then we were so afraid of losing them.' He grimaced. 'But we did anyway, didn't we? Anything else?'

The housekeeper exchanged a glance with the butler. 'She wants to obtain outdoor clothes for him, but we're so worried he might run away from her and Kitty and endanger himself. I put that to her and she said that Joe

100

and Billy have offered to help in any way they can and that if they take Charlie outside, she'd ask Billy to be with them.'

A smile spread slowly across Roland's face. 'That sounds like an excellent idea. Bennett, please tell Joe and Billy they have my full support in anything Nanny asks of them. Indeed, that goes for all the staff. I hope you know that.'

'Yes, sir, we do.'

Mrs Weston held out the two sheets of paper. 'Nanny drew round his feet. It's the best we can do at the moment to gauge his shoe size.'

Roland stood up and took the papers. 'I'll talk to my wife about this. She'll know what to do. Thank you for coming to see me. Oh, and by the way, my brother will be coming home the week after next for a few days. He'll arrive on the eleven o'clock train on the Wednesday.'

Both Mr Bennett and Mrs Weston beamed. 'That's wonderful news, sir,' Mr Bennett said. 'We'll make sure everything is ready for his arrival and I'll let Joe and Billy know to be at the station to meet him.'

Twelve

An air of great excitement began to ripple through the house but it wasn't until Kitty told her later that day as they were undressing Charlie for bed, that Lizzie understood the reason for it.

Kitty burst into the nursery, carrying clean pyjamas for the little boy over her arm, her eyes shining. 'I've just heard. Master James is coming the week after next. It's such wonderful news. Charlie adores him. He's so much better when Master James is here. He's so good with him. He – he often comes up to the nursery.' Suddenly, Kitty's cheeks were pink. She clasped her hands together. 'He's so handsome, Nanny, and so kind. He's just lovely with Charlie. You'll see.'

'Whoa, slow down, Kitty. Just who is this paragon?' Then Lizzie remembered Mr Spendlove speaking of someone called James during her interview. 'Oh yes, he's the master's younger brother, isn't he?'

'That's right. He's in the army, but he always visits us when he has a long leave.'

'Is this his home, then?'

'Not exactly. He has a bedroom here that's always kept ready for him, but I think he regards his home as with his mother.'

Lizzie raised her eyebrows. 'Oh, I hadn't realized either of the master's parents were still alive.'

'When I first came here Mrs Weston told me that the

master took over all the family's business interests about ten years ago from his father. He – the father, I mean – had a heart attack and decided to retire.' She waved her hand vaguely. 'They went to live in a little village the other side of Chesterfield. The master stayed on here to run the estate and, then, when he married, of course the mistress moved in here too. Not long after that, his father died very suddenly, but his mother decided to stay where she was. She'd already made a lot of friends in the village they'd moved to.'

'Are the mistress's parents still alive?'

'Yes, they live on the outskirts of Sheffield. Her father's quite a well-known name in the cutlery industry. I think he's got a big factory there.'

'Do any of the parents ever visit here?'

Kitty's face fell and her glance went to the little boy fighting against Lizzie trying to remove his clothes. 'Not now.' She turned away abruptly as if unwilling to say more. 'I'll get the bowl of water and towels to wash him.'

As on the previous night, Kitty watched over Charlie while Lizzie changed into her nightdress and dressing gown.

'Could you go down to the kitchen and make him a drink of Horlicks again, please Kitty?'

'Of course, Nanny. I'm sorry, I should have thought. I haven't got used to it yet.'

'No matter.' Lizzie smiled. 'And then you can have the rest of the evening off.'

When Charlie had finished his drink, Lizzie settled down with him in the big easy chair and opened the book to read. But this time, he grabbed the book from her hands and flung it to the floor.

'Oh dear. Why did you do that, Charlie? Don't you like that story?'

He gazed up at her with resentful eyes, his jaw with a determined, angry set.

She turned back the covers and set him on the floor. 'Shall we go and find another from my trunk?'

Charlie picked up the book and threw it across the room. Then he ran after it and did the same again. Lizzie stood perfectly still, watching him. After each throw, he gazed at her defiantly and then did it again. Lizzie wasn't quite sure how to deal with this; it was a little different from the lectures they'd had at college on how to deal with naughtiness. Then she remembered what one of the tutors – a tutor she had much admired and respected – had said. Follow your instincts. So, Lizzie decided to do just that. She thought that perhaps Charlie's bad behaviour was to get her attention, so instead of getting angry, smacking him or even raising her voice – reactions she didn't believe in anyway – she would just ignore him. She sat down in the chair and tucked the eiderdown around her. Although she was aware of exactly what he was doing, he thought she wasn't watching him. He threw the book three more times before coming to stand in front of her. He stood there for two or three minutes, glaring at her defiantly. Then he opened his mouth and began to scream. Lizzie allowed this to go on for five minutes and then she stood up and opened her arms to him but instead of coming to her he ran round the room, still screaming. There were no tears, so Lizzie knew this was just pure temper and not distress. When he ran quite close to her, she bent down and caught hold of him. Though he wriggled, surprising her with how strong he was, she hugged him close to her, murmuring, 'There, there, Charlie. It's all right. Come now, there's no need for all this.'

And then the tears came and she held him close,

stroking his cheek and murmuring words of comfort to him. She collected Mr Snuggles from the bed and sat down again in the armchair. Now Charlie cuddled close to her, burying his face against her neck. Soon, the crying subsided into hiccups and he fell asleep. The rest of the night was peaceful and they were both awake early. Lizzie had washed and dressed Charlie by the time Kitty appeared.

'Oh Nanny, I'm not late, am I?'

'No, no, Kitty. Right on time. Perhaps you would look after him while I get washed and dressed.'

'Of course, Nanny. I heard him crying last night. I didn't quite know what I should do. Should I have come to help you?'

Lizzie laughed. 'No, best not to make too big a thing of it. I managed fine.'

'You can always press the bell at the side of the fire-place. That rings just in the nanny's room. Well, the one that's mine now. It was for me or other nursery maids to be able to call the nanny if they couldn't cope.'

'Ah, that's good to know. Thank you.'

By the time Lizzie had completed her ablutions, dressed and returned to the nursery, Clara had arrived with breakfast.

'The doctor comes tonight,' Clara said. 'At least we'll all get a bit of peace for another couple of nights.'

'But you haven't been disturbed the last two nights, have you, Clara?' Lizzie asked.

The housemaid laughed. 'No, Nanny, but Mrs Graves says that's "a new broom sweeping clean", especially as you're spoiling him by nursing him all night. When you try to get him back into his bed, you'll soon be needing the ties back and his syrup once a week. That's what Cook says anyway.'

It was on the tip of Lizzie's tongue to say, Does she indeed!, but she didn't want to exacerbate the ill-feeling that already lay between her and the cook. She must bide her time, but at least Clara was a useful go-between. She was carrying the gossip of what she saw in the nursery to the below-stairs staff and bringing back their comments to her. Only time would prove Lizzie right and she prayed fervently that it would. She wondered where Mrs Weston – and, for that matter, Mr Bennett – stood. She needed to have Mrs Weston on her side but she, Lizzie, was the newcomer, the one they all expected to stay a short time and then leave them high and dry. Lizzie was determined to stand her ground. She would do what she believed was right for Charlie, even if it made her unpopular with the rest of the staff.

Meanwhile, Lizzie was unaware that Kitty too was struggling with her conscience. The young girl knew her loyalties should be with the nanny but she had worked with the other members of the household staff for some time now. They had been kind to her and had helped her whenever they could when she'd been left to cope with Charlie on her own. She didn't want to be disloyal to them either if it came to a matter of having to take sides.

And then there was Billy. He and his father were ardent supporters of the new nanny. They were sure already that she was going to stay. So, Kitty came to a decision. She would tell the other staff enough to let them think she was siding with them, but only what Clara would be telling them anyway. Anything that happened in the nursery that was seen by only herself would not reach anyone else's ears, except perhaps Billy's. When they could snatch some time on their own – and these times were becoming more frequent since Lizzie's arrival – she would confide in him but ask him to keep whatever she told him confidential.

The day passed uneventfully until after tea when the doctor arrived. They heard the key in the outer door and when Mrs Weston ushered him into the nursery, Charlie began to cry and ran to Lizzie, clutching at her and burying his face in her skirt. There were screams and a flood of tears from the little boy. But this, Lizzie knew, was genuine distress. It was not temper.

Above the noise, Mrs Weston said, 'Nanny, this is Doctor Grey. He has come to give Charlie his weekly dose of soothing syrup.'

'Thank you, Mrs Weston. I would like to have a talk with the doctor. Would you like to stay and hear what I have to say?'

For a moment, the housekeeper seemed non-plussed. 'Well, yes, I suppose I would, really.'

'Good evening, Doctor Grey,' Lizzie said, now turning to the newcomer. He was a tall, dark-haired man with kind eyes whom Lizzie guessed to be in his late thirties or early forties. 'Please sit down.' She gestured towards a chair near the table and also to Mrs Weston that she too should be seated.

For a moment she turned her attention to Charlie, who was still clinging to her skirt. She released his grip and picked him up into her arms, swaying to and fro and patting his back. 'There, there, Charlie. It's all right.'

As Charlie's crying subsided a little, she turned her attention to the doctor and smiled. 'Thank you for coming, Doctor Grey, but there will be no further need for your soothing syrup.'

The doctor stared at her for a moment before a grin spread across his face. 'Thank goodness, Nanny. I can't tell you how relieved I am to hear you say that.'

Mrs Weston gazed at the doctor. 'And so am I, but the rest of the staff won't be so pleased. They rely on getting a good night's sleep on Saturdays and Sundays.'

'Mrs Weston, I administered the syrup because I was instructed to do so by Mr Spendlove, but I have never been happy about it. There are disturbing reports rippling through the medical profession that the mixture can be harmful to babies and children. There have even been some deaths attributed to it if the wrong dosage has been given. I have always been most careful to give him only a very low dosage and the fact that he only has it once a week helps, but it really can't be good for him. He must get withdrawal symptoms when it starts to wear off, particularly on Mondays and Tuesdays. Have you noticed that he is extra fractious then?'

'Well . . .' Mrs Weston began and then she was obliged to say with a sigh, 'I never thought about it, Doctor, but now you mention it, yes, he is always even more difficult to handle at the beginning of the week. I never thought it had anything to do with the syrup.' She turned anxious eyes towards him. 'Oh Doctor, you don't think we've caused him lasting damage, do you, through our own selfishness?'

The doctor patted her hand. 'No, no, Mrs Weston, I would never have let that happen, I promise you, but I don't mind admitting I am very glad the practice is to stop.' He turned to Lizzie. 'You're new, aren't you? I do hope you're going to stay longer than some of the others.'

'I am, Doctor Grey.'

'Then I won't call anymore as a regular visit, but if you have any concerns at all, please do send for me.'

'I will, Doctor. And – thank you.'

As he rose and turned to leave, Lizzie noticed that his glance rested on Charlie's bed and his eyebrows rose slightly as if in an unspoken question. Then, when his gaze met hers, she was sure he had noticed that the ties had been removed. Though no more words passed between them, both Lizzie and the doctor had tacitly arrived at an understanding very quickly.

As Mrs Weston accompanied the doctor downstairs, Lizzie wondered how long it would be before news reached the other members of staff that Charlie had not had his regular Saturday night dose, nor would he be having it at any time in the future.

Thirteen

The staff reacted in different ways. Mr Bennett shrugged as if it was no concern of his. The maids too accepted what they were told without question and Joe and Billy were delighted to hear it. Only Mrs Graves banged pots and pans around until she cracked one of her favourite bowls.

'Now look what she's made me do, her and her fancy notions.'

'To be honest with you, Cook,' Mrs Weston said, 'I am relieved it's to stop. I heard the doctor himself say that the practice can be dangerous if kiddies are given too much.'

Mrs Graves looked up sharply. 'I hope you know I'd never wish the poor little lad any harm, but I must have me sleep, Mrs Weston, even if it's only for a couple of nights a week.'

'And have you heard him the last two nights since she's been here?'

Mrs Graves wriggled her shoulders as if she had been caught out. 'Well, no, I haven't. Not really. He was crying a bit last night but then it stopped. I thought she must have given him something herself without waiting for the doctor.'

'I'm sure that's not the case.'

'Is she still sleeping with him in the armchair? She's spoiling him and making a rod for her own back. She'll never get him back into his own bed.'

'We'll just have to wait and see, won't we? And now, I must see if I can speak to the mistress before dinner is served about these outdoor clothes Nanny wants for Charlie.'

The housekeeper was admitted to the drawing room, where Roland and Cecily Spendlove were enjoying a small glass of sherry before dinner.

'Do come in, Mrs Weston. My wife and I were just discussing Nanny's proposal. We'd appreciate your thoughts. If it works, it would be wonderful for him to get some fresh air and exercise, but –'

Cecily sighed. 'Yes, there's always a "but" with Charlie, isn't there?' She paused and then added, 'Just between us, Mrs Weston, what do you think of this new nanny?'

'It's early days, ma'am, but she's certainly making her presence felt. I presume you know that she's stopped his weekly dose of soothing syrup. Doctor Grey won't be coming anymore unless he's called.'

Husband and wife exchanged a glance. 'No, we didn't.'

Mrs Weston went on to tell them what the doctor had said about the mixture.

'Oh Roland,' Cecily said, her fingers fluttering to her lips as she gazed at her husband with frightened tears in her eyes. 'What have we done? Have we harmed him? Have we made him like he is?'

Before her husband could answer, Mrs Weston said swiftly, 'I asked the doctor the same thing, ma'am. And he assured me he would never have let that happen. No, Charlie's problems started way before he was ever given the syrup. It was Nanny Gordon, if you remember, who suggested giving it to him to quieten him at night.'

Again, husband and wife exchanged a glance and Roland's lips tightened. 'I am beginning to think,' he said slowly, 'that Nanny Gordon is the root of all this trouble. I am sorry, my dear, if that distresses you. I know she was your nanny too . . .'

'She was a very harsh nanny in many ways,' Cecily said. 'A strict disciplinarian. My mother thought she was wonderful, but I have some bad memories of her punishments. I – I still have nightmares about them sometimes.'

'Yes, my love, I do know about these nightmares of yours.'

'I thought that all children were brought up like that by their nannies,' Cecily said, her voice shaking a little. 'Until I went to boarding school and made friends, I didn't know that some nannies could be loving and kind and fun to be with. Nanny Gordon was none of those things.' She dabbed at her eyes with a lace handkerchief. 'How I wish I had been strong enough to stand up to my mother and defy her advice to have Nanny Gordon as Charlie's nanny.'

'Don't blame yourself, ma'am,' Mrs Weston dared to say. 'Many nannies in those days were just like you say. Perhaps today's training has a gentler approach.'

'I hope you're right, Mrs Weston,' Cecily murmured, still distressed to think of the part she might have unwittingly played in her son's condition. 'I'd like to meet Miss Ingham.'

'Wait a few more days, my dear, until we are sure she is staying.'

'Yes, you're right, Roland. I will. And now, Mrs Weston, you want to know about the outdoor clothes for Charlie. I have placed an order with my dressmaker in the village but she needs some more measurements or an item of clothing he's wearing now to know his size. As for the shoes and boots, the cobbler here has a good reputation.'

'I get my shoes and boots handmade by him,' Roland

said. 'If he needs to measure Charlie himself, then perhaps we will have to arrange it.'

Cecily looked up, startled. 'I don't think that's a good idea, Roland. He will no doubt gossip around the village.'

Roland smiled sadly. 'My dear, I think the gossip and rumours about Charlie will already have spread at least as far as the village. We can only hope our tenants and workers are as loyal to us as our household staff.'

As the door opened and Mr Bennett declared that dinner was served, Mrs Weston said, 'I'll get those measurements for you, ma'am.'

Saturday night passed peacefully and even Mrs Graves had to admit she had slept undisturbed. 'She's given him summat herself. I'd bet me life on it.'

Mrs Weston chuckled. 'I wouldn't do that, Mrs Graves. Kitty is adamant that he isn't being given anything.'

'Then she's put summat in the Horlicks when Kitty's not looking. Oh, and that reminds me, if that's going to continue every night, I'll have to order extra milk from the farm.'

Later that morning, Mrs Weston made her customary visit to the nursery. 'Mrs Spendlove is putting things in motion to provide you with some outdoor wear for Charlie. I also wanted to ask you, do you want Mr Marshall and Billy to come up this evening to help you with Charlie's bath time? He usually resists – um – quite vigorously.'

'You can say that again,' Kitty muttered.

'Does he get upset when they appear?'

Mrs Weston glanced at Kitty for the answer. 'Yes, he still cries and screams at bath time, even when he's had the syrup, so he'll be worse than usual tonight. That's why they have to come up. We wouldn't be able to handle him, Nanny. 'Specially not when he's wet and slippery.'

Lizzie was thoughtful for a moment before saying, 'Then I'd be grateful if you would ask them to come up, thank you, Mrs Weston. What time do they usually arrive?'

'About half past five, Nanny. When he's had his tea but before dinner is served.'

At a quarter past five that evening, Lizzie said, 'Kitty, will you run Charlie's bath, please, while I undress him.'

'Of course, Nanny, but it's a bit early. Joe and Billy won't be here yet.'

'I have an idea I want to try out before they get here.'

She was mystified, but Kitty did as she was asked. By the time the bath was drawn to the right temperature, Charlie was running around the nursery completely naked. Lizzie went to her trunk and took out two little wooden boats. Charlie watched as she crossed the room and went into the bathroom. Intrigued, he followed her and saw her kneel beside the bath and float the boats on the water. She reached in and pushed the boats around, while Charlie peered over the side of the bath to see them bobbing up and down on the water. Lizzie swished the water to make waves and the boats bounced around even more. Kitty stood to one side, watching.

Charlie made a sound and stretched his hand over the side of the bath, but he could not reach them as Nanny had done. He looked up at her as she smiled down at him and said, 'Do you want to get in and play with the boats?'

Charlie looked down at the boats and then back at her. Lizzie stood, lifted him up and gently lowered him into the water. At once Charlie reached for the boats and pushed them around.

'Well, I would never have believed it, Nanny, if I wasn't seeing it with me own eyes. Oh, there's Mr Marshall and Billy arriving. Shall I ask them to come in here?'

'Perhaps they wouldn't mind waiting for a few minutes. I'll let him play a bit longer, then soap and rinse him. After that, he'll be ready to come out.'

Kitty giggled. 'I don't think he will. I think he'll protest then.'

'Most four-year-olds would when they're having fun,' Lizzie said, subtly making the point that Charlie would then be no different to any other child of his age. 'Would you put a bath towel over the fireguard to warm, please, Kitty?'

'Already done, Nanny, and the nursing chair is set by the fire for you to dry him on your lap.'

Ten minutes later, Joe and Billy appeared and picked Charlie out of the water and that was when the screaming started. They carried him into the nursery and placed him on Nanny's lap.

'There, there, Charlie,' Lizzie said above the noise. 'You can't sit in there all night. You'll go pink and wrinkly. Kitty, just fetch the wooden train across so that Billy can walk around the nursery with it. It might distract Charlie.'

When Billy was moving around the room, pulling the toy along, Lizzie said, 'Look, Charlie, Billy is playing "choo, choo". Let's get you dry and in your pyjamas and then you can go and play too.'

Dressed in a clean nappy and his pyjamas and dressing gown, Lizzie set him on the floor and watched him gallop across to Billy.

'Well, Nanny,' Joe said. 'That's the easiest bath time that I can remember, even when he'd had his syrup.'

'He's not had it this week.'

'Oh, I know.' Joe chuckled. 'It's the main topic of

115

conversation below stairs, but I shall take great delight in telling them how well tonight's bath time has gone.'

'Next week might be more difficult. I want to wash his hair.'

Joe sighed. 'We've tried, Nanny, but it's got into such a tangled mess, we just couldn't manage it. What are you going to do?'

Now it was Lizzie who laughed softly and said, 'Wait and see, Joe. Just wait and see.'

Fourteen

Over the next week, Lizzie taught Kitty the rudiments of beginning to toilet-train Charlie. 'This should have been started months ago, if not years, but no matter. Maybe he'll take to it quicker than younger children.'

Kitty cast her a glance that said, I wouldn't bet on it, but to her surprise, with careful monitoring and guessing when Charlie needed to 'go', between them they caught him several times. With lots of praise when he succeeded, the little boy soon began to go towards the bathroom himself.

'Nanny, that's nothing short of a miracle,' Kitty marvelled. 'I didn't think he'd have the sense to do that.'

'Patience and praise,' Lizzie murmured, 'in all things.' It had been another mantra from her favourite tutor.

'They can't believe it downstairs. They think we're washing out his nappies up here to hide the truth. They don't believe me that he's actually going to the bathroom himself sometimes.'

Although she still settled for the night with Charlie in the armchair, Lizzie gradually began to put him into his bed when he was asleep, although she still stayed in the chair beside him. Once or twice, he woke and whimpered but she sat on the side of the bed, stroking his forehead and murmuring to him until he went back to sleep.

Although they were usually both awake and up before

117

Kitty arrived, one morning, Charlie woke up later than usual and Kitty came in to see him in his bed.

'Oh Nanny,' she said, putting her hands to her cheeks and staring wide-eyed at the little boy who was just beginning to stir. 'Has he slept all night in his own bed and without the ties too?'

'Part of it, Kitty. We're doing it very gradually.'

'But you're still sitting in the chair all night, aren't you?'

'For the time being, yes. Now, if you'll do the usual while I get dressed or Clara will be here with the breakfast before we're ready.'

The days passed. Charlie still had some bouts of crying and screaming, but Kitty told Lizzie they were much less frequent and didn't last so long as before her arrival.

'Sometimes he'd go on for hours until he was exhausted. It's so nice to see him calmer.'

Lizzie just smiled.

During the Saturday night of that week, when Lizzie could see that Charlie was soundly asleep, she took a pair of scissors and gently cut off the matted, tangled hair to a length of about three inches. Gently she moved him from side to side without waking him, so that she could reach every part of his head. When it was done, she stood back with a sigh of relief as she cleared away all the hair. Strands of it remained on the sheets, but they were due to be changed the following morning ready for washday on the Monday.

On her arrival the following morning, Kitty gaped at him in amazement. 'However did you manage it, Nanny?'

'While he was fast asleep.' Lizzie chuckled. 'He keeps touching his head, wondering where it's all gone. Kitty, please tell Joe and Billy I shall certainly need their help tonight with his bath.'

118

Kitty's eyes widened. 'You're – you're going to try to wash his hair, aren't you?'

'Most certainly. That's the whole point. It was no use even trying while it was in such a tangled mess.'

'I see that, but –' Kitty stopped and sighed. She was already dreading bath time.

Lizzie started by letting Charlie sit in the water to play with the boats.

'What do you want us to do, Nanny?' Joe asked as he and Billy entered the bathroom.

'Have you plenty of time?' Lizzie asked.

'All the time in the world, if it's for Charlie. The master's had a word with us both this week and said we're to be on call for you any time of the day or night. We intended to be anyway, as I think you know, but it's nice for us to have the master's approval.'

'I'm very grateful.'

'Oh look, Dad,' Billy said, pointing at Charlie. 'I've only just noticed. He's had his hair cut.'

'Oh my, so he has. Ah, I see now, you want us to help you wash it, don't you?'

'Right in one, Joe. But what I'd like you to do is kneel down, one on either side of the bath and play with the boats with him. Then I'm going to put a thick rolled-up towel behind him in the water, to make a headrest for him, so that when we lean him back to wash his hair, his face won't go under the water. I think he'll splash about a lot and we'll probably all get drenched.'

'Clothes'll dry, Nanny,' Joe said with a chuckle.

While Joe and Billy played with the boats, Lizzie lathered Charlie and then rinsed away the soap.

'Now, are we ready?' Gently, she eased him backwards until his neck was resting on the rolled-up towel. Holding

119

a flannel over his forehead but not covering his eyes, she gently wet his hair. All the time she talked to him with soothing words. 'There, there. What a good, brave boy you are.' But still, Charlie began to cry.

'We'll sit him up for a bit,' Lizzie said.

He sat up, his cries subsiding as he reached for the boats again while Lizzie put soap on his hair and rubbed his scalp. To distract him, Billy made waves in the bathwater so that the boats bobbed up and down. After a few minutes, they leaned him back again into the water, but this time he screamed loudly and thrashed his arms and legs about.

'Lie still, Charlie, or you'll get soap in your eyes. This won't take long. There's a brave boy.' As quickly as she could, she washed all traces of the soap away and Charlie sat up again, reached for one of the boats and flung it out of the bath. He looked up at Lizzie, defiance in his eyes. She felt Joe's eyes on her to see her reaction.

'Oh, has that boat arrived in port, Charlie?' Lizzie said calmly with a smile. 'Are you coming out too? Kitty's got a nice warm towel waiting.' She got up from her kneeling position. 'Now, Charlie, Joe and Billy are going to lift you out and bring you to me. We'll get you dry in front of the nice warm fire.'

She turned and left the bathroom. Behind her, Charlie's cries increased and he stretched out a hand towards her retreating back.

'It's all right, little fella,' Joe said, adopting the same soothing tone of voice that Lizzie had used and explaining to him what they were going to do. 'I'll lift you under your arms and Billy will take your legs. Now, up you come.'

Charlie wriggled and fought, flailing his arms and trying to kick, but the two men held him gently but firmly until they set him in Lizzie's lap. He was still crying, but not so loudly as he buried his face against her breast.

Lizzie wrapped the warm towel around him and held him close, rocking him until his sobs subsided to an unhappy hiccup. 'There, there, Charlie, all done for this time. Now, let's get you dry and see what your hair looks like.'

She towelled him dry and put on his nappy, pyjamas and dressing gown before rubbing his hair.

'May we stay and see, Nanny?'

'Of course, Billy. The more time you can spend with him having fun, the more he'll start to trust that you don't just turn up to do something he doesn't like. And I might be needing you more often soon,' she added, as she rubbed Charlie's hair dry. 'I've ordered some outdoor wear for him, but Kitty and I will need one of you to be there in case he runs away from us.'

Billy grinned as, with a sly glance at Kitty, he said, 'That'd better be me, then. I'd be quicker out of the starting gates than me dad.'

'I'll come as well if I can,' Joe put in, anxious not to be left out. 'We can teach him to play football.'

'Good job I brought one, then, in my trunk of toys.'

'Oh, if not, there'll be one in the playroom somewhere, Nanny,' Joe said casually.

She paused in drying Charlie's hair to stare at him. 'The playroom? I didn't know there was one. Where's that?'

'Across the passageway, Nanny. Next to your room, although I've heard Kitty sleeps there now. There's two rooms through there. A playroom and a schoolroom.'

'A schoolroom?' Lizzie's eyes now widened with surprise. This was something she had not expected, never mind the news that there was an actual playroom. Why on earth

121

was the poor little boy confined to his bedroom day and night if there was a separate room for him to play in?

Joe gave a deep sigh and began to explain. 'When Charlie was born, all the family, all the staff, in fact, the whole village, were thrilled. The master couldn't do enough; the little chap was to have everything they could possibly give him. A room full of toys, a schoolroom with books in readiness for the time when he would need a tutor. I believe the master even put his name down for one of the well-known boarding schools for when he was old enough. But when he was a baby, Nanny Gordon moved in and these rooms were set aside as the nursery quarters. This was his bedroom, with a bedroom for a nursery maid . . .'

'Nanny Gordon wouldn't have a maid to help her, though, would she?' Billy put in.

Joe shook his head and his voice hardened. 'He was about eighteen months old when the trouble began. She couldn't cope with a lively little boy, who had learned to walk. To be fair to her, I think she had started to suffer with arthritis. She kept him confined to this room and began tying him in his bed at night and then, as I understand it, retired to her room across the corridor. That's when the screaming started. I think she left him alone at night tied to his bed. I remember having to come and fix those ties, Nanny. It broke my heart, but there was nothing I could do. The mistress had faith in Nanny Gordon and left everything to her. He was about two years old when she told the mistress that he wasn't normal and that she could no longer handle him. She – she even advised having him taken away and put in – in some sort of institution. The master wasn't having any of that – thank goodness – but that's when Nanny Gordon left and the succession of nannies began.'

'I started here about then,' Kitty put in. 'I think it was the second nanny after Nanny Gordon who demanded a nursery maid. After that, I lost count how many we had. I can't even remember some of their names now. They all said the same thing. That – that he wasn't right and should be –' she gulped and tears filled her eyes – 'put away.'

All eyes turned to look at Charlie, who was now sitting quietly on Lizzie's lap looking up at her with soulful brown eyes.

'Oh Nanny,' Kitty breathed. 'Just look at his hair. 'It's curly and – and such a lovely auburn colour. I thought it was black.'

'He looks like a proper boy now, Nanny,' Joe said softly. 'Not a little wild thing anymore.'

A key sounded in the outside door and Clara came into the nursery carrying a mug of Horlicks. She set it down on the table and turned to look towards the others in the room. When she saw Charlie, she let out a gasp. 'Oh, Nanny. He – he looks wonderful. You've cut off all those dreadful, dirty ringlets. He – he looks normal.'

'He *is* normal, Clara,' Lizzie said and no one in the room missed the sharpness in her tone. 'He was just a little – unkempt. But not any longer.'

'Oh my, whatever will they say downstairs. And whatever will Master James say when he arrives on Wednesday?'

'More importantly,' Joe said, getting up to leave, 'what will the master say?' He touched Charlie's cheek gently with a gnarled, workworn finger. 'Goodnight, little man. You're going to be all right now.' And then he looked down at Lizzie and met her gaze as he said softly, with a catch in his voice, 'Goodnight, Nanny.'

Billy stood up too with a broad grin on his face, bade everyone 'goodnight' and, with a wink towards Kitty, followed his father out of the room.

Fifteen

It was unusual for Mrs Weston to visit the nursery more than once day, but just as Charlie was finishing his nightly drink and Kitty was tidying the bathroom, Lizzie heard the rattle of the key in the lock in the first door and then the housekeeper appeared through the second and stepped into the nursery. Her glance went at once to the little boy, and Lizzie knew she must have heard about his transformation from Clara.

'Oh!' she breathed and clasped her hands in front of her. As she came closer, Lizzie could see there were tears in the older woman's eyes. 'Oh, Charlie, you look wonderful. Nanny, what a transformation. How handsome he looks. I can see his uncle, James, in him now. More so than his father. His hair is the same colour – and curly too – and his brown eyes are so like Master James.' She paused and then asked, 'Would you mind if I tell the master? I'm sure he would like to see him straightaway. We won't be interfering with Charlie's bedtime, will we?'

'No, Mrs Weston . . .'

Almost before Lizzie had finished speaking, Mrs Weston had turned and hurried out of the room.

As they heard the outer door open and close, Kitty giggled, 'I've never seen her so excited. And for her to interrupt the master's time in the drawing room with the mistress just before dinner. Well, it's unheard of.'

It was only minutes before they heard the key in the

lock again and voices outside the nursery door. Mrs Weston came in first, holding the door open for the master who entered a little warily, but as soon as he saw his son he stopped and stared.

Charlie was sitting on Lizzie's knee. He stared up at the man he scarcely knew, but he did not cry or wriggle to get down and run to the far side of the room. He just continued to look up at him. Roland moved forward cautiously and sat down opposite.

'Hello, Charlie,' Roland said hesitantly and glanced at Lizzie.

'We say, "Hello, Papa", don't we, Charlie?' But the boy just continued to stare at his father.

'Shall we show Papa how we pull the train and say "choo, choo"?'

Lizzie lifted him down from her lap, took his hand and led him across the room to the little wooden train. 'Now, we take the string, don't we?' She put the string into Charlie's hand, but kept hers over the top of his. 'And then we pull it along like this and we say "choo, choo".'

Charlie said nothing, but with her guidance he pulled the train. He kept glancing across the room at his father and Mrs Weston.

'Good boy,' Lizzie said. 'Clever boy.'

Roland cleared his throat, but his voice was still husky as he asked, 'Does – does he say anything?'

'Not yet, sir,' Lizzie said, implying that it was only a matter of time before he did.

'Is that one of his toys?'

'No, sir. I brought a few bits with me. This train and the little boats he has in his bath.'

Lizzie saw the glance that passed between the master and Mrs Weston. 'Perhaps tomorrow morning, shall we

125

say about eleven, we should show Nanny the playroom?'
Roland said.

'Of course, sir. The maids keep it dusted, though of
course it hasn't been used for –' She paused.

'I don't think it's ever been used, has it? Not properly.'

Mrs Weston shook her head sadly. 'No, sir.'

'Then Nanny must have access to it and make use of it
as she thinks fit. But I'd like to be here when she sees it.'

'Of course, sir.'

He moved slowly across the room and squatted down
in front of Charlie. He smiled and Lizzie, close to him
now, could see tears in his eyes. He reached out and
touched Charlie's cheek tenderly. Charlie made no sound
but just stared at him.

'I'll see you in the morning, then,' Roland said, as he
stood up. For a long moment he gazed into Lizzie's eyes.
'Thank you, Nanny,' he said huskily, then turned away
swiftly and left the room.

With a nod and a smile and a quick wipe of her eyes
with a lace handkerchief, Mrs Weston followed him.

When Roland returned to the drawing room, Cecily said
at once, 'Oh my dear, what has happened? I can see
something has upset you.'

He sat on the sofa beside her and took her hand. 'My
darling, I have just seen the most wonderful thing. The
new Nanny has already achieved what I had thought
impossible.'

Cecily frowned. 'What do you mean, Roland?'

'He looks like any other little boy now. She's cut his
hair and it's brown and curly – like James's. He – he was
pulling a little wooden train along the floor. With her
help, I admit, but he was doing it. There was no crying,
no screaming and he didn't pick it up and throw it, like

126

he used to do with the other toys we bought him.' He shook his head in wonderment. 'I can't believe the changes she's made already.'

Cecily clasped her hands together. 'Oh, Roland, that's wonderful. I do hope she'll stay. Do you think she will?'

'I'm very hopeful.'

'She hasn't anywhere else to go, though, has she?'

Roland smiled. 'I don't think that would stop Miss Ingham. She seems a very determined young woman. But actually, she has somewhere to go, Cecily. She can always go to Mr Bellingham's, her family's solicitor. He told her that there was always a home for her with him and his wife.'

'That's unusual, isn't it, for a solicitor to do that?'

'Maybe, but I think he was appalled at the tragedy that had befallen her and then how her only relatives treated her. I think she will stay with us, but because she wants to. I think she has a lot more backbone than the other nannies who threw in the towel very quickly.'

At that moment, Mr Bennett appeared to announce that dinner was served.

At eleven the following morning, Roland and Mrs Weston entered the nursery. Lizzie, Charlie and Kitty were all waiting. Lizzie picked Charlie up and carried him on her hip as the three of them followed Roland across the passageway and opened the door opposite. He entered and held it open for them all to follow him in. The room was sparsely furnished with only a chest of drawers, a large toy box and shelves along the walls leaving space in the centre of the room for a child to play.

Lizzie gazed about her. 'Oh Charlie, just look at all these toys.'

A box of wooden building bricks stood in one corner

and near it a model railway was set out. It was dusty with neglect and the carriages and small figures were bent or damaged, the rails twisted. There was a heap of lead toy soldiers, painted in blue and red, but many had their heads, arms and legs broken off. There were horses with legs missing too. And on all of them the paintwork was scratched and battered.

'Most of them are broken, Nanny,' Mrs Weston said. 'It began when Nanny Gordon was still here.'

'Surely they can be mended?' Lizzie murmured as she carried Charlie around the room. 'Look, Charlie, a rocking horse.'

Charlie looked at it and put his thumb in his mouth. Gently, Lizzie removed it. 'What's his name?' When no one replied, Lizzie said, 'Shall we call him Dobbin?' She gave the horse a little push and it rocked to and fro on its wooden frame.

'Do you want to sit on it?' She made as if to lift him onto it, but Charlie's face crumpled and he began to whimper. 'All right, not just now, then.' She moved around the room again, seeing another smaller horse on wheels with a handle at the back that was designed to help a child learn to walk. 'And here's another. What shall we call this one? How about Bobo Jack? And just look at all these toys,' she went on, spying a pile of soft toys in one corner. Many of them were torn, with the stuffing poking out. 'And there's a teddy. He looks as if he needs his ear sewing back on, but he'd be company for Mr Snuggles, wouldn't he?'

Even from a distance, Lizzie could see that the teddy bear was a Steiff. No money had been spared in buying this little boy whatever he could possibly want. It was all well and good having the best of everything, Lizzy thought, but what Charlie had needed most back then was love and understanding.

'Would you like to see the adjoining room, Nanny?' Roland asked quietly. 'It's never been used at all.'

He opened the door and Lizzie, still carrying Charlie, stepped into what had been furnished as a schoolroom. There was a child's desk set in the centre of the room, with a slate and chalk, facing a table where a tutor would sit. Behind that, on the wall, was a blackboard and round the room there were shelves of books and cupboards which Lizzie guessed would hold all manner of writing, drawing and painting materials. On the walls were posters of the alphabet and numbers. Set on one of the shelves was a globe of the world. The two rooms reminded Lizzie poignantly of the playroom and schoolroom she and Bruce had once shared.

'You must use these rooms just as you wish, Nanny,' Roland said.

'I'll see that they're made ready for use, Nanny,' Mrs Weston said at once. 'If – if you decide . . .'

'And if you need anything replaced . . .' Roland began.

'I'm sure a lot of the toys could be repaired,' Lizzie said, 'but we'll take it a step at a time. Perhaps I could pick out one or two things for him to have in his bedroom to start with. This is all wonderful,' she added with a smile, 'but perhaps a bit overwhelming all at once.'

Roland smiled ruefully. 'Yes, perhaps I did go a bit over the top.'

Lizzie could imagine the proud father furnishing and equipping the two rooms with such hope in his heart for his son and heir.

'Now, Charlie,' Lizzie said briskly, 'what shall we take? How about Mr Teddy. I can stitch his ear back on. And perhaps that lovely fluffy white bunny rabbit too. We shall have to think of a name for him, shan't we?'

'Snowy,' Kitty said and then blushed as she realized

she had spoken out in front of the master. 'Oh, I'm sorry.'

'That's a lovely name, Kitty,' Lizzie said at once to spare the girl's embarrassment.

'I had a white rabbit – a real one – when I was little,' Kitty said. 'That's what I called him.'

'Then Snowy it shall be.'

As they returned to the nursery and Mrs Weston locked the door to the playroom, she handed the key to Lizzie. 'I'll give this to you, Nanny. I have a spare downstairs for the maids to use when they come to clean. Oh, and by the way, the outdoor clothes you requested should arrive early this afternoon.'

Lizzie's smile broadened.

Sixteen

Mrs Weston made her second visit of the day to the nursery early in the afternoon. She was carrying several parcels.

'Oh dear me,' she said, as she set them down on Charlie's bed. 'I should have got Clara to help me. I didn't realize they were so heavy until I got halfway up the stairs.' She was puffing a little and holding her hand to her chest as she sat in the easy chair at the side of Charlie's bed. 'Here we are, Nanny. The village dressmaker and the local shoemaker have been working very hard to deliver these. I just hope everything will fit. It's all around the village that outdoor wear has been ordered for Master Charlie. They all care, you know, in the nicest possible way. It's not gossip. You should see the little gifts that the children bring to the Manor for him at Christmas.'

'Oh, how sweet. But I suppose they don't see him?'

Mrs Weston shook her head. 'Sadly, no.'

Lizzie moved towards the parcels. 'How exciting! Come along, Charlie. Let's try everything on.'

She opened the packages, exclaiming over each one. 'What a lovely coat and a matching cap. And so beautifully made too. And look, some smart black boots. Shall we try them on?'

But Charlie ran to the end of the room and stood with the determined set to his mouth that Lizzie was coming to recognize. Lizzie turned her back on him to say, 'Thank you so much, Mrs Weston. I'm sure everything will be fine.'

With a sigh, the housekeeper got to her feet. 'It doesn't look as if I'm going to see him wearing them today. Let me know when you've had a chance to try them on.' She lowered her voice and muttered, 'If you do.'

After Mrs Weston had left, Lizzie winked at Kitty and then said loudly, 'I'm going for a little walk in the garden, Kitty. I won't be long.'

'Very well, Nanny.' Kitty was a little puzzled. She didn't quite understand what Lizzie was trying to do, but she played along.

Lizzie went into her bedroom and returned wearing her hat and coat and walking boots.

As she made for the door, Charlie ran to her with a cry and clutched at her skirt, looking up at her with tear-filled eyes. Lizzie squatted down in front of him. 'You can come with me, Charlie, but you must put on your hat and coat and your boots, just like mine. Look.' She stood up again and put her foot out from beneath her long skirt. 'We have to wear boots or strong shoes when we go out. Now, are you going to put them on?'

Charlie didn't nod or shake his head, but he did stop crying and succumbed to wearing the new clothes and boots.

'Are you coming with us, Kitty? We'll go and see if Billy is free.'

While Kitty fetched her hat and coat from her bedroom, Lizzie picked out a ball from her trunk.

'How do we get out into the grounds?' Lizzie asked when they were all ready.

'Best way is down the servants' stairs and out through the kitchen,' Kitty said. 'Then round the back of the house. We'll have to mind him on the stairs though. He's not gone down any stairs before.'

'Ah, of course not. I hadn't thought of that. Perhaps it would be best if you were to go and see if Billy is free to come and help us now.'

Kitty hurried away and returned with Billy.

'My word, Master Charlie, you do look smart,' he said. 'Now, you just come with me. Hold my hand and hold on to the bannister rail with your other hand. That's it, and down we go. One step at a time. Hold tight.'

The two women waited at the top until Charlie and Billy were safely down.

'And now we go through the kitchen,' Billy said, leading the way. 'And we can say "hello" to Cook.'

As they stepped into the kitchen, Mrs Graves turned round. She gaped at Charlie and the saucepan she was holding slipped from her hand and clattered to the floor.

Charlie jumped and clutched Lizzie's hand.

'We're just going out to play football for a little while, Mrs Graves,' Lizzie said calmly. 'Please excuse us traipsing through your kitchen. I'm sorry if we startled you.'

The cook seemed robbed of speech. Open-mouthed, she just watched them pass through her kitchen and out of the back door. As it closed behind them, Kitty was overcome by a fit of giggles. 'I've never seen her look like that before. She looked as if she'd seen a ghost.'

'Ah, here's Dad waiting,' Billy said. 'He's coming too. He can't wait to see this.'

'We'd be best on the lawn at the end of the house,' Joe said, as his gaze rested on the little boy. 'The gardener's not working there today. That's Tom, from the village, Nanny. He comes three times a week to tend the grounds and me and Billy help him out in our spare time. We have extra help in the spring and summer from young lads in the village.'

Charlie was clinging tightly to Lizzie's hand and kept

looking up at her for reassurance as Joe and Billy led them to the eastern end of the house and onto the smooth lawn there. As he looked out over the expanse of ground, Charlie began to whimper and bury his face against Lizzie's skirt.

'There, there, Charlie. We won't stay out too long today. We'll just watch Mr Marshall and Billy play football, shall we?'

'It's Joe, Nanny. Even to Master Charlie. Come on, Billy, let's show him what we do.'

For the next half an hour, the two men kicked the ball between them. Charlie watched closely, but made no attempt to join in. He still clung to Lizzie's hand.

'Billy, roll the ball to Kitty,' Lizzie said.

Kitty lifted her skirt a little and kicked it back to Billy.

'Now,' Lizzie said, 'very gently, roll it to Charlie.'

The ball stopped just in front of his feet. Charlie looked down at it and then stretched out his foot and touched it. 'Give it a little kick, like Billy did,' Lizzie encouraged.

Charlie looked up at her and then back down at the ball. Then he drew back his right foot and kicked it.

Joe, Billy and Kitty all clapped and Lizzie said, 'Clever boy. Well done.'

Charlie let go of her hand and ran to the ball, now giving it a big kick. It travelled some distance and Charlie ran after it.

'That's it, Charlie,' Lizzie shouted. 'Go after him, Billy. I don't want him to get too far away from us now he's got the idea.'

Billy caught up with him and soon they were kicking the ball backwards and forwards between them, while Joe came to stand with the two young women to watch.

'I'd never have believed it if I wasn't standing here watching it with me own eyes. Are you some sort of witch, Nanny?'

Lizzie chucked. 'If I am, Joe, I keep my broomstick very well hidden.'

As he bent over the paperwork on the desk in his study, the windows of which overlooked the lawn at the end of the house, Roland caught sight of a movement outside. He rose and moved closer to the window. What he saw shocked but delighted him.

He hurried to the drawing room. 'My dear, come quickly. There's something you must see from the morning-room window.'

The morning room was at the south-eastern corner of the house and one of its windows also looked out over the lawn where Lizzie had taken Charlie to play.

'What is it, Roland? Is something wrong?'

'Far from it, Cecily, but you must see for yourself.'

Cecily laid aside her embroidery and followed him, mystified as to what could have caused such excitement.

As they stood together by the window, Roland put his arm around her shoulders. 'Look, just look! That is our son playing football with Billy.'

Cecily stared and then shook her head. 'No, you must be mistaken, Roland. It must be a boy from the village.'

'No, no. It isn't. See there, that's the new nanny and Kitty standing with Joe to one side. Don't you see? And the little boy – *our* little boy – is dressed in the clothes you've recently ordered for him. They arrived just after luncheon and Nanny has wasted no time in making good use of them.' His voice softened. 'Such good use.'

Cecily gasped and her fingers fluttered to cover her mouth. 'It – it can't be.'

As they watched, Charlie broke away from playing football and began to run away down the lawn.

'Oh, he's running towards the lake . . .' Cecily clutched at Roland's jacket, but he only smiled as he saw Billy gallop after the boy, catch him and swing him round.

'Never fear, my darling. He's in safe hands.'

'But what if Billy hadn't been there? What if . . .?'

'I have made sure that Billy will always be there when he's needed.'

They watched as the four adults and Charlie moved back towards the house. Joe and Billy had Charlie between them, holding a hand each and swinging him into the air as they walked.

'Whatever will James make of him when he comes on Wednesday?' Cecily murmured.

As Lizzie and the others entered the kitchen, Cook set out four cups of tea and a mug of milk on the table. 'I thought you might be thirsty,' she said, avoiding meeting Lizzie's gaze. 'Please – sit down.'

'That is so kind of you, Mrs Graves. Isn't it, Charlie? What do we say to Mrs Graves?'

Charlie looked up with his solemn gaze at the cook, but said nothing.

'We say, "Thank you, Cook", don't we?'

Still, Charlie just stared but he reached for the mug and began to drink.

When Joe and Billy had finished their drinks and left the kitchen, Lizzie said, 'Mrs Graves, I need your help and advice.' She smiled winningly at the older woman.

For a moment, the cook looked startled and then, in a somewhat subdued voice, she said, 'Of course, Nanny, I'll be glad to help you in any way I can.' Although her reply was directed at Lizzie, Mrs Graves's gaze was fixed on Charlie as if she still couldn't believe what she was seeing.

'Well, you have, quite understandably, been mincing and mashing up all Charlie's food. But I wondered if you might have any ideas as to how we can gradually move on to him eating more normally for a four-year-old. He should be learning to chew his food now, don't you think?'

'I do, Nanny, but didn't they teach you how to do that at –' She paused. She had been going to say 'at that fancy college you went to', but for once, Mrs Graves bit her tongue and said, 'At college.'

'In a way. They taught us all the stages from babyhood to toddler and so on, but not quite what to do when they're already four. I would really appreciate your help, Mrs Graves.'

Kitty had to turn away to hide her giggles. She was beginning to see just how gently manipulative the new nanny could be to get her own way without the other person realizing it. Kitty, who had already become very fond of Lizzie – the new nanny had already made the nursery maid's life so much easier – now admired her even more.

'I'll give it some thought, Nanny,' the cook said and nodded.

'Thank you. I'd be very grateful.' Lizzie rose as she added, 'Now, we say "goodbye" to Cook, don't we, Charlie, and "thank you"?'

A little later, when Mrs Weston came into the kitchen, she found Mrs Graves with four or five cookery books spread around her on the table.

'Planning some new recipes, are you, Cook?'

'In a way. I'm looking up meals suitable for toddlers. Nanny has asked me to help her to get Charlie eating food that would be more normal for a four-year-old. I'm afraid, because of – well – how he's been, I have still given him baby food because I was frightened of him choking.'

Mrs Weston nodded her agreement. 'Quite right, Cook. He may well have done just that the times I've seen him crying and screaming when Kitty – or one of the nannies – was trying to feed him. But I'm hopeful that things are beginning to change.'

'I'll take it very gradually.' Mrs Graves nodded. 'Introduce more solid foods to him bit by bit.'

Now it was Mrs Weston's turn to smile and say, 'That's a very good idea, Cook.'

She too quite understood that Lizzie was subtly trying to win the cook over. And, just like Kitty, she admired the new nanny's diplomatic tactics.

Seventeen

On Wednesday morning, the anticipation seemed to ripple through the house again with heightened excitement.

'Master James is coming today,' Kitty announced, when she entered the nursery early that morning. 'Do you hear that, Charlie? Uncle James is coming.'

The little boy was sitting on the carpet, pushing at the wooden train. He looked up at Kitty, then scrambled to his feet and ran to the window that overlooked the front drive.

'Yes, that's where he'll come. Up the drive at about half past eleven. We'll watch out for him. He might wave to us.' She turned to Lizzie. 'Charlie's never run to look out before. I think he understands what I'm saying.'

Lizzie smiled. 'I'm sure he does. Now, Charlie, time to get dressed. Let's find you a nice outfit to welcome your uncle.'

For the rest of the morning, until the time James was expected, Charlie wouldn't settle. He kept running to the window and climbing onto the seat to look out, using the bars to pull himself up. At just after half past eleven he jumped up and down and pointed out of the window, making a squeaking noise.

Lizzie went to stand behind him to make sure he didn't fall. 'Hold tight, Charlie,' she murmured, as she watched the pony and trap, driven by Billy, bowling up the drive towards the front door. There was a young man dressed in army uniform sitting beside him. He was looking up at the windows of the nursery and waving.

'Wave back, Charlie,' Lizzie said. 'Like this.'

The pony and trap disappeared from their view as it neared the front door. Charlie wriggled to get down. Now he ran to the door, reaching up to the knob to try to open it.

'We must wait until your uncle comes to see us, Charlie,' Lizzie said. 'We can't go downstairs.'

Charlie's face crumpled and he began to cry. But this was not temper; these were real tears. Lizzie picked him up and held him close, rubbing his back. 'There, there, Charlie. Uncle James is here now. He'll come and see you very soon, I'm sure.' She just hoped she was right.

The minutes must have seemed like hours to the impatient little boy, but it was only about twenty minutes before they heard voices and then the key in the lock of the outer door.

'Dry your tears,' Lizzie whispered. 'Don't let Uncle James see you've been crying.'

The nursery door opened and Roland came in, followed by a handsome young man in army uniform. Just inside the door, he stopped and stared at the little boy running towards him. Then he stretched out his arms, picked Charlie up and swung him high in the air and then round and round. Then he set him down on the floor and dropped to one knee in front of him.

'Oh, my word. You said I'd see a difference, Roland, but I didn't expect this. He looks . . . wonderful.'

He rose and picked Charlie up again, then looked beyond him and straight into Lizzie's eyes. Lizzie had not expected the jolt that coursed through her as she met his gaze. Kitty had said he was handsome and he certainly was, with dark brown hair and eyes. As they'd said – just like Charlie's. He was tall and lean and his facial features were even, with a strong, firm jawline. His smile lit up his eyes with a cheeky twinkle.

'So, this is Nanny. Are you going to introduce us, Charlie?'

The little boy twisted round in his uncle's arms and reached out his left hand towards Lizzie, but he made no sound. James moved closer. 'I am very pleased to meet you, Nanny,' he said softly, his gaze never leaving her face. 'I do hope you won't mind if I spend quite a lot of time with Charlie while I am here.'

'Of course not, sir.'

James's smile broadened into a grin. 'Oh no "sir" with me, Nanny. All the staff call me "Master James".'

Lizzie inclined her head.

'Roland tells me Charlie goes outside now. That he plays football with Billy and Joe.'

'Just the once so far, Master James, but we hope it will be a regular exercise when the weather is fine.'

'Then please may I join in?'

'Of course.'

James winked at Lizzie. 'We might even persuade old Roland here to play too.'

'You never know,' Roland said quietly.

They stayed until Clara brought luncheon for the nursery, but when the two men headed to the door, Charlie began to whimper.

Lizzie picked him up. 'It's all right, Charlie. No tears now. You'll see Uncle James again very soon.'

When the two men had left, Kitty sighed, 'Don't you think he's the most handsome man you've ever seen, Nanny?'

Lizzie was quiet for a moment, thinking back to her previous life. It was not often she did so. She tried to block out her early years from her mind and concentrate on her life now. But sometimes, as now, it was impossible to wipe out the memories. She thought back to the men she had known in her life. Her brother and all the young suitors she had met during her coming-out year and then, of course, there had been Oliver. She could still picture his face and hear his voice, but the feelings she had once believed she had for him had long faded.

'Now you mention it, Kitty,' she murmured, 'I think you could be right.'

'And he's so *nice* too. He's not conceited or arrogant. Have you ever had a boyfriend, Nanny? You're very pretty.'

Lizzie hesitated. She had vowed that if she was ever asked questions about her past that she would not lie. 'Once, but it didn't work out and then I went to college. Now, let's sit down and have lunch, Charlie. The sooner we finish, the sooner we can go out to play this afternoon and perhaps Uncle James will join us.'

'We could ask Mr Bennett to let him know when we go out, Nanny,' Kitty whispered. 'I'm sure Master James meant what he said.'

About mid-afternoon, Lizzie dressed Charlie in his outdoor apparel and the three of them carefully went down the back stairs, through the kitchen and outside. Billy, who had been watching out for them, came across from the stables.

He touched his cap. 'I wondered if Charlie might like to see the horses, Nanny? I don't want him to be frightened, but I could lead the little pony up and down from a distance just to get him used it.'

'That's a lovely idea, Billy. Where should we stand?'

'I'll bring him round onto the lawn.' Billy grinned. 'The master won't mind if it's for Charlie. Besides, it's his pony really.'

'Whose?'

'Charlie's. The master bought it for him when he was still a baby.' His face clouded. 'But then . . .' He shrugged. There was no longer any need to put it into words.

'We'll go round to the lawn and wait for you,' Lizzie said.

Only moments later, Billy was leading the prettiest little Shetland pony that Lizzie had ever seen onto the lawn. He halted a few yards from them. 'I'll not bring him too close. I don't want Charlie to be frightened. What we really need is Master James.'

'And here I am,' a voice said from behind them. 'Right on cue.'

Lizzie turned to see both Roland and James appearing from the corner of the house.

'Bennett told us that you had come out and we thought we'd come and play too,' Roland said. 'But I never thought about the pony. What a good idea, Billy.'

Billy touched his cap again. 'I thought about it this morning, so I fetched him from the field into the stable – just in case Nanny agreed.'

Although he still stood beside Lizzie, holding her hand, Charlie was watching as James stroked the pony's nose.

'Shall we go a little closer, Charlie,' Lizzie said, but as she took a step he began to whimper and clutch at her hand even more tightly. 'It's all right, darling,' she said at once. 'We'll just watch from here today. Perhaps next time we'll stroke his nose, like Uncle James, shall we?' She glanced up at Billy. 'Has he got a name?'

'Dandy.'

'I'd forgotten that,' Roland said, 'but then I haven't seen him – recently. Have you still got the saddle and everything?'

'Oh yes, sir. I keep it all polished.'

After ten minutes, it was agreed that Billy should take the pony back to the stable.

'We'll try again tomorrow,' Lizzie said. 'It was so good of you to think of it, Billy. But we need to take it very slowly. Perhaps if I take Charlie into the playroom and show him the rocking horse again. That might be an idea.'

As Billy began to lead the pony away, he said, 'I'll be back in a minute to play football.'

'Does he go into the playroom now?' James asked.

Roland and Lizzie exchanged a glance. 'It's not been used for a long time, if ever, but I took Nanny and Charlie in the other day.' He paused as if allowing Lizzie to say what she had planned to say.

'Clara and Kitty are giving it a good clean and airing. In the meantime, we're taking one or two toys into his bedroom for a start.'

James nodded. 'I can see from today that everything has to be taken very slowly. But you are making progress, Nanny. Wonderful progress. Ah, now here's Billy back with the football.'

For the next half an hour, the three men played football with the little boy and by the time they went indoors, Charlie was able to kick it back to them with a reasonable aim, but all the time he kept glancing back to make sure that Lizzie was still watching.

As they returned to the house, James said, 'I'll come and see him just before we have our dinner. I expect he will have gone to bed by the time we finish.'

'Yes, Master James, he will, so that would be perfect.'

As they stepped into the kitchen, James spread his arms out. 'Dear Mrs Graves. And how's my favourite cook in all the world?'

Mrs Graves laughed and turned a little pink. 'Oh, go

144

on with you, Master James.' She turned even pinker when he kissed her soundly on both cheeks. 'You're a rascal and no mistake, but it's good to see you safe and sound.'

'And I dare bet there's pork with crackling and stuffing and apple sauce for dinner, followed by sherry trifle, isn't there?'

'Now, how would you know that, Master James?'

'Because it's my favourite meal and you always make it for me on my first night home. And now, I'd better go and take afternoon tea with my sister-in-law. I haven't seen much of her yet.'

When the two men had left the kitchen, Mrs Graves said, 'Do sit down, Nanny. I've made you a cup of tea and there's a mug of milk for Master Charlie. I'd like a word with you about Charlie's meals. I've had some ideas . . .'

Eighteen

James appeared in the nursery the following morning with Mrs Weston. Coming through the door, he held out his arms to Charlie who ran towards him to be scooped up into the air and swung round.

'Master James has volunteered to help introduce Master Charlie to the playroom, Nanny. Clara has finished cleaning it. It's all ready for use now, apart from the broken toys, of course, but you know about them.'

'Only if you want me to, Nanny,' James said. 'I don't want to interfere with your plans or your routine.'

'We'd be very glad of your company, Master James, wouldn't we, Charlie?'

'I thought if we could get him interested in the rocking horse, like you suggested, then we could show him Dandy again.'

'I'll let Clara know that the playroom needs to be cleaned and dusted regularly now,' Mrs Weston said. 'Is there anything else this morning, Nanny?'

'No, I don't think so, Mrs Weston, thank you.'

'Right then, the playroom it is,' James said.

Lizzie opened the door and James carried Charlie into the room. 'Just look at all these toys, Charlie. How's he getting on with them, Nanny? Is he learning to play with them and not to be destructive?'

'Oh yes. He now takes Mr Snuggles and Teddy to bed with him. And I took the push-along horse in there too. He pushes that around the room. We call him Bobo Jack.'

'Now, Charlie,' James said, 'let's see if you'd like to sit on the rocking horse.'

Gently, he lifted Charlie onto the rocking horse. 'Hold tight,' he said as he began to move the horse to and fro, but Charlie started to whimper and look towards Lizzie with terrified eyes. She came and stood on the other side. 'It's all right. You're quite safe. We've got you.' But his cries increased until James said, 'Not quite ready yet, are you, old chap? We'll try another day. Let's have a look at the other toys. See what can be mended, shall we?'

James stayed for a week, spending a lot of time in the nursery, the playroom and outside on the lawn with Charlie, Lizzie and Kitty. He even took over bath-time duties from Joe and Billy on the Sunday evening. Charlie still cried when he had to have his hair washed, but soon recovered when James galloped around the nursery pretending to be a horse with Charlie on his shoulders.

'Today's my last day, I'm afraid,' he said on the Tuesday. 'I have to leave very early tomorrow morning, but I would love to see Charlie riding Dandy before I leave. At least we've got him to sit on the rocking horse while it moves.'

'And playing with a lot of the toys too,' Lizzie said. 'We can ask Billy to put the saddle on the pony and try this afternoon.'

But the attempt was not a success. When James lifted him onto the pony's back, Charlie started to wail and the pony shied. Charlie held out his arms to Lizzie and James handed him to her.

'There, there. It's all right. Shush now. You're frightening poor Dandy. Let's stroke his nose, shall we? Like this.' Charlie's keening subsided to a sniffle and he watched as Lizzie patted and stroked the pony, but he clung to her and wouldn't touch the animal himself.

'I'm sorry, Nanny. That was my fault,' James said, crestfallen. 'I was rushing him too much. He's not quite ready, but I so wanted to see him on Dandy before I left.' He sighed. 'It'll have to wait until next time.'

'We'll have him riding by the time you come again next time, Master James,' Billy said.

'That won't be until Christmas, I'm afraid.'

As Billy led the pony away, James said softly, 'You're doing wonders with him, Nanny. I never thought to see even this much improvement. I'm sorry if I've tried to go too fast.'

'No harm done.' Lizzie smiled into his dark brown eyes, sorry to see the disappointment in them. 'We've something to work towards now, but please don't be disheartened. You've done so much for him this week. But may I ask one thing of you?'

'Anything, Nanny.'

'Say goodbye to him tonight and don't come up to the nursery before you leave in the morning. He'll be distressed when he doesn't see you tomorrow but I think to actually see you go would be too much.'

'I understand and of course I'll do as you ask.'

Lizzie had been right. The week following James's departure was disastrous. Charlie reverted to throwing his toys around the room. He tore the book that Lizzie read to him each night. He refused to try to feed himself and knocked the plates and dishes onto the floor. And at night, he screamed when bedtime came and she had to sleep with him all night in the chair, instead of being able to put him into his bed halfway through the night as she had been doing.

148

'I thought he was getting so much better,' Kitty said dolefully, 'but he isn't, is he?'

'Of course he is. This is just a set-back, Kitty. He's missing Master James. That's obvious.'

'Ought you to call the doctor and get him to give . . .?'

'Absolutely not,' Lizzie said firmly.

'But Mrs Graves said he kept her awake again last night.'

'I'm sorry to hear that, but he will improve again, I promise.'

And Lizzie was right again. As the days passed, although he ran to the window sometimes to look down the drive, Charlie's temper tantrums – for that was what they were – subsided. He stopped throwing his toys about. He fed himself with a spoon and he ran around the lawn after the football. And when Billy brought Dandy to see him, they didn't try to put him on the pony's back. They just encouraged him to stroke the animal's nose.

But every day he rode the rocking horse just as James had shown him.

As the early August weather grew warmer, Lizzie ordered lighter outdoor clothing for Charlie and insisted he wore a sunhat when outside in the sun. Often Roland and Cecily watched the games on the lawn from the window and sometimes Roland went out to join in.

'I suppose,' Cecily said one evening as she and Roland sat together in the drawing room after dinner, 'I really ought to meet Nanny sometime and perhaps – perhaps I could see Charlie too.'

'It would be nice if you felt able, my dear,' Roland said carefully.

Cecily's health had not been good since Charlie's birth and the worry and disappointment she felt when the boy

149

didn't develop as he should have done, further undermined her wellbeing.

'I will,' she said. 'I will try.'

'Perhaps it might be a good idea for us to take a walk on the terrace overlooking the lawn when he's out playing.'

'Yes – yes. Perhaps tomorrow.'

It was three days before Cecily plucked up the courage to take a walk with Roland. It was a surprise to everyone, not least to Cecily herself. Kitty saw them first.

'Oh Nanny, look. The mistress has come onto the terrace with the master. They're coming down the steps towards us. I think she's coming to meet you and to see Charlie.'

Just as they drew near, Charlie kicked the ball and it rolled to Roland's feet. He laughed and gently kicked it back to Charlie, but he just stood staring at them. Lizzie went to him and took his hand. 'Come and say "hello" to Papa and Mama, Charlie.'

But Charlie wouldn't move, he just stood still and stared.

'I – I thought it was time I met you, Nanny,' Cecily said hesitantly, her arm tucked firmly in Roland's. Her gaze was on her son. 'Roland has been telling me how well you're getting on. How – how much Charlie is improving.'

'It's steady progress, ma'am. It will take some time.'

At that moment, Charlie twisted his hand out of Lizzie's grasp, turned and ran across the lawn towards the lake. At once, Billy chased after him, caught him easily and swung him high in the air.

'And where do you think you're going, young man?' Billy laughed and carried him back.

'We'll go,' Cecily said, a little nervously. 'We're obviously unsettling him.'

She turned and pulled on Roland's arm to make him walk with her. Roland nodded and turned away too. As they moved away, he was disconcerted to see that Cecily had tears in her eyes. He patted her hand where it rested on his arm. 'What is it, my love? What has distressed you? He's so much better than he used to be. Surely you can see that?'

'Yes, yes, I can. We are so lucky to have such good people looking after him. I – I was expecting too much.'

'Like Nanny said, it will take time.'

When Lizzie said it was time to go in, they all trooped into the kitchen and, invited by the cook, sat down at the table. Joe was there too.

'You didn't have the pony out today?'

Lizzie shook her head. 'Not today. Perhaps we'll try tomorrow.'

'I've made you some scones with cream and jam,' Cook said, placing them on the table. 'Help yourselves. I think Master Charlie will be all right with one, won't he, Nanny?'

'I'm sure he will. These look delicious. And thank you for the meals you're sending up now. He's doing very well with them. He's learning to chew properly.'

Mrs Graves preened at the praise.

'And I'm sorry you've all been disturbed again recently,' Lizzie went on. 'I think it was a certain person leaving that upset him for a few days, but we're getting back on track now.'

She cut the scones in half and then glanced up at the cook with a grin. 'Now, Cook, is it jam first or cream first?'

Mrs Graves smiled back. 'I know there's different ideas but I think it's easier to put the jam on first and then the cream.'

151

'Then that's what we'll do.' She put the two halves of Charlie's scone in front of him and then prepared her own. She picked up one half and deliberately got a little dab of cream on her nose.

'Scrumptious!' she said and turned to look at Charlie. He was gazing up at her. She bent and rubbed her nose against his, transferring a little of the cream onto his nose. 'They're scrumptious, Charlie. You try one.'

Charlie picked up one half and bit into it. Now he had cream and jam too around his mouth. Lizzie took another bite and so did Charlie. Across the table Joe, Billy and Kitty were also tucking into their scones.

When Charlie's plate was empty except for the crumbs, he looked up at Lizzie and said, 'Scumshush.'

There was a sharp intake of breath by everyone around the table and all eyes turned to Charlie. All, that is, except Lizzie's. Although her heart was doing crazy somersaults with joy, she said, with deliberate casualness, 'You're absolutely right, Charlie. They are scrumptious.'

'Oh Nanny,' Mrs Graves breathed. 'He – he spoke. He – he said a word. A proper word.' She dragged her gaze away from the little boy and met Lizzie's eyes. At that moment, Mrs Weston entered the kitchen in time to hear Mrs Graves say, 'I owe you an apology, Nanny. I have misjudged you. Please forgive me.'

Lizzie smiled. 'Don't think any more about it, Mrs Graves. You all had a dreadful time with a succession of nannies. I understand that, but please believe me when I say that I am staying for as long as Charlie needs me.'

'That's a big commitment to make,' the cook said, shaking her head. 'You're only young. Surely, you'll want to get married – have children of your own. Have you no family?'

Lizzie hesitated. The cook was getting into dangerous

territory, but Lizzie wasn't yet sure enough of the staff at the Manor to trust them with her secrets.

Her face was bleak as she whispered, 'Not anymore, Mrs Graves. This is my home now, if you'll have me.'

Mrs Weston stepped forward, sensing that the cook's questions were getting a little too personal, though, of course, Mrs Graves didn't know why. When Lizzie had first been appointed, Roland had confided a little in his housekeeper and butler, the two most senior members of his household staff. 'Miss Ingham,' he'd said, 'is completely trustworthy and her background is impeccable, but she has recently suffered a family tragedy, which I feel she won't want to divulge at present. You will just have to trust me that I know all about it and am happy to engage her. Perhaps one day, when she gets to know you all better, she will tell you herself.'

Remembering this and trying to deflect the attention away from Lizzie, Mrs Weston said, 'Are you crying, Kitty? Has something upset you? And you too, Cook. Your eyes look suspiciously red.'

'No, Mrs Weston. We're just so happy,' Kitty said, dabbing her eyes with a handkerchief. 'Charlie spoke. He said a word.'

Mrs Weston gaped at the little boy, who was sitting in his chair munching another scone, still with the dab of cream on his nose and cream and jam around his mouth.

'What did he say?'

Kitty giggled through her tears.

'Scrumptious. It was what Nanny said about the scones. And so he tried to say it too.'

Mrs Weston glanced around the room and both Joe and Billy nodded their agreement. 'He definitely tried to say "scrumptious", Mrs Weston,' Joe said. 'We all heard it.'

'I'll go and tell the master . . .' And before anyone could say anything, she whirled around and was gone.

'Oh dear,' Lizzie murmured softly. 'He might not repeat it.'

A few minutes later, Mrs Weston returned to the kitchen followed by Roland and Mr Bennett. Joe and Billy stood up. 'We'd best be getting back to work.'

'No, no, don't go on my account. Stay and have another cup of tea and perhaps another scrumptious scone.' Roland's gaze was on Charlie as if he was trying to prompt him to say the word again for him to hear. But now Charlie said nothing, not even when Roland bit into a scone and deliberately left a dab of cream on his own nose.

'We all heard it, sir,' Joe said, as he and Billy finally got up to leave. 'It's a start, isn't it?'

'Yes, it certainly is. Do let me know if he says anything else, won't you?' Roland said, including them all.

'Of course,' they all chorused.

Nineteen

As the days passed, Charlie made no further effort to say anything else, though he improved in other ways. Bath times became easier and soon Joe and Billy were no longer required to help, though they were always on hand when Charlie played outside. Indoors, they began to use the playroom and, when he made no more attempts to break the toys, the broken ones were sent to Joe and Billy to be mended.

'It's Charlie's fifth birthday in a few days' time, Nanny. On the twenty-fifth of August. Mrs Weston and Cook wondered if you'd like to have a nursery tea party for him. Mrs Graves will make a special cake with candles and jellies and trifles.'

'That's a lovely idea. We could invite Mr and Mrs Spendlove, couldn't we?'

Kitty's face clouded. 'The master might come, but I'm not sure about the mistress. What a pity Master James can't get home again until Christmas. He'd have loved that and so would Charlie.'

The birthday tea party was a great success. Joe and Billy moved the desks in the schoolroom to the walls and set up a round table in the centre of the room and Clara and Kitty ran up and down stairs carrying all the lovely food that Mrs Graves had prepared. Joe, Billy, Mr Bennett, Mrs Weston and Mrs Graves were all invited, as were the master and the mistress. To everyone's surprise, Cecily arrived dressed in a pretty afternoon tea gown. She seemed a little nervous, but once Charlie had stared at her for a few moments, he turned away and went into the playroom where Billy was setting up the train set in the centre of the room.

'Has he said anything else since that day in the kitchen?' Roland asked.

'No, sir, I'm sorry,' Lizzie said, 'he hasn't. Sometimes in the night, he seems to be trying very hard to speak but there's been nothing as yet. I have every hope it will come.'

'Perhaps,' Roland said thoughtfully, 'he should be mixing with other children. I mean, look at today. Wonderful though it is and I – we – are so grateful for all your efforts . . .' His glance went round the room to include all his staff. 'There should be other children here, shouldn't there?'

'Would you consider him mixing with the village children?' Joe asked.

Roland glanced at his wife. 'We have discussed all sorts of possibilities. We've talked about engaging a tutor and having one or two of the local children to come here for lessons. But that would seem unfair to others. The one thing I don't want is to cause resentment among the villagers if they thought some of them were getting preferential treatment. We'd even discussed him attending the village school . . .'

'I don't think that'd be a good idea, sir, if you don't mind me saying so,' Joe said at once. 'They say the schoolmaster is an excellent teacher, but he's very strict and he's a miserable old devil. Pardon me, ma'am, but he's not the sort to have the handling of a sensitive child like Master Charlie. My mate, Bob Preston, Kitty's dad . . .'

Roland nodded. 'I know him. He's the waggoner on Home Farm, isn't he?'

'That's right, sir. Well, he was telling me in the pub only the other night that his youngest is due to start school in a couple of weeks' time and the little lad's terrified.'

Roland frowned. 'Why is that?'

'Because when the little ones start school, he lines 'em up on the first day and gives them the cane. One stroke on their hand before they've even done anything wrong. Just to show them what happens if they misbehave. Bob's little lad is having nightmares already and he's not even started school yet.'

'That's right, sir,' Kitty said. 'Our little Alfie's that frightened Mam says he's started wetting the bed and he's never been a bed-wetter.'

Lizzie was horrified, but she held her tongue. None of this was her business, not unless the master decided to send Charlie to the school. Then it would most certainly be her concern.

'There is something else you could do, sir.'

'What's that, Joe?'

'On a Saturday afternoon all the village kids congregate in the playing field you've given them opposite the school. They play football and usually Bob acts as referee. If Nanny or Kitty took Master Charlie down, he could watch and I'm sure some of the kids would talk to him.'

'I'd get my brother, Luke, to make him welcome, sir,' Kitty said. 'Luke's a good, kind lad.'

Roland was thoughtful and glanced at his wife.

'Whatever you think best, Roland,' Cecily said. She turned to Lizzie. 'What do you think, Nanny?'

'I think it's a very good idea.'

'Remind me, Kitty,' Roland said. 'How many are there in your family?'

'I'm the eldest, sir, and then there's my sister, Evie, but she's away in service now, then Luke. He's the bright one in the family. He's ten and my mam and dad are hoping he'll be able to go to the grammar school next year. And then there's Alfie. He's just turned five, like I said.' Her face clouded briefly. 'There was one between Luke and Alfie, but he was stillborn.'

'Yes, I remember that,' Roland said. 'We were so sorry.'

'You were very kind, sir, at that time. Mam and Dad have never forgotten.'

Roland gave a small smile of acknowledgement and added, 'We'll see what we can do for Luke next year, Kitty. In the meantime, perhaps he would take Charlie under his wing if he goes down to watch the football. Maybe he could even get him to join in.'

'He'd be delighted to and, being one of the oldest now, all the other kids will do whatever Luke says.'

'So, if Nanny approves, that's what we'll do.'

On the Saturday afternoon, Billy harnessed the pony and trap and drove Charlie, Lizzie and Kitty down to the village. He pulled up outside the gate leading into the field on the outskirts.

'I remember the master giving this field to the village for the kids to play on,' Billy said. 'I was about ten. It gets well used and it's safe, even for little 'uns. Not too far from their homes, you see. Looks like they're all here today. There's about twenty, including the girls.'

Lizzie smiled. 'So nearly two football teams, then.'

She scanned the field where a pitch had been marked out and there was a proper goal with a net at either end.

'The master provided it all,' Kitty said. 'And here's Dad

158

coming up the lane now.' She waved to the burly, broad-shouldered man walking towards them. She climbed down from the trap and gave her hand to Lizzy, who then turned and lifted Charlie down.

As Bob Preston reached them, he raised his cap. 'You must be the new nanny I've been hearing so much about.' He stuck out his hand, 'Pleased to meet you, I'm sure.'

'And I'm very pleased to meet you, Mr Preston.'

'Eee, no ceremony, me duck. It's Bob. Now then, young man,' Bob said gently, looking down at Charlie, who gazed solemnly up at the big man towering above him. 'Have you come to play with us?'

'We hope so, Bob,' Lizzie said, 'but we'll let him watch at first. Maybe, in a little while, one or two of the children might come and say "hello" to him.'

Understanding her meaning, Bob said, 'Aye, we'll not let them overwhelm him. I'll get our Luke over. He's the oldest here and the others tend to do what he tells them.' He turned and beckoned to the tallest boy on the field. 'Here he comes.'

Luke was tall and thin with an untidy mop of fair hair and a cheeky grin. His blue eyes were bright and intelligent, but Lizzie noticed there was a kindness in them that was perhaps unusual for a ten-year-old. She was heartened to see it.

'Master Charlie's come to watch us play,' his father explained. 'And Nanny would like you to send just one or two over to say "hello" to him. Not too many at once, mind, because this is the first time he's met other kids.' He gave a deep rumbling chuckle. It was an endearing sound. 'We don't want to frighten the little fella off, do we?'

Luke dropped to his haunches in front of Charlie. 'Hello, Charlie. It's nice to meet you. My name's Luke.

You watch us play and if you want to join in, that'd be grand, but don't worry if you don't. There's always another day. I'll send our Alfie over to meet you. He's about your age.'

A few moments later, Alfie Preston, Kitty's youngest brother, was standing in front of Charlie. ''Lo, Charlie,' he said.

'We say, "Hello, Alfie", don't we, Charlie?' Lizzie said. Charlie said nothing but just stared at the boy in front of him. He clung to Lizzie's hand and took a step closer to her skirt.

'He's just going to watch you play, Alfie, and then we'll see,' Lizzie said.

'Doesn't he talk?' Alfie said, with the candour of a young boy.

'Not much yet,' Lizzie said. She was hoping that hearing the young children talk and shout might prompt Charlie to try too.

Bob chuckled again. 'He won't get a word in edgeways with this lot. Off you go, Alfie.' He touched his cap to Lizzie. 'I'd better go and do me job as referee. We just play half an hour each way. I'll see you later.'

Towards the end of the second half, Lizzie saw Bob call Luke to him and point towards where Charlie was standing. Luke nodded and dribbled the ball towards the little boy. He stopped about six feet away and gently kicked the ball towards Charlie so that it rolled and stopped at his feet.

'Kick it back to Luke,' Lizzie said.

After a moment's hesitation and a glance up at his nanny, Charlie drew back his right foot and kicked the ball. It only rolled a couple of feet so he let go of Lizzie's hand and kicked it again. This time it landed at Luke's feet. The older boy stepped back a few feet more and, very gently, kicked it back to Charlie. Charlie moved forward again to return the ball and when they'd done this a few times, Charlie was close to the other children.

'Come on, Charlie. O'er here,' Alfie shouted.

Charlie kicked the ball again straight to Alfie.

'My word,' Billy said. 'That was a good aim. I really think he's getting the hang of this, Nanny.'

'Look, he's moving in among the children,' Kitty said excitedly, but then, 'Oh no, one of the boys has cannoned into him and knocked him over. Oh dear, shall I . . .?'

But instead of running to him, Lizzie shouted. 'Up you get, Charlie! Get the ball!'

For a moment, Charlie's lip trembled but then he looked up and saw Lizzie pointing. 'Get the ball,' she shouted again.

He scrambled to his feet and ran to the ball while all the other children stood still, afraid they were going to be in trouble. With no one to stop him, Charlie kicked the ball into the nearest goal just as he'd seen the other children do. Bob blew his whistle and beckoned all the children to gather around him, including Charlie.

'Now we'll go over,' Lizzie said and the three of them moved towards where Bob was now surrounded by the children.

'I'm sorry I knocked you over,' they heard the boy apologize, but Charlie just stared at him.

'No harm done,' Lizzie said, her smile including all the children. 'It's all part of the game, isn't it? It was so nice of you to let him join in.'

'He scored a goal, miss,' one little boy piped up. 'That means our side's won.'

'No, it doesn't. He was on our side, not yours.'

'Now, now, children,' Bob said in his deep voice and all eyes turned to look at him, even Charlie's. 'We'll call it a draw today and if Charlie comes to play again, which I hope he will, we'll put him with a team. All right?'

Several heads nodded. 'All right, Mr Bob.'

'Now,' Lizzie said, 'it's time we were going home. But what do we say to Mr Bob and the children, Charlie?' When Charlie said nothing, Lizzie continued, 'We say, "Thank you, Mr Bob, and everyone for letting me join in." '

'You're welcome, Charlie,' Luke said, as if speaking for all of them. 'Come again.'

To everyone's surprise and delight, Charlie nodded.

Twenty

Charlie was tired that evening and when bedtime came, he was almost asleep on his feet. Lizzie put him straight into his own bed without nursing him in the easy chair first. She tucked Mr Snuggles and Teddy in beside him and sat with him until she knew he was fast asleep.

Kitty crept into the nursery. 'Mr Bennett says the master and mistress would like to see you in the drawing room after dinner at about eight o'clock, but only if Master Charlie is all right for you to leave him. I'll come and sit with him, Nanny, and if there's a problem I'll ring the bell and Clara will fetch you.'

At ten minutes to eight, Lizzie removed her apron, tidied her hair and went down to the hall where Mr Bennett was waiting to show her into the drawing room.

'Come in, Nanny,' Roland said, rising to his feet as she entered. 'Please sit down. Would you like some coffee?'

It was the first time Lizzie had seen the drawing room and she glanced briefly around the large room, taking in the white marble fireplace, the comfortable sofas and chairs and the tapestry hangings on the wall. It was a grand room, yet homely too. When they were all seated and served with coffee and Mr Bennett had withdrawn, Roland said, 'We won't keep you long, Nanny, but we were just so anxious to hear how Charlie got on this afternoon.'

Lizzie told them everything that had happened, ending, 'And when Luke asked him to go again, Charlie nodded.'

'Did he? Did he really?' Cecily said, 'That must mean he understood what the boy was saying.' She paused and then looked to her husband to add, a little uncertainly, 'Doesn't it?'

'I would think so, my dear. Do you think it does, Nanny?'

'I think he understands quite a lot, but for some reason he just doesn't talk yet. But I am hopeful that being among the other children will help him. They're all very good with him, especially Bob Preston's boys, Luke and the little one, Alfie.'

'Is that the one that's so afraid of going to school?'

Lizzie nodded.

'Perhaps I should have a word with the teacher, Mr Holland,' Roland murmured, but it didn't sound as if it would be a task he would relish. 'I'm not sure that I want Charlie to attend the school if that's what the man does. I don't like the sound of him treating any of the children like that either, if I'm honest.'

'Would you give me permission to speak to him, sir?'

'Most certainly, Nanny, if you would like to. Would you like me to ask him to come here? To the Manor?'

'If we take Charlie to play again next Saturday afternoon, there may be a chance for me to speak to him then.'

She remembered that the school and schoolhouse were just opposite the field where the children played.

'Then I'll leave it to you, Nanny. Thank you for coming down.'

Back in the nursery, Kitty said, 'He's fast asleep. He hasn't stirred.'

'That's good. You can go now, Kitty, if everything's done.'

'It is, Nanny, and thank you.'

*

On the following Saturday afternoon, Billy once again took Lizzie, Kitty and Charlie down to the playing field. At once Charlie ran onto the field to join the children clustering around Bob. When teams had been picked, this time including Charlie, Lizzie said to Kitty, 'I'm just going across the road to the schoolhouse to have a word with Mr Holland. I'll watch the children playing from there. I won't be going inside, so that Charlie will still be able to see me.'

Kitty grimaced. 'Good luck with that. Watch out for his cane.'

Lizzie crossed the lane and knocked on the door of the small house adjacent to the school. It was some moments before the door opened to reveal a thin man, with a bald pate and wispy tufts of grey hair over his ears. He wore round steel-rimmed spectacles through which beady blue eyes glared at her.

'Good afternoon, Mr Holland,' Lizzie greeted him with a smile. 'I am the nanny at the Manor and there has been some discussion as to whether or not Charlie should attend your school.'

'I would have thought he'd have had a tutor,' he said gruffly, without even greeting her first.

'That suggestion has been mooted too, but it is felt that mixing with other children would be beneficial for him.'

'I'm sure it would, but would it be "beneficial", as you put it, for his fellow classmates? I've heard he's very – difficult.'

'He's getting much better now.' She half turned and gestured towards the field. 'He's playing football now with the village children.'

The man's eyebrows rose. 'Is he now?' He watched the children for a few moments before saying, 'So, you want him to come to my school, do you?'

'Only on one condition.'

Josiah Holland frowned. 'A condition? I make the conditions, not you.'

'Then I have no more to say to you, Mr Holland. I'll bid you good day.' Lizzie nodded and began to turn away.

'Wait,' he barked. It was more like an order than a request. For a moment they glared at each other in a battle of wills.

'What sort of condition?' he asked at last.

Deliberately, Lizzie kept her tone neutral. There was neither censure nor approval in her tone. 'I have heard that on the first day a child starts school, they receive one stroke of the cane, just to show them what will happen if they misbehave. Is that true?'

A cynical smile twisted his mouth. 'Keeps the little tykes in line. They know what to expect. I'm not here to be their friend. I'm here to teach them.'

'And do you think they learn any better if they're quivering in fear? Oh, I'm not talking about the older ones. They should know the score, know what's expected of them, but do you really believe that a little five-year-old needs such drastic discipline? Surely there are other punishments – if punishment is necessary? Keeping them in at playtime or after school when all their peers are outside, or writing lines in their best handwriting.'

Again, he gave her the almost pitying smile. 'You're not a teacher, are you, Miss Ingham?' She was surprised that he knew her name but then she realized that talk of her arrival would have circulated around the village. 'You've never stood in front of a class of twenty or so children, most of whom have no wish to be there and who despise and ridicule you.'

'If that is the case, Mr Holland, then I'm sorry to hear it but I still don't think caning the young ones is going to help. You're punishing them for something they haven't yet done. Where is the fairness in that? Would you like to be arrested by a policeman and incarcerated for a crime you hadn't committed?'

He glared at her, but did not answer her question directly. Instead, he said, 'School starts next Tuesday, if you decide to bring Master Charles.' And then he closed the door in her face.

When she rejoined Kitty and Billy, Kitty asked, 'How did you get on with the old misery?'

Lizzie gave a wry laugh. 'I'm not exactly sure, but I don't think I'll be taking Charlie there.'

'We can still bring him to play on a Saturday,' Billy said. 'That way he'll be able to mix with children of his own age.'

'That's true,' Lizzie said. 'I was so hoping he would have the chance to learn alongside others, but I am certainly not submitting him to that kind of treatment. I am so sorry that your little brother will have to face it, Kitty. I did my best to point out how unfair it was, but I don't think it'll have made a scrap of difference.'

'I have to admit that the kids can sometimes be very cruel to Mr Holland,' Billy said. 'He has a club foot and walks with a stick. I think they call him "Old Hop-along" behind his back.'

'He'll know what they call him,' Kitty said quietly. 'Teachers always do.'

On the first day of the school's autumn term, Luke led his little brother, Alfie, by the hand. The little boy was crying before he even reached the school gate.

'It'll just hurt for a bit, but if you behave yourself, you won't get caned again.' Luke wasn't exactly being truthful. Mr Holland was known to cane pupils for poor spelling

167

or bad handwriting, or even just if he felt they needed a "sharpener".

There was another pupil, a little girl, starting on the same day. She too looked frightened but was bravely trying to hold back her tears.

Josiah Holland stood behind his desk in front of the class.

'Good morning, boys and girls,' he said. 'You may be seated.'

When the shuffling and scraping of chairs had stopped, Josiah cleared his throat and frowned at them all over his spectacles. 'We have two new pupils joining us today. Alfie and Rosie. Now . . .' He looked directly at the two newcomers and then beyond them, half hoping to see the nanny from the Manor appear with her charge. He had given a lot of thought to what Miss Ingham had said and what he was about to do now was certainly because of her fair-minded ideas on discipline. Though he would never admit it, he felt a little ashamed of his treatment of the very young children. He had hoped she would bring Charlie today so that she could witness his change of heart. When the door remained stubbornly closed, he gave a sigh and continued. 'You may have heard that it is my custom to give you a stroke of the cane on your first day, just to let you know what will happen if you displease me.' He paused and saw the two pairs of terrified eyes staring up at him. They were such little mites, he saw now. Why had he never seen it before? Why had it taken the stern, pretty nanny from the big house to point out the error of his ways? It was a question he could not answer. Again he cleared his throat and said, 'That practice will now cease, but –' he adopted his most severe look – 'I do reserve the right to punish you for any misdemeanour in a manner I think appropriate. Luke –'

he glanced up to the back row of the classroom – 'spell "misdemeanour" for me.'

Luke stood up, cleared his throat and spelt the word perfectly.

'And now tell me its meaning.'

'It's something you do wrong, sir.'

'Very good, Luke. You may sit down.' He looked down again at Alfie and Rosie. 'So, you may dry your tears and we will begin lessons.'

It was no easy task for a teacher of twenty pupils of differing ages and abilities. He had to separate them into various groups and set them different work to do. In his classroom there was no separation between boys and girls, as was the custom, only between their abilities.

Just once more, Josiah glanced at the door. He had so hoped that the nanny would bring Charlie to his school but he feared that the determined young woman would not appear again until she heard a better report on the schoolmaster's own behaviour.

At the close of the school day, Bob Preston was waiting at the gate to meet his youngest child. He was expecting a tearful boy, nursing a hand still stinging from the stroke of the cane that morning, but to his surprise, Alfie came skipping out with a piece of paper in his hand. This was unusual; paper was expensive and most of the time the children worked on their slates with chalk that could be wiped clean and used over and over again.

'Look, Dad. I did a drawrin'. Mr Holland said it was very good and I could bring it home 'specially to show you.'

Bob looked down at the paper. He couldn't tell what it was supposed to be, but he praised it anyway. Then he glanced up as Luke approached.

'He didn't get the cane, Dad. Mr Holland said he isn't going to do that anymore, but if they do anything wrong, then they will be punished.'

'That's fair enough. I can agree with him on that.'

'He used to cane us if we couldn't spell words, but this afternoon,' Luke went on, 'Little Frank couldn't spell "machine" but Mr Holland just made him write it out twenty times in his best handwriting.'

Bob glanced up and saw that the teacher had come to the door.

'You take Alfie home, Luke. I'll just have a word with Mr Holland.'

When all the children were running and skipping towards their homes and safely out of earshot, Bob approached the teacher. 'Mr Holland, I want to thank you for your change of heart over caning. Alfie has been having nightmares for weeks leading up to starting school.'

'I still reserve the right to use the cane if I think it's appropriate,' Josiah said brusquely.

'Of course you do and rightly so, but on this occasion, I thank you.'

Josiah nodded and turned away. He was not about to admit that it had been a spirited young woman, with beautiful violet eyes, who had changed his mind.

Twenty-one

'You'll never guess what Billy's heard,' Kitty said excitedly when she appeared in the nursery on the Saturday morning after school had reopened earlier in the week.

'Now sit still, Charlie, while I put your socks on,' Lizzie said. 'There's a good boy. Sorry, Kitty, what did you say?'

'Last night, when Billy went into the village, it was all around the pub. Mr Holland has stopped caning the little ones on their first day.'

Lizzie allowed herself a secret smile, but all she said aloud was, 'I should hope so. No doubt we shall hear more about it this afternoon, if we go down to play football.'

The children couldn't wait to tell them. As soon as they arrived at the playing field, they ran across the grass and crowded around the pony and trap.

'Nanny, Nanny . . .' Alfie shouted the loudest of them all. 'He didn't cane me an' Rosie when we started school.'

As she climbed down from the trap and lifted Charlie down, Lizzie said, 'I'm very pleased to hear it, but you'll have to be a very good boy in return, won't you?'

The boy nodded vigorously. 'He told Dad that –' He hesitated and turned to his older brother for help. 'What was it he said to our dad, Luke?'

Luke pushed through the throng of excited children. 'He told him that he still reserved the right to use the cane if he thought it appropriate.'

Lizzie nodded. 'Well, I suppose we must accept that. It must be quite hard keeping all you lot in line.' She smiled at them and the children giggled in response. 'Now, is your dad coming to referee this afternoon?'

'No, Nanny,' Luke said. 'He's hurt his ankle and can't run up and down. He wondered if Billy could do it.'

All eyes turned pleadingly to the young groom. 'Oh no, Nanny. I can't. I used to play, but I don't know the rules well enough to supervise a game or keep this lot in order. *I'd* need teacher's cane.'

One or two of the younger ones looked suddenly fearful, so Billy said swiftly, 'I'm only teasing. I wouldn't do that to any of you.'

'Oh Nanny, can you do it?' Alfie asked. 'Dad's sent his whistle for you to use. We'll be ever so good.'

Lizzie laughed, remembering childhood games with her brother.

'We stick to the rules, Lizzie,' Bruce had said, 'or I'm not playing with you.'

'Oh, come on, then,' she said now. 'Let's give it a try.'

As Alfie had promised, they were all extremely well behaved.

From his window in the schoolhouse, Josiah watched the young woman in the midst of the children, lifting her skirt just above her ankles and running up and down the field. At the end of the game, he saw the children crowd around her. Some of the youngest even hugged her and all of them were smiling and rosy-cheeked from the exercise. She reminded him so much of a girl, many years ago, whom he had loved devotedly, but who had not returned his affection. He had been quite good-looking as a young man, but his disability had always been a barrier. In the street where he'd lived he'd been known as 'the cripple' and only books and learning had been his refuge from the cruel taunts of his peers.

As Lizzie, Billy, Kitty and Charlie all climbed into the trap to return to the Manor, Josiah drew back from the window, though he could still watch everything that was going on. He was sure she glanced across at his house, but then her attention was claimed by the children once again as they stood to wave goodbye.

The following Saturday, Bob was back in his role as referee and while Charlie was occupied in the game and with Kitty and Billy, who were keeping an eye on him, Lizzie crossed the road to the schoolhouse. Josiah saw her coming and opened the door as she approached.

'Please come in, Miss Ingham.'

'Just for a moment, Mr Holland, if I may sit by the window to make sure Charlie is all right.'

'He's a very lucky little boy to have such a devoted nanny, but it hasn't always been the case, has it?'

She glanced at him, but there was no sarcasm in his tone. She smiled but did not answer. Her loyalty was to Charlie and her employers. She was not about to indulge in village gossip, though she was sure everyone knew of the goings-on at the Manor.

When they were both seated by the window, Lizzie said, 'I wondered if you would allow me to bring Charlie to visit the school one day. Just for him to observe what happens, but I would need to stay with him.'

'That would be no trouble, I'm sure. I presume you want to – well – test him out, but if he wanted to sit with the other children, to join in, I'd be happy for him to do that. You could sit at the back so that you would still be near him.'

'That's extremely good of you,' Lizzie said and beamed

at him. 'But the last thing we want to do is to disrupt your classes in any way. Is there a day that would be the most suitable?'

'Perhaps a Friday afternoon, which I set aside for reading stories to the children. It's an important part of their education in literature, but it's also to allow us all to wind down at the end of the week.'

Lizzie was surprised at his words. She hadn't thought the strict schoolmaster would have thought of doing that.

'That sounds ideal,' she said. 'Thank you, Mr Holland. There is just one more question. At the training college I attended we were given basic instruction on how to begin a child's early learning. Charlie has a playroom full of toys and a schoolroom with books and – well – everything he could possibly need, but he isn't yet ready to have a tutor or to attend your school full time. He still doesn't speak, you see, though I think he does understand what is said to him.'

Josiah nodded. 'I'm sure you're right. He seems to be able to join in the football game and he must have understanding to be able to do that. Let's see how he gets on just coming one afternoon, for a start. We can soon increase his attendance. And I'll make some notes for you, if you like, on how you could begin to teach him a little.'

'That would be so kind of you.' Lizzie stood up and held out her hand. 'Thank you so much, Mr Holland. We'll see you on Friday afternoon.'

What a remarkable young woman, Josiah thought as he closed the door behind her. She is giving her young life to the care of a troubled little boy. What devotion and, yes, unselfish love.

*

Just after lunch on the Friday, Billy took Lizzie and Charlie to the school.

'What time do you want me to pick you up, Nanny?'

'If it's not raining, Billy, we'll walk back.'

'Will Charlie manage that distance?'

Lizzie chuckled. 'I think he covers more than that running up and down the field on a Saturday, don't you?'

Billy laughed. 'I hadn't thought of that, but you're right.'

Lizzie and Charlie entered the school and sat down at the back of the room as all the other pupils marched in from the playground and sat down at their desks. One or two looked round curiously at the visitors.

'Eyes to the front, children, if you please,' Mr Holland said firmly and Lizzie felt Charlie move a little closer to her and clasp her hand.

'Now, this afternoon, we are going to be reading *Alice's Adventures in Wonderland* by Lewis Carroll.' He glanced up. 'Charlie, would you like to come and sit next to Alfie in the front row?'

'It's all right, Charlie,' Lizzie whispered. 'I shall sit here at the back. I won't leave, I promise. Go and sit next to Alfie.'

Reluctantly, Charlie walked to the front and sat at the desk next to Alfie, but every few minutes he turned to make sure that Lizzie was still sitting at the back of the room. There was a ten-minute break halfway through the afternoon when the children ran about the playground to let off steam, but Charlie rushed back to sit with Lizzie.

'Will you come outside with me, Charlie?' Luke said, standing in front of them.

Charlie looked up at Lizzie and slid his hand into hers. 'You go with Luke. I'm just going to talk to Mr Holland,' she said, but Charlie just buried his face in her lap.

Lizzie smiled up at the older boy. 'Maybe next week, Luke, but thank you for asking.'

'S'all right, I 'spect he doesn't want to be rushed and he needs to be able to see you all the time, doesn't he? We'll try again next time you come.'

Josiah had come to the back of the room with a note-book in his hand and, as Luke left the room, he said, 'I've made some notes for you, Miss Ingham. Very basic, of course, but I think that's what you want, isn't it?' He opened the book. 'I've made the notes on the left-hand page, leaving the right-hand one blank for you to write down what Charlie can do.'

'That's perfect, Mr Holland. Thank you.'

'If you come every Friday afternoon, bring it with you and I can monitor Charlie's progress.' He didn't add, if there is any, though he was thinking it. Only time would tell how much of a task lay before them.

After the mid-afternoon break, the children trooped back in. Josiah set the older ones to write down as much of the story they had heard earlier as they could remember. The younger ones he set to practise their letters on a slate using chalk, and for Alfie, Rosie and Charlie he drew a circle on their slates and told them to practise copying it. Alfie and Rosie made a fair stab at it, but after a little hesitation, Charlie drew an almost perfect circle.

'My word, Charlie, that is very good. Now, I want the three of you to draw a square. Like this . . .'

By the time school ended for the day, indeed for the week, Charlie, alongside Alfie and Rosie, was drawing circles, squares and triangles.

'Keep him practising these shapes,' Josiah told Lizzie. 'They form the basis of letters.'

'Thank you so much, Mr Holland.'

As he saw them to the door, leaning heavily on his

stick, Josiah said, 'If you decide to bring him more often, Miss Ingham, he'd be very welcome.'

'Even if I have to sit at the back of the classroom?'

Josiah Holland smiled. 'Even then.'

Over the next few weeks, Charlie's weekly attendance at the school increased gradually to two mornings and three afternoons, and on the days he didn't attend, Lizzie kept him occupied in the schoolroom at the Manor. Each Friday afternoon, Lizzie took the notebook and some of Charlie's work to show Josiah.

'There's definite progress, Miss Ingham. His drawing ability is remarkable. And I see you're teaching him letters now.'

'Yes, and I read the alphabet books out loud constantly. A is for apple and so on, but –' she bit her lip – 'I have no way of knowing if he understands because he still doesn't speak.'

'But there must be understanding there, surely.' Josiah turned the pages. 'What is this drawing? A dog?'

'No, it's his pony.'

'May I suggest you write the pony's name beneath the drawing and get Charlie to copy it?' Josiah smiled as he looked up at her. 'He's making progress, Miss Ingham. I am sure of it.'

Twenty-two

'Master James is coming for Christmas and the master's mother and the mistress's parents too. Mr and Mrs Moore,' Kitty told Lizzie excitedly one day early in November. 'I've never seen the parents. They haven't been to stay for years, Cook says. Not since –' She glanced warily in Charlie's direction.

'It's all right, Kitty, I can probably guess the reason.'

'Cook's in her element. She loves to cater for all the family. She's got a mountain of recipe books around her and is making endless lists already. I think the parents are only staying over Christmas itself, but Master James might stay longer. Oh Nanny, he'll see such a change in Charlie, won't he?'

At once there was a picture of the handsome young man in Lizzie's mind. She couldn't admit it to anyone, but James figured in her thoughts quite often. And certainly, he haunted her dreams. Of course, she told herself, firmly, it was because he was so good with Charlie, but secretly she knew it was so much more than that. To her, James Spendlove stood head and shoulders above all the young men she had danced with during her coming-out season and even above her former fiancé, Oliver. She believed that if she had been engaged to James at the time of her family's scandal, he would not have deserted her. She wondered if he knew about her background – if his brother had told him. She tried hard not to think of him, not to look forward and count the days to his next visit. But it was impossible.

'Oh, we'll have such a wonderful Christmas,' Kitty was saying, breaking into Lizzie's thoughts. 'Cook says it'll be just like the old days.'

A few days after this conversation, Josiah said, 'The vicar has told me that he is hoping to hold a special family service on Friday, the twenty-third of December in the late afternoon. He has asked me if the children would be able to sing a carol. Although we have a piano in the school, I don't play so I'm afraid music lessons have not been something I have been able to do. I just wondered if you can play at all?'

Lizzie hesitated and then admitted, 'Yes, I can, but I might be a little rusty.'

'Would you consider teaching the children to sing a carol? I thought "Away in a Manger" would be suitable. The church has a Nativity scene, which the women usually set up with models of the principal characters. As part of the service, the youngest child in the village puts the baby in the manger. That might well be Charlie this year.'

'I'd be happy to,' Lizzie said. 'When would you like us to practise?'

'Friday afternoons would be the best, instead of story time. Would that be suitable for you?'

Lizzie nodded. 'That will give us four Fridays before you close for the holidays.'

The piano was not as badly out of tune as Lizzie had feared it might be, and when, on the first Friday afternoon which had been set aside for practice, she taught the children the words of the carol, she was pleasantly surprised at how good they sounded already. Charlie stood at the front with Alfie and Rosie, his gaze fixed on Lizzie, but he did not sing. He did not even try. Apart from this, the rehearsals went well and Lizzie was delighted with the progress of the 'Children's Choir', as she called them. The children were excited to think they would be the centre of attention at the service in front of almost everyone in the village.

'My mother and James will be here by then,' Roland told Mr Bennett. 'And Cecily's parents too. We all plan to attend and I hope all the staff will be there too. Tell them that if mealtimes are a little disrupted because of it, we will all understand.'

'I think Mrs Weston and Cook have got everything in hand, sir.'

Two days before school was due to close for the Christmas holidays, Lizzie asked Mrs Weston what the protocol was as regards gifts to one another.

'The master and mistress usually give us each a small gift, but we're not expected to buy for them, though we usually club together and get something for Master Charlie.' She smiled. 'You can give us some guidance on that this year, Nanny. It's been so difficult in recent years to know what to get for him. And then the staff all decided a few years ago that to buy for each other was far too expensive, so we all put our names into a hat and draw just one out and buy for that person, but we don't say who it's from.'

'That sounds like an excellent idea.'

'We'll be doing it tonight so that we all have time to buy something.' She chuckled. 'Mrs Smith at the village shop does a roaring trade at this time of the year, as none of us have the chance to go to the nearest town.'

That evening, Lizzie took Charlie down to the kitchen for him to pick out the name for her from Mr Bennett's bowler hat. Lizzie was delighted to see that he had chosen

Kitty. After school the following afternoon, Lizzie asked Billy if he would wait while she and Charlie visited the village shop that reputedly sold everything. 'I need to get one or two little gifts,' she said.

As the shop bell clanged, Mrs Smith, the rotund and smiling shopkeeper, moved forward. 'You must be the new nanny from the Manor and this –' she glanced down at the little boy clinging to Lizzie's hand – 'must be Master Charlie. Now, as this is the first time he's visited my shop, may I give him a sugar mouse, Nanny?'

'That's very kind of you, Mrs Smith. What do we say, Charlie?' Lizzie paused a moment but when Charlie did not speak, she added, 'We say, "Thank you, Mrs Smith", don't we? Now, we have come to buy a gift for one of the maids.'

After a few minutes, Lizzie settled on a box of four white handkerchiefs.

'You could embroider her initial in the corner, Nanny,' Mrs Smith suggested. 'I have some silk thread here that would do the job nicely.'

'That's an excellent idea. I'll do that. I think blue would be a suitable colour.'

After making her purchases and adding two more sugar mice as a treat for Charlie, they left the shop and travelled home in the pony and trap with Billy.

James and Mrs Spendlove senior arrived three days before the planned service. Mr and Mrs Moore, Cecily's parents, were due to arrive the following day.

'Master James asked me to tell you that he'll be up shortly to see you but he also wants to know if we can try Charlie on the pony again,' Billy said when he came to the nursery soon after fetching James and his mother from their home a few miles away. 'We haven't managed

181

to get him to sit on Dandy yet, have we? But I think Master James just might manage it now.'

It hadn't been for a lack of trying and although Charlie would happily sit on the rocking horse in the playroom and be rocked backwards and forwards, he still refused to sit on the real pony when Billy brought Dandy round onto the lawn.

'We'll try this afternoon if it's fine and if Master James is free.'

Billy nodded. 'I'll let him know, and I'll mind I'm free too.'

Although it was still cold, a winter sun lit the lawn when Billy brought the pony round the corner of the house where Lizzie, Charlie and James were waiting.

James picked Charlie up. 'Now, are you going to sit on his back today, Charlie? Just look at this lovely saddle your papa had made for you.'

For a moment, Charlie looked fearful but he reluctantly allowed his uncle to set him gently on the pony's back. 'There you are. How's that?'

Charlie glanced at Lizzie, who nodded and said, 'Clever boy. Now, shall I lead Dandy very slowly while Uncle James holds on to you?'

To their delight, Charlie nodded. Lizzie clicked her tongue and Dandy took a few very slow, small steps. It was as if the animal knew he had a very nervous rider on his back. They walked him down the lawn and then back again.

'Let's take him past the drawing room windows,' James said. 'I think Roland and Cecily are there. And perhaps my mother too.'

James led the pony round the corner of the house and along the front terrace until they were outside the south-facing windows of the drawing room. Seeing them,

Roland, Cecily and Winifred Spendlove came to the window.

'Oh Roland,' Winifred said, clasping her hands together in delight. 'You said in your letters how much improved he is. But I never thought to see this. Oh my!'

James drew the pony to a halt and waved to them, but he did not encourage Charlie to wave; the little boy was too busy holding on.

'Progress, Nanny,' James said softly. 'We're making progress.'

That evening when Charlie was in bed and Lizzie was sitting by the fire embroidering Kitty's handkerchiefs by the light of the nursery lamp, a soft knock came at the door. When Lizzie opened it, James whispered, 'May I come in?'

'Of course, Master James. Please come in and sit down.'

He sat on the opposite side of the fireplace, the flames illuminating both their faces in a soft glow.

'A Christmas gift?' he said softly, nodding towards the handkerchief in her hand.

'Yes, for Kitty. Charlie pulled her name out of the hat and I was so pleased. I know her better than I know the others.' She chuckled. 'I might have found it very difficult to buy something for Mr Bennett.'

They laughed softly together as he watched her nimble fingers. Although she carried on with her needlework, she was acutely conscious of him watching her.

'You know, Nanny, you have done wonders with Charlie already. I am so hopeful now for his future.'

She glanced up at him and although part of his face was in shadow, she could see that his brown eyes were watching her.

'There's still a long way to go, yet,' she said softly. 'But he's benefitting greatly from joining the other children at the school. With Mr Holland's guidance, I am starting to give him basic lessons in the schoolroom here, although he's not ready to have a proper tutor yet or go to school on his own. He still doesn't talk.'

'But he can speak, can't he?' He laughed softly. 'I heard about the "scumshush" scone.'

'Yes, but he's not said anything since and I have no idea how to get him to the next stage.'

'Would the doctor be able to help?'

'Maybe, but I am very wary of asking him to call, unless Charlie was ill, of course. I don't want Charlie to be reminded of the bad times.'

'Ah yes, the dreaded soothing syrup that I am sure did more harm than good.'

'To be honest, yes, but no one was to blame.'

'Only perhaps the nanny who was the first to give it to him. That was Nanny Gordon, wasn't it?'

'I believe so,' Lizzie said carefully.

James leaned closer. 'She was a right old dragon. Even I was scared of her, so what it was like to be a baby under her so-called care, I dread to think. She'd been Cecily's nanny and Mrs Moore bullied Cecily – there's no other word for it – into employing her for Charlie. Well, you'll meet Mrs Moore tomorrow. I think you'll see for yourself how it must have all come about.' He said no more, but Lizzie understood his meaning. She kept her head lowered and made no further comment.

On the Friday afternoon, two days before Christmas Day, the whole Spendlove family and all the servants from the Manor went to the village church, the family members travelling in the open-topped carriage, the servants on foot. Lizzie, with Charlie beside her, walked with the staff.

The little church was decorated for Christmas with holly and mistletoe. Candles flickered invitingly; it seemed everyone from the village was there. Roland, Cecily and James sat in the left-hand front pew, while Mrs Spendlove and the Moores sat on the right-hand side.

Lizzie and Charlie, with Mrs Weston, Mr Bennett and Mrs Graves, sat in the pew directly behind the master and mistress, with the rest of the servants behind them. The school children sat in the choir stalls, smiling and waving at their family members in the congregation. Right at the back, almost hidden from view, sat Josiah Holland. His pupils had no need of him today. They were now under the direction of the visiting organist, who played music softly as the congregation settled itself.

Roland turned round. 'Nanny, will Charlie come and sit with us?'

Lizzie looked down at him. 'Charlie, please sit with Papa and Mama and Uncle James.'

For a moment, his face crumpled and Lizzie held her breath, hoping he wasn't going to cry. She leaned towards him and whispered. 'Be a good boy. I will be right here, just behind you.' She squeezed his hand and smiled as he got up and moved past her. He walked round the end of the pew to sit between his parents but he kept glancing back every few minutes, just to make sure Nanny was still there. Lizzie saw James lean across and pat Charlie's knee. Then James glanced behind him and smiled at Lizzie. She smiled back briefly but then lowered her gaze, afraid he might see the pink blush she felt rising in her cheeks.

The vicar, Reverend Walter Lancaster, took his place and the service began. When it came to the point in the service for the children to sing their carol, Luke stepped out of the stalls and came to stand in front of Roland. 'Please, sir, may Charlie join us while we sing? And

185

afterwards, we'd all like him to be the one to place the baby in the manger in the Nativity model.'

'Of course. Up you go, Charlie.'

Charlie glanced behind him to look at Lizzie, who nodded encouragement. Then he stood up and took Luke's hand. The older boy led Charlie up the two steps towards the choir stalls and stood Charlie next to him, still holding his hand. All the children rose and, when the organist began to play, they sang 'Away in a Manger'. Only Charlie was not singing. He was keeping his gaze firmly fixed on Lizzie. With the acoustics in the church, the children's singing sounded even better than it had done in school rehearsals. When the carol ended, Luke led Charlie towards the Nativity scene and the vicar handed him the hand-crafted model of the baby. Everyone saw Luke whisper and point towards the crib. Charlie reached out and placed the tiny figure onto the straw.

'Well done,' Luke whispered again as he led the younger boy back towards his parents. Then he rejoined the other children in the choir.

As the service ended, there was much chatter among the congregation, wishing everyone around them 'Happy Christmas' and then filing out to shake hands with the vicar. Many came to the Spendlove family to wish them the 'Season's Greetings'. When the children trooped down the aisle, Luke led them all to Mr Holland in his seat at the back.

'We want to thank you for encouraging us to sing today.'

Josiah felt a warm glow spread through him. It was a feeling he had not experienced in a long time.

'You all did very well. I am very proud of you, but it is probably Nanny from the Manor you should be thanking.'

'Yes, but you allowed us and encouraged us.' Luke paused and then added, 'My mam and dad would like you to join us for Christmas dinner, that is, if you'd like to. But of course, if you have other plans . . .'

'No, no, I haven't. But – but are they sure?'

Luke grinned. 'Very sure, sir.'

Unseen by Josiah, Bob had come to stand just behind him. 'And I endorse that, Mr Holland. We'd be very glad to have you with us.' He did not add that for years they had seen the school teacher spend his Christmases alone, but then there had been resentment against him for the harsh treatment of his pupils. Now, however, that had been removed and their children were arriving home most days with excited stories of what they had been doing at school and all that they were learning from him.

'Then I would be delighted. Thank you.'

'It'll be a bit noisy,' Bob grinned, 'but, once we've had dinner, you are welcome to leave just whenever you like.'

Outside it was almost dark and promised a frost. Roland hurried his wife and parents to the waiting carriage.

'I'll walk back, Roland,' James said. 'I think Mrs Graves and Nanny might need my arm. Billy will take care of Kitty and Mr Bennett will escort Mrs Weston. Charlie, are you going to ride in the carriage with Mama and Papa?'

'That would be lovely, wouldn't it, Charlie?' Lizzie said, squeezing his hand. 'A ride in the carriage. I'll be just behind you, walking with Uncle James.' Though she said the words calmly, her heart was doing silly somersaults at the thought of walking so close to him.

As Roland, Cecily and their parents climbed into the carriage, James lifted Charlie in.

As the carriage, driven by Joe, moved away, and James

held out his arms, one to Mrs Graves and one to Lizzie, a little boy's voice rang out in the clear night. 'Nanny, Nanny.'

Everyone stood perfectly still as the words came again. 'Nanny, Nanny.'

A murmur of wonder ran through the listeners. 'That was Master Charlie. He spoke.'

Lizzie's voice was unsteady as she called, 'I'm here, Charlie. I'm right behind you.'

'Well, I never. It's a Christmas miracle. We'd better hurry,' Mrs Graves said. 'We don't want the little chap to get upset.'

'He'll be fine,' Lizzie said as they began to follow the carriage. 'The master will stop and wait for us if Charlie gets too distressed, I'm sure. But it's a good opportunity for him to learn to be without me for a short while.'

James laughed. 'Oh, you're a hard woman.'

Now Lizzie joined in his laughter. 'I'm sure a lot of people would say I'm far too soft with him.'

'I'm afraid I was guilty of thinking that, Nanny, when you first came,' Mrs Graves said, 'but I see now what you were trying to do. All the little chap needed was love and he didn't get any of that from his previous nannies.'

'I understand, Mrs Graves. You'd all had such a hard time. You just thought I was another one who was going to give up and I don't blame you for that.'

'When I think back to all the crying and screaming and being tied in his bed, I shudder. Kitty did her best, but she was too young and inexperienced to deal with it. She didn't know what to do.'

'But all's well now,' James said, giving both women's arms a quick squeeze. 'Look, the carriage has reached the front door and Roland is lifting Charlie down. I hope he doesn't let go of him.'

There was the last bit of the driveway before they reached the terrace in front of the Manor. Roland was standing on the steps leading up to the front door, holding on to Charlie's hand, though Cecily, her parents and Mrs Spendlove had gone inside. As he saw them gain the terrace Roland released Charlie's hand and the little boy galloped towards them to fling himself against Lizzie.

'Nanny, Nanny.'

Lizzie took her arm from James's and picked Charlie up, holding him tight and saying, 'Here I am. Now, did you have a lovely ride in the carriage? What a good boy. Now, we must go up to the nursery in time for a late tea, mustn't we? And then it will be bath time.'

Because Christmas Day fell on a Sunday this year, Lizzie had decided that Charlie should have his bath on the Friday evening in readiness for the celebrations.

'Oh, may I come up and help with that?' James said. 'I do like sailing those boats in your bath, Charlie.'

Lizzie's heart skipped a beat but she said, surprisingly calmly, 'That would be nice, Master James. We'll see you later, then. About six o'clock, if that suits.'

'Perfect.' James reached out and tweaked Charlie's nose gently, wishing that he was bold enough to do the same to the nanny.

Twenty-three

The following morning, Christmas Eve, Roland sent for Lizzie.

'Do you think Charlie would be able to have luncheon with the family tomorrow? We have it a little later on Christmas Day, at about three o'clock. I would ask you to join us, but the other staff . . .' He made a helpless gesture with his hand.

'No, sir, it wouldn't be right, but perhaps if I stayed in the hall, close at hand to the dining room, just in case.'

Roland smiled with relief. 'That's a very good idea. By the way, we'll be putting the Christmas tree up in the hall this evening and it is our custom to exchange gifts then before our dinner when everyone can be present. We used to do it on Christmas morning,' he explained. 'But it made things very difficult for the staff. Especially for Mrs Graves. You'll bring Charlie down, won't you?'

'Thank you, sir. I'm sure he'd enjoy that.'

Decorating the tree and the present-opening ritual was held in the hall after nursery teatime but before the grown-ups' dinner time.

Lizzie dressed Charlie in the smart dark blue sailor suit which Cecily had ordered for him. It fitted perfectly.

'Oh, don't you look smart, Master Charlie?' Kitty said, clapping her hands.

190

Removing her apron, Lizzie said, 'Right, I think we're ready. We'll go down.'

The servants were already assembled and as Lizzie, Kitty and Charlie reached the bottom of the main staircase, the family emerged from the drawing room.

'Bennett,' Mrs Moore's imperious tones rang out. 'I shall need a chair.'

'Of course, ma'am,' Mr Bennett said and at once moved a chair from the side of the hall nearer to the tree.

'You may begin, Roland,' she said.

The whole family and the staff joined in decorating the tree. Roland took the lead and Cecily, her parents, Roland's mother and James all hung baubles onto the branches and then each member of staff was invited to contribute. Lizzie helped Charlie to fasten some trinkets onto the lower branches. As they all stood back to admire their handiwork, Roland climbed the stairs and leaned over the bannisters to attach the star to the topmost branch.

'And now,' he said, descending the stairs, 'it's present time.'

He began to hand out the gifts to the staff from himself and Cecily, while Cecily handed presents to James, her own mother and father and to Roland's mother. Then all eyes turned to Charlie.

Mr Bennett moved forward. 'Sir, with your permission, we, that is the staff and I, are delighted to be able to give Master Charlie a gift this year. We weren't sure what to get, but Joe and Billy came up with the idea of repairing all the toy soldiers and then building a fort for them. Joe, perhaps you and Billy would bring it in, if you please.' As Joe and Billy left the hall for a few moments, Mr Bennett went on, 'We didn't put it under the tree, sir. It was rather too big to wrap.'

The two men returned carrying the wooden fort between them. They set it on the ground and then Billy handed some wrapped parcels to Charlie. Lizzie squatted down beside him and showed him how to unwrap the presents. Inside were the once-broken lead soldiers from the playroom, all now mended and freshly painted.

'I wondered where they'd all gone. I thought Clara must have thrown them out but how wonderful that you've mended them, Joe. Just look, Charlie. Won't we have fun with this?'

Charlie was staring at the fort and the soldiers and then he glanced up at James, who smiled down at him and said, 'I'll show you how to play with them tomorrow, Charlie.'

Lizzie stood up. 'Thank you so much, Joe and Billy, and indeed all of you. It's such a kind thought and a wonderful gift.'

There was a loud sniff from Mrs Moore. 'Just make sure he doesn't break them all again and smash up the fort.'

The present-giving gave Lizzie the chance to observe Charlie's grandparents properly. Roland's mother, Winifred Spendlove, was a dear: plump and with her round face always smiling. She wore her grey hair in neat curls on the top of her head and her manner, especially towards Charlie, was gentle and kind. In contrast, Beatrice Moore was angular, with sharp features and a sour expression. Her hair was drawn back tightly into a bun at the nape of her neck and her beady eyes missed nothing. She seemed constantly to be giving a sniff of disapproval. But to Lizzie's surprise, Beatrice's husband, Lewis Moore, was the epitome of a doting grandpa. He was rotund and sported brightly coloured waistcoats with his tweed jacket during the day time, but, like Roland and James, he wore more formal black for evening wear. He had a bushy white moustache and sideburns and he made no secret of enjoying a good single malt whisky.

After the excitement of decorating the tree and the opening of presents, Charlie was over excited. It took Lizzie longer than usual to undress him for bed and James arrived to read him a story before the little boy was in his pyjamas.

'Let's try him on the rocking horse for a few minutes,' James suggested. 'That might just calm him down and then I'll read to him. Come on, old chap. Up you come.'

He carried Charlie through to the playroom and rocked him gently. Then he lifted him up and took him to his bed, sitting beside him to read to him until, at last, Charlie's eyes began to close. Closing the book and laying it aside, James tiptoed across the room to sit near the fire with Lizzie.

'I understand Charlie is to have luncheon with the family tomorrow,' he said softly. 'I wish Roland had included you.'

'It wouldn't be proper, Master James. I get on very well with the other members of staff now and I wouldn't want anything to spoil it. Besides, it will be good for Charlie to be separated from me a little.'

'I don't blame him for wanting to be with you all the time,' he said quietly. 'I would too if I was in his shoes.'

Lizzie was glad of the dim light as she felt the colour rise in her face. There was silence between them until James said, 'You said you get on well with the other staff *now*. Didn't you at first?'

'They were wary. Understandably so. They had had so many nannies come and go and poor Kitty was exhausted. They weren't getting any sleep because of his screaming, hence the use of that syrup. I can't – and don't – blame them.'

'Yes, I remember. He was like a little wild animal. But they're all right with you now? Even Mrs Graves? Fond though I am of her, I know she can be a bit of a tartar.'

'She's been great,' Lizzie said carefully. 'She's helped me to move him on to eat proper food rather than baby pap.'

'I'm glad.' He paused and then, reluctantly, he stood up. 'Well, I'd better leave you in peace. I'll be late for dinner and then there'd be gossip. I don't mind for myself, but we have your reputation to think of. A little boy of five and fast asleep is not quite the chaperone Mrs Moore would expect. I hope I haven't compromised you.'

She laid aside her needlework and rose too. 'It's probably your reputation that is more at stake than mine,' she teased him gently. 'Consorting with the nanny, indeed. Whatever next?'

He stood close to her and reached for her hand. 'Whatever next indeed?' he whispered. He raised her hand to his lips and kissed her fingers. 'Goodnight, Nanny, and thank you from the bottom of my heart for all you are doing for Charlie.' And then he was gone, closing the nursery door softly behind him. Lizzie stood for a long moment holding the fingers he had kissed to her lips.

Twenty-four

Christmas Day dawned bright and frosty and Charlie awoke early. Lizzie was now able to sleep in her own bed in the adjoining room, but she always left the communicating door open and she woke at once if Charlie stirred during the night.

'Good morning, Charlie. Happy Christmas,' she called, as he appeared in the doorway between the two rooms. She held out her arms to him and he ran towards her and took a flying leap onto the bed.

She held him close. 'We're going to have such a lovely day today, playing with your new toys and then this afternoon at three o'clock you're going to have Christmas luncheon with Mama and Papa, Uncle James and your grandparents.'

He drew back from her and looked into her eyes. Guessing what he was trying to ask she said, 'I shan't be far away. I shall sit in the hall just outside the dining-room door.' She touched his cheek tenderly. 'You will be fine. I promise I won't move from there. And now we must get up. Kitty will be here shortly.'

Lizzie washed and dressed Charlie in his play clothes. Toilet training was complete. Once he had begun to understand what was needed of him, he had taken to it very quickly.

'And this afternoon, we'll dress you in your smart new sailor suit.'

Once Kitty had arrived and taken Charlie into the playroom where the new fort had been set on the floor, Lizzie had a few moments to herself to wash and dress. Then, sitting quietly by the fire, she thought about her own family. She wondered where Bruce was now and hoped he was safe and well. She dwelt on the happier times they had had together, the Christmases at Ancholme Hall. They had always gone to midnight mass on Christmas Eve, in the church where her mother and father now both lay in the churchyard. Occasionally, there had been a white Christmas when she and Bruce had built snowmen in the garden and pelted each other with snowballs. They had gone back indoors wet through, but laughing and joyous. What happy times they had been. She smiled pensively. If it had been a white Christmas today, she imagined that James would have built a snowman for Charlie and maybe even engineered a snowball fight. She gave her head a shake and tried to put thoughts of him from her mind.

In a clean, blue uniform and snow-white apron, Lizzie descended the main staircase with Charlie at ten minutes to three that afternoon. Mr Bennett was prowling in the hall as the staff carried the first course into the dining room.

'The master said to take Master Charlie into the drawing room, Nanny, and I've put a chair for you near the dining-room door as requested.'

'Thank you, Mr Bennett, and Happy Christmas to you. It's the first time I've seen you today.'

'And the same to you, Nanny. If you'll excuse me . . .' he said and hurried into the dining room to supervise the placing of the dishes.

Lizzie knocked on the door of the drawing room and,

hearing 'Come in', she opened it and ushered Charlie into the room. At once, James came towards them and picked Charlie up.

With his back to the rest of the room, he winked at Lizzie but said in a formal tone. 'Thank you, Nanny, I will look after him now.'

Lizzie nodded. 'Thank you, Master James.'

As she turned to leave, Charlie made a noise in his throat and stretched out his hand as if to prevent her leaving.

'I'll be just outside in the hall,' she reminded him quietly. 'Be a good boy, now.'

James turned and carried him towards his parents as Lizzie slipped out of the room. Ten minutes later, Mr Bennett announced that luncheon was served and the family crossed the hall into the dining room. This time, James was leading Charlie by the hand, but the little boy wriggled free and dashed across the space to where Lizzie was sitting.

'Roland,' came Mrs Moore's imperious voice, 'can't you control the boy?'

'Oh Beatrice,' Roland's mother, Winifred, said, 'he's only a little boy and this is his first Christmas with us. Don't be so hard on him.'

'You're too soft with him,' Beatrice said. 'He needs some discipline. It's such a shame Nanny Gordon grew too old to care for him. He'd know what good behaviour is by now if she'd still been here.'

James crossed the hall to stand in front of Lizzie. 'He'll be fine with me, Nanny,' he said softly and then he stooped down to Charlie and whispered, 'Nanny will stay here all the time, I promise. Now, come with me, there's a good chap.'

Beatrice swept into the dining room without a glance

197

at Lizzie, though she'd made sure the nanny had heard every word of her criticism. With another conspiratorial wink at Lizzie, James led Charlie into the dining room. When the first course had been eaten and the dishes cleared away, Charlie climbed down from his chair, ran round the table and out of the dining room to Lizzie.

'It's not finished yet,' she told him, giving him a quick hug, 'you must go back and sit in your chair.'

For the first time ever, Charlie shook his head. Had the circumstances been different, she would have rejoiced at another sign of his understanding, but now was not a good time. She rose and took his hand, leading him back to the dining-room door. 'In you go,' she said. 'Go and sit back in your chair, next to Uncle James.'

Reluctantly, he obeyed her but between each course Charlie ran out into the hall again.

'Roland, I really must insist you control the boy or he leaves us altogether,' came Beatrice's imperious voice again. 'His behaviour is quite spoiling our luncheon.'

To everyone's surprise, it was Cecily who spoke up, 'Mama, it's Christmas. This is his first time with us and he's doing no harm.'

'Cecily! I'm surprised and disappointed in you speaking to me in that way.'

'I don't want to quarrel with you, Mama, but I think you should know that both Roland and I think that Nanny Gordon was the root of all Charlie's – problems.'

'Nonsense. She was an exemplary nanny.'

'She was cruel and vindictive,' Cecily said.

'She was a disciplinarian, I grant you, but that's what all children need.'

'Not sensitive, nervous children. She smacked me for the slightest misdemeanour. She locked me in a dark cupboard for an hour when I spilt some milk. I was only five. Oh, I could go on, but know one thing, Mama, the only happiness I had as a child was the time you sent me to boarding school because when I came home for the holidays, thankfully, she had gone by then. I grew up into a shy and anxious adult, frightened of my own shadow, and if I had not had the good fortune to marry a man as kind and understanding as Roland, I dread to think where I might be now.'

Beatrice was staring at her daughter open-mouthed. When at last she found her voice, she said, 'Then if she was so very dreadful, why did you employ her as nanny for Charles?'

'Because you demanded it and until this moment I have never dared to stand up to you. But I will now, for my little boy's sake. I have not been the best of mothers but, with the help of the wonderful nanny we have now, things will change.' She turned to speak to the butler. 'As long as he doesn't get in the way of the staff serving us, Mr Bennett, please allow Charlie to run in and out to see Nanny between the courses.'

Mr Bennett inclined his head in acknowledgement and left the room with a huge grin on his face. Within minutes, all the staff in the kitchen knew what had been happening in the dining room.

When he returned minutes later, he crossed to where Lizzie was sitting. 'The staff have asked me to invite you to join us for our Christmas dinner tonight, Nanny, and to bring Master Charlie too. On Christmas Day the family only have a cold collation set out in the dining room in the evening and help themselves, so that we can have our own celebrations in the servants' hall. We eat at six o'clock, so we should be finished in good time for Master Charlie's bedtime. Besides . . .' He smiled. 'It's Christmas. Being late to bed for once won't matter, will it?'

'Oh, that is so kind of you all, Mr Bennett. We'd be delighted to join you. Thank you.'

He gave a small bow. 'We shall look forward to it. Some of us feel we haven't got to know you as well as we should.'

Lizzie nodded but bit her lip. She hoped she wasn't going to be asked any awkward questions about her past.

The servants' hall had been decorated with holly and mistletoe by Joe and Billy and the table groaned under the weight of the food. There were all the traditional dishes that the family had eaten earlier in the day, but all were freshly cooked for the servants.

'The master always does us proud,' Mrs Weston said. 'I think it's always been his way of saying "thank you" to us. Now, I've put you and Charlie in the centre of the table alongside Kitty. Mr Bennett sits at the head of the table and I sit at the other end. We've put a chair with a cushion on it for Charlie. We'll all be here. All the household staff and Joe and Billy too. Even Polly.'

Polly was the only member of staff whom Lizzie didn't know well by now. Although she was the head housemaid and doubled as Cecily's lady's maid, she did not live in, like the rest of the staff and so Lizzie didn't see her very often.

'Polly is allowed to live with her widowed mother in the village and come each day to the Manor,' Mrs Weston had explained. 'The poor woman is not in good health and the master and mistress are very understanding.'

'It all looks grand,' Lizzie murmured now. The servants at Ancholme Hall had always had their own Christmas celebrations in much the same way, but she couldn't remember ever seeing such a lavish spread for them as there was in front of her now. She wondered briefly how they were all getting on with their new master and mistress. Any contact with her old life was only through Mr Bellingham, who still wrote to her regularly. Up to now, he had always remembered to address letters to her as Miss Ingham.

As they all sat down, they pulled the crackers set beside each plate. Each person turned to their left to pull it with the person sitting next to them, so that everyone pulled a cracker twice. Charlie blinked at the sound but didn't seem fazed by it. He even allowed Lizzie to put the paper hat on his head.

'This is something new,' Lizzie remarked. 'I've never seen paper hats inside a cracker. It's usually just a sugared almond and a motto.'

Charlie gazed around the table as everyone else donned their hats too. Then he looked across the table at Mrs Graves, who was sitting directly opposite him. She was wearing her paper hat at a comical angle. Charlie stared. Then he smiled and then – to everyone's amazement – there came the gurgling sound of a real chuckle.

Now it was Mrs Graves who stared open-mouthed at Charlie. Tears welled in the cook's eyes. 'Oh Nanny,' she whispered. 'He's laughing. He's really laughing.'

'He is indeed.'

'Has he – has he ever done that before?'

'No, it's another step, Mrs Graves, thanks to you and your funny hat.'

It was a merry party in the servants' hall that evening and Charlie's eyes were closing by the time Billy carried him up the stairs to the nursery.

'Now, you two,' Lizzie said to Kitty and Billy. 'Off you go and enjoy the rest of the evening. I won't need you to come back, Kitty. I can get ready for bed while he's asleep. He's had such an exciting day, I don't think he'll stir.'

'If you're sure, Nanny, that would be lovely. We haven't been able to have much time together at Christmas in the past, have we, Billy?'

Billy grinned and shook his head. 'But just in case you're worrying, Nanny, we won't do anything we shouldn't. I love Kitty too much to hurt her.'

Lizzie nodded. 'I trust both of you and I also know that because you are given more leeway in this household than is usual, you will also respect the master's faith in you.'

The two young people nodded solemnly and then left the nursery hand in hand.

Lizzie smiled pensively as she undressed the sleepy little boy and tucked him into his bed, putting Mr Snuggles and Teddy on either side of him. Then she sat beside the fire's flickering flames and dared to day-dream of the master's handsome young brother, who was at this moment only yards away from her downstairs in the drawing room.

Twenty-five

Lizzie was up and dressed the following morning and just washing and dressing Charlie when a soft knock came at the nursery door.

'Come in,' she called and was surprised to see James appear.

'Happy Boxing Day,' he said. 'I don't know if that's what we're supposed to say, but I'm saying it anyway.'

Lizzie laughed. 'And we'll say "Happy Boxing Day, Uncle James", won't we, Charlie?'

'I thought he might like to ride his pony this morning. It's not so frosty underfoot.'

'I'm sure he would, but doesn't the master hold a Boxing Day shoot on his land? I thought it would be a tradition here and that you'd be involved in it.'

James shook his head. 'We used to do years ago, when our father ran the estate and Roland continued the tradition for a few years, but after Charlie's problems began, he stopped doing it. He didn't want nosey parkers spreading gossip around the whole county. We have to bear all the villagers knowing, but that's as far as any of us wanted it to spread.'

'I think their interest is kindly meant. Look how they treated him at the children's service just before Christmas, involving him in the choir and the Nativity.'

'Yes, that was quite an eye-opener for me, I must admit.'

Then he added softly, 'But I rather think you had a lot to do with that, Nanny.'

'Oh, I can't take the credit for that. I think it was mainly Luke, Kitty's brother. He's a grand lad and very bright. Even Mr Holland says so and he doesn't hand out praise easily. I know Luke's family are hoping he will be able to go to the grammar school next year.'

'You should have a word with Roland about that. He likes to help where he can.'

'I had heard that and, yes, I will have a word with the master before long. And now we must have our breakfast, mustn't we, Charlie, if we're going riding?'

'I'll leave you to it, then. I'll see you on the lawn about ten. Will that be all right?'

'Perfect.'

As he began to turn away, he added softly, 'I'm sorry I didn't come up to the nursery last night. It was – um – difficult to get away from the family without remarks being made. Mrs Moore is like a dog with a bone if she thinks something is going on that, perhaps in her eyes, shouldn't be. I hope my previous visit didn't embarrass you, Lizzie.'

Her heart felt as if it did a somersault as he used her Christian name for the first time. 'Not at all,' she managed to say evenly. 'You were here to see your nephew.'

'But – he was asleep.'

Lizzie chuckled softly. 'But no one else knows that, do they?'

James stared at her for a moment and then burst out laughing. 'Then that shall be our little secret. I'll see you later.'

Charlie rode Dandy around the lawn, with James leading him and Lizzie walking beside him.

'Just look how she mollycoddles him,' Mrs Moore said,

watching from the morning-room window. 'You were riding your pony on your own at his age, Cecily. Nanny Gordon saw to that.'

With her newfound strength, Cecily said, 'Yes, I was and if I fell off, all she said was "Get up. You're not hurt" without even checking if I was or not. Mama . . .' Cecily bit her lip. It was so hard to throw off a lifetime of obedience, even though she was now an adult. She glanced at her mother-in-law for tacit support. Winifred gave an imperceptible nod and Cecily drew in a deep breath. 'Mama, I have to say this. Roland and I have complete faith in what Nanny Ingham is doing for Charlie. He has improved immeasurably since she came. We are both now hopeful there are better things still to come.'

Beatrice turned with a smug smile. 'Are you *sure* she's the right nanny for Charlie? Are you aware of who she really is?'

Winifred was glancing from one to the other, puzzlement on her face, but Cecily said calmly. 'We know all we need to know about her.'

'I have been making some enquiries about your paragon of a nanny,' Beatrice went on. 'She's not what – or who – she claims to be. I thought the name "Ingham" rang a bell, so I made it my business to dig a little deeper.' She moved across the room and rang the bell to summon one of the servants. It was the butler who answered.

'Bennett, please ask your master and my husband to join us.' She glanced out of the window to see James and Lizzie laughing together as they guided the pony around the lawn. 'And that's something else you should keep an eye on. James is getting far too familiar with the nanny.' She frowned towards Winifred. 'I'm surprised you don't guide your son in a more suitable direction.'

Winifred bristled. She was a warm-hearted, gentle crea-
ture, who, most of the time, wouldn't say the proverbial
'boo to a goose', but if anyone dared to criticize her boys,
then she could turn into a veritable tigress. She drew in
a deep breath and her bosom swelled. 'Beatrice, my sons
make their own decisions. Roland is a respected land-
owner and also runs the mine the family owns. When my
husband died, his will left everything jointly between our
sons. James has chosen the army as his career, but he
knows his duty. If he were needed, he would come back
here to help his brother.'

'He should marry and produce an heir to run the estate,
seeing as Charlie will never be fit to do so.'

It was at this point that Roland and Lewis came into
the room. Roland, catching Beatrice's final words,
frowned. 'What will Charlie never be fit to do?'

'Run the estate and the mine, but I didn't call you in
here to discuss that. I want you to be aware of exactly
who your "wonderful" nanny is.'

Roland turned to the butler. 'That will be all, thank
you, Bennett.'

'I think he should stay. I'm sure the staff don't know
who she really is.'

'Thank you, Bennett,' Roland repeated firmly and the
butler withdrew with an acquiescent bow. There was some
sort of trouble brewing. He could feel it and it was to
do with the nanny. But whatever it was, he didn't think
it could change the servants' opinion of her. Not now,
when she had already done so much for Charlie and
made all of their lives so much easier. He would stand
by her whatever it was and he would do his best to see
that all the staff under him followed his example.

'No matter,' Beatrice said as the door closed behind
the butler. 'They'll find out soon enough, I've no doubt.'

Unwittingly, Roland echoed his wife's earlier words. 'Cecily and I know all we need to know about Nanny.'

'I doubt very much that you do. As you know, I am well respected throughout Derbyshire. I am on several committees for good works, so I have connections not only in this county but also in neighbouring counties, including Leicestershire. I have it on good authority that your nanny is Lady Elizabeth Ingham, the daughter of the fifth Earl of Ancholme. And surely you remember the Ancholme Scandal a few years ago?'

Roland and Cecily listened calmly, but Winifred gave a little gasp and her fingers fluttered to cover her mouth. Lewis stared at his wife but said nothing while Roland moved to take a seat beside Cecily.

'Miss Ingham was very open when I interviewed her,' he said. 'She told me everything I needed to know about her past. She was an innocent victim in a family tragedy.'

'But do you really want your son brought up by a person with that disreputable background?'

Roland shrugged and said pointedly, 'Does it really matter if, as you say, he is never going to be fit to be my heir? As far as our household is concerned, she has brought about a vast improvement already. The staff get their sleep at night and Cecily and I now have hope for the future. It might never be what we once believed it would be, but it's certainly going to be a lot better than we've dared to hope recently.'

'I'm disappointed in you, Roland,' Beatrice sniffed. 'I thought my daughter had married a man of impeccable propriety. You are not the man I thought you were.'

'Now, just a minute, Beatrice. That is grossly unfair.' Everyone in the room was startled as Lewis spoke. He rarely contradicted his wife, but now he moved forward. 'This is not our concern, but from what I have seen over the last few days, this nanny – whoever she is – is making remarkable progress with the boy. I have never interfered with your running of our household or the bringing up of our daughter, but I am beginning to wonder if Nanny Gordon was the epitome of virtue you believed her to be.' Beatrice was gaping open-mouthed at her husband, but could find no words to answer him. Lewis now turned towards Cecily. 'My dear, I can't tell you how sorry I am to hear that you suffered under Nanny Gordon and that, worse still, you felt compelled – as I'm sure you did – to take your mother's advice over a choice of nanny for Charlie. Let's hope it is not too late to put right the damage that has been done.'

'Well really, Lewis. I am only trying to advise what I think is best for our family.'

'I'm sure you are, my dear. No one would doubt that for a moment, but we don't always get it right, do we?'

Beatrice rose, almost majestically, and moved towards the door. 'You can think that if you like, but I know I am right.'

Beatrice closed the door behind her and then paused for a moment in the hall. Then, with a smug smile, she went towards the door leading down to the kitchen.

Outside on the lawn, Lizzie said, 'I think that's enough for today. It'll soon be time for luncheon and Clara will be bringing ours up to the nursery.'

'Yes, you're right,' James said, 'and I should be ready for when the gong sounds or I shall be in trouble. I'll see you later. I'll come up to the playroom this afternoon and set up the fort with Charlie, if that would be all right. I want to spend as much time with him as I can. I'm afraid I have to leave tomorrow morning.'

Lizzie felt her heart plummet but she managed to keep

her feelings from showing on her face. 'He'll miss you,' she said quietly and, very softly, James murmured, 'I do so hope he won't be the only one.'

They returned to the house and entered by the kitchen as usual. Tea and biscuits were waiting on the kitchen table, but Lizzie was aware of a strange silence in the room. Mrs Weston and Mrs Graves were both sitting at the table while Mr Bennett was hovering near the door to his pantry. Nelly darted into the scullery. But, strangest of all, Kitty was standing to one side of the kitchen just staring at Lizzie.

James didn't seem to notice anything odd and took his leave. 'I'd better go up. I don't want to be late for lunch. Mrs Moore would not approve. I'll see you later, Charlie.' He ruffled the little boy's hair and then left, while Lizzie lifted Charlie into the chair that had been placed for him in front of a glass of milk and two biscuits on a plate.

Still, no one spoke or even moved, even though it was almost time for the dishes for luncheon to be prepared. Joe and Billy came in from the yard and stood to one side of the kitchen. But, stranger still, neither of them spoke either.

'What is it? Has something happened?' Lizzie said, her gaze resting on Mrs Weston, but it was Mrs Graves who said harshly, 'So, have we to start calling you "m'lady", then?'

Lizzie felt a jolt run through her. So, they had found out her secret. The next few minutes would determine whether she could stay here or not. She lifted her chin and returned Mrs Graves's stare steadily. 'Most certainly not. What have you been told?'

'That you're Lady Elizabeth Ingham. The daughter of an earl.'

'And?'

Mrs Graves shrugged. 'And that you're not a suitable person to have charge of Charlie, though –' here Mrs Graves paused and sighed – 'though why she would say that after all you've already achieved with him, I just don't know. Do you, Mrs Weston?'

Mrs Weston had tears shimmering in her eyes and her voice was unsteady as she said, 'Not really. When the master appointed you, Nanny, he confided in Mr Bennett and me that you had suffered a family tragedy, but he didn't give us details though I presume you told him everything.'

'Yes, I did, when I came for the interview and I expect he would have told his wife too.'

'Ah, so that's how the old beezum got to know, is it?' Mrs Graves said.

There was a question in Lizzie's eyes as she looked at the cook. 'Mrs Moore,' Mrs Graves said. 'Who'd you think?'

Lizzie frowned. 'I'd be surprised if the mistress told her, though I suppose it's possible. She is her mother after all. So, what exactly has she told you?'

'Just that you're the daughter of an earl and there was a family scandal. In her view, you shouldn't be working as a nanny and certainly not bringing up Master Charlie.'

'I see. And did she give you details of the scandal?'

The servants glanced from one to another. 'No.'

'Very well, then I will tell you everything and you can decide if you want me to stay here or not. But I'd be very sorry to leave.' She stroked Charlie's silky curls as he drank his milk. 'Not only Charlie, but all of you too.' She took a deep breath. 'Did you hear of the Ancholme Scandal, as it was called in the newspapers almost four years ago?'

'Yes,' Mr Bennett said. 'I remember reading about it

but I don't know if anyone else did.' He glanced around the room, but was answered by a lot of shaking of heads.

'I'll be as brief as I can because I know you have luncheon to prepare. My father, the fifth Earl of Ancholme, owned an estate in Leicestershire which had been handed down through the generations . . .' She went on to tell them everything from her brother's wayward behaviour through the loss of her family's wealth and the deaths of her parents to Mr Bellingham's kindness in helping her to plan her own future.

'But for him, I doubt I would be sitting here. So, there you have it in a nutshell.' Lizzie got to her feet. 'I'll let you discuss it among yourselves and I'll come down this evening for your decision, because if you're not happy for me to stay, then I will leave voluntarily even though I will be devastated to leave Charlie.'

Joe, who had not said a word since coming into the kitchen, moved forward. 'I don't know about everyone else, but I want you to stay, Nanny. In fact, if you leave, so will I.'

'And me,' Billy said.

'And I go with Billy,' Kitty piped up. 'I wouldn't stay here without you, Nanny. You're the best nanny I've ever worked with. I don't want to go through all that turmoil we had before you came. Not again. Please, not again.'

Lizzie felt herself blushing and cast a grateful glance at the three of them. Now Mr Bennett spoke up. 'We should perhaps discuss it, I suppose, but I for one agree with Joe, Billy and Kitty. You've worked nothing short of a miracle with Master Charlie. No one could have done more. It sounds to me as if the tragedy that happened to your family was none of your doing. You were a victim in all of it. What are your feelings, Mrs Weston? And you, Mrs Graves?'

211

The two women glanced at each other.

'We agree with all of you,' Mrs Weston said and Mrs Graves added, 'We want you to stay, Nanny.'

Lizzie felt tears of gratitude prickle her eyes. 'Thank you. Thank you, all,' she said huskily. 'And now Charlie and I must get out of your way. You have luncheon to serve. Come along, Charlie.'

The little boy looked up at her and, suddenly, he smiled and quite clearly said, 'Old beezum.'

Twenty-six

Lizzie and Kitty were still giggling helplessly as they climbed the back stairs to the nursery. 'We can't – even tell – the master that, can we?' Kitty spluttered. 'He spoke – quite clearly – and two words too, not just one. But we can't tell them.'

'No,' Lizzie said. 'We'll just have to hope he says something again very soon. Something we *can* tell them.'

When Clara brought their luncheon, she was grinning. 'You should hear what's going on downstairs. They're all debating – the senior members of staff, that is – as to what Mr Bennett ought to tell the master about what's happened. He thinks Mr Spendlove should be told that we all know about you now. He asked me to ask you if you had any objection, Nanny?'

'None at all, Clara. I'm quite relieved in a way that it's all out in the open now and so very grateful to you all that you want me to stay. I've become very fond of all of you. You're my family now.'

'Oh Nanny, that's a lovely thing to say. I'll tell Mr Bennett.'

After luncheon, which had passed mostly in an uncomfortable silence, had finished in the dining room, the three women retired to the drawing room and the three men to Roland's study. Mr Bennett knocked on the door. 'I wonder if I might have a word with you, sir?'

'Of course, Bennett. Come in.'

'Well, perhaps – er . . .' He glanced uncomfortably at Lewis and James. 'Another time, sir.'

'It's all right. I think I can guess what it's about. You've heard about Miss Ingham's background, is that it?'

'Yes, sir.'

Roland sat up suddenly in his chair, spilling some of the whisky in the glass he was holding. 'Oh my God, she's not leaving, is she?'

At that, James looked up too, an anxious frown on his face.

'No, sir,' Mr Bennett said calmly. 'We all want her to stay and we have told her so. I just wanted you to know that we have all now been appraised of the facts by Nanny herself.'

As the butler left and closed the door behind him, Lewis said, 'Roland, I must apologize for my wife's behaviour. I have no doubt that she was the one who took great pleasure in telling your staff. I am relieved it has not caused any serious problems.'

'It's probably for the best that they all know the truth,' Roland said.

'I agree,' Lewis said. 'But I don't think that is what my dear wife –' there was obvious sarcasm in his tone – 'intended and for that I am truly sorry.' He turned towards James who had remained silent. 'Did you know about all this, James?'

'I did, yes. Roland confided in me the first time I came home after her appointment. I am just relieved that the staff have taken it so well.'

'Oh, so am I,' Roland said with heartfelt thankfulness.

'There's just one thing you'll have to be ready for – and so will Nanny,' James went on. 'The news will spread to the village. There's nothing that goes on in this house that they don't find out about eventually. And now, if you will both excuse me, I have promised to play soldiers with Charlie and his new fort.'

James spent the whole afternoon on his knees in the playroom showing Charlie how to line up his soldiers for inspection and march them in and out of the wooden fort, which Joe and Billy had constructed with such love for the little boy. When nursery tea was served, Mrs Graves had sent up enough for James to join them. He stayed until it was time for Charlie to settle down for bedtime. He tucked him into bed and then sat in the easy chair and read him a story. As Charlie's eyelids grew heavy, James laid the book aside and tiptoed across the room to where Lizzie was sitting by the fire.

'I'm afraid I must go down now in time for dinner and I don't think I should come back later. I don't want to compromise you. By the way, I do know what's gone on today, but I have always known about your background. Roland told me the first time I came home after your appointment.'

'I'm glad you know,' Lizzie said softly. 'I didn't like having such a big secret from you.'

'Well, your home is here with us now.'

'Until Charlie can do without me.'

'I think that is some time off, Lizzie, but I don't know whether to be pleased or sorry about that as his recovery would take you away from us. Though of course I want him to make a full recovery.' He hesitated and then asked, almost wistfully, 'Do you believe it's possible that, one day, he'll be just like any other boy?'

'I do, Master James.'

As he stood up to leave, he reached for her hand and pulled her to her feet. Standing close to her he said, 'Do you think you could bring Charlie down in the morning to wave me off? I'd like that very much.'

Lizzie was a little hesitant. 'We could try, but he got very upset last time when you weren't here the following morning.'

'Perhaps that was because I just disappeared without a word. Perhaps if he waves me off, he'll understand better.'

Lizzie nodded. 'We can but try.'

The following morning, just after breakfast, Lizzie took Charlie down the back stairs to join the staff before they all went through to the hall where the family, including the visiting parents, were assembled to see James leave. Only Billy was missing. He was already sitting outside the front door waiting with the pony and trap to drive James to the station.

James was resplendent in his uniform and he came at once to Charlie and lifted him up. 'Now, old chap. I have to go back to my real soldiers, but you keep playing with your toys and imagine it's me you're moving about. Have me marching up and down with them all, won't you?'

He set him down on the floor next to Lizzie and she took Charlie's hand. James exchanged a swift smile with her, but his eyes held a sadness that was mirrored in her own.

'Goodbye, Nanny,' he murmured and then he turned to wish each and every member of the staff goodbye. Then he turned to his family. He shook hands with Roland and Lewis and kissed the three ladies on the cheek. As he turned to go out of the front door, which Mr Bennett was holding open, Charlie let out a cry, twisted his hand out of Lizzie's grasp and ran forward.

James bent, picked him up and hugged him hard. 'I have to go, Charlie, or I'll miss my train. Be a good boy now . . .' He tried to set him down on the floor, but Charlie clung to him and his cries grew louder until he was screaming. Lizzie moved forward. In a sharp tone that she had never used with him before – and which none of those present had ever heard – she said firmly, 'Charlie, stop that silly noise at once. Let go of Uncle James. He has to leave.'

Charlie's screams stopped instantly and he turned to look at Lizzie with a shocked expression. His grip loosened on James, who set him on the floor, but the boy's gaze was still on Lizzie.

'Now, we say we're sorry for being so silly and wish Uncle James "God Speed", don't we?'

Still, Charlie gazed up at her. Then, with a sob, he flung himself against her and buried his face in her skirt, but everyone present heard his muffled, 'Sowwy, sowwy, Nanny.'

Lizzie picked him up. 'We'll go out onto the terrace and wave as the pony and trap go down the drive. But no more silliness, do you understand?'

Charlie nodded vigorously.

'I'm so sorry, Nanny,' James said. 'That's my fault, I shouldn't have suggested he came down here this morning. It's too much for him.'

'He has to learn, Master James.'

'But – he'll be all right?'

'He'll be fine.'

James hesitated and then glanced at his brother. He would dearly have liked to ask Lizzie to write to him, but he didn't want to embarrass her in front of everyone, so instead he said, 'Roland, please write and let me know how he is.'

'Of course, I will.' Roland promised, his own eyes troubled.

James turned back to Charlie and touched his cheek gently and his gaze met Lizzie's briefly. She saw the mute apology and there was something else too that she couldn't quite define, but it was something that made her heart miss a beat. Then James turned and ran down the steps to climb into the trap.

Lizzie carried Charlie out of the front door and they waved as the trap moved away. Lizzie felt someone wrap a cloak around them both and she glanced up to see Joe.

'It's cold and you could be standing here a while,' he explained, 'if you're going to watch him out of sight.'

'Thank you, Joe. That's so thoughtful of you.'

He stood with them until the trap disappeared down the drive and then towards the village. They were still watching when it turned towards the station and they could no longer see it.

Lizzie set Charlie on the ground and the three of them went inside. The family and servants were still waiting. Kitty and Mrs Graves were both in tears and Mrs Weston's eyes looked suspiciously watery. Charlie, though quieter now, continued to hiccup miserably and cast sorrowful glances at Lizzie as he clung to her hand.

'All that child needs is a good smack. He's a naughty little boy, who is just seeking attention,' Mrs Moore's voice rang out. 'That young woman doesn't know how to be a proper nanny.'

Lizzie ignored the remark and led Charlie up the main stairs.

'She doesn't even know her place,' the accusing voice continued. 'Taking the main staircase indeed. If she wants to be a servant then she should act like one.'

But Lizzie carried on as, below her, the rest of the servants went back to their duties. Once in the safety of the kitchen, Mrs Graves gave vent to her anger. 'I nearly gave that wretched woman a piece of my mind, but it would have meant instant dismissal if I had, and I know Nanny wouldn't have wanted that.'

'She certainly wouldn't,' Mrs Weston agreed. 'I don't know what has upset me the most. Seeing poor Charlie so distressed, or how Nanny had to be so firm with him. It almost broke my heart.' She put her hand to her head. 'Oh dear. I think I'm getting one of my headaches.'

Kitty was crying openly. 'I've never heard her speak crossly to him. Not ever. She's always so gentle. Oh dear. I don't know what to do. Should I go up or – or not?'

'Sit and have a cup of tea and calm yourself first, Kitty,' Mrs Graves said. 'Maybe they're best left alone for a while. In fact, I'll make tea for all of us.'

'It was hard to watch,' Mr Bennett put in soberly, 'but I think Nanny managed it perfectly. There was bound to come a time when he had to be handled firmly and I think we've just witnessed it.'

'Poor little boy,' Mrs Graves said as she set out cups and saucers. Then, pausing a moment as if just remembering, she added, 'But he spoke, didn't he? He said "sorry, sorry, Nanny".'

They all glanced at one another. 'He did,' Mrs Weston whispered. 'He really did.'

'Now, Kitty,' Mrs Graves said more briskly. 'Dry your tears. Have your tea and then take a cup up to Nanny and see what's happening. I want to know how things are.' She glanced around. 'I think we all do, so you come back and tell us.'

Everyone present nodded and then sat down to have a welcome drink of tea, but their thoughts were still with the distressed little boy in the nursery.

In the morning room, Beatrice continued her tirade. 'How can a young woman, who was brought up in upper-class society and was even presented at Court, know how to behave as a nanny? She is far too lenient with him. Roland, if you take my advice, you will dismiss her at once. I'm sure I could soon find you a suitable replacement.'

Before Roland could answer, his mother – the normally quiet and gentle Winifred, but now with her eyes glittering with anger – said, 'Over my dead body, Beatrice. It seems to me that all Charlie's troubles have stemmed from the nanny whom *you* recommended so highly. A nanny, it turns out, who treated your own daughter so cruelly. Cecily says so herself. How can you even think of repeating it?'

Beatrice opened her mouth, but before she could utter a word, Lewis said, 'As a matter of fact, I completely agree with Winifred. The boy is making obvious progress with Miss Ingham. It doesn't matter how she is doing it, what matters is that it's happening. Perhaps . . .' He regarded his wife with his head on one side before adding pointedly, 'Perhaps all the little chap needed was love.'

'Love, indeed,' Beatrice almost spat. 'What children need is discipline.' She rose. 'I am afraid we will have to leave, Cecily. Please arrange for your maid to come and help me to pack and ask Marshall to be ready to take us home in the carriage this afternoon.'

Mildly, Lewis said, 'You go if you wish, Beatrice, but I shall be staying until after the New Year as we were invited to do. I know there was no Boxing Day shoot organized and there won't be a proper New Year's Day shoot either, but Roland has said he and I will go out shooting tomorrow. I am looking forward to that and have no intention of missing it.'

Beatrice paused, glared at her husband and then left the room without another word to anyone. Cecily rose from the sofa and went to her father. 'Oh Papa, are you sure? You're very welcome to stay, of course, but – but she won't speak to you for days now.'

But Lewis only shrugged. 'It won't be the first time and I doubt it will be the last. No, I will stay with you, if you'll have me.'

Cecily kissed his cheek. 'Of course we will and Roland will make sure you have a lovely day's shooting. I'm only sorry that James wasn't able to stay for it too.'

'Mrs Moore's leaving this afternoon,' Mr Bennett announced a few minutes later, having received Cecily's instructions. 'Joe, you're to take her home to Sheffield in the carriage this afternoon.'

'Just her? Not him?'

'That's what the mistress said and Clara, can you find Polly and ask her to go now and help Mrs Moore to pack.'

Clara grinned as she turned to leave the kitchen, 'It'll be my pleasure.'

'And I'd better go up and see what's happening in the nursery,' Kitty said. 'I'll let you know how things are.'

When Lizzie and Charlie had arrived back in the nursery, she had sat down in the easy chair next to his bed and taken him onto her lap, holding him close and murmuring, 'There, there, it's all over now.' She had stroked his hair and rocked him until his sobs subsided. 'But you have to learn to be a good boy. We don't want any more of those tantrums, now do we? And to see you like that upset Uncle James when he had to leave. You don't want Uncle James to be sad, now do you? And Mrs Graves and Mrs Weston too. You don't want to hurt them either, do you?'

'No, Nanny. Sowwy.'

Lizzie held him even closer and felt the tears fall from her own eyes. Having to speak severely to him had wounded Lizzie just as much as it had distressed Charlie, if not more. But it had been necessary and the right thing to do. And it seemed it had even brought about a further small breakthrough. He still wasn't saying very much, but at least he was now answering her.

Twenty-seven

When Kitty came into the nursery, she saw Charlie sitting on Lizzie's lap, her arms around him and his cheek against her shoulder. Lizzie looked up and smiled. 'Here's Kitty, now run and give her a hug too.'

Kitty placed the cup of tea she had brought up for Lizzie on the table, then knelt down and held her arms out wide. Charlie scrambled from Lizzie's lap and ran towards her to be enveloped in a bear hug. Kitty's tears began again. She couldn't help it. 'Oh, Master Charlie.' She looked up at the nanny, a question in her eyes.

Lizzie smiled. 'Everything's all right, Kitty. Charlie's very sorry he behaved badly.'

'Everyone's so upset downstairs, Nanny. May I just go back and tell them everything's all right now?'

'You may, and say that perhaps we will come down a little later this afternoon to see them all.'

'By the way, Mrs Moore is leaving this afternoon.'

'Oh, I'm sorry if it's caused them to leave.'

'Not *them*, Nanny. Just her. He's not going.' Kitty wiped away her tears and smiled. 'He wants to stay to go out shooting with the master tomorrow, Mr Bennett said. Mr Bennett also said he overheard quite an argument going on in the morning room before she flounced out and said she was leaving.'

'Oh dear.'

'Don't worry, Nanny. We're all glad to see the back of her.'

Lizzie tried to stop her own smile, but failed. 'I think,' she said slowly, 'from now on we ought to be careful what we say in front of little ears.'

Kitty nodded, understanding at once. 'You're right. He picked those words up very quickly, didn't he?' She planted a swift kiss on Charlie's curls and then said, 'Right, Nanny, I'll just run downstairs to tell them he's all right. I won't be a minute . . .'

After nursery tea, when Charlie was in his pyjamas and dressing gown but just before the family would be having their dinner, Lizzie took Charlie down to the kitchen. Mrs Graves and Nelly were busy preparing dinner but they both stopped and stared at Charlie when he came in.

Mrs Weston and Mr Bennett were there too and Lizzie said, 'Charlie has come to say how sorry he is for being a silly boy this morning.'

'Oh, Master Charlie.' Mrs Graves put down the saucepan she was holding with a clang and came towards him. She squatted down and enveloped him in a hug. 'We didn't like seeing you so upset and getting into trouble with Nanny. But she was right to be firm. You were getting so much better. Are you all right now?' She drew back a little and looked down into his upturned face. To her delight, he nodded and then after seeming to struggle for a moment, said, 'Sowwy.'

'Oh, you little darling.' Mrs Graves hugged him again. Then she stood up. 'I must get on now, but tomorrow, if it's fine and Nanny takes you outside to play, I'll have some of those scones you like ready for you when you come in. Would you like that?'

There was a small frown on Charlie's face as he seemed

to be thinking hard. Then, suddenly, he smiled and said, 'Scumshush.'

'Oh, bless you,' the cook said and ruffled his curls. She glanced up at Lizzie. 'Fancy him remembering that. Oh, he is coming on, Nanny. And don't you worry about the old –'

Swiftly, Lizzie put her finger to her lips and then pulled her own ear. Mrs Graves stared at her for a moment and then, understanding, she chuckled and altered what she had been about to say. 'About her leaving. Mr Bennett says the atmosphere's lighter upstairs already.'

'In that case –' Lizzie turned to the butler – 'Mr Bennett, please would you ask the master if I may bring Charlie to see him.'

'Of course, Nanny. They're all in the drawing room awaiting dinner but there's still time before Mrs Graves will be ready for us to serve. I'll go this minute. Perhaps you'd like to come up to the hall, because I am sure he will say yes.'

Lizzie and Charlie followed the butler up the stairs and waited in the hall while Mr Bennett entered the drawing room. They heard a brief murmur of voices and then the butler opened the door and beckoned to them. When they had moved into the room, the butler withdrew and closed the door behind him.

Now Lizzie and Charlie faced the four members of the family who were awaiting the announcement of dinner being served, but she was relieved to see they were all smiling at Charlie.

'Charlie just wanted to say how sorry he is for his silly behaviour this morning.' She glanced down at him. 'Now, Charlie, say, "Sorry, Papa".'

'Sowwy, Pap-pap.'

There was a moment of stillness before Roland set

down his glass of sherry and took a few steps towards Charlie. Then he dropped to one knee and spread his arms wide. For a moment, Charlie hesitated but then he pulled his hand away from Lizzie and ran towards his father to be scooped into a bear hug.

'Oh Charlie, my boy, my boy,' Roland said, his voice unsteady.

Both Cecily and Winifred held delicate lace handkerchiefs to their eyes and Lewis cleared his throat noisily. Then he looked at Lizzie. 'That is such a step forward, my dear,' he said gruffly. 'And – for my part – don't worry any more about this morning's little – um – episode. He's only a little chap and he's obviously very fond of his uncle. I thought you handled it admirably. And I am so sorry about my wife's – um – interference in your private life. You were open and honest with Roland when you applied for the post and that's all that matters. It is no one else's business, though I would just like to add how grieved I am that you have suffered such tragic events in your young life.'

'Thank you, Mr Moore,' Lizzie said quietly. It was the most she had ever heard the quiet man speak and she guessed that when his wife was present it was easier to remain silent. Already, she could feel that there was a more relaxed atmosphere in the room.

Now Lewis turned to Roland. 'We're not doing anything the day after tomorrow, Roland, are we?'

'There's nothing planned, no. Why?'

The older man smiled. 'Then I should like to supervise Charlie riding his pony if the weather is clement.'

'That's a great idea. We'll do it together, but I'll make sure Billy is on hand should Charlie run off. I don't think either you or I could chase after an energetic five-year-old.'

There was a discreet knock on the door and when the

butler appeared, Lizzie realized he was wanting to announce dinner.

'It's time we were going, Charlie. Say goodnight to everyone.'

As Roland released him and stood up, Charlie ran back to Lizzie and took her hand. Then he turned back to look at everyone in the room. He did not speak again, but waved at them and gave a beaming smile that brought fresh tears to the eyes of the two ladies present.

The morning after next, just as they had promised, the two men were waiting on the lawn with Billy and Dandy when Lizzie took Charlie down from the nursery. He allowed Roland to lift him into the saddle and then walk beside him while Lewis held the bridle and led the pony.

'Let's go and stand on the terrace between the bay windows,' Billy suggested to Lizzie. 'He'll still be able to see you, but it'll be sheltered there. I can gallop after Charlie if I need to. It's a lovely morning for the last days of December, but chilly. No Kitty this morning?'

'No, I'm sorry. Mrs Weston wanted her to dust the playroom.' She laughed. 'I'll be able to give Kitty some time off this evening after she's helped me get Charlie ready for bed.'

'You don't seem to get any spare time, Nanny. To be fair, don't you want Kitty to sit with him some nights while you have some time for yourself? I mean . . .' He stopped, anxious not to be thought prying.

'There's nothing I really want to do at the moment, Billy. I used to enjoy walking, but not on dark, cold nights. I love reading, but I can do that perfectly well sitting with Charlie as he sleeps.'

'I suppose you haven't had chance to make any – well – friends here.'

'I have all the friends I need among the staff.'

'Yes, but you're not getting a chance to meet . . .' He faltered and then blurted out, 'You're a very pretty young woman – beautiful, in fact. You ought . . .'

'Billy,' she said with a sad smile, 'you're sweet to think of it, but I had a young man once upon a time. We were engaged, but he broke it off when the family scandal hit us.'

Billy looked at her, appalled to think that any young man in his right mind could do such a thing to someone as lovely as Lizzie. 'That's awful. The master would never have done that to the mistress. And I don't think Master James would treat his young lady like that. Not that he has one, as far as I know.'

'No,' Lizzie said pensively, as she watched Charlie riding his pony with far more confidence now. 'I don't think he would.'

New Year's Eve was a relatively quiet affair in the Manor's household. Mrs Graves prepared a special dinner for the master and mistress and their two remaining guests and then the staff had their own celebration in the servants' hall.

'Mrs Weston has said I can go to see my family tomorrow, if it's all right with you, Nanny,' Kitty said. 'And Mr Marshall has said Billy can go with me. It won't be until the afternoon anyway. Only thing is, we won't be on hand to take Master Charlie outside.'

'Don't worry about that. One day won't matter. As far as I'm concerned, Kitty, you can have the whole day off to be with your family. We can have a nice quiet day in the playroom, can't we, Charlie?' The little boy didn't answer. He was engrossed in playing with the toy soldiers in the fort.

'Oh, thank you, Nanny. I'll ask Mrs Weston.'

With the housekeeper's approval, Kitty was given the day off and it was arranged that Billy would join her at her family's cottage in the village during the afternoon.

Left alone, Lizzie played with Charlie in the playroom but after about an hour she opened the door into the adjoining schoolroom. She was saddened to think how Roland and Cecily must have given so much thought to equipping the room and with such hope in their hearts at that time. As she stood looking around, she felt a tug on her skirt and turned to see Charlie looking up at her. She took his hand and together they walked further into the room to look at all the books on the shelves, the maps and pictures on the wall. Lizzie opened one of the drawers in the chest and took out a drawing pad and pencils. Then she pulled up a chair near the child's desk. Without direction from her, Charlie climbed onto the child's chair and rested his arms on the desk, just like he did at school.

'What shall we draw today?' Lizzie asked. Before this moment, Lizzie had encouraged him to draw shapes, just as Josiah Holland had suggested, but she had always taken paper and pencils into the nursery. This was the first time she had brought him into the schoolroom in the hope that he would sit at the little desk. 'Or,' she added now, 'shall we learn how to write your name? That would be such a nice surprise for Mr Holland when we go back to school next week.'

Slowly Lizzie wrote out Charlie's Christian name at the top of a large sheet of paper. Then she handed the pencil to him. 'Now you copy that underneath.'

He took the pencil in his right hand and carefully wrote 'c' and then 'h' and the rest of the letters in his name. He had been practising writing the letters of the alphabet for some time now, but this was the first time Lizzie had thought to teach him his name.

'That's very good, Charlie. That's your name.' She pointed to each letter and spelt it out phonetically, ending, 'But "c" and "h" together are pronounced "ch" for Charlie. Now, let me see if you can write it again without copying.'

She took away the first piece of paper so that he could no longer copy the word and gave him a blank sheet. 'Can you write "Charlie" now?'

After a moment's hesitation, he bent his head over the paper and carefully wrote out the name almost perfectly. Only one letter – the 'r' – had been written backwards.

'Well done, Charlie.' She kissed the top of his head and he leaned against her shoulder as she murmured, 'My clever, clever boy.'

Twenty-eight

A few days before the village school was due to open again for the spring term, Roland sent word that he would like to see Lizzie in his study. Winifred and Lewis had left just after New Year's Day and the house was gradually getting back to normal. The Christmas tree and all the decorations had been taken down and packed away for another year.

'I'm going down to talk to your papa in his study,' she explained carefully to a solemn-faced Charlie. 'Kitty will be here and Billy is coming up to play with you in the playroom. I promise I won't be long.'

Downstairs, she waited in the hall until Mr Bennett announced her.

'Ah, Nanny,' Roland said, getting up from behind his desk. 'Please come in and sit down. Bennett, please would you ask Clara to bring coffee for us.'

As the door closed behind the butler, and before she sat down, Lizzie said, 'I've brought these to show you.'

First, she handed him the sheet of paper on which she had written Charlie's name. 'I wrote the top line and then, as you can see, Charlie has copied it four times. And then this . . .' With a smile of triumph, she produced the paper with just Charlie's writing. 'He wrote it entirely by himself without copying and without any prompting from me. I didn't even tell him the letters.'

Roland held both pieces of paper in his hands, looking

from one to the other. 'Oh, Nanny. Really? He really wrote his name all by himself. That's remarkable and it's a coincidence that you should bring this to show me this morning because it's about his future education that I wanted to talk to you. Oh, do sit down and we'll wait until Clara has been.'

When the maid had served their coffee and closed the door behind her as she left the room, Roland leaned back in his chair.

'School starts again on Tuesday and I wondered how you felt about him going for five mornings plus Friday afternoon, which I understand is story time, to start with, but with a view to him going full time if he settles.'

'I would have to talk to Mr Holland first to see how we can gradually get Charlie to be in the classroom without me being there.' She chuckled. 'I don't think the teacher would want me sitting at the back of his classroom full time.'

'Are there any children Charlie has made friends with?'

'He sits beside Alfie Preston and a little girl who started at the same time in September. Rosie. And then there's always Luke.'

'Ah yes, Luke. Now, I wanted a word with you about him too. He's the one you say is suitable to go to a grammar school in September, isn't he?'

'Mr Holland says he's a very bright lad and deserves the opportunity.'

'What about his parents?' Roland pulled a face. 'Some families – in fact, most families – want their eldest son to go out to work as soon as possible to contribute to the family purse. I would be willing to meet the expense of Luke attending the school, but I couldn't raise his father's wages. That would be unfair on the rest of my farm labourers.'

'I understand that. Perhaps I could have a word with Mr Holland first and make sure that he definitely recommends Luke for a grammar-school education, and then you could talk to Bob Preston.'

'That sounds like a very sensible idea. We had a boy from the village who attended Chesterfield Grammar School, but he's finished now and is at university, I believe. He's Matt Naylor's son and Matt used to take him every morning and evening in his own pony and trap. That was his choice, mind you. With Luke, I would suggest him boarding in the week and I'd allow Bob to use one of the farm's vehicles to fetch him home on a Friday evening and take him back on Sunday evening. We're only about five miles or so from the school, but it's still a lot to do every weekday.'

Lizzie rose. 'I must get back to Charlie. Although I want him to get used to being away from me, I must do it by degrees. Once he knows I'm always going to come back when I say I am, then I think separation from me will get easier.'

Roland nodded but, as the door closed behind her, he was deep in thought. Would Nanny always be able to be there for Charlie? That was a question for them all, not just his son.

On the Saturday afternoon before school was due to reopen, the game of football was also recommenced.

Billy drove Lizzie and Charlie down to the field.

'I'll come and fetch you later, Nanny, if you want.'

'Only if it rains or snows, Billy,' she laughed.

But Billy didn't laugh. 'It was trying to snow this morning and the sky looks very grey.'

As Luke ran across the grass to greet them, Lizzie bent down and said, 'Now, Charlie, I am going across the road

233

to visit Mr Holland. You'll know where I am and I'll be back here by the time the game finishes. Luke will look after you.' She straightened up. 'Hello, Luke. Did you have a nice Christmas?'

'Great, Nanny, thank you. Mam and Dad invited Mr Holland for Christmas Day, seeing as he was on his own and d'you know what, he was nothing like he is in school. He bought us a board game called Ludo and played with us all afternoon. He's really quite nice when you get to know him outside school. Right, Charlie, come on. They're picking teams and I want you to be on my team today.'

Lizzie watched Charlie for a few moments to make sure he was happily engaged in the game before she turned and crossed the road to the schoolhouse. Josiah had been watching from his front window and opened the door just as she raised her hand to knock.

'Happy New Year to you, Mr Holland.'

'And the same to you, Miss Ingham. Please come in. I have already made tea in the hope that you would come across. You don't want to be standing there for an hour in this weather. Now, you go and sit by the window so you can keep an eye on Charlie and I'll bring the tea.'

They spent the next hour discussing plans for Charlie and for Luke.

'I want Charlie to be able to stay in school without me being there all the time, but it may take us a while to achieve that.'

'We can do it slowly and I did have another idea, if you would be agreeable.' He cleared his throat in embarrassment before saying hesitantly, 'I am afraid word has got around the village about your – erm – about the tragedy in your family.'

Lizzie sighed. 'I expected it would, Mr Holland. Are you trying to tell me that feelings towards me have changed? That perhaps I am no longer welcome to be with their children?'

'Oh, Heavens no, Miss Ingham. Quite the opposite, though I have to admit that if everyone had known from the start, their attitude towards you might have been different. But they have got to know you and . . .' Here Josiah paused as he gazed at her lovely face. He had been about to say the word 'love' but coming from a crusty, middle-aged schoolmaster, it sounded indelicate. He cleared his throat and continued, 'Like you for yourself and not who you are in terms of your standing in society.'

Lizzie nodded. 'I'm glad. Of course, Mr Spendlove and his wife knew from the start, but my colleagues at the Manor have only learned of it recently.'

'So I understand,' he said softly, but added no more.

There was a short silence before Lizzie prompted, 'So, what is your idea?'

'Oh yes, that. Sorry, I got side-tracked. I am assuming that because of your upbringing you are perhaps a competent needlewoman.' He smiled at her over the top of his spectacles. 'I did wonder how you came to be so proficient on the pianoforte. Now I understand, so I wondered if you would be willing to teach needlework to the girls.'

He was surprised by the smile that lit up Lizzie's eyes. 'Oh, I would. What a wonderful idea. But what would the boys do during that time?' She chuckled. 'I rather think there wouldn't be any takers among them to learn sewing and embroidery.'

Josiah gave a small bark of laughter. 'No, I think not. Oh, I'd find something suitable for them to do. I thought you could have one of the mornings when Charlie is here. Perhaps you'd give it some thought and let me know what materials I need to order for you.'

'I will and I'll let you have a list. How many girls are there?'

'Nine.'

Lizzie glanced out of the window. 'Ah, it looks like the football game is coming to an end. That hour went very quickly.' She placed her empty cup on the tray and stood up. 'Thank you, Mr Holland. I look forward to seeing you on Tuesday morning.'

'And I you, Miss Ingham.'

The weeks following Christmas and New Year passed uneventfully and to everyone's delight, Charlie made steady progress. He began to say more words, though he still didn't string them together to make a full sentence.

'We'll have to mind our Ps and Qs now,' Mrs Graves chuckled. 'No more calling a member of the family an old beezum.'

Josiah had obtained the needlework materials which Lizzie had suggested and each Wednesday morning the girls moved their chairs to the back of the classroom to sit in a circle around her. Meanwhile, Charlie sat with the boys as they did extra lessons in practical mathematics.

When they heard about the new arrangement, several of the villagers offered their expertise if needed.

'Matt Naylor has offered to talk to the boys about his trade as a wheelwright and blacksmith,' Josiah told Lizzie. 'And since many of them will, no doubt, end up working on the land, I've asked Mr Spendlove's farm bailiff if he would give them a talk. Not all of them are suitable grammar-school pupils.'

'They should be encouraged to believe that their practical skills are just as valuable and praiseworthy as academic achievements,' Lizzie said. 'Everyone has a talent, it's just a matter of finding out what that is and encouraging it.'

Josiah smiled quietly. He wasn't sure he agreed with her wholeheartedly but it was a wonderful philosophy to have. Throughout his teaching career he had been aware that some children did not reach their potential because they were not given the chance. But here, in this village, thanks to the philanthropy of the master at the Manor, each and every child would at least be given the opportunity to follow whatever path in life they chose. For the first time in his life, he felt privileged to be a teacher and able to guide youngsters to achieve the best that they could. And it was this remarkable young woman who had shown him that.

Gradually, Lizzie began to leave the school for brief periods while Charlie was there.

'I'm just going across the road to the village shop,' she told him halfway through the lessons one Monday morning. 'I won't be long. You sit with Alfie and Rosie. You're going to learn numbers today, so that you can do sums like Luke.'

He made no sound, although later Josiah confided, 'He didn't concentrate very well while you were gone, Miss Ingham. He was forever turning round to watch the door for your return. However, I think you're doing the right thing. It will get better, I'm sure.'

'Ah, just the person I wanted to see,' Bob Preston greeted Lizzie one morning as she walked to the village shop on yet another fictitious errand. 'Mr Spendlove sent for me yesterday to see him about Luke going to the grammar school in September.' His grin broadened. 'It's all arranged and I think I've you to thank for that.'

'Not really, Bob. It's been done before, I understand.'

'Well, yes, but the master's doing a bit more for us than was necessary for Daniel Naylor. His dad used to take him every day so he wasn't a boarder. But Mr Spendlove has offered for our Luke to board in the week and just come home at weekends. He's even said I can have use of one of the traps belonging to Home Farm to fetch him and take him back. And he's paying for Luke's board at the school.'

'I'm so pleased. What is Daniel Naylor doing now?'

'He's in his second year at university studying science and doing ever so well, so he won't be coming back to work with his dad. One of their younger boys is dead keen to do that though – work with his dad, I mean – so it all works out very nicely for Matt Naylor. So, we've high hopes for our Luke, but whatever he decides to do, Miss Ingham, we'll be proud of him.'

'He's a wonderful, caring boy and very sensible too. I'm sure he'll make the right decision. He's already a credit to you and your wife, Bob, as are all your children. And Alfie is already doing very nicely, Mr Holland tells me.'

'Ah, now I definitely have cause to thank you for that, Miss Ingham.' They smiled at each other, remembering little Alfie's fear when starting school. Bob raised his cap to her as they parted and said, 'I'll see you Saturday afternoon at the football, weather permitting.'

When Lizzie and Charlie arrived home at the end of morning lessons, there was great excitement running through the household.

'Master James and his mother are coming for the weekend,' Mrs Graves said, almost before they'd got through the kitchen door.

Twenty-nine

James and his mother arrived on the Saturday morning, the first weekend in February, and as soon as he had greeted his brother and sister-in-law, James bounded up the stairs to see Charlie.

The nursery was empty so he looked in the playroom, but there was still no sign of his nephew. Then, just as he was about to turn and go back downstairs, he heard a scuffle in the next room. The door into the schoolroom opened and a little body hurled itself at him. He picked Charlie up and swung him round.

'Football,' Charlie said.

For a moment, James was startled but he glanced up to see Lizzie standing in the doorway. 'That's a new word. Hello, Nanny. How are you?'

'Well, thank you, Master James.'

He turned back to Charlie. 'Yes, we'll play football this afternoon.'

But Charlie shook his head and pointed vaguely in the direction of the village.

'Ah, I think he might be trying to tell you that we go down to the village on a Saturday afternoon to play football with the other children,' Lizzie explained.

'Ah, yes. I'd forgotten. May I come with you to watch?'

Charlie nodded vigorously.

So, after luncheon, James drove the trap down to the village and tethered the pony at one end of the field, while the children gathered to play. Bob was, as usual, in charge. Several of the fathers of the children now came to watch if they were not working. Each one of them greeted James and shook his hand.

Josiah watched from the window. It was unlikely Miss Ingham would cross the road to talk to him today, but, to his surprise, just after the teams had changed ends signifying half-time, he saw Lizzie touch James's arm and gesture in the direction of the schoolhouse. James glanced behind him and then nodded, but only Lizzie stepped across the road to knock on his door.

'I'm sorry, I haven't prepared tea today. I didn't think you'd come over, but do come in.'

Lizzie smiled at him as they sat down together in the front window. 'No matter. I just wanted to tell you that Charlie said a new word today when Master James arrived. "Football". He was trying to tell him that we would be coming here this afternoon to play. He still doesn't string words together to form a proper sentence. I think the most he has ever said was two words.' She smothered a giggle as she remembered just what two of those words had been. She could hardly repeat them even to the teacher. 'But his writing is coming on very well, I think.'

'Yes, I have noticed he's improving all the time. I even think he can read more than he's letting on. And don't worry about the speech. I think it will come in time. Some children don't say more than they have to in order to get what they want. You might try pretending not to under-stand something to encourage him to tell you what he wants.'

'Ah, I see what you mean. Maybe I have been remiss in always understanding his needs.'

Josiah smiled and said gallantly, 'I don't think you have

240

been remiss in anything, Miss Ingham. You are doing amazingly well with him. You've only been here, what is it now, about seven months?'

Lizzie nodded. 'Yes. I suppose, looking back, he has improved a lot.'

'I don't think anyone – most of all his parents – ever believed he would – or could – be like he is today.' He nodded out of the window. 'Just look at him running up and down, kicking the ball straight and true. He doesn't even make a fuss if he falls. He just jumps up again and runs after the ball. Master James must see a huge improvement in him every time he visits.'

'Master James has helped a lot. He's very good with him and devotes most of his time to playing with him when he's here. The only downside is that Charlie hates it when his uncle leaves.'

'That's only natural.'

There was a pause between them until Lizzie said, 'I understand it's all arranged for Luke Preston to attend the grammar school in Chesterfield from September?'

Josiah nodded. 'Thanks to Mr Spendlove's benevolence. But the boy is worth his patronage. He's a hard worker.'

'Well, thank you for your part in it all,' Lizzie said.

Josiah chuckled. 'Don't forget I have an ulterior motive. It's a feather in my cap if one of my boys goes on to the grammar school and even more so if they take their education further like Daniel.'

'I am sure his parents would back him if Luke wanted to do that too.'

'They're a very nice family,' he said pensively as he gazed out of the window at the children and their referee. 'They gave me the best Christmas I've had in recent years, Miss Ingham, if not ever. I was an only child and my parents weren't what you would call gregarious.'

Lizzie was reminded sharply of the Christmases at Ancholme Hall when she and Bruce had been young. They had been joyous, happy times. She stood up. 'I think the game is coming to end and I must go, but I'll see you on Monday.'

'Do you think Charlie could have Sunday luncheon with us?' James asked Lizzie. It was the custom in the Spendlove household to have a late Sunday luncheon and then a cold collation on Sunday evening. The staff were then able to have a more leisurely dinner in the evening.

'Not all employers are as thoughtful as Mr Spendlove,' Mrs Weston had said when she had first told Lizzie of the routine. 'But then this is rather an unusual household.'

'Of course, it will be better this time.' James grinned saucily. 'There'll be just my mother and me as guests.'

'Yes, and this time I'll see if I can be in the kitchen and not sitting in the hallway. Perhaps we can use the opportunity to take another step forward.'

On Sunday afternoon, just before three o'clock, Lizzie took Charlie down to the kitchen. 'Now, you're to have luncheon in the dining room with Mama, Papa, Uncle James and your grandma and I shall be in here all the time. I promise I won't go anywhere else.'

'You come,' Charlie said, stringing two words together.

'No, darling. Nannies do not eat in the dining room. They eat in the servants' hall.'

Charlie frowned and then his gaze fell on Kitty. 'You come.'

But Kitty shook her head. 'No, Master Charlie. I can't eat in the dining room either.'

Charlie pouted. 'Then I eat here.'

Lizzie counted in her head. Four words. He'd strung four words together, just like Josiah had said he might when he wanted to get his point across. Hearing the conversation, Mrs Graves said, 'If you're a good boy and eat your dinner in the dining room, you can come down here afterwards for one of your favourite scones with jam and cream. How would that be?'

Charlie seemed to be considering this before saying, 'Uncle James come too.'

Another four words. Lizzie felt a thrill of triumph run through her.

'Of course,' Mrs Graves laughed. 'Master James is always welcome in my kitchen. Now, off you go upstairs to the dining room. We'll look after Nanny while you're gone. We'll keep her here with us, I promise.'

The luncheon with his family went well. Charlie only followed Mr Bennett back to the kitchen once between courses, just to make sure Lizzie was still there. No one around the table in the dining room mentioned it and at the end of the meal, Charlie slipped down from his chair and tugged on James's sleeve.

'Come. Scones.'

The four grown-ups glanced at each other in puzzle-ment, until Mr Bennett said, 'Mrs Graves told him that if he was a good boy having luncheon with you, he could go down to the kitchen for scones with jam and cream and Master Charlie wants you to go too, Master James.'

'Then how could I resist one of Mrs Graves's scones? Lead the way, Charlie.'

Now that luncheon was over, there was a much more relaxed atmosphere in the kitchen. As James and Charlie entered, the little boy rushed to Lizzie to clasp her knees in a hug. Then, satisfied he was back with her too, he climbed onto his chair at the table.

'Come in, Master James. Please sit down,' Mrs Graves said. 'Eh, this is just like the old days when you were a bairn and you'd come down to my kitchen for scones.' Her gaze wandered fondly over James and then onto Charlie. 'And now Master Charlie is carrying on the tradition. I never thought I'd see the day, you know.'

James nodded. He knew exactly what the cook meant. She'd never hoped to be able to see Charlie sitting at her kitchen table like this. 'Those bad times are gone, Mrs Graves,' he said softly.

'God willing,' Mrs Graves murmured and poured James a cup of tea and pushed a plate of scones towards him and Charlie.

'I'll do my best, Mrs Graves, to do them justice,' James grinned, patting his stomach, 'but after that delicious lunch, I'm not sure I have room.'

The cook chuckled and her red face was wreathed in smiles. 'I'm sure you'll find a little corner.'

She cut three scones in half, smothered them with strawberry jam and cream and passed one each to James, Charlie and Lizzie.

Charlie bit into his scone, leaving a dab of cream on his nose. 'Scumshush,' he said.

Although Joe and Billy were rarely needed to help with bath time now, they often came to the nursery on Sunday evenings to play with Charlie, but when they arrived that evening, James was sitting on the floor of the playroom with Charlie, moving soldiers around the fort. Lizzie was in the nursery. She had taken the opportunity to let Charlie get used to being without her close by, although she always made sure he knew exactly where she was.

'Do you need us at all, Nanny?' Joe asked.

Lizzie smiled and shook her head. 'Not tonight, Joe, but thank you for asking. Master James has promised to come back a little later and read Charlie a bedtime story.'

In a soft tone, Joe said, 'Master James is leaving to-morrow morning, isn't he? What about Charlie? Him saying "goodbye", I mean?'

'He must learn to say goodbye without creating a fuss like he did at Christmas. I don't mind him shedding tears. He's only a little chap – that's understandable, but I cannot allow the screaming.'

Joe and Billy glanced at each other. 'It broke our hearts when you were so stern with him,' Joe said.

'Mine too,' Lizzie admitted softly, 'but it was necessary. I shall have a talk with him in the morning. If he prom-ises to behave, we shall come down when Master James leaves.'

'Ah yes, of course. Billy will take Master James to the station early and be back in time to take you and Master Charlie to school. He's going to take Mrs Spendlove home later in the morning.'

When bath time was over and Lizzie was sitting in front of the nursery fire with Charlie on her lap, drying his curly hair, James arrived back to read to Charlie. As the little boy's eyelids drooped James tucked him into bed, kissed his forehead and tiptoed back to the hearth to sit with Lizzie.

'Does he know about tomorrow?' James whispered. 'I've only got such a short leave this time.'

'Not yet. I didn't want to say anything tonight just before he went to bed, but I'll explain in the morning.'

'Shall you bring him down to see us off?'

'Yes. He has to learn to behave.'

'I know,' James said worriedly. 'But I hate seeing him upset. I don't know which was worse, him being distressed at me going or you being cross with him.'

His anxious brown-eyed gaze met hers across the hearth. After several moments, James cleared his throat. 'I'd better be going. I'll see you in the morning, then.'

As he rose, Lizzie stood up too. 'Thank you, Master James, for all your help this weekend. Charlie loves having you home.'

'And I love being with him.' He seemed about to say more, but then stopped. 'I'd better go,' he said abruptly. 'Goodnight, Nanny.' Then he left the nursery, a little hurriedly, Lizzie thought.

She sat down again and gazed into the flickering flames. It wasn't often she longed for the old days. She was very happy and contented in her life at the Manor and she loved Charlie as if he were her own child. But just some-times – as tonight – what wouldn't she have given to have been downstairs in the drawing room, sitting on the sofa beside James and being treated by the family as an equal.

The following morning, Kitty asked hesitantly, 'Are you taking him down to say goodbye to Master James?'

'Yes, I am, Kitty. We've had a little talk this morning, haven't we, Charlie?' she said, as she smiled down at the little boy and helped him to fasten the buttons of his jacket. She was now teaching him to dress himself. 'He understands that his uncle has to come and go because he is in the army, like Charlie's toy soldiers. We're going to play that they all go on leave at different times, but they always have to come back to the fort to do their duty. Now,' she added as she stood up from her kneeling position, 'we're ready.' She held out her hand.

Downstairs in the hall, the staff had all gathered to wave James off. He was already shaking hands with them as Billy waited outside with the pony and trap.

Charlie stood very still, his gaze on James, who now turned to him and picked him up.

'Now then, old chap. We have to go, but Grandma and I will come again as soon as we can. Are you going to stand on the terrace and wave me off?'

Tears welled in Charlie's eyes, but he made no sound. Instead, he put his arms around James's neck and hugged him tightly.

James's gaze met Lizzie's eyes. 'Nanny will look after you,' he whispered, 'and you must take good care of Nanny, too. Promise?'

Against James's neck, Charlie nodded. Then James turned and carried him out of the front door, across the terrace and to the top of the steps, where Billy was waiting at the bottom. James set Charlie down, gave him a quick kiss on the top of his head and ran down the steps. Lizzie had followed them out and now stood just behind Charlie. As the trap moved away, the little boy waved but he made no move to follow them nor did he make any sound. They stood watching until the trap had gone down the drive, then down the lane and disappeared round the corner towards the station.

Lizzie touched his shoulder. 'And now we must have breakfast and get ready to go to school when Billy comes back with the trap.'

Charlie turned and looked up at her. Tears were rolling down his cheeks, but still, he made no sound. Back in the nursery, Lizzie hugged him hard. 'Good boy. I'm very proud of you.'

Thirty

The weeks turned into months and every day Charlie improved a little more. Soon, it was July and Lizzie had been at the Manor for a whole year. The difference between the wild little boy she had first encountered and Charlie now was unbelievable. He was speaking more and doing quite well at school, although Josiah confided in Lizzie that Charlie would never be an academic. 'I doubt he'd even cope with a place at the grammar school. He'd be unhappy there.'

'I don't think that being unable to go to a grammar school will matter,' Lizzie had said with a smile. 'His future is here as the next master of the estate alongside his father and his Uncle James.'

'Oh, he'll do that all right. As he grows, his father will teach him and he'll be loved by all his tenants.' This time Josiah used the word 'loved' quite naturally and without embarrassment. It was what all the villagers would feel about Charlie.

On that last day of the summer term, there were celebrations at the school. Luke was leaving to start at Chesterfield Grammar School in September.

'You will be sorely missed,' Josiah said, shaking his hand. 'I have treated you as something of a "head boy" in the school and I have written a glowing testimonial about you to your new headmaster. Work hard, Luke, and I know you will do well. Thanks to Mr Spendlove's generosity, you have a wonderful opportunity. Don't waste it.'

'I won't, Mr Holland, and thank you for all your help. I know you have given me extra tuition and guidance and I'm very grateful.'

Josiah shrugged. 'It's been my pleasure. Don't forget it's a feather in my cap too that you're going to the grammar school. I don't think your little brother will follow in your footsteps, but he's doing well. He tries his best, which is all I can ask. And he's become great friends with Charlie, which I think is helping them both enormously. Alfie has your kindness, Luke. He'll do all right in life, never fear.'

And so Charlie lost his greatest ally at school, but fortunately, by now, he fitted in with the other children. After the Easter holidays, he had begun to attend the school for the full five days each week and Lizzie no longer needed to sit at the back of the classroom to be near him, although she did visit on a Wednesday afternoon to teach needlework to the girls. When that was happening, Josiah took the boys to visit the local wheelwright or one of the tenant farmers to introduce them to the sort of practical work they might wish to undertake when they reached school-leaving age. Another huge step forward was when Charlie agreed to Billy taking him to and from school in the trap, and also down to the village on a Saturday afternoon for football, which, in the summer months now became cricket, all without Lizzie. And whenever he could get leave, James visited, often bringing his mother too.

But Cecily's parents no longer visited at all.

For Charlie's sixth birthday in August, Roland decided that he should have a proper party on the Sunday afternoon and invite all the children from the school.

'Do you think Mrs Graves could cope with the catering?' Roland asked Mrs Weston. The housekeeper smiled. 'She'll be in her element, sir. And we'll all help, but if I might make one suggestion . . .'

'Please do.'

'I think you ought to ask one or two of the parents to come too. Twenty children running about the grounds will be a handful.'

'That's a very good idea, Mrs Weston. Thank you. I'll talk to Bob Preston. I think he might agree to come and because he has charge of all the children who play sport on a Saturday afternoon, they'll respect his authority.'

They were lucky with the weather, for even August could be wet. But the day dawned clear and warm, so that trestle tables could be put out on the lawn for the children to eat outside. All the staff were involved and Bob Preston and his wife and one or two other parents came too. Dandy was in great demand to give rides, and games, instigated by Bob, were played on the lawn. Billy was posted at the end of the lawn to stop any child venturing too near the lake.

Both Roland and Cecily came out too. Roland joined in the games and even Cecily, alongside Lizzie and Bob's wife, Martha, helped to supervise the children at the table. The plates of sandwiches, jelly and cakes disappeared as if a flock of gannets had flown in.

'Ee, I love to see bairns with a good appetite,' Mrs Graves said as she watched all her carefully prepared food disappearing.

'It's a wonderful spread, Mrs Graves,' Martha Preston said. 'Thank you to all of you for such a grand party. What a shame Master James couldn't be here.'

'He tried to get leave but couldn't this time,' Cecily

said. 'Maybe next year.' Already, Cecily was planning that this should be an annual event.

All the children went home happy, each clutching a little bag of home-made sweets, courtesy of Mrs Graves.

After dinner that evening as Roland and Cecily sat together in the drawing room, Roland took her hand in his. 'My love, I truly believe we now have the son we always wanted.'

'Thanks to Nanny. She really is a remarkable young woman.' Suddenly, Cecily was anxious. 'She won't leave us yet, will she?'

'I don't think so. She has said she will stay as long as Charlie needs her and he still does at the moment.'

'But what about when he's old enough to go to boarding school? That was always your dream, wasn't it?'

'Originally, yes, but I don't know if it would be suitable for Charlie now. I will have a talk with Mr Holland and seek his advice. I am sure he will give me an honest opinion.'

When school reopened in September, Roland sought a meeting with Josiah. After the two men had shaken hands and Roland had enquired if there was anything the school needed, he came straight to the point of his visit. 'I would appreciate your advice about Charlie. Normally, I would put his name down for a public school and he would become a boarder at somewhere between eight and ten years old, but I'm really not sure it would be the right thing for him. What is your opinion?'

'You want me to be frank?'

'Of course.'

'Then I think it would be the worst possible thing you could do. He needs the stability of home and familiar surroundings. In short, at present he still needs Miss

Ingham, although she is doing her best to help him to become more independent of her. I think she will succeed, but I think it will still take some time yet.'

'Do you think a tutor would be beneficial? No offence to your teaching capabilities, but you do have twenty children in your charge. You can't possibly give individual attention to each of them.'

Josiah smiled. 'None taken, sir. It isn't easy, especially in a small village school where they're all different ages and abilities. But to answer your question . . .' He paused. 'I think, at present anyway, he's gaining so much more by being among his peer group.' He smiled wryly. 'Much as it pains me to admit it, I think he learns as much from them as he does from me.'

'So we'll leave things as they are for the moment and perhaps think again when he's older.'

Josiah nodded. 'I give you my word that if at any time I think there should be a change in his education – either for him to have a tutor or to go to a different school – then I will let you know.'

And with that, for the moment, Roland had to be content. The plans were not those he had once had for his son, but he was honest enough to admit that they were a lot better than he had recently thought they might be.

So life at the Manor and in the village settled down into a routine. Charlie continued to grow and flourish; Luke came home every weekend and joined in the sports on the field every Saturday afternoon, and James and his mother visited as often as they could. On his last night, James would help to see Charlie into bed, read him a story and then sit with Lizzie in the glow of the nursery fire. Always, when he left her, he would look deeply into her eyes and then raise her hand to his lips and gently kiss her fingers. Long after he had gone, she would sit gazing into the fire and dreaming of what might have been.

'Nanny –' Clara burst into the nursery one morning just after eleven-thirty while Charlie was at school – 'Mr Bennett sent me to tell you that there's a gentleman arrived asking to see you.'

Lizzie looked up in surprise. 'Did he give a name?'

'Mr Bellingham.'

Lizzie's eyes widened. Since she had been at the Manor she had exchanged letters with her family's former solicitor, but if he had come in person today, then whatever he needed to see her about must be important and serious.

Lizzie smoothed her hair and quickly changed into a clean apron. Mr Bennett was waiting in the hall and showed her into Roland's study. At once both Roland, sitting behind his desk, and Mr Bellingham rose.

'I'll leave you together,' Roland said. 'I hope you will stay for luncheon, Mr Bellingham. It's a long journey back for you.'

'That's most kind of you, Mr Spendlove.'

As the door closed behind Roland, Mr Bellingham held out both his hands to Lizzie.

'My dear, I am pleased to see you, but I regret to say I am the bearer of sad tidings.'

Lizzie stared at him as she put both her hands into his. 'Tell me quickly, Mr Bellingham.'

'It's your brother. He went to South America to try to escape his pursuers, but I'm sorry to say they caught up with him anyway.'

The colour drained from Lizzie's face and her hands trembled in his grasp. 'Please sit down, Miss Ingham. This is a dreadful shock for you.'

When they both sat down again, Lizzie whispered, 'You – you mean, he's dead?'

Mr Bellingham nodded. 'I'm afraid so.'

Lizzie was silent for a long time. At last she said, 'I presume he's been buried out there?'

'Yes. I'm so sorry we couldn't bring him home to be buried beside your parents, but . . .'

Lizzie was shaking her head. 'Please, don't apologize. It's for the best. Bruce made his own choices. We were very close when we were young and those are the times I like to remember. I really don't recognize the man he became later in life as my brother. I – I find it hard to forgive all the trouble he caused, though I had hoped he'd found a life abroad. I never wished for this to happen to him.'

'Of course you didn't.'

'So, is there anything I have to do?'

'Not that I know at present, but I will keep you informed, of course.'

'Thank you for coming all this way to tell me in person. I am very grateful.'

'How are things working out here?'

'Very well, I think. Charlie – the little boy I'm nanny to – is still improving every day.'

'So, will there come a day when you're no longer needed here?'

'I expect so, but I think it will be a while yet before that happens.' Lizzie didn't want to think about it. She would miss everyone here, especially Charlie.

And, of course, James too.

Thirty-one

It was Mrs Graves who first noticed that Mrs Weston wasn't well.

'Are you all right, Mrs Weston? You look as if you've lost your balance. You were weaving about all over the place when you came into the kitchen just now. Is it one of your bad headaches again? Here, have a nice cup of tea.'

The housekeeper sat down heavily and stared up at the cook with frightened eyes. Her mouth worked but no proper words came out, just a gurgling and sounds that made no sense.

'Nelly!' Mrs Graves shouted to her scullery maid. 'Fetch Mr Bennett this minute and then go up and ask Nanny to come down.'

The butler arrived in the kitchen within minutes and Lizzie only moments later, closely followed by Kitty.

'She's having a seizure,' Mr Bennett said at once. 'That's how my old dad was. Nanny, ask Billy to go at once for the doctor and ask Joe to come in here. We may need his help.'

As Lizzie hurried out of the back door to find both Billy and Joe, Mrs Graves said, 'Should we get her to her bedroom?'

'That's what I want Joe for. Kitty, run upstairs and tell the master. He'll know what we should do.'

Kitty lifted her long skirt and ran up the stairs to the

hall. She rapped urgently on the door of the master's study, but when there was no answer she raced across the wide hallway to knock on the drawing-room door. Cecily's voice said, 'Come in.'

'Oh ma'am,' Kitty said breathlessly. 'I'm sorry – Mrs Weston's been taken ill. I was looking for the master.'

At once Cecily cast aside her embroidery and rose. 'The master's out riding, but I'll come down. Where is she? In the kitchen?'

'Yes, ma'am. Mr Bennett thinks it's a seizure. He's sending Billy for the doctor.'

When they entered the kitchen it was to see Mr Bennett holding Mrs Weston from falling out of the chair.

Cecily sat down opposite her and took her hands. 'Don't worry, Mrs Weston. We'll take care of you.' She glanced up at the butler. 'Do you think we could get her upstairs to a bedroom? You'll never make it to her own room on the next floor, but if you can manage it to the first floor, put her in Master James's room. The bed is always kept aired in there and it'll be handy for the staff looking after her.'

'Ought she to go to hospital?' Mrs Graves was making no effort now to hide her anxious tears.

'We'll see what the doctor says, but I think she'd be better here where we can all look after her.'

Lizzie and Joe entered the kitchen. 'Billy's gone for the doctor, ma'am. Is there anything else we can do?'

'Yes, there is. Joe, could you help Mr Bennett take her upstairs into Master James's room? It would be better if she was in bed when the doctor arrives, I'm sure.'

It took quite a while for the two men to get her up the stairs. The right side of Mrs Weston's face had dropped and she was dragging her right foot. She was a dead weight between them. Just as they reached the bedroom, Roland came bounding up the stairs. 'I've just heard. Can I help? Cecily, I'm so sorry I wasn't here . . .'

'No matter, Roland. We've managed this far, but perhaps you can help get her onto the bed. Billy has gone for the doctor and Nanny and I will undress her, if we can. Kitty, draw back the bed covers.'

'I wondered why there was no one in the yard,' Roland murmured, as he bent to lift Mrs Weston's legs to help manoeuvre her onto the bed. 'We'll be just outside if you need help, though I am conscious of preserving the poor woman's modesty.'

It was over half an hour before Billy arrived back with Doctor Grey, who had been out on a call in the village. Both Cecily and Lizzie stayed in the room while he examined his patient.

'Yes, it is a seizure and the next few hours will be critical. Are you happy for her to remain here? I think moving her would be very unwise.' He glanced at Lizzie, but it was to Cecily he spoke. 'I can, of course, find a nurse for you, Mrs Spendlove, if you wish, but I think Nanny, with my advice, would do perfectly well.'

'Whatever you say, Doctor,' Cecily said. 'But we want whatever is best for Mrs Weston. She is very dear to all of us.'

He nodded. 'Then my decisions will be guided by that. I will visit every day and I am convinced that being here at home will be far more conducive to her recovery than being cared for by strangers, professional though they might be.'

Before he left, he gave Lizzie detailed instructions on what should be done, promising to call again the following morning.

'Has she any relatives?' he asked, as he sat in the

drawing room at Roland and Cecily's invitation. 'Because if so, I think you should let them know.'

Husband and wife glanced at each other. 'Not that we know of. No close ones certainly,' Roland said. 'She's been here since she was young. She started as a housemaid for my parents and worked her way up into the position of housekeeper. She's a very valued member of our household.'

'She's never been married?'

Roland smiled. '"Mrs" is a courtesy title given to housekeepers and cooks. Mrs Graves has never married either.'

Doctor Grey nodded. He had heard of the custom in big houses.

'We'll ask Mrs Graves and Mr Bennett about any relatives she might have,' Roland promised. 'They may know.'

All the staff were united in their care of the housekeeper. When Billy had fetched Charlie home from school later that day, Lizzie explained gently to him that Mrs Weston was poorly and staying in his uncle James's room.

'See her?' he asked.

'Only if you promise to be very quiet and we won't stay very long. Now, there's something else I must explain to you. The doctor has asked me to look after Mrs Weston so although I won't be far away, I won't be here in the nursery as much. But Kitty will be here with you all the time.'

She watched as Charlie bit his lower lip and she could see that he was trying to be very brave. She stroked his hair. 'You will be doing your bit to help Mrs Weston get better.'

'See you?'

'Of course. Every day. I'll work something out with Kitty. Now, wash your hands in the bathroom and we'll go to see Mrs Weston.'

As they left the nursery, Charlie picked up Mr Snuggles and tucked him under his arm. They went along the passages to the opposite end of the house though on the same floor. As they reached the bedroom where Mrs Weston was, the doctor emerged.

'I thought I would call in again this afternoon, just to see how she is,' he explained. 'Hello, Charlie. My word. You've – altered since I last saw you. I'm sure you've grown.'

For a moment, Charlie shrank back against Lizzie's skirt and Doctor Grey laughed. He put up his hands and wriggled them. 'It's all right, Charlie. Look. No nasty syrup. So, how are you?'

'Say, "Very well, thank you", Charlie,' Lizzie prompted.

Charlie glanced up at her and then looked back at the doctor. 'Very well. Thank you.'

If Lizzie had needed any further approbation for the progress Charlie had made in her care, she had it now. The look of surprise on the doctor's face was worth a hundred testimonials. He glanced at Lizzie with admiration in his eyes. Then he squatted down in front of Charlie. 'I am so pleased to hear you say that. Now, are you going to see the patient?'

Charlie nodded.

'You can just go in and say "hello" to her,' Doctor Grey said. 'But you must be very quiet. She is very poorly.'

'Mr Snuggles,' Charlie said, wriggling the soft toy tucked into his arm.

'Is he going to look after her?'

Charlie nodded.

'That's very good,' Doctor Grey said as he stood up. 'I will call again tomorrow morning, but if you have any concerns in the meantime, Nanny, send Billy for me at once. I have left some written instructions for you on the dressing table.'

'Thank you, Doctor.'

As Doctor Grey left, Lizzie opened the bedroom door and she and Charlie tiptoed inside. The curtains were half drawn against the bright sunlight but there was still plenty of light for them to see Mrs Weston lying in the bed. She was lying with her head turned to the left. Quietly, they moved to stand where she might be able to see them. It seemed that she could, for she smiled lopsidedly when she saw Charlie. Solemnly, he placed Mr Snuggles beside her on the pillow.

'Mr Snuggles. Look after you,' he said.

Mrs Weston's mouth moved and she made a sound but no one could guess what she was trying to say.

'We'll leave you to rest now,' Lizzie said softly, 'but Charlie wanted to see you.'

Again, an unintelligible sound but, although her right arm lay motionless on top of the bed covers, she raised her left arm and wriggled her fingers in a wave.

It was arranged that Kitty would stay with the housekeeper until after Charlie had gone to bed and then Lizzie would sleep in an easy chair at the side of Mrs Weston's bed. Kitty would get Charlie ready for school in the morning and then take over in the sickroom while Lizzie snatched a few hours of proper sleep in her bed.

The following days were critical. Mrs Weston was in a deep sleep for much of the time, but Doctor Grey was pleased. 'It's the best thing for her,' he told Lizzie. They were speaking quietly outside the bedroom door. Doctor Grey had warned that everyone should be careful what they said in the room. 'We're not sure whether patients can hear and understand what is being said, even when they appear to be unconscious, so it's best to be careful. I can't detect that she has had a further seizure, but it will still take a long time for her to recover and she might never regain the full use of her limbs or her speech.' He paused and then asked, 'What will happen to her?'

'I honestly don't know,' Lizzie said, 'but I can't imagine that Mr and Mrs Spendlove will see her go into the workhouse.'

'I sincerely hope not. They're grim places.' He paused and then added, 'I must be going. I have other patients in the village to see. I will call again tomorrow, but be sure to call me if you need me.'

Downstairs he was greeted in the hall by Mr Spendlove and his butler, both anxious to know any news.

'She's holding her own at the moment,' was all the doctor could say.

Roland had written at once to tell his brother, and five days after Mrs Weston had fallen ill, having somehow wangled leave, James came home. He sat by the house-keeper's bed holding her hand and talking quietly to her. He insisted on taking turns with Kitty and Lizzie to sit with her, so that both women could get some proper rest.

On the second day, Mrs Weston stirred and seemed to recognize James. She smiled again lopsidedly and squeezed his hand but still, she could not speak. Only gurgling sounds came out. It was during the third night that Lizzie heard a gentle tap on her bedroom door. Pulling on her dressing gown, she opened the door to find James standing there.

'Lizzie, you'd better come. I – I think she's gone in her sleep.'

At once Lizzie tightened the belt on her dressing gown, closed the door behind her and followed James. As she approached the bed, she was holding her breath. In the light from the candles, Mrs Weston appeared to be sleeping, but when Lizzie felt for her pulse, she couldn't find one. Then she fetched a hand mirror from the dressing table and held it in front of the woman's face. She wasn't breathing.

'Shall I fetch the doctor?' James whispered. 'I can go. There's no need to wake anyone else.'

'Perhaps you should, though I think you're right. I'm sure she's gone.'

James hurried away and Lizzie settled herself in the chair at the side of the bed. Although there was nothing else she could do for the housekeeper, she wasn't going to leave her. But what dreadful news awaited the rest of the household in the morning, and however was she to explain it to Charlie?

Thirty-two

It was just under an hour before James returned with Doctor Grey who, sadly, confirmed their suspicions. Mrs Weston had passed away in her sleep.

'Perhaps it's the kindest thing for her,' the doctor said. 'She might have been partially paralysed for the rest of her life.'

'My brother would have made sure she was properly cared for,' James said. 'He's always said he would never see any of his employees in the workhouse and I know he means it.'

Doctor Grey nodded his approval. 'That's good to hear. Of course, families look after their own when they can, but sometimes it's just not possible, especially in a case like this where we don't even know if she has any relatives.'

It was so hard for both James and Lizzie to impart the sad news the following morning.

'I'll tell Roland and Cecily,' James said, 'and everyone else, but I'll have to leave you to tell Charlie. I just wouldn't know where to begin.'

'I'm not sure I do,' Lizzie murmured, as she picked up Mr Snuggles from the bed. 'But I must do it straight away when he wakes up.'

'Shall you keep him off school?'

'I'll see how he copes with the news. I don't want to

keep him at home, but I'll go with him to school and tell Mr Holland what has happened.'

As she helped him to wash and dress, Lizzie explained with a sad smile, 'Mrs Weston was so very poorly that she passed away in the night. But she is at peace now and out of pain. We must remember that.'

'Will she go to Heaven?' Charlie asked, his brown eyes anxious.

'Most definitely. If anyone deserves a place there, it's Mrs Weston.'

'That's all right, then.'

Lizzie was surprised how well Charlie had taken the news but it wasn't until she had spoken to Josiah that she understood why.

'One of his classmates, Rosie, lost her grandmother a couple of weeks ago. Poor child was crying such a lot in class that I asked the vicar if he would come in and talk to all the children. He was wonderful. He explained all about life and death and how we all go to Heaven when we die. It definitely helped Rosie and I expect Charlie has remembered it.'

'Then I must thank you too. It's certainly made things easier for me and explains why Charlie took the news so well.'

The rest of the household was shocked and Mrs Graves was inconsolable.

'We've been friends and work colleagues since we both came to work here at about the same time. Neither of us had any family. We both came from orphanages, though not the same one, and we became like family to one another. If only she'd lived, I'd have looked after her and been glad to do it.'

Lizzie put her arms round the distressed cook. 'We'd all have taken care of her, but it wasn't to be. At least she's at peace now. I don't think she'd have liked to have been an invalid, do you?'

'No, no, she wouldn't. You're right about that, Nanny, but, oh, I'll miss her so much.'

'We all will. She was a lovely person and ran this household so perfectly.'

The funeral was arranged within four days so that James could attend before he had to leave. Everyone from the Manor would attend and many of the villagers too. They had not known Mrs Weston well, but they were all familiar with her from her regular attendance at church. She was to be buried in a shady corner of the churchyard.

Lizzie had debated for a long time about whether or not Charlie should attend the funeral. When she had still not decided by the evening before, she tapped on the door of the drawing room just after dinner, completely forgetting that she should have asked Mr Bennett first.

'I'm sorry to bother you,' she said apologetically to the three family members gathered there. 'But I would so much appreciate your thoughts on whether or not I should take Charlie to the funeral tomorrow.'

James stood up and came towards her. 'Come and sit down, Lizzie, and we'll discuss it,' he said, putting his hand under her elbow.

'Oh no, Master James, I couldn't . . .'

Hearing James's use of Lizzie's Christian name, Roland and Cecily exchanged glances, but all Roland said was, 'Yes, please do. You are quite right to come to see us. Has anything been said to Charlie?'

Lizzie shook her head as she took a chair. 'No, sir. I didn't want to broach the subject until I knew how you felt.'

'Do you think he would behave well?' Cecily asked. 'I mean, we don't want him to get – well – very upset,

265

do we?' They all knew she was thinking back to the tantrum he had displayed when James had left just after Christmas.

'May I make a suggestion?' James said. 'If I sit with Charlie and Lizzie in the pew behind you two, I think he'd be all right and if he isn't, I can soon carry him outside.'

'That sounds like a sensible suggestion,' Roland said.

'Right, that's settled, then,' James said, standing up. 'And now, I'll come back with you, Lizzie, and we can tell him together. Then you can get him ready for bed and I'll read him a story.'

As the two of them left the room, Roland and Cecily were left staring at the door.

'Did you notice?' Cecily said softly, 'that James calls her "Lizzie"?'

'Yes, I did, and I've been aware for some time now of how he looks at her.'

'Of course, she is still a servant in our household despite her birth. And then there is the scandal surrounding her family. If James wants to marry her, it would cause a lot of gossip in the neighbourhood.'

'I know. But I want my brother to marry for love – just as I did. Perhaps my reason is also quite selfish. It would keep her here with Charlie longer than she otherwise might stay.'

'Oh Roland!' Cecily pretended to be shocked, but her eyes were twinkling.

'And there's something else I've been thinking about too. Not yet, of course, it's far too soon – we must leave a respectful gap – but we will need to get another house-keeper in due course and I just wondered . . .'

'If Nanny would do it,' Cecily finished for him. When he nodded, Cecily went on as if thinking aloud. 'I'm sure she would be capable and she's not needed to be Charlie's full-time nanny now, is she?'

'Kitty could continue as nursery maid. That's all he'd need if he continues to progress as he has done.'

'But her training was to be a nanny. Perhaps she wouldn't want to become a housekeeper. And what about when you send Charlie to boarding school? That's if you do.'

Roland shook his head. 'I don't think that would be a good idea in his case. He has improved beyond my wildest hopes and I wouldn't want all that to be undone. No, I think we should keep him at home. Get the best education we can for him here and I can begin to teach him all he needs to know about running the estate and the mine.'

'Perhaps we could be a little crafty,' Cecily said. Roland glanced at her, reflecting on the recent change he had seen in his wife. Not only had Charlie improved beyond what they had dared to hope, but Cecily too was so much better in health and temperament. She didn't seem so anxious now. Perhaps, as well as Charlie's obvious improvement, standing up to her imperious mother had given her a new self-confidence.

'Go on,' he prompted.

'We-ell,' she said slowly, 'we could ask Nanny if she would help out in a small way with the duties of house-keeper. We can say – quite truthfully – that we feel we don't want to replace Mrs Weston with unseemly haste. It would give everyone time to accept a new regime and to see if Nanny herself would take to the role in a more permanent capacity.'

'And it would keep her here for Charlie.'

'Exactly.'

'Cecily Spendlove! I never knew you could be so

devious. And now I'll suggest something too. Shall we ask James what he thinks of that idea?'

Despite the sadness that still pervaded the house, Cecily laughed. 'Oh Roland, yes. Do let's.'

The day of the funeral was overcast and threatened rain, which seemed fitting to the sorrow of the day. Charlie, though solemn-faced, behaved impeccably sitting between Lizzie and James during the service and standing at the graveside afterwards. He even threw a flower picked from the garden at the Manor into the grave and then walked all the way back holding Lizzie's hand on one side and James's on the other.

Roland and Cecily, riding in the carriage driven by Joe, invited Mrs Graves to ride with them. 'And before you refuse, Cook, we know how upset you are. Let's not stand on ceremony today of all days.'

'If you're sure, sir, then I'd be very grateful. It's a long way back. Thank you.'

Despite her distress, Mrs Graves had prepared a cold buffet to be laid out in the dining room for the three members of the family and also in the servants' hall for the staff. On the drive back home, Roland said, 'Let's just have it all in the servants' hall, Mrs Graves. We'll come down and join you. We should all stay together today.'

'That's kind of you, sir, but then you've always been thoughtful and generous employers. We all say so.'

'We have reason to be. You have all been so devoted to us in our troubles with Charlie.'

'We always did our best, sir, but it wasn't until this nanny came that he started to get better. She's an angel sent by God to a troubled little boy. I thank Him every night in my prayers for sending her to us. And her with

268

such troubles of her own, too. I just dread the day when she might leave us.'

Roland said nothing, but he and his wife exchanged a conspiratorial glance.

Life settled back into its normal routine. Mrs Weston was sorely missed but her way of running the household was well known to all of them. The maids knew their duties and carried on as the housekeeper would have wished. It was just that there was no one at the helm.

'You know, Nanny,' Mrs Graves said one morning as they sat together over a cup of coffee. 'I don't really want another stranger coming in to reorganize everything. I was wondering how you would feel about me suggesting to the master that you should take Mrs Weston's place.'

Lizzie blinked. 'Me? But I'm not trained as a housekeeper.'

Mrs Graves chuckled. 'Neither was Mrs Weston. She grew into it. As I did in the role of cook.' Her eyes took on a faraway look as she remembered. 'We both came here as youngsters, both from orphanages. Me as scullery maid and Florence as laundry maid.' She smiled wryly. 'The lowliest positions in the servants' ranks. We shared a bedroom right up in the attic then that's not even used now. But we worked hard and progressed. I learned all I could from the cook. She was a nice woman. She was very strict, though, and could be quite sharp and demanding, but she was fair in sharing all her secrets with me. She wasn't possessive of her knowledge like I've heard some cooks can be. And Florence progressed too. She rose through the ranks of the maids until she was ready to take over from the housekeeper when she retired and went to live with her sister in Cornwall.'

'What happened to the cook?' Lizzie asked.

'The Spendloves are good people. Of course, it was

Mr Roland's parents in charge then, but they gave the cook a cottage in the village where she lived rent free. She died a few years ago, but I'm hoping that's what they'll do for me when my time comes. So, what do you think? Master Charlie won't need you much longer as a nanny and if they decide to send him to boarding school – which, frankly, I hope they won't, but it's nothing to do with me – you wouldn't be needed here at all. And . . .' She paused and, with a sheepish smile, added, 'And I don't want you to leave. None of the staff do. I'm sure we could do it between us.'

'But would the master and mistress agree, d'you think?'

'They'd be daft not to.'

'But what about Mr Bennett? Would he be happy with such an arrangement?'

Mrs Graves's smile widened. 'It was him that suggested it.'

Lizzie's mouth dropped open. 'Really?'

The cook nodded. 'Him and Florence always got on so well and he can't bear the idea of someone new coming in and throwing her weight about. If the butler and housekeeper don't get on, it upsets the whole feel of the household.' Lizzie's background was hardly ever spoken of, but now Mrs Graves said tentatively, 'But I expect you know that.'

Lizzie gave a deep sigh. 'There was a time when I was about twelve when we had a new housekeeper and she and the butler were at daggers drawn. You're right, it affected everyone. Even me and – my brother. She didn't stay long, thank goodness, and we got a very nice woman after that. She stayed right until things all went wrong. I think she's still there, as far as I know, working for the people who bought the estate.'

'You must miss the life you had,' Mrs Graves said gently.

'To be honest and to my surprise, I don't. It was all very – superficial. Parties and balls with only one intention. Finding a husband.'

There were only the two of them sitting at the kitchen table and Lizzie decided to confide in the cook.

'I was engaged at the time the scandal broke and Oliver asked me to release him from our engagement. I was hurt at the time, but now I'm glad it happened. I soon realized that I wasn't in love with him.'

Mrs Graves said nothing, though she too had been aware of the looks that sometimes passed between Master James and the nanny. If only . . . she thought, but her attention was drawn back to what Lizzie was saying.

'I'm very happy here and no, I don't want to leave either. You've all become my family. But you're right, Charlie won't need me for much longer and Kitty is quite capable of looking after him even now.'

Mrs Graves chuckled. 'I don't think Master Charlie would agree.'

Lizzie smiled fondly. 'Probably not.' And deep in her heart, she admitted that there was another person she'd miss so very much: James.

'So, shall I have a word with the mistress?' Mrs Graves asked.

'Yes, it would be better coming from you.'

'Right, then,' she said, standing up. 'No time like the present. I've half an hour to spare before I need to prepare luncheon, so I'll ask Mr Bennett to see if the mistress is free.'

Ten minutes later, Mrs Graves was standing in front of her master and mistress in the morning room as they were finishing their own morning coffee.

'Is there a problem with the menus for the week, Mrs Graves?' Cecily said. 'I thought we sorted all that out on Monday as usual.'

271

'No, ma'am, everything is fine. It's just – it's just . . .' She bit her lip and then the words came out in a rush. 'About the position of housekeeper.'

'Ah, yes, that,' Roland said with a sigh. 'We've been discussing that too. Have you any suggestions?'

The cook took a deep breath. 'As a matter of fact, yes. I wondered if you'd consider Nanny taking the position. Master Charlie soon won't need her so much as a full-time nanny and me and Mr Bennett could advise her. The truth is, sir, we don't want her to leave. We all love her, both for what she's done for Master Charlie and for who she is. She's such a lovely, caring young woman.'

'But would she want to? She's trained as a nanny.'

'I think so, sir. She doesn't want to leave here either. She says we've become her family.'

'You've spoken to her about it?'

The colour flooded Mrs Graves's face. 'I didn't think it was any use putting the suggestion to you, sir, if she wasn't agreeable. So, yes, I have. I'm sorry if I've stepped out of line.'

'You haven't, Mrs Graves.' Roland smiled. 'In fact, my wife and I had come up with the same idea. We all know how a new member of staff can upset the equilibrium of a household.' He grimaced. 'We experienced that with the succession of nannies, didn't we?'

'We did indeed, sir,' Mrs Graves said with feeling.

'So, we'll have a word with Nanny ourselves and, if she agrees, we'll ease her into the position gradually.'

Mrs Graves smiled genuinely for the first time since her old friend had died. 'I think it's what Mrs Weston would have wanted too, sir. And it's certainly what Master Charlie will want.'

'There's no doubting that, Mrs Graves. Not for a minute.'

Thirty-three

So a new regime was established, though the routine was very little different in practice. With advice from both Mrs Graves and Mr Bennett, Lizzie made sure she ran the household just as Mrs Weston had done. The only person she needed to explain things to was Charlie. He was growing so rapidly now that she no longer took him onto her lap but sat with him in front of the nursery fire.

'Not going away?' he said anxiously.

'No, but Kitty will look after you more.'

He frowned and then pointed to the bedroom next to his own. 'Still sleep there?'

'Yes, I think so. For a while anyway.'

Out of respect for the former housekeeper and also to stay nearer Charlie at night, Lizzie had decided not to move into the housekeeper's bedroom yet, although she was now using Mrs Weston's sitting room downstairs where Mr Bennett and Mrs Graves often joined her for a nightcap. It was a tradition they all wanted to keep.

'Come for bath time?'

'Yes, I'll come and help with that. We have fun, don't we, with your boats?' Even though he was growing, he still liked to be a little boy at bath time and play with his boats.

Charlie nodded.

*

When James next came to stay for a few nights, he was delighted to hear about the new arrangement which had been implemented.

'It's a brilliant idea, Lizzie,' he said when he visited the nursery. 'Charlie still needs you to be here but not perhaps as a nanny for much longer. Do you mind, though? Do you feel as if all your training has gone to waste?'

'Not really. I am very happy here. I don't want to leave and besides, like you say, Charlie still needs me a little.'

'I think he always will,' James said quietly. They were standing together on the terrace watching Charlie ride his pony. Billy was close by, but the young boy no longer needed to be led around the lawn.

'He's riding quite well now, isn't he?' James remarked. 'He sits well.'

'Your brother spends quite a bit of time with him. He's been teaching him.'

'Do you ride, Lizzie?'

'I – used to.'

'Then we must go out riding together.'

Lizzie was tempted by his invitation. She would so love to go riding with him, but she was obliged to say softly, 'You know that wouldn't be possible, Master James, but I thank you for offering.'

They looked at each other and his gaze softened. 'Maybe one day, Lizzie. Maybe one day.'

Life moved on and eventually, Lizzie moved into Mrs Weston's old bedroom and also had use of the house-keeper's sitting room on the ground floor. Kitty still stayed in the bedroom that previously had been designated as the nanny's bedroom and, for the time being, the room next to Charlie's was no longer used.

When the school reopened for the autumn term in

September 1907, Roland rode down at the end of afternoon lessons. Billy had come to fetch Charlie home in the trap, but it was Mr Holland whom Roland wanted to see.

'We'll go into the schoolhouse, Mr Spendlove. You can tether your horse outside. May I offer you a drink? Tea, coffee or something stronger? A glass of sherry perhaps, now that my working day is finished?'

'That would be most acceptable. Thank you.'

When they were both seated in the window, Roland said, 'I would like your advice about Charlie and I want you to be completely honest with me. Brutally so, if necessary. Normally, I would have sent my son to boarding school this month, now that he has just turned eight, but in Charlie's case I don't think it would be the best thing for him.'

'Neither do I. Considering how he once was and the problems he had, he is doing remarkably well, Mr Spendlove, but he will never be academic.'

'Not even grammar-school material?'

'I'm afraid not, but he is very gifted in one way. He can draw and paint well beyond his years. Miss Ingham has been bringing his efforts to show me for some time.'

'Although I have seen his work, I must admit I didn't realize how good it was. How very remiss of me. How can I help to foster his talent?'

'I can only take him so far, but there are young artists who tutor on the side, so to speak, to earn money to fund their ambitions. You might find one who would be prepared to travel here every so often to help Charlie. And, of course, there is the Sheffield School of Art. Perhaps a student from there might be willing to help. In time, Charlie might be good enough to go there himself and be able to board in the week, rather like Luke does at

Chesterfield Grammar School. It wouldn't be as harsh as being sent to boarding school at eight years old.'

'Mr Holland, you have given me hope for his future.'

'Surely his future is to run the estate and the mine you own, isn't it?'

'Yes, it is and I'm sure he will eventually, but I am not planning on dying just yet and I'd like him to have something that is his own. To become an artist would be ideal. It is something he could always do.'

'It is indeed.'

Roland stood up and held out his hand. 'Thank you, Mr Holland, not only for your advice today, but for all that you have done to help Charlie.'

Back at the Manor, Roland sent for Lizzie. 'I've been to see Mr Holland to ask his advice about Charlie's future. He tells me he is quite gifted at drawing and painting. I would like to encourage that and perhaps find someone who can give him some tuition. What do you think?'

'It's a wonderful idea. I think he's very good, but then I'm biased.' She laughed. 'I used to do watercolour paintings years ago as part of a young lady's upbringing, but they were just that. Very watery. I was always better at sewing and embroidery, which has served me very well, both as a nanny and now helping the young girls at the school too.'

Lizzie still went down to the school one afternoon a week to teach the girls needlework.

'I want you to know how very pleased both Cecily and I are with your work as housekeeper. With no disrespect to Mrs Weston, we haven't really noticed any difference.'

'Thank you, sir. With the help of both Mr Bennett and Mrs Graves, I am trying to run everything just as Mrs Weston did.'

Roland nodded. 'Then you're obviously succeeding and, possibly even more importantly, you're still here for Charlie. And speaking again of Charlie, perhaps you'd like to bring him down after afternoon tea with some of his artistic work to show us. If I think it appropriate, I will make some enquiries.'

When Charlie and Lizzie arrived in the drawing room just prior to dinner, both Roland and Cecily were stunned by their son's artistic abilities.

'These are magnificent, Charlie. Just look at this, Cecily. That's Dandy to a T and he's even got a likeness for Billy. And this one of the house. He's even got the perspective accurate. Oh, how I wish I'd known before.'

Quietly Lizzie said, 'I don't think he'd have been ready any earlier, sir. Now is just the right time.'

With his eyes still on his son's drawings and paintings, Roland murmured abstractedly, 'Yes, you're probably right, Nanny.'

'Don't we call her "Mrs Ingham" now she's our house-keeper?' Cecily laughed.

'Oh, yes, I was forgetting. Sorry.'

But it was Charlie who took hold of Lizzie's hand and said firmly, 'Still Nanny.'

Roland glanced down at his son and smiled. 'Yes, you're right, Charlie. She's still Nanny too, so is that what we should call her?'

Charlie nodded his head vigorously and the three adults laughed together.

Roland interviewed three students from the Sheffield School of Art and the one who appeared to be the most suitable, mainly because Charlie liked him, said he could cycle the distance from the outskirts of the city, where he still lived with his parents, as long as he didn't have to bring any art materials.

Henry Croft was a young man of twenty, in his second year at the art school. He had fair curly hair, bright blue eyes and a beaming smile.

'I will supply everything you need,' Roland said, 'if you give me a list and, if you wish to stay overnight at any time, we can make the room next to Charlie's bedroom available for you. You will also have full use of the schoolroom and have your meals with Charlie.'

'That's very kind of you, sir. I might very well take you up on that offer, especially when the weather is bad. Although I love cycling, even eight or nine miles in heavy rain isn't pleasant. I don't have classes on a Friday so I could come over in the morning and spend Friday afternoon and maybe Saturday morning with Charlie, if that would be suitable.'

'That would fit in very nicely. Mr Holland – the school teacher – said Friday afternoon would be the best. He is willing to change the afternoon the children do art work to a Friday to coincide with our arrangements. He doesn't want Charlie to miss story time, which is an important part of their English lessons. Charlie joins in the football or cricket games on the village playing field on Saturday afternoons. I wouldn't want him to miss that. It's good exercise and teaches him to be a member of a team.'

'That sounds ideal, then, Mr Spendlove. I have already spoken to my tutors at the college and they have given me some tips on how to encourage a boy of Charlie's age and, perhaps, a little later on, you wouldn't mind me taking some of Charlie's work to show them. They're all very keen on children being taught correctly from a young age.'

'I wouldn't mind at all.'

And so Henry Croft became an important part of the household. Clara, who was a similar age, thought he was the most handsome young man she'd ever seen and always contrived to be the one to deliver the meals to the school-room on Fridays and Saturdays.

'Fancy starving in a garret with a struggling artist, do you, Clara?' Mrs Graves teased. But Clara would not be put off, especially when there were wedding bells for someone else in the air.

'Mr Bennett,' Billy said politely to the butler one Saturday afternoon after he had fetched Charlie from the football game. 'Would you be kind enough to ask the master if Kitty and I could see him, please?'

Mr Bennett guessed what this could be about. He didn't really approve of the young servants being allowed to walk out together, but then this had been an unusual household ever since Charlie's birth. He recognized that the master and mistress felt they owed a debt of gratitude to both Kitty and Billy for their devotion to Charlie. So the butler swallowed his own rigid ideas on what the household's rules should be and inclined his head. A little later he told Billy that the master would see them both in his study after dinner.

As they waited outside the door, hand in hand, Kitty whispered, 'My knees are trembling.'

'Mine too,' Billy said softly as Mr Bennett opened the door to the study and ushered them inside.

'Hello, you two. Come in and sit down. How can I help?'

Nervously, they sat on chairs opposite Roland. Billy took a deep breath. 'We would like to get married, sir, but we would so like to stay on here at the Manor.'

Roland was smiling. 'Well, I would hope so, indeed.

279

Charlie would be devastated if either of you left.' Then his expression sobered. 'I am aware that this has been an unusual household. Followers are not normally allowed, but you both have played such an important part in Charlie's life – especially you, Kitty, through the most difficult times – that I bent the rules. I knew I could trust you both and you have never betrayed that trust. So, have you thought about where you might live?'

'Dad says we could live with him over the stables, if you were agreeable.'

'I have a better suggestion than that. One of my cottages in the village – the one next to the schoolhouse – is to be vacated soon. You could have that, if you like. I'd have to charge you a small rental so that it's not unfair on my other tenants.'

Billy and Kitty glanced at each other. They could hardly believe their good fortune. 'That would be wonderful, sir. Thank you.'

'When were you thinking of getting married?'

Now Kitty spoke up. 'We thought a June wedding next year would be nice, sir.'

'I'll talk to Mrs Spendlove about holding the reception here for you.'

Now Kitty was pink with pleasure. 'Oh sir. How kind that would be. There wouldn't be many guests. Just Billy's dad and my parents, my sister and two brothers and, of course, the staff here.'

'You'd have a few friends from the village, wouldn't you?'

Billy and Kitty glanced at each other again. 'Our best friends are here, sir,' Billy said. 'In this household.'

Roland found his simple words quite moving and silently vowed to give the young couple a grand wedding they would never forget. He knew Cecily would agree.

Thirty-four

The wedding was set for the first Saturday in June 1908 and great excitement rippled through the Manor for months beforehand. Billy and Kitty were overwhelmed when Roland told them that he would be delighted if they would accept his offer for the reception to be held in the ballroom at the Manor – a huge room that had not been used in recent years – and added that they were to invite as many guests as they liked. 'I'm sure we could accommodate the whole village if needs be,' he said, with a smile.

'How generous they are,' Kitty and Billy said time and again.

'It's no more than you deserve,' Mrs Graves said firmly. 'You have been – and still are – loyal members of the staff here and you've helped more than anyone else with Master Charlie, apart from Nanny of course. Now, you must both let me know what you would like for the wedding breakfast, because it looks like I'm going to be busy.' But she was smiling as she said it. Cook liked nothing better than showing off her skills.

The weeks leading up to the Big Day, as everyone referred to it, were hectic for everyone.

'Isn't it sad,' Mrs Graves said with a tear, 'that Mrs Weston is missing this? She'd have loved it.'

'She would,' Lizzie said. 'I just hope I am doing her justice.'

'Oh, you are, Nanny. You're doing a grand job.'

'Mrs Spendlove is being most helpful with advice and telling me what she wants doing. And did you know, she's getting her own dressmaker to make Kitty's dress and one for Clara as bridesmaid?'

'I think the mistress is enjoying it. She's been so much better in health recently too, hasn't she?' Mrs Graves said. 'And Master Charlie is loving all the excitement, though I think he's a little worried that Kitty won't be sleeping in the room near him anymore.'

'I've been thinking about that too,' Lizzie said. 'I'm not going to say anything yet – just see how it goes. I could always move into the room Kitty's been using, but only if he began to get really distressed.'

'Normally, he would have been away at boarding school by now,' Mrs Graves remarked.

Lizzie nodded. 'I know and this is a good opportunity to take another step towards him becoming more independent of a nanny or a nursery maid – if it would work. Kitty will still be here in the daytime, of course.'

'You can but try. The door to the nursery quarters is no longer locked. He'd be able to trot along to your room if he really needed you in the night. Oh, and by the way . . .' Mrs Graves beamed. 'Have you heard that Master James has got leave to be here for the wedding?' She chuckled. 'He and his mother have both been invited.'

'That's lovely,' Lizzie said, trying to keep her voice steady and to quieten the sudden rapid increase in her heartbeat. 'What about the mistress's parents?'

Mrs Graves pulled a face. 'I expect they'll have to be invited or it would look odd, but whether or not they'll come is a different matter.'

*

'What a beautiful day for a wedding,' Lizzie declared as she drew back the curtains in Charlie's bedroom on the June morning. 'Up you get, Charlie. We've so much to do.'

The hours passed in a flurry of activity throughout the Manor, but by eleven-thirty everyone was ready to walk to the church for the service at noon. Joe drove the master and mistress and Mrs Spendlove senior down in the specially decorated carriage and Mrs Graves had been promised a ride back after the service. Kitty, of course, had spent the night at her parents' house in the village and Billy walked down with his father and friends from the Manor.

'I wonder if Kitty's as nervous as I am,' he confided to Lizzie as she walked beside Charlie and James, who had elected to walk with the staff rather than ride in the carriage.

James chuckled. 'You're not afraid she's not going to turn up, are you?'

At that, Billy grinned. 'No, it's not that. It's just that I'm not used to being the centre of attention in front of the whole village. Neither of us are.'

'But they're all your family and friends, Billy,' Lizzie said. 'They'll be there because they all love you both.'

'Have you got your speech ready?' James asked.

Billy groaned. 'Oh, don't remind me about that. I'm not going to say a lot. Just thank both our parents and the master and mistress, of course, and sit down quick.'

'Will Joe say much? He's acting as your best man, isn't he?'

'I'm hoping not. I think he's as nervous as me.'

The church was full. As Roland had predicted, the whole village was there. They couldn't miss seeing one of their own being given such a grand wedding and to be invited to the Manor afterwards for a sumptuous feast was something to be relished and remembered for ever. Even Mr Holland had taken his best suit out of mothballs and was sitting at the back of the church. As Roland entered he spotted the schoolmaster, his walking stick propped against the pew. As he passed him, Roland put his hand on the man's shoulder and bent to whisper, 'We'd be delighted to take you to the Manor in the carriage after the service, Mr Holland, and see that you are taken home later.'

Josiah glanced up. 'Thank you, sir. That's most kind of you.'

As everyone settled to await the bride, the organist played softly until given the signal that Kitty had arrived at the church door with her father and her bridesmaid, Clara. Kitty was a pretty girl, but today she looked beautiful and there were gasps of admiration as she walked down the aisle on Bob's arm. Billy, rather red-faced, was nevertheless grinning as he watched her moving towards him. His nerves fell away. This was the day they had both waited for, for so long. The service went smoothly and soon they were all on their way back to the Manor, the bridal pair choosing to walk at the head of the procession. As they and their guests flooded into the ballroom, everyone looked about them in amazement. The room had been decorated with flowers and ribbons. Trestle tables, covered with pristine tablecloths, were arranged with a top table and three others set at right angles to it. The meal, cooked by Mrs Graves, was served by Mr Bennett and the rest of the servants, apart from Kitty and Clara of course.

'I tried to persuade the staff to allow me to bring in outsiders to serve, but none of them would hear of it,' Roland told James and his mother, who, although not on

284

the top table, were seated at the head of one of the three tables opposite each other. 'They insisted that they should serve Kitty and Billy themselves. They are going to sit at the end of these tables, though, when everyone is served.'

Winifred Spendlove laughed. 'Unusual, my dear, but a very good idea.'

Roland chuckled. 'Since when has anything been "usual" in this house, Mama?'

Cecily, sitting beside her husband, smiled too. 'My mother – had she come – would certainly not have approved.'

Cecily's parents had politely declined the invitation. Though secretly Lewis would have loved to have been there, he didn't want to suffer the weeks of disapproval from his wife that would inevitably have followed.

When everyone had finished eating, Bob Preston stood up to make a short father-of-the-bride speech, followed by Billy, who, as he had promised, kept it short and then it was Joe's turn as best man. He, too, didn't waste any words. He did not tell embarrassing tales about his son or Kitty, but at the end he added, 'There is just one more thing I would like to say and this is with the blessing of both Kitty and Billy. As well as the usual toast to the bride and groom, which it is my pleasure and honour to propose, I would just like to make a very special toast to Master Charlie. We are all humbly grateful for his recovery from what was a very difficult time for him, his parents and indeed for all of us who care for this family. And we give thanks for the remarkable young woman who came into our midst and made it all possible. Please raise your glasses to the bride and groom and to Master Charlie and Miss Lizzie.'

As everyone toasted them, Lizzie felt herself blushing and she dropped her head. James, who was sitting one place away from her, reached in front of Charlie and grasped her hand. It was a gesture that did not go unnoticed by those sitting nearby. And then, to everyone's surprise and delight, Charlie stood up and said loudly and clearly, 'Thank you,' to which there was spontaneous applause.

And then came the moment for the triumphal entry of the magnificent cake which Mrs Graves had begun preparing the moment she heard about the wedding arrangements.

If the guests had thought the room and the meal had been wonderful, then the cake was Cook's pièce de résistance. Mrs Graves was pink with pleasure as Kitty and Billy cut the cake together and slices were passed around.

It had been a wonderful day and when Kitty and Billy were driven to their new home in a flower-decorated carriage, the rest of the villagers followed on foot. Even Josiah insisted that he could manage the walk if he took his time. Luke offered his former teacher his arm and they walked together, chatting about Luke's progress at the grammar school.

After a day which the whole neighbourhood would always remember, life settled back into a routine that was little altered. Kitty and Billy still worked at the Manor and came every day. Charlie continued to attend the village school and to have art lessons on a Friday and Saturday with Henry Croft and no more was discussed about the boy going to boarding school. He still continued to improve slowly and by the time he reached twelve, he was tall and broad-shouldered with curly dark hair and soft brown eyes. It was at this time that Roland began to take him with him around the estate and to see the mine.

James visited as often as his duties in the army allowed

and he and Lizzie grew closer. Now that Charlie did not need to be with Lizzie every minute of the day, James was able to have her to himself occasionally. They took long walks together and spent many hours chatting in the evenings. One morning, just after Christmas in 1911, James entered his brother's study and closed the door.

'May I have a word with you, Roland?'

'Of course. Shall I send for coffee?'

'That would be nice. Thank you.'

When Bennett had served them both and left the room, Roland said, 'Now, how can I help?'

James took a deep breath. 'You know that I have to seek the permission of my commanding officer to get married.'

'I do. Go on.'

'Well, I have received his blessing, but now I need yours.'

'Do you? Why?'

'This may come as a surprise to you because it is Lizzie to whom I wish to propose.'

Roland smiled. 'That's hardly a surprise, James.'

James blinked. 'It isn't?'

'Anyone with eyes in their head must have seen the growing closeness between you. My only comment is that I wonder why it's not happened before now.'

'Charlie has needed her and the household has too after the sudden death of poor Mrs Weston.'

'But now you feel we could all manage without her?'

'I – am hoping so.'

'Where would you live?'

'That's a problem we'll have to solve. I don't want her to follow me wherever I go. Some of the accommodation, even for officers' wives, is pretty dire, but I can't see any other way.'

'There is, if you would both agree to it.' James frowned as Roland went on. 'This is a big house and there are a lot of rooms that are hardly ever used, especially at the west end of the building. We could have some alterations done quite easily to provide you and Lizzie with your own accommodation. There's even room enough for you to have your own servants if you wished to live entirely separately.'

'That's incredibly generous of you, Roland, but I don't think my army pay would run to the employment of servants.'

Now Roland laughed out loud. 'Don't tell me you have forgotten the arrangement we made when Father died?'

'No, to be honest, I don't recall. It was so long ago now.'

'Do you really think our father would have left the entire estate and the mine to me without providing for you too?'

'Well, I – er – just presumed that you, being the eldest, would inherit everything. I've never minded,' he added hurriedly. 'It's the way of the world.'

'Not in our world, James. We're not, and never were, aristocracy. Father left it so that once all the expenses for the running of the estate and the mine had been paid, any profit was to be used to pay an annuity for Mama and the rest was to be divided equally between us. So, according to his wishes, I have been paying an annual sum into an account he set up in your name. I'm sorry, James, I thought you knew all about it. You must have been receiving regular bank statements?'

James laughed. 'I'm not very good with paperwork, Roland. I just gave it all to Mama and asked her to look after it.'

Roland fished in a drawer and drew out a folder. 'I

have a copy sent to me because it's involved in the estate's accounts.' He opened it up and pushed it across the desk towards his brother. 'Here's what you're worth.'

James's mouth dropped open as he read the figure. He looked up at Roland and then dropped his gaze again. 'Good Lord. I could buy several houses with this.'

'But there's no need. By rights – and it's in Father's will too – you own half of this house. Mother could have continued to live here too but she preferred to stay where they'd retired to. She'd already made a circle of friends there.'

James's mouth twitched. 'Indeed she has. She's never at home for long, not even when I'm visiting.'

'So you see, you're entitled to live here and so is your wife and family. And besides, we'd like it. There's something else I think I should say too. Although Charlie is much improved, far more than we had ever dared to hope, I don't know yet whether or not he will be able to run everything. He may need your help and guidance in the years to come.'

'If I outlive you, of course, but you must also remember that army life is precarious. If we were to be involved in a war . . .'

'Is that likely?'

'Not that I know of at present, but alliances among the European countries can make things volatile. I understand that we have a longstanding pledge to go to Belgium's aid if it were ever threatened.'

Roland shrugged. 'I really wouldn't know, politics and international affairs have never interested me much. I just concentrate on looking after my own little corner of the world.'

'Which you do incredibly well.'

'Just remember that if you feel you'd like to leave the

army there's always a home and a job here for you. I have to admit running everything sometimes gets a little onerous. There are occasions when I'd love to have another person to discuss matters with. Cecily's a very good listener but she doesn't understand what it takes to run both the estate and the mine.'

'So, you have no objections to me proposing to your housekeeper and former nanny?'

'None whatsoever. In fact, I am delighted. And we'll have another wedding here just like we had for Billy and Kitty.'

Thirty-five

'Lizzie, will you take a walk with me down to the lake?'

'Of course, but I must be back here by the time Billy brings Charlie back from school.'

They left the house by the side door and strolled down the lawn. James took her hand and tucked it through his arm. As they reached the edge of the lake, they stood for a moment looking across the stretch of water to the line of trees on the far side. Then James turned and took both her hands into his. Looking down at her he said softly, 'Lizzie, darling Lizzie, you must know that I have fallen in love with you. In fact, I've been in love with you for years. Dare I hope that you feel something for me too?'

Lizzie looked up into his eyes. 'Of course I do. I think I fell in love with you the first moment I saw you.'

He kissed her fingers. 'Then – will you marry me? Please?'

It was the fervent 'please' that was her undoing. Tears flooded down her face. 'Yes, James, I will, but are you sure? I have such a scandalous family history. I don't want to bring disgrace on you or your family.'

James touched her cheek tenderly. 'You are the sweetest, most honest person I know. No one in their right mind could ever blame you for any of the humiliation your family suffered.'

'But . . .'

As his lips sought hers, all doughts were driven from

her mind. For a brief, idyllic moment it was as if they were the only two people in the world and nothing and no one else mattered.

As they walked back towards the house, James told her of his conversation with his brother and the offer Roland had made.

'It sounds sensible,' Lizzie said. 'But I wouldn't see as much of you living here, as if I lived in married quarters, would I?'

'No, but we still have to think of Charlie for a few more years at least. I don't think he's ready for you to leave just yet. And perhaps . . .' He hesitated for a moment at the enormity of what he was about to suggest. It was something he had never envisaged, but his brother had put the idea into his head. 'I should consider leaving the army.'

'Would you really want to do that? It's your whole life.'

James chuckled. 'Not anymore, my darling.' And he bent his head to kiss her again.

'Look, just look.' Mrs Graves pointed out of the kitchen window. 'I told you so. Didn't I tell you, Kitty?'

'Tell me what?' Kitty said, coming to stand beside her. 'Oh my!' she added as she saw James and Lizzie with their arms around one another.

The two women stood watching the couple. 'Well, now, isn't that the best news ever?' Mrs Graves said, beaming. 'Another wedding at the Manor.'

'Is it good news? This means she'll be leaving us. Army wives live in married quarters, don't they?'

'I doubt it. She'd not leave Master Charlie. Not yet. And Master James wouldn't want her to, I'm sure of that.' She turned away from the window. 'They're coming in. Let's not be caught spying on them.'

Kitty laughed. 'They'll know we've seen them. You won't be able to keep that big grin off your face.'

The cook laughed. 'You're right there. I won't.'

'Fancy, Master James marrying the housekeeper. Whatever will folks think?'

'If you think about it, Kitty, she's from a class higher than him and it weren't her fault it all went pear-shaped for her, now was it? Besides, if I know the village folk here, they'll all be delighted. Everyone loves Master James and they all love Miss Lizzie now too.'

Kitty had been quite right. When the couple walked into the kitchen they could see immediately that their secret was out – if it had ever been a secret at all.

Soon, the whole household knew but there was one person whom James and Lizzie agreed they should tell themselves. As she always did, Lizzie went to the nursery to say goodnight to Charlie and to reassure him that she was just along the corridor now that Kitty no longer slept nearby. But tonight, James was with her.

'There's something we want to tell you, old chap,' he said, as the three of them sat in front of the fire. 'Nanny and I are going to get married. Are you happy about that?'

For a moment Charlie was silent, looking from one to the other. Then his gaze rested on Lizzie. 'Are you going away?'

It was James who answered. 'No, your papa has said that we can live here. We'll have our own rooms at the other end of the house. I shall have to be away quite a lot – like I am now – but Nanny will still be here.'

Again there was a silence until Charlie asked, 'Are you getting married here? Like Kitty and Billy?'

'Yes,' James said.

And then Charlie began to smile.

*

'Whatever can you be thinking of, Cecily, to allow this to happen? Your brother-in-law to marry a *servant*?' Mrs Beatrice Moore, on one of her now rare visits, was not slow to voice her disapproval. 'I am most disappointed in Roland. He is not the man I thought he was. When you married I thought you were marrying into a reputable family, one that might, at some stage, be honoured with a title of some sort. I fear that will never happen now.'

'I doubt very much whether it would have anyway, Mama.' Cecily was no longer in thrall to her mother. Alongside Charlie's improvement, Cecily had thrived both mentally and physically. She no longer blamed herself for her son's problems, though she still felt guilt that she had allowed her mother to dictate who should be the boy's first nanny, a decision Cecily now bitterly regretted. Although there was no proof, she believed Nanny Gordon's treatment of the very young child had been the root cause of his problems. But all that was in the past and she vowed never to heed her mother again. Even her father, it seemed, had found a new strength in standing up to his wife's opinions and demands.

'Well, I'm delighted to hear the news, Cecily, my dear,' Lewis said. 'James is a fine young man and she is charming and obviously well bred. I hope we will receive an invitation to the wedding. I, for one, shall attend this time.'

Beatrice gave a loud sniff of disapproval, but said no more.

As plans moved forward for the wedding to be held in the summer of 1912, Cecily said, 'Is there really no member of your family you wish to invite, Lizzie?'

'The only relatives I have are my aunt and uncle, and after their treatment of my mother and me at the time the tragedy happened, I have no wish to invite them.

However, there are two people I would dearly love to ask, if you have no objection.'

'Of course not, Lizzie. Who are they?'

'Mr and Mrs Bellingham, the solicitor and his wife, who were so very good to me.'

'Of course you must invite them and we can arrange for them to stay here at the Manor for a night or two. But is there really no one else? No friends from your childhood?'

Lizzie thought briefly about her former dearest friend, Alexandra. But she too, along with all the rest, had deserted her. Lizzie had no wish to look back into her past. There was no one there who could possibly compete with all her newfound friends here in the Manor and in the village.

'No one,' she said firmly. 'No one at all.'

'So who are you going to ask to be your bridesmaids and who will give you away?'

'I thought I would ask Kitty to be my matron of honour and as for who would give me away . . .' She took a deep breath. 'Who else could possibly do it but Charlie?'

'What an absolutely stupendous idea, darling,' James said. He was home for a short leave and the talk was of little else but the wedding. 'Being tall for his age, he's quite the young man now.'

'Yes, he's as tall as me now, but you don't think he'd be nervous?'

'He'll do it splendidly. I shall be asking Roland to be my best man, so Charlie will be surrounded by family, but more than anything . . .' he touched her cheek tenderly – 'he'll be close to you. Now,' he added, tucking her hand through his arm, 'let's go and look at all the alterations Roland is putting in place for our new home.'

*

The weeks seemed to fly by and soon it was the day of their wedding. Just as for Billy and Kitty, the weather smiled benignly on them and once again, the whole village was invited to attend.

'They all love you just as we do,' James told Lizzie.

'They love the Spendlove family,' she said modestly. 'I suspect they always have done.'

'My father brought us up to care for all our tenants and employees and Roland has followed in his footsteps.'

The arrangements were much the same as they had been for Kitty and Billy, except for one or two minor changes. Charlie, dressed in a morning suit and smiling proudly, escorted Lizzie up the aisle. When asked, 'Who giveth this woman . . .?' he answered clearly and gave her hand to James. Then he moved back to sit beside his mother in the front pew. Roland handed over the ring at the right moment and after the register had been signed, they were walking out of the church as man and wife and there, the biggest surprise of the day awaited them. All the children of the village, dressed in their Sunday best, were lining both sides of the church path and throwing rose petals.

Then, once again, everyone walked to the Manor and entered the ballroom, decorated in the same way as before. After the meal came the speeches and Charlie stood up to speak in loco parentis of Lizzie's father.

Everyone in the room held their breath. How would Charlie manage? As he stood beside her, Lizzie put up her hand and he held it and raised it to his lips just as he had seen James do. Then in a clear and steady voice, he said, 'My dearest Nanny. You do know I planned for Uncle James to marry you so that you would never leave, don't you?'

There was a ripple of surprise around the room, though

not at what he said but at how he was speaking. Many of them had never heard him talk with such clarity or in such long sentences. And then, when they realized exactly what he had said, there was more laughter, the loudest being from James.

'Now you are really one of the family,' Charlie went on, 'and I suppose I should call you "Aunt Lizzie".'

When it was James's turn to speak, he began by saying, 'I never realized I was being manipulated by my nephew but I want everyone to know that I am more than happy to fall in with your plans, Charlie, and to keep this wonderful woman in our midst. Darling Lizzie, today you have made me the happiest man in the world.'

'And me,' Charlie piped up and the entire room burst into laughter again.

It was the most joyful of days and when it came time for James and Lizzie to retire to their new quarters, Charlie went to bed happy in the knowledge that his beloved nanny was only just at the other end of the house.

Thirty-six

In many ways, life at the Manor was little changed. James decided to stay in the army for at least another year.

'I'll put in an application to leave at the end of 1914,' he told Lizzie and his family. 'I'll have served fifteen years by then and leave with the rank of major.'

Lizzie resumed her role as housekeeper and only took time off when James was at home on leave. It was an unusual arrangement but, as Roland had often remarked, 'what's usual about our home?' As long as everyone was happy – and they were – what did it matter what anyone else thought? Not even Beatrice Moore. She visited her daughter less and less, though Lewis now came sometimes on his own, especially if Roland organized a shooting party.

The school-leaving age was twelve, but Josiah was able to allow Charlie to stay on for another two years until he was fourteen. Charlie had grown and flourished and the schoolmaster knew he had played a part in him now being like any other boy of his age. During those last years at the school, Charlie adopted the role that Luke had once held; that of unofficial head boy. He watched over all the children, especially the little ones. Although there was now nothing to fear from the schoolmaster as long as they behaved, starting school was still an ordeal for some of them. In the July of 1913 when Charlie finally left the school, Josiah offered to give him private tuition on two nights a week as long as he, Josiah, wasn't expected to walk to the Manor.

'Charlie is doing very well, now, Mr Spendlove,' he'd said, 'I really don't think he would have been happy at the grammar school, even if you had paid for him to go there.'

'No, neither do I. But I'd like to take you up on your offer of private tuition. I shall of course, pay you and I won't take no for an answer. He's no longer having art lessons now. Mr Croft has moved away. He completed his college course and has taken a post as an art teacher in London, I understand. He did a lot to help Charlie and he still writes to him now and again. He did say that we might think about sending Charlie to the art college when he is older. He thought Charlie's work would be good enough.'

'Then that's something to work towards, isn't it?'

But in June 1914, their peaceful existence and all their plans for the future were cruelly shattered. With the assassination of Archduke Ferdinand, the heir to the throne of the Austro-Hungarian Empire, and his wife in Sarajevo, the clouds of a war in Europe gathered. Suddenly, there was no hope of James being able to leave the army at the end of the year.

'So, can you tell us what it's all about?' Roland asked over dinner when his brother had a short leave in July. Lizzie now ate with the family, as did Charlie. 'For a start, why was the archduke killed?'

James sighed. 'It's all so complicated, I'm not sure I understand it myself, but here's what I *think*. There has been unrest for some time, particularly in the Balkan states. There have been a couple of skirmishes and rivalry for control of the Balkans.'

'Yes, I remember what they called the Balkan war a couple of years ago,' Roland said.

'There was another last year too. We weren't involved then, but I very much fear that this time we might be.'

'But why?'

'Although not directly caught up in the Balkan wars, Austria-Hungary became weaker with the enlargement of Serbia. It's almost looking for an excuse to go to war with Serbia and the assassination of its heir by a Bosnian Serb student has provided it. Sadly, Austria-Hungary also has Germany's backing and because of that, other long-term agreements between several countries will come into play.'

'Including ours, I presume,' Roland said.

'Yes. It's believed that Germany now has the best-trained army in the world and it's also trying to rival our navy.'

'Ah yes,' Roland said. 'I remember reading that when we built the battleship, the *Dreadnought*, Germany immediately built a similar one.'

'And, of course, military weapons are being improved all the time.'

Although they hadn't joined in the conversation between the two men thus far, Cecily and Lizzie exchanged an anxious look. It all sounded very frightening to them and Lizzie was prompted to ask now, 'Who are we allied with, then?'

'France and Russia. We're called the Triple *Entente*, but we also have an old treaty with Belgium guaranteeing its neutrality, so if they're threatened . . .' James fell silent but his listeners understood his meaning.

'And who would be opposing us?'

'The Triple *Alliance*. Germany, Austria-Hungary and Italy.'

300

'So what's going on now? Do you know?'

'Not really. There are a lot of rumours and conjecture, as you might expect, and there's heightened tension rippling through the ranks. I'm sorry to say it, but parts of Europe are like a tinder box. It only needs one spark to ignite a conflagration.'

'And you think the assassination of the archduke might just be that spark?' Roland said quietly.

'Yes, I do. Like I said, it's my opinion that Austria-Hungary is just looking for an excuse to go to war with Serbia.'

When James bade Lizzie a tender goodbye, he warned her, 'Leave will be spasmodic now, to say the least, but we will write to each other every week and, if war does come and I am sent abroad, as I'm sure I will be, I will always be honest with you, though I am afraid I won't be able to tell you exactly where I am.'

'I understand. Just – just take good care of yourself and come home safely.'

The family and all the servants stood outside the front door to wave James off, Lizzie and Charlie standing together. Little did they know then that it would be many months before they saw him again.

After James's departure back to his regiment, Roland, Lizzie and even Cecily began to read the newspapers with a greater interest. At first, Roland had thought to shield his wife from unpleasant news, but Cecily was showing remarkable fortitude in the face of an impending disaster over which none of them had any control. Indeed, to everyone's surprise the news seemed to invigorate her. Over dinner one evening, she explained the reason to Roland and Lizzie.

'I have never been able to participate fully in the running of the estate and the mine. The household has always been so expertly run by Mrs Weston and now by you, Lizzie, that I am not needed.'

'Oh, Cecily . . .' Lizzie began, but Cecily smiled as she held up her hand. 'Please, let me finish. When Charlie was born, I thought I would be able to undertake some of his care myself, but Nanny Gordon was adamant that we should stick to tradition – that I would be too soft with him, she said, and spoil him.'

'My dear Cecily,' Roland said softly, 'how I wish you had.'

Cecily sighed. 'I know. I bitterly regret not standing up to her. He was *my* son, it was *my* household and I should have taken control.'

Roland reached across the table and covered her hand with his own. 'You only did what you thought was right – what you thought was best for Charlie. We both did.'

'Exactly,' Lizzie said firmly. 'You must not blame yourselves. Either of you. But go on with what you were saying, Cecily.'

'But if war does come, there is so much I could do to help the villagers and the war effort too.' She glanced at her husband. 'I know you will take care of them. They will still be housed and fed, but if any of our young men volunteer – as I am sure they will – there will be anxious mothers and fathers aplenty. And they, in turn, will want to feel they are doing their bit to help their young men at the Front.'

'You want to form some sort of committee, do you?'

'I'm not sure yet what will be needed, but I think your mother, Roland, and her friends would have some ideas. And I shall consult the vicar too.'

'You can always use the ballroom for any meetings,' Roland said.

Cecily shook her head. 'Thank you, darling, for the offer, but we'd need something in the village. That's partly why I want to talk to the vicar. I think we could use the church hall for something like that and although it was built by your father, Roland, for the villagers to use as they wished, it is only courtesy to ask Reverend Lancaster.'

'What sort of things do you think will be needed?' Lizzie asked.

'It's summer now, but just think if the conflict goes on into the winter, how bitterly cold it will be for the soldiers.'

Lizzie's face brightened. 'They'll need extra-warm clothing. Gloves, socks, balaclavas – that kind of thing. I can help with that.'

'Most of the women in the village – probably all of them – will be able to knit and sew. It's part of their job as wives and mothers. And . . .' Cecily went on, her eyes twinkling at Lizzie, 'thanks to your tuition at the school, even the little girls will be able to do something to contribute.'

Towards the end of July, Roland read about the ten-point ultimatum which had been handed to the Serbian government from Austria-Hungary.

'It says here that the demands are humiliating and would destroy Serbia as an independent country,' he told Cecily and Lizzie. 'And that if Serbia does not agree to *all* the demands without exception, Austria-Hungary will invade without further ado.'

'What about Serbia? Are they mobilizing?' Lizzie asked.

'I expect so and they have Russia as an ally, you know.'

'But Austria-Hungary have Germany and Italy on their side, don't they?'

'It seems as if James was right. Austria-Hungary are looking for an excuse to start a war and I don't know what James would say now, but I see the hand of the Kaiser in all of this.'

At noon on 28 July, Austria-Hungary declared war on Serbia. Britain immediately ordered its warships to various war bases, the Home Fleet assembling at Scapa Flow in the Orkneys from where it could dominate the North Sea and prevent the access of Germany's fleet to other oceans. Over the following few days, events escalated. Bulgaria and the Netherlands declared their neutrality, while Germany mobilized its navy. Czar Nicholas ordered a partial mobilization and Austro-Hungarian warships bombarded the Serbian capital of Belgrade. Britain and France were drawn further into the conflict by Germany's refusal to accept Belgium's neutrality. Even though Italy now declared its neutrality, events had gone too far and on 4 August Britain declared war when Germany rejected their ultimatum to leave Belgium.

'This will involve most of the world before it's over,' Roland said solemnly. 'You mark my words.'

Thirty-seven

'There's great excitement in the village,' Billy and Kitty told the rest of the staff when she and Billy arrived for work. 'The vicar's organized for an army officer to hold a recruitment rally on the playing field.'

'Has he indeed?' Mrs Graves snapped. 'I wonder what the master will have to say about that.'

'D-do you think I should tell him?' Billy asked.

'At once, Billy, if you know what's good for you.'

Later Roland told Cecily and Lizzie what Billy had told him. 'The vicar, of all people, is leading a recruitment rally here in the village. There's no need for any of our men to go. No one is going to be conscripted yet and, even if they are eventually, agricultural work will be classed as a reserved occupation, I'm sure.'

'You don't think the war's going to last long, do you?' Cecily asked.

'The newspapers say it'll be a quick skirmish that'll be over by Christmas.'

'Let's hope so. It's bad enough that people who are already serving in the armed forces, like James, will be involved, without civilians being caught up in a wave of – of . . .' She sought an appropriate word, not knowing quite what it was.

'Ridiculous nonsense,' Roland said firmly. 'If they're called up, that's different – they must answer their country's call – but just to volunteer on a whim, to allow

305

themselves to be swept along on a tide of jingoism, is foolish and dangerous.'

Even amidst the seriousness of their talk, Cecily chuckled. 'I was going to say "patriotism".'

'They'll be properly trained though, won't they?' Lizzie put in.

'I expect so. I *hope* so.'

'I had a letter from James this morning, written three days ago, just after he'd heard the announcement about the declaration of war. He said they expect the British Expeditionary Force to be sent to France any day and he thinks he'll be going.' She paused and then added quietly. 'Perhaps the reason behind the call for volunteers is to make sure we – the British – are stronger than our foes. Presumably a lot more troops are needed if we are to be in a war situation. At the moment, we only have the regulars.' There was silence as the three of them thought about the one who was already missing from their midst.

Roland sighed heavily. 'I think you're right, Lizzie, but it's just the rush to take up arms that I'm worried about. These young men really don't know what they're letting themselves in for. I saw in the paper yesterday that Lord Kitchener is asking for one hundred thousand volunteers. Hence, I suppose, the recruitment rallies.'

Lizzie gasped and her eyes widened. 'That's an awful lot of young men.' There was silence around the table until she added quietly, 'Kitty has already been in tears. Billy has vowed to attend the rally.'

It seemed all the young men of the village were keen to attend and some of the slightly older ones too. Some went because they genuinely wanted to serve their country; some because they were caught up in the fever of patriotism and a few because they didn't want to be left out or thought of as cowardly.

'They're not asking for married men, are they?' Joe insisted as he and Billy stood together waiting for the appearance of the officer. 'So what exactly are you doing here?'

'I'm not going to be seen as a coward, Dad.'

'No one'd think that of you, lad. Nor of anyone else in this village.' He glanced around him at all the young men there. He knew each and every one of them and their fathers too, many of whom had come along, just as Joe had done, to be a steadying influence.

But as the army officer spoke eloquently about the need for their beloved homeland to be protected, and about the atrocities that were reported to be happening in Belgium to women and children that could soon be happening here in England's green and pleasant land, it was not only the young men who surged forward to sign their names. That evening, tears were shed in several of the cottages in the village over husbands as well as sons.

Joe had not enlisted, but he had not been able to prevent Billy from signing up. In truth, he had not wanted to do so. While Billy went home to face Kitty, Joe trudged back up the hill to his quarters over the stables with a tumult of emotions. He revelled in the pride in his son but it was tempered by the fear of what Billy would have to face. Joe would have loved to have gone with him, to be at his side, as families and friends were being promised that they would stay together and fight together, but Joe knew he was needed at home. There would only be him to look after the stables and the carriages and, no doubt, to help fill other gaps on the estate left by more volunteers. The family needed him, but he couldn't prevent a stab of guilt that he was sending his son off but not going himself.

Roland was having much the same thoughts, only it

was his brother who would be involved and, thankfully, not his son. Rationally, he knew his place was at home, running the estate and providing work and food for all his tenants and employees. And perhaps, though God forbid that the war would go on for very long, there would be other ways in which he could help the war effort. He would just wait and see what would be needed.

The exuberance which had greeted the declaration of war was soon tempered by the disastrous defeat of the British and the French at Mons at the end of August. Lizzie knew that James would have been there and, as an officer, would have led his men into the thick of the fighting. He had told her that he would be one of the first to go and though they did not speak of it openly, Lizzie knew that Roland had guessed the truth too.

Billy left home at the beginning of September to go to training camp and, although he would not be sent abroad for some months, Kitty still wept copious tears.

'How could he do it? How could he leave me?'

'Not pregnant, are you, lass?' Mrs Graves asked bluntly.

'No,' Kitty wailed. 'I only wish I was. Perhaps he might not have gone then.'

The cook sighed. 'I don't think it'd have made any difference. Men do what they want to do.'

Roland and Lizzie scoured the newspapers that were delivered to the Manor before handing them on to Mr Bennett and any of the staff who wanted to read the war news. When the casualty lists began to appear, they read the names with trepidation.

'Our boys – the volunteers, that is – won't have gone overseas yet,' Mr Bennett tried to reassure them. 'They'll still be in training.'

'Master James will have gone. He'd have been one of the first. Lizzie said so,' Mrs Graves reminded him tartly.

James was as dear to her as one of her own would have been had she been blessed with marriage and children.

On her marriage to James, Lizzie had suggested that from now on all the staff should call her 'Lizzie'.

'We don't want the confusion of another Mrs Spendlove. I'm no longer "Nanny" nor even the housekeeper, really. And,' she'd added with a smile, 'it's what I would like.'

As the war touched them all, the household drew closer. Cecily, with a shudder, refused to read the papers. 'Just tell me if there's anything I really should know.'

Roland and the rest of the household treated her with care, anxious that she should not regress. But to their surprise, Cecily threw herself into organizing local fund-raising activities and knitting and sewing parties to send extra comforts to the troops. While she did not want to read the details, she guessed what must be happening and, along with her mother-in-law, who now visited the Manor more frequently, she became a leading figure for the war effort in the community. All the women in the village, as well as everyone at the Manor, followed Cecily's lead, and Mrs Spendlove senior rounded up her friends to help too.

'Our forces retreated as far as Paris, but they are doing better now,' Roland told her in September, keeping his wife informed but without too much detail.

The retreat was finally halted with the help of the French and by the beginning of September, a counter-attack against the Germans was launched along the River Marne to stop them reaching Paris. The German armies retreated to the River Aisne and began to dig in.

'You know what will happen now, don't you?' Roland said over dinner. Charlie now dined with them most evenings, so Roland was doubly careful how much he said about the war news. 'Both sides will dig trenches but at the same time they'll both try to reach the Channel coast to secure a port. We'll just end up with long battle lines on both sides and that's probably where they'll all stay at least through the winter.'

Charlie listened with interest, but he said very little. He had grown and developed into a tall, broad-shouldered young man. He still slept in the same room, but the nursery, the playroom and the schoolroom had been transformed into rooms for fifteen-year-old Charlie's use. The nursery had become his bedroom with the bathroom still attached. The playroom was now a small sitting room for him and the schoolroom was his studio, where he could draw and paint undisturbed.

When Billy had enlisted, Kitty had offered to move back to the Manor but Roland had insisted she should stay in the cottage in the village. 'There's no one else needing it, Kitty, and you should both have somewhere to be on your own when Billy comes home on leave. It's your home. But, of course, you are welcome to stay here overnight if you want to at any time.'

Charlie was much changed from the disturbed little boy he had been and anyone meeting him for the first time would not have guessed at his troubled past. Like his father, he now read the war news avidly. Not only was his uncle out there, but many of his boyhood friends were on their way to the Front too; boys he had sat beside in school and played football and cricket with on the playing field every week. He so wished there was something he could do to help with the war effort.

'Papa, may I talk to you,' he said, knocking on the door of his father's study one morning.

'Of course, my boy. Come in and sit down. Now, how can I help you?'

Charlie spoke well now, but he still found stringing

310

long sentences together challenging. 'What can I do to help the war effort?'

Roland frowned. 'You are helping. In a way. You come around the estate with me and then we discuss what crops we should grow and how we should make the best use of our land.' He smiled. 'Perhaps you don't realize how much of a help to me you have become. It's so nice to have someone else to talk to about what we should do. Your uncle never took a great interest in the estate and the mine, but he was always there if I needed to ask his opinion.' Roland sighed deeply. 'Now he isn't.'

'I do find it all interesting, but . . .' Charlie faltered.

'You don't see how it's helping the war?'

Charlie shook his head. 'No.'

'If the war goes on for any length of time, Charlie, there will begin to be food shortages. Our main focus will be to keep all the villagers and our workers well fed, but after that, we will be able to produce food for the rest of the country too. It will be just as important as volunteering to be a soldier.'

'I wish I could volunteer like Billy.'

Roland's face blanched. 'Oh Charlie,' he said in a strangulated whisper. 'Please don't say that.'

Charlie smiled. 'It's all right, Papa. I know I'm not old enough.'

Roland said no more but he was thinking, not at the moment, no, but if this war goes on . . . He dared not look too far into the future.

Thirty-eight

Thankfully, neither Cecily nor Lizzie seemed to give any thought to Charlie ever going to war. Perhaps in their minds he was still a little boy, who needed loving care and attention. Their days were now filled with what they could do for the war effort and how they could galvanize the local women into helping.

'We can use the village hall for meetings. Charlie can design some posters for us to put up advertising the date and time.'

The first gathering in the village hall took place one Friday afternoon at the end of September. Lizzie marvelled at the way Cecily stood up in front of them all. She was indeed changed; she now had a purpose. The hall filled quickly. All the female servants from the Manor were there, even Mrs Graves, who had been granted the privilege of travelling down in the pony and trap with Cecily and Lizzie.

'We need your expertise on what food we could send to the boys out there,' Cecily had told her, 'and it's a long way for you to walk both ways.'

'I appreciate it, ma'am. Thank you.'

As Cecily and Lizzie stood at the front, Lizzie spotted Martha Preston talking to Mary Grey, the doctor's wife, and Sarah Smith, the owner of the local shop, who also ran the village post office. No doubt her services would be much in use soon for sending letters and parcels to the boys away from home. Lizzie recognized quite a few of the women, although she didn't know many names. There were mothers and daughters and even grand-mothers all anxious to do their bit, especially if a member of their family had already volunteered.

Cecily banged on the table to bring the meeting to order and waited a few moments while everyone found a seat and settled down.

The discussion was lively, almost everyone making a contribution with ideas about what they could do.

'I can knit and crochet. They'll want socks and maybe small blankets.'

'I can bake cakes. They'll never say "no" to extra food, I bet. But . . .' Lily Naylor hesitated and seemed unwilling to carry on.

As if guessing what could be troubling her, Cecily said swiftly, 'That's an excellent idea. I'll open up an account with Mrs Smith and you must all charge whatever ingre-dients and materials you need to it.'

Sarah Smith's hand shot up. 'I don't think you should be paying for everything, Mrs Spendlove. Maybe we could hold events in the village to raise money. Fetes and Christmas fairs. That sort of thing.'

There was a murmur of assent around the room.

'But if you all let me know what you'll want,' Sarah went on, 'I'll order extra supplies.'

'Any other suggestions?' Cecily asked.

'We should send tobacco, cigarettes and chocolate.'

'What about packs of cards and maybe even board games? I bet there's times when they're bored rigid.'

The ideas flew thick and fast and Lizzie, who was trying to write everything down, had a job to keep up.

At the end of two hours, Cecily brought the meeting to a close. 'Thank you, ladies, for coming. May I suggest we meet each week on a Friday afternoon, if that suits you? In the meantime, get knitting and baking.'

Despite the seriousness and, indeed, the anxiety that lay behind their proposed endeavours, the meeting ended on a joyful note.

'Well, I think that went very well,' Cecily said, as she climbed into the trap with Joe's help. 'There were a lot more ladies there than I'd expected.'

'There were fifty-three,' Mrs Graves said. 'Kitty counted them.'

'That's very good for a small village.'

'I think all the women were there, ma'am,' Kitty said. 'Only poor old Mrs Davidson was missing, but she's bedridden now. Her daughter and granddaughter were there, though. I saw them.'

'It's a very good start. Let's just hope they continue to be as enthusiastic as they've been today.'

'I'm sure they will. It's for their lads, isn't it?'

'I'm very proud of you, my dear,' Roland said, as the family gathered in the drawing room just before dinner. 'Lizzie tells me your first meeting was a great success.'

'Everyone was certainly very keen to help. I think we'll set up an office for Lizzie and me to use in the morning room. I have the large bureau there already where I write my correspondence. I envisage there might be quite a lot of paperwork as we progress.'

Roland smiled indulgently. He was happy to see the change in his wife, although he was sorry for its cause. 'Just let me know if I can help in any way.'

'You – and Charlie,' she added, with a glance at her son, 'are already playing your part on the estate, but, thank you. Lizzie and I needed to have our own little enterprise for the war effort.'

'Well, just as long as neither of you overdoes it. Lizzie still insists on keeping her position as housekeeper.'

'The house almost runs itself,' Lizzie said and then added swiftly, 'Oh, I don't mean that to sound disparaging to poor Mrs Weston. It was she who set all the routines in place and the standards. She is still the reason everything runs so smoothly.'

'And because we still have all our loyal staff with us.' Roland sighed. 'All except Billy. I do wish he hadn't felt the need to volunteer.'

Everyone at the Manor read the news constantly, watching the progress of the war.

'Two more boys have gone from the village,' Cecily reported after another Friday meeting at the beginning of November. 'They were brothers and one of them is only seventeen. He'd no need to go at all yet, but he was determined not to be left behind.'

'I'm surprised they took him,' Roland said with a frown.

'It seems that they aren't too fussy about age,' Lizzie said quietly, 'if they look strong enough and pass the medical.'

'I read yesterday about the King of Belgium ordering the opening of the canal and sea-defence sluice gates between Nieuwpoort and Diksmuide to flood the land, in an effort to halt the German army's progress,' Roland said.

Lizzie sighed and shook her head. 'That's dreadful. This war's going to have a lot to answer for when it's all over.'

'I think the Germans were trying to get control of Ypres. There's a major battle going on there now,' Roland said.

Lizzie's eyes widened in fear as she whispered, 'I think that's where James is.' At first she had heard regularly from James. Although sometimes the letters were late arriving, he was still assuring her that he was fit and well. But soon after Roland had told them about the battle near Ypres, James's letters had stopped suddenly. Lizzie was not one to panic, but now the sick feeling of foreboding grew and she would rush down to the hall when she knew the post had been delivered only to be disappointed when there was no word from him.

'We'd have heard if anything had happened to him,' Roland tried to reassure her, but his words were no comfort. Though not admitting it out loud, Roland was anxious too.

'If he's in this latest big battle – and I'm sorry to say I think he will be – it must be awfully difficult to write letters, let alone get them mailed.'

'I'm sure you're right,' Lizzie said, 'but the waiting and the not knowing is just so hard.'

At last, four letters from James arrived together towards the end of November, the last one being written only a few days earlier.

The worst of the fighting seems to be over, his most recent letter said, *but now we have snow to contend with. Please ask all your wonderful ladies to send more socks, gloves and balaclavas to the Alstone boys. Warm woollen underwear would be a Godsend too. It seems as if our side has been victorious in this latest battle, though at great cost. Now, with the apparent onset of winter, both sides are digging in and I think lines of trenches will eventually stretch from the North Sea to the Swiss border.*

When James sent his letters home, to save having to write more than one with the same news, he sent them to Lizzie but designed each one so that certain pages could be read by everyone – including the servants – but one page was for her only and filled with loving messages.

'I'm surprised this has all got past the censor,' Roland remarked as he read the 'family' pages.

'He's very careful how he phrases things,' Lizzie said. 'He doesn't actually name the place where they are. He knows we follow the news and that we'll know where the current battles are.'

'Yes, but this bit about the lines of trenches being dug . . .'

Lizzie, able to smile once more now she knew James was safe, said, 'If both sides are keeping pace with each other, the enemy will already know, won't they?'

Roland gave a wry laugh. 'Yes, Lizzie, you're right. Now, about all this underwear he's suggesting . . . Cecily, if you'd like to raise the matter at your next meeting, suggest that all the wives and mothers let us know what they want and sizes, I will pay for whatever is needed.'

'That's very generous of you, Roland. You're already doing such a lot . . .'

Roland shrugged. 'They're our boys,' he said simply. 'I view the staff here and all the villagers as extended family.'

'Papa,' Charlie said to Roland as they rode together around the estate on horseback one morning, 'the young men who are about to be sent abroad have a photograph taken in their uniform for their families –' He paused as if gathering his thoughts. Roland waited patiently. They all knew not to try to rush Charlie, even now. He still needed time to formulate his words for lengthy sentences. 'Mrs Smith's son, Donald, is going, but instead of a photograph, she's asked me if I'd do a painting of him.'

The villagers had, of course, been aware for some time of Charlie's artistic talents. Whatever happened at the Manor the locals were sure to find out about it one way or another. When Henry Croft had been seen cycling through the village on his way to and from the Manor every week, it could not possibly go unnoticed. It hadn't taken long for them to find out exactly who he was and what he was doing.

'What a splendid idea,' Roland said. 'How do you feel about it?'

'I'd like to do it, but I don't want to charge them anything.'

'Quite right. It's the least we can do.'

'He'd need to come up to the Manor to sit for me.'

'Of course. Do you want to use any particular room?'

'No, no. My studio will be fine. I could do a portrait in a day. He won't have a very long leave.' Charlie smiled. 'Thank you, Papa. I'll let Mrs Smith know.'

The painting was completed the day before Donald Smith was due to return to his regiment.

'It's wonderful,' Donald said as he stood in front of it.

'I can't let you take it yet,' Charlie said. 'It's not dry, but I'll make sure it's delivered to your parents.'

'Thank you so much, Master Charlie. Mam will love it. She's already got a place for it above the mantelpiece in the front room.'

'Wouldn't it be better in the kitchen where she can see it all the time?'

Donald chuckled. 'Probably, but she's so afraid of it getting damaged by the smoke from the range.'

Charlie laughed. 'Tell her not to worry. I can always do another. I want her to enjoy it.'

'I'll tell her.'

Donald left early the next morning. A week later, Joe helped Charlie deliver the painting and to hang it in Sarah's kitchen.

'Oh, Master Charlie, it's perfect,' she said with tears in her eyes. 'It's so lifelike. It's as if he's sitting there. You have a wonderful gift. I ought to hang it in the shop for everyone to see.'

The next time Lizzie visited Sarah's shop, that's exactly where the painting of Donald was hanging and before long Charlie was inundated with requests from the parents or wives of those who had volunteered.

Charlie's life was suddenly very busy.

Thirty-nine

'It's going to be a very different Christmas this year,' Roland remarked. 'What can we do to make everything a little easier for everyone?'

'We've already sent out extra parcels to our boys,' Cecily said.

'Christmas cakes, puddings, mince pies . . .' Lizzie reeled off a list.

'And the extra-warm clothing James asked for.'

In the days leading up to Christmas, James's letters were once again spasmodic, but Lizzie received one on Christmas Eve:

> *Little progress is being made at the moment and we don't expect much activity now over the winter months. The weather is atrocious for all of us. Please don't worry about me and try to enjoy Christmas . . .*

His letter ended with a loving message to all of them and his plea was heartfelt, but it was impossible for those who loved him to enjoy the festivities, imagining what he and all the men out there were enduring.

'What a start to a New Year. The war is already nearly six months old and there's no sign of an end to it,' Roland said with a sigh. 'I expect the fighting will start up again in earnest as soon as the weather improves.'

*

Charlie was sitting on the window seat in his bedroom one morning in March when he saw a soldier coming up the hill towards the Manor. The figure was too far away to recognize, but thinking it could be James home on leave he ran down the stairs and flung open the front door in welcome.

It was not James; it was Luke, dressed in a brand-new army uniform, coming to attention in front of him and saluting smartly with a big grin on his face.

Charlie moved towards him, holding out his hand, grasping Luke's and pulling him inside the house. 'I didn't know you'd joined up. Your dad never said.'

'They didn't know until I arrived home yesterday. I enlisted in Leeds a while ago and have completed my training.'

'But – but you haven't finished your course yet, have you?'

Luke shook his head. 'Several of us are going. The university has said there will be a place for us when we come back and we can finish our studies then.'

'What have your parents said?'

Luke pulled a face. 'Not much. Very – stoic, I think the word is. This is what they call an embarkation leave. I'm off abroad next week.'

'To the Front?'

Luke shrugged. 'Don't know till I get there. They don't tell you much in case you tell your families.'

'Will you write to me, Luke? Please. I'd like to hear from you.'

'That'd be great. And you'll write back?'

Charlie nodded. 'Of course.'

'It'll be nice to get letters from home.'

'Now, come down to the kitchen. I'm sure Mrs Graves will find us something to eat.'

Before he left, an hour later, Luke had shaken hands with everyone at the Manor. Even Cecily, who said, 'Your mam is a stalwart of the village ladies' group. They're all furiously knitting socks and balaclavas, besides packing up parcels by the dozen to send out there.'

'I expect anything you send out, Mrs Spendlove, will be gratefully received.'

On a sudden impulse, Cecily gave him a hug. 'Take care of yourself, Luke. We'll never forget how good you've always been to Charlie.'

'We'll soon give the Hun a bloody nose, get this war won and all be back home, don't you worry.'

They stood watching him march back down the hill and give them a cheery wave as he reached the village and turned towards his parents' home.

Over the next week, Charlie painted a portrait of Luke from memory to present to Bob and Martha.

'It's perfect, Master Charlie,' they both said. 'How clever you are.'

In April Lizzie read with growing horror of the use of chlorine gas by the enemy for the first time. A month into the battle, which was again being fought near Ypres, the first telegram giving the worst possible news arrived to a family in the village. The Preston family. The wording was stark and brutal:

> *Deeply regret to inform you that Private Luke Preston was killed in action 28 April. The Army Council express their sympathy.*

'What a terrible waste of a fine young man,' Roland said in private but when he led the tributes in the church the following Sunday he spoke only of Luke's fierce patriotism, his courage and the pride they all had in him. The whole village grieved for Luke, but none more so than Josiah Holland. The schoolmaster had thought of Luke as the son he had never had. Overnight, Josiah seemed to age ten years and, although he carried on teaching – it was the only life he knew – his heart was no longer in it.

While Kitty shed tears for her brother, Charlie was solemn-faced. He did not weep openly, but for many nights he lay in bed staring into the darkness and remembering all the good times he had shared with Luke. Lizzie mourned the young man's death too and the fears of everyone in the household for Billy and for James were doubled. In May a badly written letter from James arrived addressed to Lizzie but intended for them all saying that he had suffered in a gas attack and that he was in a hospital on the French coast awaiting transportation back to England.

'Can we go and fetch him home?' Lizzie asked Roland frantically. 'We can look after him here, can't we?'

'Of course we can, if they will allow us to, but he's still the responsibility of the army. Sadly, we have to obey their rules too.'

Lizzie scanned the letter again. 'He says he'll let us know when he's back in England and he hopes we'll go and see him wherever he is.'

'Of course we'll do that and we'll ask if we can bring him home, but you must be prepared in the event that they might not let us.'

With that, for the moment, Lizzie had to be satisfied.

Two weeks later, when the major battle – which came to be known as the Second Battle of Ypres – was deemed to be over, Lizzie received a letter from James saying he was back in England. He was due to board an ambulance train which he hoped would eventually bring him to Sheffield. 'It will be easier for you to visit me there.'

After another week, early in June, word arrived by telegram – the delivery of which caused great alarm until it was opened and read – that James was in hospital in Sheffield. The following day, Joe drove Lizzie and Roland into the city. Their search for him in the hospital took a while. They were both overwhelmed and dismayed to see all the wounded men being brought in, many of whom were so badly injured that they would never return to the Front or perhaps even be able to work again. At last, a nurse took them to the ward where James was. As they entered, the noise that greeted them was frightening. The men's breathing was laboured and noisy. In a bed at the far end of the ward, they found James propped up against pillows. His face was ashen and shiny with sweat. As they stood looking down at him, unsure whether or not they should disturb him, he opened his eyes.

'Lizzie . . .' he gasped. 'And Roland.'

Lizzie moved at once to sit beside him and take his hand but Roland stood at the end of the bed, twirling his hat between shaking fingers. He didn't know what to say. He didn't know what to do. He felt as helpless as when he had looked upon his distressed little boy all those years earlier.

'I'll – er – see if I can speak to a doctor, Lizzie.'

She nodded absentmindedly. Her whole attention was on James.

It took a while before Roland could find a doctor who had time to speak to him.

'Can we take him home?'

'Have you the facilities to care for him? He needs proper nursing care and a doctor on hand who knows what he's doing. I suggest you leave him here for a while, but give me your name and address and I'll be sure to let you know when it might be possible for him to come home.' He pulled a wry face. 'To tell you the truth, we'd be glad to release a bed.'

'His wife is not a nurse, but she's a trained nanny.'

The doctor smiled briefly. 'Better than nothing, I suppose. What about your local doctor?'

'I'll have a word with him to see what he thinks. We want the best for James, whatever that is.'

'Naturally,' the doctor murmured. 'Please excuse me. I have an urgent amputation awaiting me.'

'I'm sorry to have taken your time.'

'Please, don't apologize. I'm sorry to be rushing off. Look, have a chat with your local doctor and write to me here. My name is Doctor Latimer. When I know what care would be available for him at home, I can assess where would be best for him.' He was about to turn and hurry away when he glanced back and asked, 'If the facilities you can offer are adequate, have you room to take one or two more convalescents?'

For a moment, Roland was startled but then he said, 'Yes, I'm sure we have. We'd be happy to help however we can.'

The doctor smiled. 'Thank you. I'll bear that in mind.'

They stayed with James for as long as they were allowed and Joe, who had brought Lizzie and Roland there, was able to see him for a few minutes before they drove home again. All of them were quiet, lost in their own thoughts and trying to deal with the enormity of James's suffering.

He had not been physically wounded by bullets or shrapnel but his breathing was laboured and painful. Over dinner they told Cecily and Charlie what they had seen.

'The doctor said he is sure that James will recover but that he may well be left with breathing difficulties.'

'Will he have to go back to the Front?' Charlie asked.

Lizzie sighed. 'That's for the doctors to decide. Unfortunately, we have no say in the matter.'

'I must see Doctor Grey,' Roland said. 'Get his opinion to see what we can do to take care of James if he's allowed to come home.'

'We've got enough room to take three more soldiers in upstairs bedrooms, I would say,' Cecily said. 'We must do our bit.' She was thoughtful for a moment before adding, 'Perhaps, if we turned the ballroom into a ward, we could take more.'

'Accommodation on the ground floor would be easier for those who could not manage stairs,' Lizzie put in. 'So the ballroom would be ideal.'

'You're already busy with the local war effort, my dear,' Roland said. 'Please don't try to take on too much. We can always hire extra staff if needed.'

Cecily waved away his tentative objection. 'The ladies of the village are quite capable of running the committee themselves now it's all been set up. They don't need me if I could be more useful here.'

Roland glanced at her. He was anxious she should not overexert herself, but he had to admit that she seemed more animated than he had seen her in recent years. Her next words allayed any fears he might have.

'It's good to feel there's something we can do. Something positive. I felt so useless and helpless over Charlie, but now, I know exactly what's needed. We can do this, Roland, and you'll help too, won't you, Lizzie?'

'Of course I will, but if James is allowed to come home, my first priority will always be him.'

'That goes without saying. Roland . . .' she turned back to her husband – 'please ask Joe to take a message to Doctor Grey and ask him to visit us as soon as he can to discuss something we want to do to help the war effort.'

Charlie had been very quiet throughout the discussions, but now he asked, 'May I go to see Uncle James the next time you go, Papa?'

'Of course, but you must prepare yourself for some dreadful sights.'

'I will wait until we can welcome him home,' Cecily said. 'And, hopefully, one or two soldiers more with him.'

As the meal ended, Lizzie rose. 'I'll go down and tell the others what we found today. I know they're all worried. Mr Bennett, what time would be convenient when you'll all have finished your dinner?'

'About nine o'clock, if that would suit you.'

'I'll see you then.'

When Lizzie explained all that they had seen in the hospital, Mrs Graves shed tears and Kitty, still grieving for her brother and worried sick about what might happen to Billy, buried her face in her hands and wept silently.

'Mrs and Mrs Spendlove are hoping to talk to Doctor Grey about what we could do, not only by having James brought home but also perhaps by way of offering to have a few less seriously wounded soldiers to convalesce here.' She glanced around. 'Would you all be willing to help?'

There was an immediate chorus of 'Yes' and 'Of course'.

Mrs Graves dried her tears. 'I'd have to find out what sort of food they could eat.' Already she was planning her part in the care of the injured.

Doctor Grey arrived the following afternoon. He now had a small car to help him on his rounds, covering an area which included all Roland's lands and beyond. There were often many miles to travel in a day.

'Such a wonderful invention, except when it breaks down,' he told them with a wry laugh. 'But there's usually someone who comes to my rescue. Now, how can I help you?'

Roland, Cecily, Lizzie and Mr Bennett sat together in the drawing room. At four o'clock Clara served afternoon tea to them all, though Mr Bennett felt extremely awkward in being asked to join them.

'These are extraordinary times, Bennett,' Roland reassured him. 'The old niceties and traditions must be laid aside where necessary for the good of the country and the wellbeing of our brave boys.'

'I know, sir, but will they ever come back after it's all over? That's what worries me.'

'Even I can't tell you that, but now, to the business in hand . . .'

The discussions lasted over two hours.

'If you were to bring Master James home and, say, three or four other patients to start with – just to see how it goes – you would probably need some nursing care, at least to be on call, if not living in,' John Grey said. 'Now, you may not know, but before we married my wife, Mary, was a nurse. In fact, she was a staff nurse. She's been itching to get involved in some way . . .'

'Yes, she's joined our group,' Cecily said.

John Grey smiled. 'Yes, I'm getting quite used to the sound of clacking knitting needles every evening after dinner.'

Cecily laughed. 'Oh, so that's where our nickname comes from, is it? Mrs Grey has christened us "The Clackers".'

'Guilty!' John grinned.

'So, would she be able to help us?' Lizzie asked.

'I'm sure she'd be delighted to.'

'If needed, your wife could use the bedroom where Kitty used to sleep before she married. It used to be part of the nursery quarters, but we've changed all that now.'

John nodded. 'I don't think she'd want to live in permanently, but it would be useful to know she could stay overnight if necessary.' He paused and then added quietly, 'I have been feeling rather guilty that I wasn't doing more to assist in the war itself. I'm in my mid-forties, so I suppose I could volunteer, but doctors are needed here. Civilians still get sick. But this way, if I could care for the patients here, I would feel I was helping the war effort too. So, I'll go to Sheffield and meet with Doctor Latimer and find out for myself what we can do.'

Forty

Once John Grey had visited the Sheffield hospital, had talked to Doctor Latimer and had followed up these discussions by contacting the necessary authorities to obtain official approval for the Manor to become a convalescent home, events moved swiftly.

Doctor Grey's wife, Mary, came to the Manor to give advice on what would be needed. 'Of course, if you only have the walking wounded, first-floor bedrooms will be fine,' she said, 'but in here . . .' She spun round in the middle of the vast ballroom, with her arms outstretched, 'you could take at least twelve beds, six down each side. It's a marvellous space and you could have wheelchair patients too, who could be taken out through the French windows onto the terrace for fresh air.'

Roland and Cecily exchanged a look. Roland raised his eyebrows and Cecily gave a little nod. They knew each other so well that they didn't need to speak to know what the other was thinking. Besides, they had already thought of this themselves.

'We would certainly be willing to do that,' Roland said, while Cecily added, 'But wouldn't that require more nurses?'

'Not necessarily. I'm only talking about men who don't need a lot of actual nursing care coming here. With me coming here most days, I think you'd have plenty of staff. That is, if your current staff are all willing to help.'

'Oh, they are,' Roland and Cecily chorused and everyone laughed.

There was little furniture to be moved out of the ballroom and within two weeks, it was cleared and twelve beds installed.

'It's good to see it being used again,' Cecily said. 'It's a lovely room and has beautiful views of the grounds from the long windows.'

Three bedrooms on the first floor were designated for patients who were almost ready to be discharged, either to go to their own homes or to return to duty, and who were fit enough to climb stairs. James, of course, would have his own room within his own living quarters. Lizzie would have sole charge of him, except when she needed Mary's expertise, but she would also help out with the other patients.

Roland had only one stipulation. 'There is to be no difference made between any of them because of their rank. In here, they're all to be assessed by their individual needs as patients. That must be made clear to all of them when they arrive.'

By August they were ready to accept patients. The first to arrive, of course, was James.

'Oh, darling Lizzie,' he said grasping her hand. 'It is so wonderful to be home.'

'It's wonderful to have you home and – and comparatively safe. You've still a long way to go and you'd better know now, James, that no one in this house is going to let you go back to the war.'

James, pale with exhaustion after the journey, lay back against the pillows. 'Sadly, my love, that decision won't rest with you or anyone else here. Not even Roland. He might be master of all he surveys around here, but his authority will cut no ice with the British Army.'

Lizzie, so much happier now that she had James under her care, chuckled. 'Then I shall enlist the help of Mrs Graves.'

James, though his eyelids were drooping with fatigue, managed a weak smile. 'Now, there's a thought.'

His eyes closed and he fell asleep. Lizzie kissed his forehead and tiptoed from the room.

Opening up the Manor as a small convalescent home was a huge upheaval and change for everyone, but they were all willing to help in any way they could.

'Only thing is,' Mrs Graves said, 'I don't like to think of any of them being sent back into the fighting. Haven't they done enough? Even those who haven't been badly wounded physically must be suffering torment in their minds after all they've witnessed.'

'I quite agree with you, Mrs Graves,' Lizzie said, 'but that's the rules of the army. I dread the day when the doctor might decide that James is fit enough to go back.'

Mrs Graves glanced at her sharply and said quietly, 'Then we'll just have to mind that he isn't.'

Lizzie smiled to herself as she thought of her recent conversation with her husband. She didn't envy the commanding officer who might have to stand up to Mrs Graves and her rolling pin.

When James had rested for a couple of days and was able to leave his bed to sit in a chair by the window overlooking the grounds, one by one, everyone in the Manor visited him. They were heartened to see him and so relieved to have him home, yet distressed by the sound of his rasping, laboured breathing.

Charlie, too, played his part. Every day he would visit

James and also sit with the other patients in the ward. Often, he would draw their likeness for them.

'You know, Charlie,' Edward Driscoll, one of the soldiers in the ward, said, 'You've got a wonderful talent. If you were a bit older, you could volunteer as some sort of war artist. We had a chap out there with us and he did some marvellous paintings of us lads, as well as scenes of the war. He was there of his own accord, you know, unofficially, but I think his family were going to try to get his work exhibited back home somewhere. I reckon you're every bit as good as him.'

The patient in the next bed – an officer – said, 'They ought to appoint official war artists.'

'Why would they do that?' another patient – a private – butted in. 'They've got photographers and film-makers. What would they need artists for?'

The officer, Captain Montgomery Fitzwarren – known as Monty to all – wrinkled his brow. 'I can't really answer you that one. But there's something about a drawing or a painting that has more *feeling* to it.'

The private laughed. 'I reckon you're getting a bit fanciful there, mate.' But Edward said seriously, 'I can see what he means.' He glanced at Charlie. 'If ever you feel like volunteering, I reckon that's the route you should go. See if they'll take you on as a war artist. How old are you?'

'Sixteen.'

Monty smiled. 'You're a bit young, yet, but you might get in if the only weapon you're going to carry is a paintbrush.'

Charlie nodded and gathered up his artwork. As he left the room, he was lost in thought.

*

As autumn progressed, thoughts turned towards preparations for Christmas.

At their weekly meeting in the church hall at the beginning of October, Cecily addressed the gathering. The attendance of all the ladies in the village had not dropped off; in fact, there were three more attendees: the wives of the two tenant farmers, one bringing her grown-up daughter too. They arrived together in a pony and trap.

'Last Christmas – the first of the war – was a bit of an odd one, wasn't it?' Cecily began as she opened the meeting. 'We all thought the fighting would be over by then and when it wasn't, we were all a bit at a loss to know quite how to handle it. But this year's different. We have a definite purpose. One, to send even bigger parcels to our boys still out there and two, to make sure those who come home on leave have a wonderful Christmas with their families.'

A hand at the back of the room shot up. 'My boy's coming home. He reckons there's quite a lot being allowed home this year for a Christmas leave.'

'My lad reckons it's a lot quieter on both sides over Christmas.'

'Aye well, they celebrate Christmas same as us, don't they? We got the idea of Christmas trees from Germany, didn't we?'

'Sort of. It was Prince Albert who introduced the tradition into this country.'

'Actually, it was Queen Charlotte, the wife of George the Third, who first put up some sort of a Christmas tree, but you're right. Prince Albert certainly made it more popular.'

'Ooh, showing off your knowledge, Mrs Smith?'

Sarah Smith sniffed and then smiled good naturedly.

'I like history. I read a lot of books about our kings and queens.'

'There you are, then. Queen Charlotte was German, wasn't she? Like I said, they'll celebrate Christmas as much as we do.'

'Ladies, ladies, may I please have your attention,' Cecily said. She loved these meetings, but sometimes people got side-tracked and she had to call the gathering to order.

'At least Billy'll get home,' Kitty said. 'He's finished his training, but he's still in this country.'

'Have you heard?' someone said. 'They're bringing in conscription in the New Year. We were all a bit upset when our lads enlisted before they needed to, but they'd have had to have gone soon now anyway, wouldn't they?'

Cecily banged on the table and the chattering died down at last. By the end of the afternoon, several new ideas had been suggested and everyone left with a long 'to do' list.

The occupants of the three bedrooms on the first floor at the Manor were discharged and sent home before Christmas.

'Are they going to be sent back to the Front?' Mrs Graves asked Cecily worriedly.

Cecily sighed. 'Doctor Grey thinks that two will definitely have to go back but he says he's sure the third won't be fit enough yet. If ever. He has a leg wound which won't heal properly, though he's well enough to go home with care from his local doctor.'

Mrs Graves gave a huge sigh. 'That's something, I suppose. Now, ma'am, about the meals for Christmas Day. Do you know how many soldiers will still be with us?'

'There'll be eight left in the ward for definite, but

Doctor Grey doesn't think they'll send any more to us until the New Year now.'

'Right. That's helpful. Kitty says Billy will be home too. What family will be visiting, ma'am?'

'Just Mrs Spendlove. My parents have declined our invitation, though my father has said he'd like to come for a few days on his own after New Year.'

It was a lively Christmas – probably the noisiest any of them could remember, but it was good to see the wounded well enough to enjoy themselves. At Roland's suggestion, three of them were able to invite one or two of their family members to visit on Boxing Day.

'I'm sorry your folks can't make it,' he said to those who wouldn't have any visitors. There were different reasons. Some lived too far away, some had young children and travelling would be difficult, or there was sickness or infirmities in the families.

'Ne'er mind,' Edward Driscoll said philosophically. 'We'll all be going home soon anyway. We can just have our family Christmas a bit late, that's all.'

It was the best Christmas for Kitty and Billy. They joined in all the celebrations at the Manor, as well as helping with the work, but sneaked off to their cottage as soon as they could to be on their own.

'The master wouldn't let me give up the cottage. I did offer, but he said we should still have our own home. He's so good to us, don't you think?'

'Mmm,' Billy said as, with the door firmly closed behind them against the rest of the world, he pulled Kitty into his arms.

Forty-one

One morning in February Kitty arrived at the Manor with red and swollen eyes. 'Billy's gone.'

Mrs Graves stared at her with startled eyes. 'What d'you mean? Gone?'

'Abroad. To the fighting. He came home on an unexpected forty-eight hour pass that he said was embarkation leave. That means he's going abroad.'

'Oh, so that's why you weren't here yesterday.'

'I did send word. I asked Alfie to bring you a message.'

Mrs Graves sniffed. 'Well, it never arrived. Ne'er mind, lass, we managed. Don't worry any more about it.'

'He must have forgotten. I'll box his ears for him when I see him,' Kitty said. 'I'd never stay away without letting you know.'

'I'm surprised Billy didn't come to say goodbye to all of us. 'Specially to his dad.'

'He couldn't face it.'

Mrs Graves laughed wryly. 'Sooner face the Germans, eh? Ah well, I suppose I can understand it.' She paused and then added, 'How's Alfie doing now? Not thinking of doing anything daft like volunteering, is he?'

Kitty shook her head. 'I don't think so. He's happy working on the land alongside Dad. Besides, he's the same age as Master Charlie. He's not old enough to go.'

'Thank the Good Lord for that,' Mrs Graves murmured and continued beating pancake mixture with extra vigour.

'Has anyone seen Charlie this morning?' Lizzie asked in the kitchen. 'James is asking for him. I haven't time to go looking for him. Mary and John are due any minute and I must do the rounds with them.'

It had become the normal routine for Lizzie to accompany Mary as she visited each patient on her arrival at the Manor each morning. Three mornings a week, Doctor Grey came too and the three of them would spend the morning talking to each patient and assessing their needs.

'Can't say I have,' Mrs Graves said. 'Clara, was Master Charlie at breakfast?'

'No, Cook. I haven't seen him.'

'Just nip upstairs and see if he's in his bedroom or his studio.'

Clara hurried away and came back moments later to say, 'He's not there. His bedroom and his studio are ever so tidy.' This was unusual. Charlie was not the tidiest of people. 'And – and I think some of his clothes are gone.'

'What do you mean "gone"?'

'His best suit isn't in the wardrobe and there's a lot of his underwear not in the chest of drawers. And the small suitcase he keeps at the back of his wardrobe. It's not there. I think a lot of his recent drawings and paintings are missing too. You know, the recent small sketches he's done of the patients. And that big folder thing he carries his drawings in – it's not there either.'

'His portfolio, you mean?' Lizzie said.

'Yes, that's it. I knew it had a fancy name.'

'Oh dear. I don't like the sound of this. I'd better find Roland.'

'What about . . .?' Mrs Graves began, but Lizzie had gone, running up the back stairs. She arrived in the hall just as Mr Bennett was opening the front door to welcome John and Mary Grey.

'Good morning,' Lizzie said hurriedly. 'I have a problem. Please could you see the patients on your own?'

'Is it James?' John Grey asked at once.

'No – no. He's fine. Well, no worse, if you know what I mean. I must see Roland – Mr Spendlove.'

They could both see how anxious Lizzie was even though, as yet, they didn't know the cause. John said immediately, 'Don't let us detain you, Lizzie. We can manage very well. Mary will fill you in later.'

Lizzie turned to the butler. 'Do you know where the master is, Mr Bennett?'

'In his study. Shall I . . .?'

But Lizzie was already running to the door, knocking and entering the room before waiting for an answer.

Without greeting her brother-in-law she burst out, 'We can't find Charlie!'

Roland stared at her as he rose slowly. 'What d'you mean?'

Lizzie explained swiftly about the brief search that had already been made and what had been discovered.

'Some of his belongings are missing.'

'That's – odd. Hasn't he said anything to anyone?'

'Not that I can find out so far.'

'Have you spoken to Joe? He might know something. See what you can find out and come to the drawing room. I'll meet you there. I must tell Cecily.'

They separated to go in different directions, but met a short time later in the drawing room.

'Joe's not seen or heard anything,' Lizzie said, while Cecily, with wide frightened eyes, was wringing her hands.

'He wouldn't go off without telling you, would he, Lizzie?'

'I didn't think so, but . . .' She bit her lip. 'I've been so busy lately with James and – and the other patients. Perhaps I have neglected him.'

'You mustn't blame yourself, Lizzie,' Roland said firmly. 'He no longer needs a nanny and we shouldn't molly-coddle him. He's a young man now.'

'Maybe he's just gone for a day out sketching and painting,' Cecily said, clutching at straws, 'and forgotten to tell anyone.'

'But why would he take some clothes with him?' Lizzie asked reasonably.

'I – don't know.'

'Have you asked James? He talks to him a lot now, doesn't he? And the other patients. He's been drawing them.'

'I . . .' For a moment, Lizzie seemed uncertain what to do.

'What is it, Lizzie?' Roland asked.

'I don't want to upset James.'

'He'd want to know,' Roland said gently. 'He might even have some information we don't. If not, we'll ask around further. Someone must know something.'

James knew nothing, but, as Lizzie had feared, he became agitated, his breathing becoming more rasping.

'He's not – done – something stupid – has he?'

'What do you mean?' Lizzie asked, her heart taking a leap of fear.

'Like – like enlisting.'

'He's only sixteen. He's not old enough.'

James shook his head. 'Wouldn't – matter. They don't –

always ask. He's a big, strong lad . . .' He fell into a painful fit of coughing before being able to gasp, 'Ask the patients.' He waved his hand in dismissal. 'Go – go. I'm fine.'

Lizzie arrived in the ballroom that was now referred to as 'the ward' just as John and Mary had finished talking to each of the patients there and were about to go upstairs to the single rooms, which were all now filled again with the 'walking wounded' as they were called.

'What's wrong, Lizzie?' John asked.

'It's Charlie. We can't find Charlie. Some of his clothes and his drawings are missing. I want to ask the patients if they know anything.'

'Edward Driscoll might,' John said. 'He's got a drawing of himself that Charlie did propped up on his bedside cabinet. They've obviously been chatting. In fact . . .' He paused as he glanced around the room. 'Most of them have a drawing of themselves by their beds, now I come to look. We'll be upstairs, Lizzie. I'll be leaving then but Mary is staying the rest of the day.'

Lizzie nodded and moved towards Edward, curbing her anxiety over Charlie enough to ask, 'How are you feeling?'

'Fine. Doc says I might be able to go home next week.'

'That's wonderful.'

Edward pulled a face. 'I've to go back to the hospital in Sheffield first. They're still the ones with the final say-so. Only trouble is, they might say I'm fit enough to go back on duty.'

'Yes,' Lizzie agreed soberly. 'I'm sorry to say there's always that. Anyway, you know we all wish you the very best of luck and hope that at least you won't have to go back to the Front.'

'Aye well, Lizzie. What will be, will be. We're all in the same boat.'

'Can I ask you something? Have you seen Charlie? He seems to have gone missing.'

Edward stared at her for a moment before saying. 'Oh Lord! That could be our fault, Lizzie.'

'How?'

Before answering her, Edward raised his voice. 'Monty, can you spare a moment, please?'

Monty swung his legs off the bed, reached for his walking stick and hobbled across the room.

'Morning, Lizzie. How can I help you?'

'Charlie's missing.'

'Charlie? The lad who does the wonderful drawings.' He and Edward now exchanged a worried glance. 'Oh dear. D'you think we had something to do with that?'

Now they both turned to look at Lizzie, whose anxiety was growing by the minute. 'What? Please tell me.'

'We were telling him how good his drawings are and that he would be good enough to be a war artist.'

'I didn't know there were such people,' Lizzie said.

'There weren't until recently. A chap went out to the Front and sent or brought back – I don't know which – some wonderful drawings and watercolours. Now the authorities have just appointed someone as an official war artist. I think he's going out to the Front very soon. In May, I think.' He paused and looked worriedly at Lizzie. 'And you think Charlie might have volunteered his services in a similar capacity?'

'I think it's possible,' she said flatly.

'I'm sorry if we have caused this, but if what I've heard is true, he won't be sent out there as a soldier. He might be given an honorary rank, but he won't go for training or be taught to shoot.'

'He'll go to the Front, though, won't he, if he's to draw and paint realistic pictures?'

The two men couldn't deny that.

As Lizzie turned away, Monty said, 'I'm so sorry if we're the cause of this.'

She turned back to force a smile. 'It's not your fault. He'd have heard about it sooner or later. He reads the newspapers avidly.'

She found both Roland and Cecily with James and so was able to tell them all together what might have happened.

'What can we do?' Roland said.

'You could get Joe to ask at the station if anyone saw him getting on a train,' James suggested.

'But where to?' Roland's anxiety was growing by the minute. 'Where would he go?'

'Sheffield?' Cecily suggested.

'Wouldn't he ask Joe to take him there?'

'Not if he didn't want any of us to know,' Lizzie said. 'We could make enquiries, Roland, like you suggest. Otherwise, I think we'll just have to wait to hear from him. But I'm sure that's what he's done.'

Forty-two

Charlie arrived home three days later on the last train of the day to pass near the village.

'Are my parents and Aunt Lizzie still up?' he asked Mr Bennett when the butler opened the door to him.

'Oh, Master Charlie, thank goodness. Your parents and your Aunt Lizzie are in the drawing room. Shall I take your things for you and would you like something to eat? I can bring a tray.'

Charlie smiled. 'Thank you. I haven't had much to eat today.'

At that moment, the door into the drawing room was flung open. 'There you are, Charlie! And just where have you been? You've had us all very worried.'

Charlie crossed the floor towards him. 'I'm sorry, Papa, but if I had told you what I planned to do, you would have tried to stop me.'

'More than likely,' Roland said, dryly. He held the door wider. 'So, come and tell us what exactly you have done.'

When they were all sitting together and Mr Bennett had brought in a sandwich and a drink, Charlie said, 'Ever since Luke went to war, I've wanted to volunteer. And then, when Uncle James came home so badly wounded, I knew that – somehow – I had to do my bit.'

'You've volunteered, haven't you?' Cecily said, her voice trembling.

'I have, Mama, but not in the usual way. Edward and

344

Monty were telling me about the recent appointment of a war artist. So I took my drawings to show the men at a recruitment centre in Sheffield. They advised me to go to London. So I did.'

The three of them gaped at him. 'You – you've been all the way to London on your own?' Cecily said. 'Oh my!'

Lizzie said nothing, but her emotions were very mixed. She was proud of Charlie for his initiative and for travelling so far on his own – something he had never attempted before – and yet she was fearful of what he had actually done.

'And what happened?' Roland asked.

'I saw several people. I felt rather like a parcel being passed from one person to another until, at last, someone interviewed me properly and studied my work. I'll get a letter in a week or so, but they think I could be useful as an artist.'

'At the – at the Front?' Lizzie whispered.

'Perhaps eventually, but they're going to try me out behind the lines to start with. If it's approved, of course.'

'Well, Charlie,' Roland said. 'I don't know whether to be filled with pride or worried sick.'

'You're not old enough,' Cecily said. 'Did you lie about your age?'

'I didn't need to, Mama. They never asked. Besides, I look eighteen, don't I?'

Cecily sighed heavily. There was no denying that.

'I'll be seventeen in August. They'd soon have been calling me up anyway.'

Roland nodded. 'I suppose that's true enough.' He was well aware that since the Military Service Act had been passed in January, conscription applied to all single men between eighteen and forty-one apart from certain exemptions. He looked at his son. Although this brought new fears – different fears – he would never cease to give thanks for Charlie's remarkable recovery. He was now what Roland had always wanted: a son to be proud of. And, with the best will in the world, neither he nor anyone else could regard Charlie any longer as 'medically unfit' for service.

Charlie met his father's gaze steadily. 'If I do get accepted to do this, I won't be called up as an ordinary soldier.'

'You'll still be in danger, though. You're bound to be, if you're observing the fighting.'

'Yes, I will, but I won't be going "over the top" like the soldiers here talk about and charging towards the enemy with a gun in my hands.'

There was silence between them all until Lizzie stood up and said, 'I must go and tell James that you're back safely. He's been worrying. He's in bed now but I doubt if he's gone to sleep.'

'I'll come with you,' Charlie said. 'I want to explain everything to him myself.'

James accepted Charlie's news more philosophically than the young man's parents – and even Lizzie – had done.

'You'd have to – go next year. I think this way will be marginally safer. There's always the shelling – but get yourself into a dug-out – when anything – kicks off. Promise me – you'll remember to do that, Charlie.'

When Charlie visited the ward the following day, Edward and Monty were full of apologies for having put the idea into his head.

'I'm glad you did. This is something I really want to do. Even my family have realized that I'd probably be called up next year anyway.'

346

They too gave him more ideas as to how he could keep himself comparatively safe.

'And never . . .' Edward added, with a wry look at his senior officer – 'volunteer for anything. Although you will have to obey orders, of course, you're out there to do a particular job. Just you mind the officers know that.'

As Charlie left the room, Monty said softly, 'Of course you do realize, Edward, that they'll probably ask him to act as a stretcher bearer.'

'Aye, they will, but let's just hope that's only when the shooting's stopped.'

The rest of the household were appalled at what Charlie had done.

'He can't possibly go,' Mrs Graves wailed, in floods of tears. 'Lizzie, can't you do something? Can't you go and tell them how he used to be? Tell them how very precious he is to all of us.'

Lizzie took the cook's hands. 'Dear Mrs Graves, of course he is, but so are all the other boys who have to go. They're all precious to someone. And at least this way, he won't be called up next year to go as a fighting soldier, now will he?'

'I – suppose not, but, if he hadn't got better . . .'

'Oh come now, you wouldn't really wish him still to be like he was, would you?'

For a few moments, Mrs Graves struggled with conflicting emotions. At last she gave a huge sigh and whispered, 'No, of course not, but isn't there some way we can think of to keep him safe? I mean, the war might all be over by next year when he'd be called up.'

'It might, but if it isn't, then he'll be obliged to go and go wherever they send him. This way, he is marginally safer. Given all the circumstances, I think what he has done is for the best.'

'Perhaps you're right, Lizzie, but, oh, I'm so afraid for him.'

With a break in her voice, Lizzie said softly, 'We all are, Mrs Graves.'

Charlie received a letter telling him where to report and he left for France a month later at the end of June.

I wear a British Army uniform, he wrote in his first letter to his family a week later, *just so no one thinks I'm a spy*. He did not add the words 'in case I'm captured', but everyone realized the underlying meaning. *I'm being sent to where the fighting is, but I'm armed with pencils, paints and paper, not guns and grenades.*

The very next day the newspapers delivered daily to the Manor told of the horrific battles taking place near the Somme and of the catastrophic losses which had been suffered by the British Army on 1 July. A few days later, Kitty received a telegram to say that Billy had been killed on that day. It was the news she had dreaded for months, but that didn't lessen the awful blow. She and Joe tried to comfort one another, but there was nothing that could console either of them, though they bravely carried on with their duties at the Manor.

'It's all I have left now, Kitty,' Joe said. 'I'm lucky to have a roof over me head and work to do.'

'I'm coming back to live here at the Manor. I can't bear living in the cottage on me own without – without . . .' Tears flooded down her face. 'Without Billy. I need to keep busy.'

'What about going back to live with your mam and dad? You could still work here every day like you've been doing since . . .' He stopped as the enormity of what was happening to them hit him afresh.

'I don't want to do that. They're worried sick now that

Alfie will go next year when he's old enough. With Luke gone and now my Billy, it's not a very happy household. At least here, there's so much going on, I won't have time to think.'

'Try to stop Alfie from going, Kitty,' Joe said. 'He's no need to go. He's in a reserved occupation working on the master's farm. Talk to Mr Roland. He'll put a stop to it. Your family's given enough.'

Although Billy had been buried in the nearest military cemetery to where he had fallen, a memorial service for him was held in the local church. Charlie, devastated by the news, sent a moving letter which he asked his father to read out for him at the service. The whole village were present to hear his words.

I will never forget Billy's kindness to me, Charlie wrote, *or the part he played in my recovery. He mended my broken toys, taught me to play football and how to ride my pony. He was always there for me whenever I needed him, even at bath time.* This brought a fond smile to those from the Manor who remembered those times only too well. Charlie ended his letter by saying, *His devotion to me and my family was unsurpassed. He will be hugely missed by us all, but loved for ever.*

Kitty, clinging to Joe's hand but smiling through her tears, whispered to him, 'Wasn't that lovely?'

Joe nodded, unable to speak for the lump in his throat.

The officers and soldiers who were deemed fit enough to return to duty, were soon removed from the Manor, Edward and Monty among them, but more took their place very quickly. More and more wounded were arriving back in England every day, especially after the carnage of the Somme.

'I'm not letting James go back,' John Grey told Lizzie quietly. 'He's itching to return, but his breathing is still not normal, though I may not be able to stop an army doctor visiting to assess him.'

James had improved enough to come downstairs for his meals with the family, to take short walks in the garden and to mix with the other invalids, but to Lizzie's mind he was far from well.

'I understand that. I'm just so afraid he will make out he's much better than he really is.'

'They're all medical men,' John reassured her. 'They won't be deceived.'

A doctor, authorized to decide if a soldier was fit enough to return to duty, arrived to see all the patients at the Manor. Most had only recently arrived and, although not needing constant nursing care, were still decidedly unfit to return to duty.

'There are one or two who should be well enough to go back in a few weeks. I'll visit again, Mrs Spendlove, to discharge them,' the visiting doctor told Lizzie, 'but your husband is not among them. I'm sorry to tell you that I believe his lungs are permanently damaged. Gas is a despicable weapon and I am disgusted that our side decided to use it as well in retaliation.'

Lizzie didn't know whether to be pleased that James would not be returning to the Front or devastated that he had a permanent injury. James, when they talked about it, was as philosophical as ever. He took her hand and kissed her fingers in the gesture that had always spoken of his love for her.

'I've had a good career in the army and now I have you. I'm sure I shall improve and Roland will help me to find something useful to do around the estate.'

Forty-three

The name of Charles Spendlove soon became known throughout the art world and beyond. He wrote home to say that he understood there was to be an exhibition of his work, which had already been sent back to England, in a gallery in London.

'We must go to see it,' Roland declared.

It was decided that Roland and Lizzie should go. James was not fit enough and Cecily shuddered at the thought of the trains crowded with soldiers. 'I'll stay here and man the fort,' she joked. 'But you must be sure to tell us all about it.'

Roland and Lizzie, as Cecily had predicted, travelled on trains packed with soldiers, though gallantly they always gave up their seat for Lizzie. In the city they found their way to the gallery where the exhibition of war artwork was being held.

'I don't think there are many war artists yet,' Roland said, 'so how big it will be I don't know.'

They wandered through the rooms showing the usual kind of paintings, portraits, landscapes and still life, which had nothing to do with the war, until they came to a large room devoted to pictures sent home from the Front. And there, covering the whole of one side wall, were drawings and watercolours by Charles Spendlove. In the centre of them all was a large oil painting.

'Oh Lizzie, just look. Aren't they magnificent?' Roland stood gazing around him in awe of his son's work.

Lizzie smiled. 'Lessons with Henry Croft were certainly not wasted.'

'Henry always said Charlie was good enough to go to the art college. Maybe he still can after all this is over.'

There were sketches of soldiers at rest; some were sleeping, their guns still at their side; some were writing letters, others playing cards. Then there were paintings of the trenches with men lined up waiting for the order, but the oil painting was the most arresting.

'It must be what they call no-man's-land after a battle,' Lizzie whispered.

'It looks as if stretcher bearers are picking up the wounded. Just look at all the bodies of the dead. Oh Lizzie, how awful it must be out there.'

'James won't talk about it. None of the soldiers we have staying with us will.'

'The memories of what they have been through – all they have seen – will stay with them for the rest of their lives.'

'Lives that will never be the same again,' Lizzie murmured. 'Even for those who come home relatively unscathed. The hurt will be to their minds. I wonder if at some point in the future the medical profession will recognize damage to the mind as well as physical wounds. I read recently that they're starting to treat shellshock as an injury now and not accusing men of cowardice like it's said they did at the outset of the war.'

But Roland wasn't listening. 'I thought they'd only recently appointed official war artists.'

'That's what Charlie said.'

'Well, look at these on the wall opposite Charlie's work,

there's a painting here done in 1914 and at least two in 1915.'

'Don't you remember Charlie saying that one or two had gone of their own volition before official appointments were made?'

'Yes, I do, now you mention it. But as early as 1914?'

'Maybe they were soldiers who were already out there, who happened to be artistic as well. Rather like the serving soldiers who are writing war poetry.'

'These are all very good though, aren't they?'

'But Charlie's are the best,' Lizzie said loyally.

Back home, Roland and Lizzie did their best to describe what they had seen to Cecily and James. They did not, however, mention the reason for their trip to London to the other patients. 'Best not to revive bitter memories,' Roland said.

But James said, 'I only wish I could have seen them for myself.'

Two weeks later, James's wish was granted in a small way. A big, well-packed parcel arrived containing five paintings with a note from the curator of the gallery where Charlie's work was being exhibited.

Mr Charles Spendlove has asked that any works which we are unable to accommodate should be sent to you. We have several of his paintings here on show at the gallery . . .

Roland wrote back at once, acknowledging safe receipt of the paintings and telling the curator of their visit. He received another letter by return in which the curator promised to keep in touch with him and to let him know if more, or different, paintings by Charlie were added to the collection, in case the artist's family might like to visit again.

'We must have these framed,' Roland said.

'But perhaps not displayed yet until our patients have left,' Cecily said.

'Ah yes, you're right, my dear. I hadn't thought about that. I'm just so very proud of Charlie's work.'

'So am I, but we must consider the feelings of others at the moment. But it doesn't seem to bother James. You can get one or two done for his and Lizzie's apartment. The other patients don't visit their quarters. And we could hang one or two in our rooms where the patients don't go. Although, we must be sensitive to poor Kitty's feelings. She often goes all over the house in the course of her work. Maybe Lizzie could have a word with her. And now I must go. Joe is waiting for me outside with the pony and trap. I'm needed to join the worthy ladies of the village in packing up more parcels to send out to our brave boys.'

Cecily bustled away and Roland watched her go with a fond smile on his lips. How very different she was now. She had a spring in her step, a new purpose. The only cloud was her anxiety over Charlie's safety.

'Kitty . . .' Lizzie, sitting at the kitchen table, broached what might be a tricky conversation. Only Mrs Graves was present. 'I want to talk to you about something. You know that Master Charles has gone to the war zone as an artist?'

Kitty pulled in a deep breath and stared at her. 'Oh no, Miss Lizzie, don't tell us he's been hurt or – or . . .'

'No, no,' Lizzie said hastily. 'Nothing like that. As far as we know he's fine. You are aware that there is some of his work on show in London. That's where Mr Spendlove and I went a couple of weeks ago.'

Kitty nodded.

'Well, the gallery evidently doesn't need all the work he is sending back, so they have sent some of his drawings and paintings to us.'

Kitty smiled. 'Oh, that's lovely, Miss Lizzie. Can we see them?'

Now it was Lizzie's turn to smile, this time with relief. 'That's what I wanted to talk to you about. Mr Roland and Mr James would like to have them framed and hung around the house but we didn't want it to upset anyone – particularly you. We are going to be careful that the patients don't see them.'

'Oh, I'd like to see them. I want to know what my poor Billy – and Luke – had to face. It wouldn't be honouring their sacrifice if we just shy away from the truth. I think my mam and dad would like to see them too, if that wouldn't be being too cheeky.'

'Of course it wouldn't, Kitty. Don't ever think anything like that.'

Mrs Graves, who had been privy to the conversation, said, 'You know, Lizzie, I think perhaps you underestimate our guests. Some of them might well be pleased to see the paintings. They might be glad that someone has taken the trouble to record their courage. Although the pictures won't make pleasant viewing, they'll surely want people to know the truth. They might even hope that it would help prevent such a catastrophe happening again.'

'Perhaps you're right, Mrs Graves. I hadn't looked at it like that. We were just anxious to protect anyone who might be distressed by being reminded of what they'd suffered.'

'There's one way to find out, Miss Lizzie. Just ask them.'

'But I certainly want to see them,' Kitty said firmly. 'So you just tell Mr Roland to hang them wherever he likes in the house as far as I'm concerned. The sights will make me sad, I know, but I'd rather pay my respects to my Billy and Luke and all their comrades than try to brush it away and forget all about them.'

Lizzie talked the matter over with Mary and John Grey before approaching the patients. They agreed with Mrs Graves. 'Just ask them,' John said. 'They'll tell you the truth, but I rather think most of them will say they'd like to see them. I know many of them don't want to *talk* about their experiences themselves, but I'm not sure whether that's for their own sake or to save their families' distress. A bit of both, would be my guess.'

'A lot of them have nightmares. We hear them calling out.'

'Maybe they always will,' John said with a sigh.

So one morning Lizzie went into the ward and broached the delicate subject just as she had to Kitty.

One of the men, who had been with them for several months, laughed wryly as he said, 'Well, it was partly our fault that Master Charlie went. I remember the captain and Edward talking to him about it.' He glanced around at the other patients, some of whom had arrived after Charlie had left and hadn't met him or known about his art work. 'Master Charlie, Mr Spendlove's son, is a grand lad and he's very clever with his art. Without even seeing his war paintings, I know he'll have done us all justice and shown the world just what we've been through. So, for my part, I'd be glad to see them, but I do understand if some of the lads would rather not. Maybe you can hang them somewhere where we don't normally go. And you'll need to ask the chaps in the single rooms upstairs.'

Lizzie nodded. 'Yes, that's a good idea. I'll talk to Mr Roland and James.'

In the end, two were hung in Roland's study, two in the morning room and the rest along a corridor on the first floor leading to James's and Lizzie's quarters, where none of the patients would see them accidentally. They were told, however, that if they wished to see any of the pictures, they were most welcome to do so.

Life settled into a routine once more. Patients came and went quite frequently, for the Manor was the last place they stayed before either going home or being returned to duty.

The village and its inhabitants were luckier than many. They were almost self-sufficient. Even the commandeering of many of their horses for the Front was overcome. They were allowed to keep six to cover the whole of the estate and while the workload for those left was much heavier, everyone made sure the horses were well cared for, recognizing that the health of these animals was vital for their own wellbeing.

As James continued to improve, Roland involved him more and more in the running of the estate. One morning when they were in Roland's study discussing the affairs of the estate, James said, 'Have you thought of investing in another steam engine? I know you already have one for harvest time, but ploughing needs two.'

Roland frowned. 'I've heard about it, but never seen it in action. It might be a very good idea. I've got a horrible feeling we might lose more horses yet.'

'You need two engines, one placed at each end of the field and each with a winch to pull the plough backwards and forwards. You still need men to operate everything, of course, but no horses are required.'

By the time Roland had purchased a second steam engine, more men had gone from the village and now women began to work on the land to fill the places left.

'I don't like to see women doing such work,' Roland said.

James chuckled. 'I wouldn't worry about that, Sir Galahad. The ones I've seen are thoroughly enjoying it. It's getting them out of the kitchen. We haven't forced anyone to do it or even asked them. They're all volunteers. Even Kitty has asked for time off from the house to work in the fields one or two days a week.'

'Has she? I didn't know.'

'I think Lizzie and Cecily have both approved it.'

Roland shrugged. 'Well, household management is down to them.'

The war ground on through 1917 with no end in sight. The arrival of the first Americans in France in June brought hope to the Allies, but they lacked the numbers and training to go into combat immediately. There would be more to follow, but meanwhile, from the end of July to November, once again near Ypres in Belgium, a gruelling battle was being fought in atrocious weather conditions for the village of Passchendaele.

The curator of the London gallery wrote once more to Roland.

One of the rooms in our gallery has now been dedicated to your son's work. He has sent some magnificent paintings but their content is distressing to say the least. Please let me know if you intend to visit as I should very much like to take you to lunch. I am sending, under separate cover, another package of drawings and paintings, which we are unfortunately unable to accommodate.

Roland and Lizzie once again travelled to London. While they admired his craft, they were appalled to see the sights depicted in Charlie's work.

'He must be in the thick of it all,' Lizzie said as they journeyed home.

'He must,' Roland agreed quietly. 'Otherwise he couldn't paint it, could he?'

'Did you see all the mud? And the men and horses floundering in it?'

'I've read somewhere that if they fall in the mud, they can't get out. Men and horses alike. They're drowned rather than shot.'

By the middle of November, British and Canadian forces finally took control of the village of Passchendaele, securing a victory for the allies.

'Perhaps now the enemy will capitulate,' Lizzie said hopefully, but the Central Powers, as Germany and its allies were now known, had other ideas.

Forty-four

In the spring of 1918, the Germans began a series of offensives. Roland and James discussed their fears endlessly, usually in Roland's study or when he accompanied James on a gentle walk where they could not be overheard.

'It's not that I want to keep anything from Cecily or Lizzie,' Roland said. 'They know what's happening. They read the papers too. It's just . . .' He paused but James finished his sentence for him. 'You don't want to exacerbate it.'

'I know they're so desperately worried about Charlie.'

The brothers stood together on the terrace overlooking the empty lawn but, in their mind's eye, so vivid were their memories that they could almost see the ghostly figures. Charlie chasing the football and kicking it to Billy, with Lizzie and Kitty standing on the terrace where they were now. They could see again Billy leading Dandy around and then, as time had gone on, Charlie able to ride the pony alone. And then Billy chasing after Charlie as he ran off towards the lake, scooping him up and swinging him high in the air.

They were happy memories that were now tinged with sadness. Billy would never come home again, poor Kitty, a young widow, was wrapped in her grief and Charlie was in constant danger.

'Now that the Russians are no longer in the war,

Ludendorff' – James referred to the German General – 'has more men at his disposal as he can move them from the Eastern Front. I think they outnumber us now.'

'But we have the Americans with us now. Surely . . .?'

'We do,' James agreed. 'But it's my belief that Ludendorff is planning a string of offensives as a last-ditch effort. I'm sure he knows, deep down, that Germany can no longer win the war with America's might on our side.'

'That's despicable. Why not end the conflict before thousands more lives are sacrificed? On their own side as well as ours.'

'That's not the way he or the Kaiser thinks, though, is it? Surrender is a disgrace.'

Roland sighed heavily. 'I know you're right, but it just seems so stupid.'

'It's all been stupid, Roland. But all we can do now is pray that Charlie stays safe and all our boys from the village who are still out there come back.'

Roland and James continued to follow the daily news. Over the next few weeks and months, the war swung this way and that. Ludendorff's enlarged armies advanced on a fifty-mile front on the old Somme battlefield and then began a bombardment on Paris with huge, long-range artillery.

'The French will want to protect their capital above all else, I reckon,' James said gloomily.

'Can't blame them. We'd do the same if it was London, wouldn't we?'

James couldn't argue with that. Instead he said, 'I was talking to one of the new arrivals in the single accommodation on the first floor. He's a pilot. He reckons air support will help our troops on the Somme.'

A few days later the German General realized he could not gain victory on the Somme and switched his next offensive to an area near the River Lys, on a narrow front towards the Channel ports through which the British received their supplies, causing the British Commander-in-Chief to issue the directive 'each one must fight on to the end'. With French troops arriving, the enemy's attempt failed. But far from giving in, Ludendorff began planning a third offensive.

It was a hard time for those waiting at home for news. Charlie's letters were now as spasmodic as James's had been, though Roland was heartened to hear from the curator of the gallery in London, who contacted him regularly now, that new art work from Charlie was still arriving, some of which he sent on to the Manor.

'He must be all right if he's still sending drawings and paintings home,' James said, more with ardent hope than definite knowledge.

At the end of May, yet another German offensive brought them within eighty miles of Paris, but the American Expeditionary Force sent reinforcements to the Aisne River. Only a few days later, another section of US forces went into action on the Marne River and although Ludendorff called off these offensives, he nevertheless continued to plan more. The skirmishing continued and it wasn't until July that sections of the German army began to retreat. By August large numbers of German troops began to surrender and the enemy collapsed.

'It's got to be over soon now,' James said. 'It's just got to be.'

But he was wrong. The Germans fell back to the Hindenburg Line and then to its 1914 positions. By October the Turkish Government and the Austrian Empire were asking for a ceasefire. Only Germany continued to fight but, by degrees, internal revolution made a continuation of the war impossible and when the Kaiser fled to Holland, the war was truly over.

At last, after a silence of several weeks, a letter arrived from Charlie.

> *I'll soon be home now, but I want to stay another week or two just to capture the aftermath of the war . . .*

'At least we know he's safe,' Roland said thankfully.

But their euphoria was short-lived. An unseen enemy, more deadly even than bullets and bayonets, crept stealthily across Europe and arrived on Britain's shores. No one, not even doctors and nurses, realized at first how catastrophic this influenza-type sickness would be.

The first wave of the illness which had begun in the spring of 1918 was mild in comparison, but by August a more deadly strain had emerged that turned quickly to pneumonia and resulted in death in many cases. Just as the news came that the war was finally over in November 1918, a wave of this far more serious form of the disease spread through Britain as more and more soldiers returned home, bringing the unwelcome gift with them.

The wounded were still needing treatment in the hospitals and at the Manor.

'We can't just close our doors,' Roland said, 'because the war has ended. The suffering still goes on.'

There were several cases of the influenza at the Sheffield hospital and, inevitably, a patient who came to the Manor fell ill on the day after his arrival. The infection spread quickly among the other patients and on the same day that Charlie was due to arrive home, the first death in the ward occurred. But even that – sad though it was – could not dampen Lizzie's joy at Charlie's return. She stood at the nursery window watching for Joe to appear driving him home from the station. When she saw the pony and trap, she picked up her skirt and ran down the stairs, flung open the front door and was down the steps and running down the drive to meet him, arms wide, tears of joy and relief flooding down her face. Lizzie rarely cried, but this was one occasion when even she could not hold back the tears. Charlie leapt down from the trap and gathered her into his arms, swinging her round, just as, all those years ago, she had swept him into her loving embrace so many times.

But what should have been a celebration of his home-coming and the end of the hostilities was instead a time for increased anxiety, for Lizzie had dreadful news with which to greet Charlie.

'James has the influenza and in his weakened state, he could be very ill,' she told him gently after he had greeted his parents and all the household staff.

'I must see him . . .'

'No,' Lizzie said, trying to dissuade him, but it was a different Charlie who had come back from the war. A determined young man who now made his own decisions.

'Aunt Lizzie, I have come this far without catching it and if I do, I am younger and fitter. I will get over it. Now, I wish to see my uncle.'

Lizzie gave a wan smile. Although she was afraid for him – afraid of anyone catching it – she was filled with pride at the young man he had grown to be.

'Very well.'

It was a shock for Charlie as he entered the bedroom to see James propped up against pillows, his face wet with sweat, his breathing the worst Charlie had ever heard it – far worse than the damage the gas had wrought.

James's eyes, when he forced them open, were dull and lifeless, but there was a spark of recognition.

'Home . . .' he gasped. 'Safe.'

'Yes, Uncle James. I am and without a scratch. I've been very lucky. And now I'm back to make sure you get well again. Get some rest. I'll see you again very soon.'

Another soldier in the ward died that night and the family's fears for James grew, but Charlie refused to have any doubts. 'He has the best nurse,' he declared, glancing at Lizzie. 'And Doctor Grey and his wife are on hand. He has everything to live for. We won't let him die. We just won't.'

Charlie stayed with James day and night. He helped to feed him, if he could take a sip or two. He helped Lizzie to wash him and he sat with him during the few times he could persuade Lizzie to get some rest herself. James was never left alone. It was as if by the strength of both their wills, Lizzie and Charlie would keep James alive.

Lizzie lay beside her husband every night, her arms around him, listening to his painful breathing. She prayed as she had never prayed before and then, one morning, he seemed a little brighter, his breathing not quite so laboured. He even managed to drink a little soup which Mrs Graves made freshly every day in the hope that he would take just the smallest sip.

As darkness fell, Lizzie lay beside him as usual.

'My darling wife,' he murmured.

'Just rest, my love.'

'No, I must say what I need to say. I loved you from that very first moment I saw you with Charlie in the nursery and I've never stopped loving you since. I just want to say that if – if I . . .'

Lizzie put her fingers gently against his lips. 'Please, don't say any more. I have something to tell you. Something you must get better for. Something you must live for. James, we are to have a child.'

For a moment, she thought he hadn't understood, but then he let out the deepest sigh of sheer contentment. She felt his whole body relax as he nestled his head against her shoulder, his hand resting lightly upon her stomach. He closed his eyes while Lizzie held him, the tears running silently down her face.

'Let him live,' she prayed fervently. 'Please – just let him live.'

Epilogue

Lizzie was sitting in front of the window in the nursery overlooking the driveway, her three-month-old baby nestling in her arms. She was deep in thought, her mind going over the traumatic events of the last year. How very ill James had been and how she and Charlie had taken it in turns to sit beside him through the long nights willing him to live. And then there had been the birth of her child, a joyous event and yet . . .

Her thoughts were interrupted by the sound of footsteps in the corridor and, when the door opened quietly, she held out her hand.

'Perfect timing,' she said. 'Your daughter needs a cuddle from her papa.'

James tiptoed across the room. Gently he took the baby in his arms. They sat contentedly together for some minutes before James said softly, 'You know, now I'm so much better, we should think about Katherine's christening.'

'Only when you feel up to it.'

'Of course, but we should discuss godparents, don't you think? Now, tell me again, what is the tradition for a girl?'

'Two godmothers and one godfather, but you can have more if you wish.'

'So have you any ideas?'

'Cecily for one, of course, and if you have no objection, I'd like to ask Kitty.'

'That's a lovely idea. She'll be thrilled.'

'You don't think Roland and Cecily will have any objections? I mean, she's still a servant here.'

James chuckled. 'Since when have this family had any regard for society's conventions? Besides, she's Katherine's nanny now, isn't she? What could be better?' He paused and then added, 'And the godfather?'

'There's really only one person, isn't there?'

They smiled at each other as they said in unison, 'Charlie!'

Acknowledgements

My special thanks and love, as always, to Helen Lawton and Pauline Griggs for reading and advising on the first draft. Your comments in the early stages are always so very helpful.

My grateful thanks to my marvellous agent, Darley Anderson. I wouldn't be where I am today without the fantastic support and help of you and your team.

And then, of course, there is the amazing team at Pan Macmillan, headed by my editor, Lucy Brem. Thank you to each and every one of you for all the hard work you do.

As always, this is a work of fiction; the characters and plotline are all created from my imagination and any resemblance to real people is coincidental. This time, even the house and the village are fictional, although in my imagination they are set somewhere between Sheffield and Chesterfield.

A Mother's Sorrow

By Margaret Dickinson

Three young women. Two families united.
A bond that can't be broken . . .

Sheffield, 1892. Patrick Halliday rules his family with a
rod of iron. He's hard on both his wife and his elder
daughter, Flora, but he spoils his youngest, Mary Ellen,
because she reminds him of his beloved mother.

When Mary Ellen, aged seventeen, finds that she is
pregnant, Patrick throws her out of the family home, and
Flora goes with her. After wandering the Derbyshire countryside for miles, they find shelter on a farm, working for
their keep.

When Flora must return to her job as a buffer girl in
Sheffield's cutlery trade, she is reunited with her friend,
Evelyn Bonsor. As both young women find love and fall
pregnant, the Halliday and Bonsor families are united,
despite the many trials that cross their paths.

Then comes the Great War. Through hardship and
tragedy, these two families must stick together to weather
the storm . . .

The Poacher's Daughter

By Margaret Dickinson

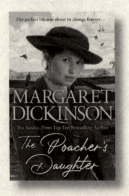

'I'm going to live in that house, Dad.
One day, I'll be mistress of Thornsby Manor . . .'

1910, the Lincolnshire Wolds. Young Rosie Waterhouse lives with her father, Sam, well known as the local poacher, in a cottage on the Thornsby estate. The land is owned by William Ramsey, a harsh and heartless man who is determined his only son, Byron, should marry well and produce an heir.

Rosie is quick to learn the tricks of her father's trade and it's when she's poaching fish from the estate's stream that she meets Byron. As their friendship blossoms, they realize that they are destined to be together, but William will stop at nothing to ensure that they never meet again.

As the years pass and the threat of war becomes a reality, Sam is involved in a tragic incident that will affect both his and Rosie's lives more than they could ever have imagined. Life will never be the same in Thornsby, but will Rosie find the happiness she yearns for?

Wartime Friends

By Margaret Dickinson

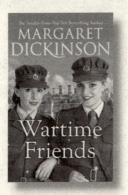

*Courage, love, friendship and
hidden secrets among a family at war.*

It is 1940 in coastal Lincolnshire and the storm clouds of
war are gathering over Britain. Two brave young women
discover the value of true friendship, as they deal with
troubles of their own while the lives of those they love
are put at risk.

Carolyn Holmes is keen to do what she can for the
war effort. Raised on the family farm, she battles with
her mother, Lilian, to further her education – although
nothing is too good for her brother, Tom. Phyllis Carter,
a bitter widow from the Great War, lives close by with her
son, Peter, who works on the farm. When Peter decides to
volunteer, a distraught Phyllis blames Carolyn, who leaves
to join the ATS. There she meets Beryl Morley, who will
become a lifelong friend.

Carolyn and Beryl are posted to Beaumanor Hall in
Leicestershire as 'listeners', the most difficult of signals intelli-
gence gathering. As the war unfolds and their work becomes
even more vital, Carolyn and Beryl's friendship deepens,
and in the dangerous times that follow, they support each
other through some of the darkest days they will ever know.

The People's Friend

If you enjoy quality fiction, you'll love "The People's Friend" magazine. Every weekly issue contains seven original short stories and two exclusively written serial instalments.

On sale every Wednesday, the "Friend" also includes travel, puzzles, health advice, knitting and craft projects and recipes.

It's the magazine for women who love reading!

For great subscription offers, call 0800 318846.

twitter.com/@TheFriendMag
www.facebook.com/PeoplesFriendMagazine
www.thepeoplesfriend.co.uk